INFINITY LEGION

A LEGENDS OF INFINITY NOVEL

INFINITY LEGION

A LEGENDS OF INFINITY NOVEL

MYAH BAWADI

THE SEVEN REALMS OF INFINITY

The Unknown
The Glass Castle
The Castle of Lex
The Lost Wing
Army Blockhouses
The Bridge
The Battlefield
The Armoury
Academy Fortress
The Wall
THE REALM OF LEX

The Prophecy of the Invisible

At the dawn of the realms The Books of Infinity were formed.

Bound in eternal light they join naught.

At the alignment of the realms, one will seek to bind the books.

To destroy and rebuild the realms anew in undying majesty.

Only one in invisibility can halt the demise of the seven realms.

Forged in everlasting light, they alone will have the power to last the realms.

The power to bind existence for eternity.

PROLOGUE

18 YEARS EARLIER

Seven Knights were seated at a round table, the air around them thick with magic—the power, and promise, of war.

Here, the Knights—not rulers but nobles—discarded their crowns on the stone table. Their immortal forms, perfection and beauty incarnate, were adorned by only the most intricate of gilded thrones. In this circle of power, the ebb and flow of its magnitude a physical being, each Knight took up their own breadth of space equal to the power they claimed for themselves in their reign.

Their goblets, promising salvation and servitude to the endless depths of the contents within, lapped with violet liquid at the brim. The matching jug, painted with scenes of battle and council, war and peace, lay in the center of the table.

Not one Knight had taken a drink yet, they simply listened.

"Omnis has held The Book of the Bound for far too long." The grey-haired knight spat, standing slowly. "Nearly one hundred millennia, and what do they have to show for it?" He stared around the table, making, then breaking eye contact with each knight. Despite his anger, the Knight had enough sense to avoid the gaze of the immortal directly across the table. The Knight shook his head and a tuft of grey hair fell into his face. He swiftly pushed it back, careful to remain in his personal width of space.

"Will no one answer me?" His tone remained clipped and his grey eyes froze over with anger. "Isn't it obvious? They have *nothing*—nothing to show for it. Nothing but their precious gardens and useless artwork. No real advancements have come from Omnis' reign as binder of the realms," he paused. Whether unsure of how he wished to proceed, or simply for the dramatics that the grey-eyed Knight so loved, the other Knights would never know, for he continued swiftly.

"I suggest, a *change* in powers." The whorls of magic in the air halted and six Knights held their breath.

The grey-eyed man directed his icy gaze to the slightest of the Knights. A woman with slick black hair and soft features. "You! You understand—the *shifts*—the star cycles! You must!" The air was released from the lungs of the immortals and the magic flowed again, unsure in its path but flowing, nevertheless.

The woman reached for her goblet, meeting his stare with all of his own intensity and more—the power of the stars. She took a long drink of the wine from her goblet, not once veering her eyes from the challenge. She swallowed her drink and deliberately set the goblet down on the table, exactly where it had been before.

To the first to dare drink at the council of The Infinite Knight Court...

"The *shifts?*" She asked lazily, stretching out each sound to the point of fault.

...goes the power.

"Yes. And as Lady Knight of Aetas you—" the Knight began, flustered.

The woman had let her eyes amble to her other Knightley companions as she had no need to think. Eventually, when she deigned to disrupt the words of the immortal pestering her, not an ounce of her mental space would be occupied by the task. "As the Lady Knight of Aetas I need not listen to you. Not now, nor in the next thousand millennia. As the Lady Knight of Aetas, I have seen the stars and the only thing they have told me is that this millennium is coming to a close. I am not a *seer* Lord Acastus."

Lord Acastus balled his hands into fists at his sides, his knuckles going white with unbridled fury. Though, as if Infinity had blessed them all, his words came out cordial, unbothered even. So different from the bitter remarks he had made only moments ago. "I never said you were, Lady Kala. I am only suggesting that we," he paused again, finding strength for his continued composure in the correct words. "*Ponder* for a moment, on the connection between the star cycles which you so incessantly study, and the potential for a shift in powers." He stopped again, this time reeling the dark-haired Lady Kala in for retort.

"I fail to see—" Lady Kala began.

Lord Acastus stopped her in her tracks. His grey eyes lightened with the possibility to turn the tide of this council meeting. "You, fail? *You*, Lady Kala, *fail* to see?"

To her credit, Lady Kala's face remained completely smooth, devoid of any sign that she was ever *reeled* into anything. "I *fail* to see your point, Lord Acastus. As you *fail* to see the effect that your words have on this council. We are at the cusp of a new millennium." Her words were cool and calculated, each one enunciated with control and a steady calmness that flowed out of her and through the room. Through the magic that swirled around each immortal. "This is not the time to question the abilities of Omnis as the holder of The Book of the Bound. Omnis has had many advancements in—"

Any control Lord Acastus had in that moment shattered into a thousand jagged pieces flung about the council room. The swirls of magic that contained the secrets of a hundred millennia were shred and left to hang in tatters.

"Advancements!" Lord Acastus scoffed. "Advancements!" He laughed humorlessly. "The only advancements that our dear Lord Eric has made as sworn Knight of Omnis have been to this castle's decoration!" He turned his head to the Knight whose gaze he had been avoiding for the duration of the council meeting, and finally met his piercing blue eyes.

Lord Eric—*the* High Knight of The Infinite Knight Court—lounging casually on his throne, grabbed for his goblet of wine. He took a quick yet deep gulp of the dark violet liquid, holding Lord Acastus' scowl. His quip was quick on his tongue and yet he drank and mindlessly swirled his drink, veering his gaze to watch the liquid shimmer and dance in its iron cage.

"I am quite glad you enjoy my decorating, Lord Acastus. In fact, you are the first to notice it. One would think that the pointed eye gets dull with age, but here you are, pointing out *every* detail." Lord Eric chuckled, flashing a crooked smile. As if Lord Eric's confidence was a healing power unto itself, 'the magic stitched itself back together, erasing Lord Acastus' outburst just as though it never occurred at all. "I would so enjoy it if you shared your secrets one of these days. But until then…" He quickly rose to his feet, not worried about the air he stirred, the magic that shifted in his wake. Dark hair spilled onto his forehead; he made no move to adjust it. "A toast!" He lifted his goblet in the air with his right hand and gestured theatrically with his left. "To Lord Acastus, Knight of Lex, for being the most *observant* Knight of the council. For noticing my decorating but missing the clear and simple message of this meeting." The High Knight turned his head, this was for Lord Acastus only. "You will *never* be the High Knight of this court. Not if I die tomorrow and you live another hundred millennia. Even if I have to curse it into your bloodline and into you land, Lex will crumble before it becomes the binder of the realms."

A gasp came from Lord Eric's left. The doll-like Lady Psyche, Knight of Spiritus stared—green eyes unblinking—at the jug of wine in the center of the table. Her nose scrunched in cringing, distorting the freckles that spotted her pale skin. Lord Nasim, Knight of Entis—a living, breathing shadow—shifted and tensed to her left.

Lord Acastus' face flipped. "You insolent child—"

The air from Lord Acastus' lungs ceased to exist, filled instead with Lord Eric's ever mysterious and all-consuming power. Lord Acastus grabbed at his neck, at the invisible and intangible rope twining its way around his throat. Lord Eric held on, watching Lord Acastus' grey eyes go feral. With half a thought, the High Knight released his grip on the lesser Lord and simply found his position in his throne once again.

One, two, three, seconds passed before anyone dared to speak. To every Knights surprise, it was Lady Psyche who broke the lull. "I do not believe that this argument is wise. We mustn't burn bridges." Her eyes darted nervously to Lord Nasim.

"I agree with Psyche, it is crucial that we keep our doors open in this time of change. We must keep a connection between the books." Lord Nasim lifted his head to meet Lord Acastus' gaze, but it was focused on another Knight entirely.

Lord Acastus huffed. "Burn bridges? We had blown them to nothing! And the doors along with them. Damn them both, they have ceased to exist!" He directed his next words at the green-eyed immortal on his left. "And you! I once considered you ally *and* friend. Now you dishonor me *and* your realm."

Lord Vale, Knight of Tellus—a lean and angular man—let his head hang towards the floor. His light brown hair fell in waves, forming a shield around his face. He focused on the weathered brick beneath his feet. "You know

I have nothing to do with this. This belongs to Lady Kala, and Fable even, it is not my jurisdiction…" His words trailed off as if the thought had vanished as quickly as the connection he once shared with the grey-eyed Knight.

Lady Fable, Knight of Ingenium who sat to Lord Vale's left, quickly turned her head to him in an attempt to catch his eyes. Fruitless, as they remained on the floor. The Lady abruptly lifted her head to Lord Acastus, her brown eyes flaring with the wisdom of the worlds. A sight to behold against her skin of deep umber, radiant with an eternity of knowledge.

When she spoke, her tone was eloquent and imperial, demanding and eternal. "Lord Acastus, you have presented your thoughts to The Infinite Knight Court. We have all had a chance to listen and, *ponder*, your ideas. With the permission of Lord Eric, we will call a vote. A simple majority and no one may abstain. *This* will decide if further discussion is warranted." She turned to Lord Eric. "High Knight of the Infinite Knight Court, do you give your consent for this vote?"

Lord Eric smiled widely, clearly amused by the sudden turn of events. "Wonderful proposal Lady Fable! Why *yes*, I will give my consent for this vote. Rules are as Lady Fable stated, a simple majority will carry, no one may abstain. Any objections?" He waited, making, then breaking eye contact with all six Knights around him. Each gave a curt nod in reply. Including Lord Acastus, who, even in the face of certain loss, understood the game of power.

When Lord Acastus spoke, his words were cold. "I am not dull, I understand your ploy, but know this. I, in the last five hundred years of my reign as Lord and Knight of Lex on this court, have not forgiven easily. This will be no different." He met Lord Eric's gaze, the chill of his grey eyes returning. "The tides are turning; the star cycles are shifting. The power of Lex has grown, and The Book of Law no longer serves our interests. If you do not wish to grant me what I seek, fine. But do remember," power rolled off of the Lord's form. *"I will find a way."*

Lord Eric barely regarded him before continuing. "Well then. All those in favor of continuing the discussion on Lord Acastus' proposition for a shift in who holds The Book of the Bound, raise your goblet."

Lord Acastus lifted his goblet into the air. *Defiance,* even in the face of certain loss.

"All those in favor of ending the discussion on Lord Acastus' proposition for a shift in who holds The Book of the Bound, raise your goblet."

Six goblets rose in unison.

PART I

THE STUDENT

CHAPTER

ONE

A *stone table.*
Seven ornate goblets.
Seven gilded thrones.
Seven shining Knights.
A pair of piercing blue eyes.
"I will find a way."
One goblet lifted.
Six goblets rose in unison.

The images flash in my mind, one after the next, quick and shimmering in their efforts to pull me from battle.

Our swords clash. I will not be distracted.

Again, and again Nova drives at me, relentless in her speed—her strength. But I am faster, I am stronger, and soon I'm on the offensive. I begin driving, gaining ground on our makeshift battlefield. My arms don't falter, my mind doesn't surrender.

The clash of steel rings out in my ears, a joyous sound. The sound of home. The same home that relentlessly whips its biting winds at my body, winds as cold as death itself.

Winters always are the worst on Lex.

Nova's starbright eyes swirl with determination, shimmering with her thoughts as always. Even when she tries to hide them, I simply need to look to understand. I see her plan before she knows it herself.

I won't give her the chance to try it.

I reel her in, allowing her to believe that I am *losing.* As if I could ever lose. She realizes a moment too late and as her blade pushes down on mine, I unsheathe the dagger at my thigh and drive it towards her unguarded right side.

"I win." I smile, letting the tip of my dagger poke lightly into Nova's side.

"I knew what you were doing, Soleil." Nova counters, shifting her weight so that it no longer bares down on me.

"Only a moment too late, Nov." I laugh, sheathing the golden dagger back at my thigh. Nova sticks her tongue out in mocking and I only laugh harder. "Come on, I'm freezing." I walk to the weapons rack and hang up my sword, Nova follows.

"Breakfast?" Nova asks as we walk away from the battlefield.

"Mmhm." I hum quietly, wrapping my cloak around my body to find reprieve from the biting wind—it doesn't help. I glance at the towering stone structure ahead.

On the barren wasteland of Lex, with its horrendous winters and thin air, lies The Fortress, an extensive brick structure home to The Academy of The Undying Army.

My home.

As the military force of The Seven Realms of Infinity, Lex trains students at The Academy to become members of The Undying Army the moment they graduate. The top students become highly ranked members of The Army, moving into The Castle of Lex to live among the other nobles. The rest of the graduates—named foot soldiers—live in stuffy blockhouses and barracks along the outskirts of Lex, near the barricade of The Wall.

The Wall, said to be built by the first Knight of Lex, is an all-encompassing oval made of giant brick that rises hundreds of feet and spans miles, creating Lex proper. Brick by giant brick, built and bound together by magic, the goal was for it to keep the harsh weather out of the central city of Lex.

The stories say that it worked for a while, but as the millennia have come and gone, the magic that originally held the weather out, has vanished. Exacerbated by the fact that each Knight of Lex in the last ten millennia, has been born with less and less of the magic that the immortals of Lex once gripped so tightly.

So, I grit my teeth against each merciless gust of wind, with no reprieve from the monstrous winters.

As I ponder the history of my realm, my mind wanders back to my dream from earlier. I recall the flashes that pull me from sleep every night, the ones that threatened to pull me from battle only moments earlier.

A stone table.

Seven ornate goblets.
Seven gilded thrones.
Seven shining Knights.
A pair of piercing blue eyes.
"I will find a way."
One goblet lifted.
Six goblets rose in unison.

The same as any other night. Always the same. The six goblets rise—I wake.

My head spins as I try to decipher the dream that has plagued me for eighteen years, but I can't pull my mind from those brilliant blue eyes. They have always been bright and stabbing as they pierce into my soul. But last night they flared with an intensity that I have not seen—or not noticed—before. I let my mind conjure up the picture again, so real as if I am truly staring into them.

I shake from the intensity of the image and find that my body has grown numb with cold in my mental absence. I pull my cloak tighter around my body. It's no use. The cold penetrates my mind and the blue eyes find me once more.

"So, what's on the schedule for today?" I ask offhandedly, knowing that Nova hasn't gotten a chance to look at the sheet tacked to our sleeping chamber door yet, either.

"The usual, I suppose. Breakfast, history lesson, training." Nova pauses. "Maybe we'll get lucky and finally have training with a fun squadron." Nova's pristine curtain of bright blonde hair swishes as she walks.

I can't help but laugh at her dramatics. "Who are you thinking of?"

"Male Group 7G." She giggles and jumps, loud enough to wake *all* of Lex. I wave her along as we step into the doors of The Fortress.

Male Group 7G is one of the ten male squads in our year; it holds twenty men out of the two hundred in year seven as a whole. One member of Male Group 7G makes it *particularly* special to Nova.

"You know I don't exactly care for *him*. You could do so much better Nov."

She rolls her eyes. "Soleil, you have made your point very clear. But *he* is our best friend."

I roll my eyes in return, heaving a sigh. "That is exactly why you shouldn't feel for him. You have seen every stupid thing he has done in the last seven years. And *still…*" I shiver, a mix of cold and disgust.

"Agree to disagree then." Nova lets go of her cloak, letting it flow behind her. I do the same even though the only difference between being inside of The Fortress, and outside of it, is that we now have two feet of stone shielding us from the wind. The biting cold however, remains. Still, I'll take what I can get.

I laugh and catch Nova's eyes. "Sounds good to me."

Beams of sunlight peak brightly through the windows of The Fortress as gusts of cold air sneak through the cracks and crevices of the crumbling stone walls. Each whistle of wind, a reminder to the immortals of Lex of the power they once gripped so tightly. Whatever the reason for their loss of power—I feel the effects of it every day.

I catch my reflection in a window and pause to adjust myself. I never considered myself particularly vain, but power *is* in presentation, and I wish to be powerful. If only for the sake of *being* powerful. Whether that makes me a bad person, I have never truly cared.

As I tighten my scabbard around my thigh—matte white leather stamped with whorls of gold and embossed with my name—I think back on my life in Lex, utterly invisible as one of the *Lost* children, yet somehow granted an impossible gift… I pull out, shine, and reinsert my dagger; an impeccably sharp thing with a shining gold blade.

I adjust my clothing, ensuring that my white thermals lay smoothly across my body and that my cloak falls nicely around my shoulders. I pull my hood down and split my soft curls—windswept from the mornings battle practice with Nova—down the middle. I watch them fall in dark and curling tendrils to my waist.

Nova is next to me adjusting herself as well. She smooths out her black thermals over her thin and lean form, doing her best to release the wrinkles in her cloak that formed from bunching it to her body.

I am just about the same height as Nova—taller than most girls, and some guys too. But where Nova is lean and angular, I am all curves. My muscle, unlike the sharp and cutting exteriors of most, is held under the softness of my hips and thighs, under the curve of my arms.

I look up and meet my own eyes in the glass, a deep and endless brown. My thick eyebrows are out of order so I roughly slick them down with my fingers. My tan skin glows with the light sheen of sweat, a rare sight in Lex's stale air. I put my hood back up and nod to Nova—shadow-like in her all-black ensemble—and we continue our trek.

I set my jaw against the raw blasts of wind, still somehow assaulting me through feet of stone, and walk alongside Nova, our steps in perfect sync and the gentle click, clack of our boots the only sound in the still sleeping Fortress. Hoods up, we are a sight to be seen, our cloaks liquid with the momentum of our steps and our scabbards at our thighs.

We keep our hoods pulled over our heads and our eyes down, as soldiers usually roam The Fortress at this early hour. They start the fires in the various sleeping chambers and make breakfast for the students, jobs reserved only for the lowest of the foot soldiers in The Army. Most are incredibly bitter and wouldn't mind bothering some seventh-year students. *Nothing to lose*, I always assumed.

Being a soldier in The Undying Army means constant vigilance, something that Nova and I have perfectly adapted to after all these years. So our limbs are loose in case we have to reach for our daggers sheathed at our thighs.

"Infinity knows that winters on Lex get more brutal every year—*I know it*. And still, I'm shocked when the end of the year rolls around and the air bites again." Nova whines, voice hushed so as to not echo down the halls.

"You act as if summer exists in this Infinity forsaken realm. It's better if you cut your losses and pretend that we simply exist in perpetual winter." I tease.

"All I'm saying is that some temperate weather would be much appreciated." Her mood turns gruff. "Maybe when we become soldiers in The Army, we can take the portals and ditch this place."

"Where to Nov? If it wasn't completely illegal and grounds for execution, I would still stay. I'd rather live through a thousand of Lex's winters before I end up in Omnis." I retort.

Omnis, the shining jewel of The Seven Realms of Infinity, home to the Infinitely blessed, and the Infinitely protected.

"It's not so bad, I hear the weather's nice. The sun actually *shines* there." Nova replies scornfully.

"The sun is *shining* today." I glance out of the window. Sure, the sun is a rare sight on Lex, but there it is. "Omnis is not worth the abyss of pretentious artists and self-proclaimed diplomats. I would rather *do* something with my training." I stop there, not wishing to pick a fight with Nova. We have two very different ideas of what *doing something with our training* means.

"Spoken like a true self-proclaimed diplomat, Sol. Maybe you *would* fit into Omnis just fine." Nova counters. I scoff and nudge her lightly with my shoulder.

Past the war rooms and storage closets, male sleeping chambers and council rooms, down the spiraling stairs and after the classrooms, Nova and I finally make it to the dining hall. The smells of rich food encompass us quickly and the gentle hum of voices and the light clatter of dishes fill the hall.

The grand dining hall is expansive, incredibly tall and long with rows and rows of stone tables and benches. On the far wall is the only thing that could possibly be considered art in the entirety of The Fortress, a colossal stained-glass portrait of a long-forgotten Knight of Lex.

He raises a sword into the sky, The Castle of Lex, The Fortress, The Wall, and a far-reaching army behind him.

His face is contoured in fury. A battle cry—magic enough to shake the realms.

In front of the stained-glass window lies a stage about ten feet off the ground with a set of stairs on either side. When it comes time to address The Academy as a whole, the dining hall is the only place big enough to do it. Two grand clocks sit on either end of the stage, they read *0730*.

Running along either side of the hall are food stations serving a rotating menu based on the time of day. *0500* to *1100* is designated breakfast, though most opt for the extra sleep instead of a meal. Nova and I never do, instead relishing in all we can get done in the quiet hours of the morning.

A grand fireplace, twenty times as big as the ones that roar in our sleeping chambers, has its home on the left side of the hall. The dining hall is empty at this hour—as usual—and only a few of the endless rows of tables and benches are at all filled.

Nova and I walk to the food stations on our left, each taking our trays and utensils. We go down the stations, piling our plates high with food. We often miss lunch, using the time for extra hours of training or private lessons with professors, so breakfast is often the only meal we have until dinner.

My stomach rumbles with hunger as I scoop an assortment of rich foods onto my plate. Salted meats and fluffy scrambled eggs, soft bread slathered with butter and fruit preserves, thin cakes drizzled with sweet syrup and a tall cup of orange juice all make their way onto my tray. I nearly topple over when I hear a voice from behind me.

"Morning." The voice is deep and rough with sleep. I quickly spin around, considering for a moment, reaching for my dagger. But I know that voice.

"Hey Arche!" Nova flutters, batting her eyes.

"Ladies…" I look up into the grey eyes of Arche Inconnu, who towers over me by at least half a foot. "Planning on eating all of that, *Soleil?*" He drags my name out beyond recognition, sending a—very unwanted—chill down my spine.

"Yes. Maybe if you tried it someday, you could work up…" I pause for effect. "Half? Of the muscle I have." I stick my tongue out in mocking. Arche squints his steel gray eyes and runs a hand through his icy white hair.

"Ouch. Harsh Sol." He turns to Nova who blushes. "Did she wake up on the wrong side of the bed this morning?"

"Same as usual." Nova laughs.

Arche Inconnu—the anonymous moon in the tongue of old—completed our galaxy seven years ago when Nova and I met him at The Academy during our first year. Arche was born and raised in Lex to parents who were servants in The Castle. For years, he was on track to follow the paths of his parents and become a servant as well.

They passed when Arche was twelve—from one of the more horrible sicknesses to spread through our land. The whispers say that he was Infinitely blessed for the claws of sickness never touched him. The whispers say that I am too. But if it were left up to the whispers, everyone would be Infinitely blessed.

Infinitely blessed or not, Arche begged the headmistress for weeks to allow him into the first-year class. After proving his skills, she relented and Arche entered The Academy in the same year as Nova and I. He is a year older than me, two older than Nova, but we get along well. Our own mismatched galactical family.

Arche Inconnu also *happens* to belong to Male Group 7G.

"Good point. Speaking of points, did you hear that Lord Acastus is giving a speech at *oh eight hundred hours?*" Arche asks casually.

Lord Acastus, Knight of Lex, is a cold man. As one of the immortals, he is blessed with the gift of everlasting life. But apart of the royal bloodline of Lex, his *magical* powers are non-existent. Still, it thrums in his veins, manifesting in icy waves that beg for release when anyone comes near. Lord Acastus must be hundreds of years old at this point in his reign, not the oldest of the Knights currently serving on The Infinite Knight Court, but certainly old enough.

"No, I didn't hear that. I wonder why." I answer.

Nova turns to me. "Whatever it is, it must be serious. Lord Acastus hasn't personally given remarks to The Fortress in years." Nova's eyes shift to Arche.

"You guys haven't seen your schedule yet?" Arche asks, raising an eyebrow.

"We left the sleeping chamber well before it was posted." I reply.

"Well, our squadrons are facing each other during battle simulation at *seventeen hundred hours.*" Arche flashes a wide grin.

"Nice!" Nova exclaims.

"What a great chance to show off, then." I bump Arche's shoulder. "But what does that have to do with the Lord's speech?"

"Our battle simulation isn't the only thing of note. I was talking to some of the guys, all of our schedules are out of order. We don't have the classes we used to. I wouldn't think twice about it usually, but it's happening to *everyone.*"

"Hmm…" I ponder.

"Let's go get seats, I'm sure people are going to rush out of bed to hear whatever the Lord is saying. Especially when they see their schedules." Arche leads Nova and I to an empty table a few rows from the stage. When Nova and I settle, he goes to get food for himself.

"Any idea what the Lord is going to talk about?" Nova asks me quietly.

"No, I don't." My words come out bitter and unfeeling, though I don't mean them to. Nova seems to take the hint though, and she doesn't push me anymore. Always the reasonable one, the water to my flame, Nova knows exactly when I need a moment to cool down. So I let my mind wander to Lord Acastus as I race to figure out what he could possibly wish to discuss.

Arche eventually walks back to the table, plate stacked with thin cakes and heaps of fruit preserves, chocolate spread, butter, and syrup. He sits next to Nova—across from me—and digs in quickly, his mouth sloshing with the sounds of food. My stomach churns at the noise. I reach over to him and take his chin in my hand, pressing it up and closing his mouth. He slows his eating and keeps his mouth closed after that.

Nova and I eventually begin eating our own food and the room around us begins to buzz. I hear conversations all wondering the same thing I am.

What is Lord Acastus going to talk about?

Arche and Nova talk idly on the other side of the table, something about the stables out on the grounds, I think. But I remain in my own mind—a fortress of its own—with my thoughts bursting through the walls in bitter gusts of wind, like the winds of Lex.

"What do you think, Sol?" Arche asks.

"About what?" I respond, my thoughts slowly fading into the background. In my mental leave, the dining hall has filled almost to the brim. Everyone is here to listen to Lord Acastus speak.

"The horses in the stables. Do you think they bring them inside The Castle for the winter?" Arche meets my eyes. Is he seriously asking me about horses?

I remain distracted, watching person after person pool into the dining hall, each in a different color cloak.

"You know what Arche, that's a great question, follow it up with the headmistress and get back to me." My voice is monotone, completely detached from their conversation. Nova giggles and Arche retreats.

I am unblinking, staring at the bumps and divots in the cold stone table I sit at. I find a particularly deep dent and trace it with my finger, calming my thoughts in the repeated motions. The volume of the hall grows with each tracing over the stone, until I can no longer hear myself think.

Two pounds of a staff on the ground. The room goes silent. Two more pounds and the hoods of our cloaks come down, a symbol of respect no soldier or student of The Undying Army dares to disobey. Another two pounds and our eyes are on the stage. Two final pounds—a total of eight—and we know that Lord Acastus, Knight of Lex is ready to speak. But it isn't the Lord that appears on stage.

The hall is eerily silent, I swear that I can hear my own heartbeat in the quiet. Then a woman—tall and skeletal—her long black hair falling in a curtain behind her, walks onto the stage. Wraith-like in stature, the woman is clearly an immortal, but not a direct blood relative of the royals of Lex.

Madam Alessia Hadu, headmistress of The Academy of the Undying Army, walks to the center of the stone stage and regards the room before speaking.

"Students of The Academy of the Undying Army, I bid you good morning." Her gaunt face ripples with each word, her raspy voice straining to muster up the power to fill the expansive hall. "Today is a momentous day. As you may have noticed, your schedules look quite different. Rather than your usual rotation of lessons and battle training after lunch, each of you now have large amounts of allotted free time." The room shakes with possibility, the amount of battle training that I can do in that time is incomprehensible. The Headmistress goes on. "This is not the only change that has been made to your daily schedules. To tell you more, Lord Acastus Knight of Lex, is here to explain."

The already quiet room silences further, any energy floating about, clipped quickly. A tall man with grey hair and matching eyes walks up the stairs, the click of his boots, and the clack of the Headmistress' heels, the only sounds daring to fill the hall.

Lord Acastus is a stately man. Tall, broad shouldered, and muscular, he is the embodiment of a perfect soldier. Despite his age and grey hair—though some say that his hair was white, even in youth—he is blessed with the gifts of the immortals and his skin remains clear and smooth. Handsome and eternal, Lord Acastus is what every soldier wishes to be… *Power itself.* Though he looks mortal at first glance, he walks with the calm demeanor of an immortal—no rush—for he has all the time in the realms.

The fine features of his face are only accentuated by his exquisite clothing. A gambeson of grey and long black pants with matching black boots, align imperially with the grey of his eyes and hair. His chin is strong and the line of his jaw sharp. He *is* classically handsome, a true Knight.

As he walks across the platform—his power flowing off in waves that crash throughout the hall—all eyes follow. He finally makes it to the center of the stage with the perfect balance of noble command and the nonchalant manner of the immortals. After taking account of the crowd, he speaks, his voice commanding and smooth. There is a slight rasp to it, a mortal quality that shocks me for a moment. For any other immortal, this would soften his appearance. But *this* is the Knight of Lex, and he will not be diminished.

"Welcome students and soldiers of The Undying Army." His voice ripples across the hall effortlessly. "I have come to discuss changes with your schedules. But first, I must attend to another order of business." An air of confusion drifts through the hall. "We are but a short three-star cycles away from the end of this millennium and the beginning of the next. With this, comes The Alignment of the Realms."

The Alignment of the Realms is of colossal importance to the citizens of The Seven Realms of Infinity. Something that most never get to experience in their lifetimes, The Alignment is the advent-of-the-millennia phenomenon where the realms perfectly align with each other. Usually in constant motion, once a millennium, the realms stop for seven minutes of complete perfection. In those seven minutes, the Knights of The Infinite Knight Court perform The Convergence of The Books. This is the only time where The Books of Infinity—a collection of seven books with an unfathomable amount of power—come together. This process tethers the realms together for another millennium.

"With this historic event, comes The Eternal Dance. A ball full of festivities and attendees from across the seven realms. As stated by The Infinite Order, in this, The Alignment of the Realms for the hundredth millennium, the realm of Lex will host The Eternal Dance." The energy of the room spikes once more. The Eternal Dance is a legendary tradition of honor and light, and the opportunity to attend—well it even piques my interest. Lord Acastus continues, reigning in control of the hall once more.

"At the exact moment of The Alignment, all seven of The Knights of Infinity will perform The Convergence of the Books of Infinity for all of the attendees to witness. Preparations are already underway and you are *all* invited as representatives of The Academy or The Army." If attending the ball isn't a gift in itself, seeing The Convergence with my own eyes is unimaginable. The sheer power all in one place is something that most *Knights* don't get to see more than once.

"I understand that this is an exciting time for the realms." A smile then from Lord Acastus, charming and wide, showing off his bright white and perfect teeth. "However, we must return to the original order at hand. Beginning today, you each have an allotted hour of battle simulation on your schedules. Coupled with another squadron in The Academy, you will get the chance to show off all you have learned." A pause as Lord Acastus scans the room. "The chance to prove yourselves, *to me.*" Shocked intakes of breath come from the students and soldiers alike. Lord Acastus rarely spoke at The Academy, *but to watch us train...*

"As you may already know, my second in command, General Cadel Aldera has chosen to retire after generations of service to my family, this realm, and its army."

The legends of Lord Acastus and General Aldera over years of war and battle, are endless. The General is known for being a quiet man, but his mind is said to be endless. He was blessed by Infinity and born as one of the immortals as well. Other than the royal bloodline of Lex, General Aldera and Madam Alessia are the only other immortals left in the realm. Forbidden from continuing their own line, once they choose to participate in The Flight, the royal bloodline of Lex will be the only immortal line in the realm.

"As General Aldera has no heirs, I must find a replacement for him. So, I look to you, students of The Academy of the Undying Army, to find my next second in command. I will watch all of you, but my second will be chosen from the graduating class of tenth years."

Blood pounds in my head; this is it. All of the power I want and *more*. The chance to prove myself, to earn my name, to show everyone that I am not a *waste*. That the blessings bestowed upon me when I was but an hour old were not wrongfully given. That my decision, my path, is the right one. I know I am the best, all I have to do is show him. But I can't. He will watch me and yet—he won't consider me. I boil.

My chance is here and I can't have it.

My chance is here and I want it more than anything.

My chance is here and I will take it.

Before I can think—I stand, no longer in control of my movements. The eyes in the room shift to me, including those of Lord Acastus. I feel Nova's gaze pierce through my skin, but my sight remains steady on the Lord.

"Name yourself." He says to me.

I have no right—none—to stand and interrupt the Lord. But I do it anyway. I feel my heartbeat in my fingers.

I am here, I want power, I want more.

I meet his stare and speak, sending a silent prayer to Infinity that my voice will carry.

"My name is Soleil Yamanu, I am in my seventh year at The Academy." My voice is proud and strong, crystal clear as it echoes off the walls of the hall. Infinity knows how I have received the strength of the realms in voice, but I have it. I relish in the power but crush under the weight of it all the same. A familiar feeling, so I settle into it.

"*Soleil Yamanu,*" Lord Acastus regards me slowly. "Why do you stand? Why do you interrupt me in my speech?"

His eyes are cold, but there is an edge of curiosity in his voice.

I gamble, choosing to capitalize on his interest, and praying to Infinity that it leaves me enough space to be heard. "I have a grievance with your words my Lord." He nods then, gaze softening and curiosity winning out. Something about his features—his eyes—ignite a feeling in my core that refuses to leave. "The opportunity to be your second in command is one for honor and glory unmatched in all of the realms. It should not be restricted to those in the tenth year. There are plenty of gifted students in The Academy that *aren't* in their tenth year. If you are watching us all, then respectfully, *consider us all.*"

His mouth curves into a smile as I speak. "Why yes, *Soldier Yamanu*, you present an interesting point." A chill goes through my bones at the title. *Soldier*, a word only used to address students at The Academy for the most serious of matters. "I will consider all students of The Academy in years—seven through ten. A *treat* for being so bold. A character I quite like to see in my soldiers." I believe him done after that, but he speaks again, his words chilling my bones. "Do not disappoint me." These words are not for The Academy as a whole, but for me alone.

My heartbeat roars in my ears. It is all I can do to remain standing, knees locked, back straight, and shoulders squared. But I am not done yet, for now I am on Lord Acastus' radar, and I must remain benevolent. "Thank you, my Lord, for your generosity. I will not forget this." My words come out with the grace of a thousand Knights.

Lord Acastus holds my stare. "Neither will I, *Soldier Yamanu*." His eyes flare with interest and I feel them as they survey my body. And then a chill, as if his power is wrapped around me, probing me too, deciding whether or not I am worthy of his thoughts.

I sit down, my movements controlled and calm. I continue to hold the Lord's stare until he breaks it himself. My breaths are shallow—too quick to take effect in my body. I keep them quiet, in an attempt to avoid drawing any more attention to myself.

Nova reaches for my hand from across the table, taking it in hers. I look up. *Okay spitfire let's see what you've got.* I read the words in her eyes. I allow myself a glance at Arche who has his brows furrowed in frustration. *Fair,* I did just put myself on Lord Acastus' radar. Nova keeps her grip tight on my hand as the Lord continues to speak.

"All students of The Academy in years seven through ten will be considered for the role of my second in command of The Undying Army. If anyone else has any—" a stop, and a look in my general direction. "*Grievances*, speak now." The students of The Academy shuffle in discomfort, looking around for the next person to speak up. Of course, no one does.

"Very well. I will consider you all for the next star cycle; twenty-eight days. At the end of this time, on the first day of the *ninth* star cycle, I will announce my new second in command. An honor for the ages, they will be carved in timeless splendor and honored at The Eternal Dance." Lord Acastus' eyes flicker over the audience. "I expect great things to come from my search." He meets my eyes once more before walking off the stage and out the back doors of the dining hall. A chill crawls relentlessly down my spine.

When the Lord is finally gone, talk in the hall resumes at a shrill volume. Nova and Arche finally turn to me.

Arche is pale and oddly nervous as he speaks first. "So, now that you have the power of the realms in your hands. What will you do with it?" His words fly over my head as my mind drifts to Lord Acastus' bitter eyes and his words directed only to me.

Do not disappoint me.

I will not.

CHAPTER
TWO

Though the clatter of dishes rings out as thousands of students rise and leave the dining hall, I remain plastered to my seat. I can't shake Lord Acastus' eyes out of my mind, so I begin comparing them to the ones I see so often in my dreams. Lord Acastus' aren't as blue, and they are much colder than the ones that live only in my mind, but the burn of emotion is the same.

"Sol? Are you ready to go?" Nova asks me, an air of concern in her voice.

I shake my head attempting to rid myself of the pair of eyes that follow me relentlessly. "Yeah, I'm ready." My voice comes out shaky—unsure—but I don't bother explaining myself.

"Hey, are you alright? I know that was rough." Arche's concern spills out into his voice.

"Yeah, I'm fine. I feel great. I think I'm coming off an adrenaline rush." I try to sound as okay as possible, but my tone is still off. Whatever blessing from Infinity I had during the conversation with Lord Acastus, seems to have worn off by now.

"*Okay.*" Nova stretches out the word. "How about we get to history early? Shake you out of that—*adrenaline rush.*" Nova clearly sees right through me, as she always does, but she also knows better than to bring it up in front of Arche. There is no need to get him worried.

"Yeah, that sounds good." I stand and collect my dishes. I lift the soft hood of my cloak over my head, hoping to block out any prying eyes. I *did* just announce myself to the entirety of The Academy. I don't need any more eyes on me.

I pick up my tray and walk it to the bins at the front of the hall, avoiding eye contact with anyone who crosses my path. Of course, I hear the whispers. A blood red cloak isn't exactly traditional and people seem to have put the pieces together easily enough.

I turn around to Nova and Arche. "Let's get going before people arrive to the history lesson." I move to address Arche alone. "See you in battle simulation?"

He smiles, cocky and bright. "Maybe—or maybe I will be so quick that you *won't* see me."

"Ha. Ha. Ha." I laugh sarcastically. "See you then. Come on Nov." As Nova and I walk out of the dining hall we are quickly hit by the crisp air of Lex.

"So, *if you are watching us all, then consider us all?*" Nova is casual, almost skeptical. Still, the gleam in her eyes tells me that she is struggling to find the correct words.

I make it easy for her. "Yeah." I take a moment, searching for exactly what to say.

"I guess that puts me in the running too." She lets out a breath, as if the situation is so unfathomable that she must steady herself. "And Arche, too."

"Listen, Nov I have waited for a chance like this for my whole life. And I saw it, it was *right there*. But he won't consider me for the job because I am in my seventh year? I couldn't let it go by. And I know it was a rash move but—"

Nova cuts me off. "Soleil, I trust you. Truly. But you made yourself known to the Knight of Lex; you must watch what you do now. I know you want this Sol, but you have to be *careful*."

"Nova, I am going to get this job. I know it." I set my jaw in determination.

"I know you are Sol, that's what terrifies me." She turns to me. I laugh when I meet her eyes and she joins me soon after.

When we finally reach Female Sleeping Chamber G, it is alive with excitement. I skip to the fire and I rub my hands together to soak up the warmth. My knuckles are incredibly rough and red from Lex's dry air. As I make a mental note to go down to The Castle of Lex for some of Alma's homemade lotion, I hear a voice coming from the door frame.

"*Soleil Yamanu*, what a *bold* thing to do today. I always thought you were a little spitfire, but I didn't think that it would extend to Lord Acastus. I'm surprised that you were not executed on the spot." The voice is venomous, slick with invitation.

I am friendly with all the seventh-year girls in The Academy—when you live with them for so long it happens—but the other years, not so much. I turn to the door and find Fay Enyo, a rat faced tenth year who has long despised me for consistently outranking her, despite my being three years younger. Her straight black hair falls just to her chin in a pristine curtain that swishes as she speaks.

"Maybe Lord Acastus was just *feeling generous*." I pause, walking to her. "Or maybe, what I said had *value*. You wouldn't know that feeling though, would you? Considering you haven't said a valuable thing in the last ten years." My words are casual, conversational, but it is hard to miss the taunting that I weave through them.

Fay swings at me, I dodge it quickly and her fist collides with the stone doorframe. She lets out a gasp. Fay is shorter than me, and skinnier by far, so I spin around, easily sweeping her into a headlock. I quickly unsheath my dagger to press it to her throat. The shining blade sits against the center of her neck with pressure enough to let her know that I will slice if I have to. For a moment, I want to.

"You still haven't learned your lesson, Fay? Listen to me. You are going to leave me alone and you will not come back to this chamber again. Got it?" Fay shakes in my arms, trying to yank herself free. I adjust myself to remind her who is in control. "*Uh uh uh*. No. Don't do that, Fay." I coo. "Now, I am going to let go, and you are going to leave. If you don't," I pause, bringing my mouth to her ear, so only she can hear. "This dagger will be in your neck before you can say another word about how *bold* I am." I am shocked by the confidence of my own words, by the poison lacing them.

Fay struggles again and I let go. She springs away from me, heaving to catch her breath. I point my dagger at her, reminding her that I am not making an empty promise. She meets my glare, her eyes feral, and collects herself before walking swiftly down the hall to her own sleeping chamber. I let out a breath and slip my dagger back into its home at my thigh, suddenly disgusted by its capability for creating fear.

I turn around to face the rest of the sleeping chamber and find nineteen sets of eyes on me—including Nova's whose face burns hot with fury. I simply walk to my trunk and gather my things for history; my textbook titled *History of the Seven Realms of Infinity*, a black leather-bound journal, and my pouch which holds some fountain pens and lead pencils. I shove my things into a black leather satchel and walk out of the sleeping chamber. I am only about twenty or thirty feet out when I hear the clacking of Nova's boots trailing after me.

"Soleil!" Her voice echoes down the hall. I keep walking, my face going red with embarrassment. Nova is clearly going to scold me for what I did, but in the moment it felt right. At the very least Fay won't bother me again, and after seven years of torture from her, maybe some fear will be a welcome sight. I hear Nova's steps quicken behind me, slowly getting louder until she is beside me, her steps matching my own.

"Soleil! Stop!" She is truly angry now. She grabs my wrist, forcing me to stop walking. She takes her stance in front of one of the windows, the light of the sun radiating around her in a golden halo.

"What?" I look off to the side.

"Soleil. Look at me." Her voice is stern and commanding in a way I rarely hear it.

I relent and turn to face her. "Yes?"

"Do you care to explain what that was about? Fay has been bothering us for years and *now* you hold a dagger to her throat?"

I stop her there. "That is the point Nova. Fay Enyo has been messing with us since our first day at The Academy. Why not stop it now?"

Nova and I entered The Academy in the same year. Both orphaned on Lex, we found home in the cold and calculating strategy and steel that The Academy offered. The two of us were a part of the *Lost* in the realm of Lex. We were the unwanted, the abandoned, the anonymous. Nova Ignotus—*the unknown star*, in the language of worlds past—was deserted at the doorstep of The Castle of Lex in the middle of winter. I was left in a similar way as a newborn—found in an abandoned army blockhouse at the edge of Lex. Lord Nasim—Knight of Entis and ruler of The Door of the Dusk—must have felt merciful then, for my soul remained put and my heart continued to beat to the pounding of the wind. A blessing and a curse—an Infinity-blessed life that I far from deserve.

When I was finally found and brought inside The Castle to The Women of the Lost, they stripped the layers of fabric and makeshift clothing from my body, finding a piece of paper that—in a rushed scrawl—read "*Soleil Yamanu.*"

Each of the Lost receive a new surname upon arrival—usually some twist on the words abandoned, anonymous, or forgotten. A cruel joke for the immortals of the realm.

The Women of the Lost however, chose not to change my surname, even though *Yamanu* was a word none of them had heard before—made up, or from a language so old and obscure it was simply forgotten. *Soleil,* on the other hand, was easy. Another word from the languages of the old world, it means sun. Ironic in the desolate land of Lex.

Maybe I avoided the fate of being forever unknown like every other orphan in Lex, but it was never that simple to me. I always felt that I have to earn my name, my uniqueness. So, *Lieutenant Yamanu* became synonymous with a bright future, one where I earned the right to have a name so different from those in my same situation. That was the path I set out on, the only path I have ever known. The path that put me in front of the Lord of Lex today.

Nova and I are the rare bright spots in Lex. The rare light surrounded by endless night. Despite being smothered by the dark and cold, Nova and I shone anyway. I became the sun, and she, the stars.

When I made the decision to attend The Academy of the Undying Army, at eleven, instead of The School of the Unfading in Ingenium, Alma—Nova and I's caretaker—was concerned for me. I had grown up loving to read and by the time I left The Castle, I had devoured Alma's library twice over. Alma simply assumed that I would attend The School as she once did, but something called me to The Academy.

Seeing it outside my window for my entire life, watching the calculated steps of the soldiers and the decorated lieutenants walk by, I was drawn to it. Drawn to the possibility of *earning* what had been so easily given to me. But Nova was a year younger than me. At ten, she would traditionally remain in The Castle with The Women of the Lost for another year before picking her path. But Nova begged and pleaded with Alma to let her join me, even if she would be younger than anyone at The Academy.

After weeks of pleading and convincing, Alma softened, and agreed to speak with the headmistress of The Academy to see if it was even possible. For weeks Alma met with the headmistress, and day after day Nova and I begged for information asking her how the meetings went, but it was always the same.

"The meeting was fine; we will continue to talk tomorrow."

Always in the same brusque tone, always without meeting our eyes. Then the next day she would go back to The Fortress to speak to the headmistress once again. This went on for weeks until Alma finally returned one day, two letters in hand. She handed one to me and the other to Nova. I recall inspecting it for long seconds.

The envelope was cream colored, a dark grey wax seal that read *Lex* was stamped to close it. On the back, was my name, in a cursive script. I was far from submitting my confirmation to either The School or The Academy so it never crossed my mind that it could be an admission letter.

I tore through the envelope, the wax seal landing on the ground in a soft thud. I grabbed the letter and—in my haste—the torn envelope fell to the floor as well. I unfold-ed the paper and read the words.

> SOLEIL YAMANU,
> ON BEHALF OF THE ACADEMY OF THE UNDYING
> ARMY, WE ARE DELIGHTED TO GRANT YOU ADMISSION TO
> OUR INCOMING FIRST YEAR CLASS. WE EXPECT GREAT
> THINGS FROM YOU.
> REGARDS,
>
> ALESSIA HADU
> HEADMISTRESS OF THE ACADEMY OF THE UNDYING ARMY

I was at a loss for words, I couldn't speak or think. The admissions processes for both The Academy and The School were notoriously rough—essays, training courses, physical evaluations, and entrance exams were the usual. But in this brief and to the point letter, *I was in.* My heart thudded in my chest; I saw my life laid out before me. My first day at The Academy, the battle simulations, re-lentless training, my graduation, being named lieutenant and leading a squadron into battle. I saw a life where I deserved my name, where I had proven myself worthy of being more than just another one of Lex's *Lost.* I saw the world where the lucky hand that I was delt wasn't wasted.

In my fantasy, I had forgotten about Nova.

I turned to her. She was holding her letter, completely frozen. I dropped mine to the ground and snatched hers out of her hands. I scanned through it wildly, attempting to get the gist of the words. Her letter was longer than mine by far, so I jumped to the last sentence.

> THIS BEING SAID, WE ARE DELIGHTED TO GRANT YOU
> ADMISSION IN OUR INCOMING FIRST YEAR CLASS.

I turned to Nova, and suddenly she was in my life ahead as well. It was the both of us walking into the dining hall for our first day at The Academy, both of us in battle simulation, both of us being broken and rebuilt by the relentless training, both of us graduating and being named lieutenants. The two of us *together* leading our squadrons into battle. All of it, with my sister at my side. What better way to earn my name, to earn my blessing from Infinity, then to have Nova next to me?

Nova looked at me and I was sure she saw it too.

"How did you do it?" I asked Alma, my voice shaking with excitement and disbelief.

Alma looked down at me. "It took a lot of convincing, believe me. But Madam Alessia seems to believe that having both of you would be to her benefit. Admissions numbers for girls at The Academy have been down in recent years and having two girls from Lex who *aren't* taking their first chance to escape to The School, is a rare sight indeed." Alma cracked a mischievous smile. "Of course, Nova will have to go through the training course for evaluation purposes because she is so young. But both of you will attend The Academy by the end of the year."

So together, Nova and I entered the doors of The Fortress two days before the start of the term. Nova passed the training course with flying colors, and I, opting to take the entrance exam even though I didn't need to, received the highest score out of the entire entering class. Arm in arm, our leather satchels filled with our most precious belongings, we entered our new lives *together*, as we did everything.

It was the middle of the year; the day unseasonably warm for Lex. Nova and I had just put in our orders for our thermals and cloaks. Nova chose black, a customary color among The Army and I chose a deep blood red that seemed to suck the light around it.

We went down to the dining hall for breakfast, the smell of the food intoxicating. Nova and I loaded our trays with sweet thin cakes, loads of syrup, and piles of fresh cut fruit. We each got a mug of thick and steaming coca. Food in The Castle was okay, filling but flavorless. But the two of us had never seen so much variety of food in our entire lives. When our trays were close to toppling, we began walking to a table. The dining hall was nearly empty, Nova's habit of rising early winning out even then. We were stopped by a girl who was much shorter than me but still looked to be a few years older.

Her features were sharp and disproportionate, eyes too close together, nose too small, her lips too thin. Her face had a downward slope, the look of perpetual anger and disgust. She hadn't spoken a single word to me or Nova, she simply regarded us slowly and continued walking in between us. As she passed in between Nova and me, she let her hands out, flicking each of our trays up and onto our bodies. Nova and I were a sticky mess, drenched in coca and syrup we quickly left the hall.

Only days later, we saw that girl again in our first round of battle training where we learned her name, Fay Enyo. She was relentless, messing with Nova and I for outperforming her in everything we did. I remember everything and, until today, I never fought back.

"Why not now Soleil? You may not realize it, you may have just entered Lord Acastus' radar today, but there is no way that he is not having you watched. You know as well as I do that this Fortress has eyes and ears. Every brick is watching and listening and you just held Fay Enyo in a headlock, dagger to her throat." As Nova talks, it becomes incredibly clear that my choice was a bad one. There *are* soldiers and spies everywhere in The Fortress, and while I know the girls in my squadron well enough, there are no promises that Fay won't speak.

"Okay, okay. I get it. It wasn't the best idea. But Fay is off our backs now." Despite my growing nervousness at the situation, I continue to shift to the bright side.

"Sure, but if she speaks? Infinity knows what would happen then."

I think of every way I can prevent her from speaking—I can't—but I *can* come up with a contingency plan. "Fay has messed with every single girl in our year. *If* she speaks, she will have to set the scene, the other girls who saw would be brought in for questioning. None of them would be on her side. Fay must know that and that's why she *won't* talk. *If* she does though, we use every horrible thing she has done to us and turn it on her. Let the girls use their pent-up rage to flip the story. She started it anyway." I shrug. My voice is hushed. The Fortress listens and in a moment of ignorance, I forgot that. I can't afford to do it again.

Nova quietly considers my logic and her eyes swirl with possibility. Moments later, she replies. "You know that when it comes down to picking a side, I will always pick you. But that is as far as I go on this. I see your reasoning and I am fairly certain she won't talk, but if she does—"

I cut her off. "*If*, Nova, that is a big *if*. We'll be fine. Now let's get to history before we're late." I turn around and begin walking down the hall.

"Our intention *was* to be early to history lessons, wasn't it?" Nova queries, lifting her hood and following me.

"Yeah, it was." I respond, laughing humorously.

CHAPTER
THREE

I have always adored the scent of old books. Simply radiating the scent, the fourth-floor lecture hall is one of my favorite rooms in The Fortress. Large, with rows and rows of wooden tables and chairs set atop of risers, it is lined on either side by bookshelves packed to the brim with novels and memoirs, textbooks and epics. In this early hour, the sunlight has not yet made its way to the thin windows set between the bookshelves.

To my delight, there aren't many people in class yet, which makes sense considering that they all happened to be in the sleeping chamber when I chose to *put on a show*. Nova and I walk down the levels of risers to our seats in the first row of the lecture hall. I reach into my satchel and pull out my textbook, journal, and a lead pencil, arranging them neatly in front of me.

"Did you do the readings for today?" Nova asks quietly—her usual small talk, safe enough for the prying ears of students, professors, and soldiers alike.

"Yeah. It was *interesting*." The reading was about the fall of Lex's empire. Technically it was a bit less direct than that, but our professor has her own supplements and annotations.

"Okay sure. If you consider Professor Clara's subversive comments about Lex to be *interesting*."

Professor Clara Holden is a well-known *insurgent* in The Academy. While she is a mortal—like Nova and I—some say that she must have been blessed by Infinity, for she is one of the brightest minds the realms have ever seen. While I tend to disregard the musings of the people of Lex, and who they deem *Infinitely blessed*, with Professor Clara, it is quite obvious. With her jet black hair and pearlescent skin, she often looks out of place among the mortals here. Many believe that she would have been better off teaching where she studied at The School of the Unfading in Ingenium, but her capacity for strategy and her love for steel must have won out. Professor Clara is the only superior in The Academy who requests that we call her *Professor*. All of our other superiors got their training here in The Academy and were sent to The Undying Army where they earned their ranks. If they decide to teach or supervise, we are to call them by that rank.

"They *are* interesting." I counter.

"Sure, sure. But at the end of the day our final examinations are on what the textbook says." Nova rolls her eyes at me. I see history as an art, a way to learn from the past and strategize for the future. Nova, however, has had an aversion to history since she was a toddler.

"Good morning students." Professor Clara walks into the lecture hall, carrying a large stack of books, her long silver hair flowing down her back. She wears a simple emerald dress that sweeps the floor. "I trust that you have all done today's reading." The lecture hall buzzes over Professor Clara's voice.

"Excuse me!" Her voice is controlled and the volume of the room softens almost instantly. "Very well, it seems as if Lord Acastus' speech is going to ruin the whole lesson if we don't air our concerns. Now, why don't you all tell me what the big deal is. From my knowledge, he was very much to the point." No one speaks. "Well go on, I won't start the lesson like this."

Lyra, a pale skinned girl with strawberry blonde hair speaks up, her voice unsure. "Well Professor, it isn't exactly *Lord Acastus' speech* that has us concerned." My face grows hot.

Wonderful. If it isn't about what happened with Fay—which I am sure it's not—then I am about to relive my entire conversation with Lord Acastus, narrated in the third person. The room fills with the giggles of eighteen girls. I tug my hood further down my head and sink into my chair, my eyes fixed pointedly on my textbook.

"I see." Professor Clara has an inquisitive tone to her words. "Well then, let me just say this. Without the actions of your fellow soldier, none of you would have even the *slightest* chance to be Lord Acastus' second in command. Simply by your actions at this moment, it is clear that many of you *still* won't have one. I understand that you are all friendly with each other, as is the byproduct of growing up together, so use this time not to *ridicule* your fellow soldier for speaking up when none of you had the fortitude to do so, but to actually attempt to *impress* the Lord. It might be to your benefit. This job is one that people have killed for in the past, and Lord Acastus may as well have you all on the execution block simply for laughing at his decision."

For the first time, I feel hope from someone other than myself. Professor Clara was always a favorite of mine, her insights a rare breath of fresh air from usual black and white history lessons. Hearing what she really thinks about what I did, makes me stop second guessing myself in an instant. My face cools and I lift my head. I meet Professor Clara's eyes. Not a usually expressive woman, I am shocked when I see an inkling of a smile on her face. The room finally falls silent, as if the students truly realize what is at stake.

"Well then, let's begin our lesson."

I reach to open my journal, hands lingering on the soft leather cover. I crack it open and date the page, 1/8/999/99, the first day of the eighth star cycle, in the nine hundred ninety-ninth year of the ninety-ninth millennium. Picking up a piece of chalk, Professor Clara begins her lecture with passion flowing from her voice. She is *not* an expressive woman—not unless she is lecturing.

"Each year you learn the history of the realms, and each year I am disappointed in the lower-level professors for being so incredibly vague. I will assure you that not a single one of you is aware of the true, unabridged and uncensored history of even this realm."

I am confused for a moment. I turn to Nova who only shrugs. We learn the same history of the realms every year. What else could we possibly know about Lex?

Professor Clara continues. "At the beginning of our time, after the death of the old world, and the deaths of worlds before it, The Seven Books of Infinity were formed. These books were scattered about our universe, each one forming a realm to call home and an immortal Knight sworn to protect it.

"Each of the books holds a mystifying amount of power, but they each specialize in one thing. In the realm of Ingenium lies The Book of Wit. The Book of Wit holds the knowledge of this world and every world past. So much knowledge that only the Knight of Ingenium can handle reading it all. From The Book of Wit comes many smaller books in The Boundless Library, so that anyone may get even *some* of the knowledge that The Book of Wit holds. Students of The Boundless library belong to The School of the Unfading, a prestigious academy for only the brightest.

"The Book of Law belongs here in Lex, and it has the power to forge laws that restrict anyone, even the strongest of the immortals. It is only used by the Knight of Lex, and only with the full approval of The Infinite Knight Court. The Undying Army's authority comes from the power in The Book of Law, and its job is to uphold the laws of the realms.

"The Book of Age is under the jurisdiction of the realm of Aetas. It has the power to control and manipulate time, as well as maintain its flow. The Ageless—a group of master time holders who study the flow of time via the star cycles—led by the Knight of Aetas, are the only beings who know the full extent of the book's power.

"The Book of Life in the realm of Spiritus, controls the cascade of spirits flowing into our realms as lives, through The Door of the Dawn. The Book of Element, which has a home in Tellus, creates the matter of our realms—the air we breathe and the ground we walk on. These elements are studied in The Lab of the Realms.

"The Book of Death lies in the realm of Entis where it controls the waves of those exiting life and becoming spirits once more through The Door of the Dusk. Finally, The Book of the Bound, which ties the realms together, lies in Omnis. The home of the Infinite Knight Court where the Seven Knights of Infinity meet once a star cycle to make decisions that affect each of the realms."

My hand remains still and my paper empty. As students of The Academy, we get the same lecture on the realms each year, this information is nothing new. I quickly tune out from Professor Clara's lecture, not wishing to subject myself to the eternal torment of listening to her speak on something I already know. She may add her flourishes—bits about forgotten Knights or insights of the old world—but I can live without hearing them. I truly love Professor Clara, but some lessons are better than others.

As Professor Clara goes on about the importance of the Infinite Knight Court, my mind travels to The Castle of Lex. I see my old room with the Lost, the pallet that Nova and I shared. I see Alma's room, and the two fluffy chairs that we sit on when I visit. But my mind continues to move until I see Lord Acastus' eyes.

I attempt to fit them into the eyes that haunt my dreams—it is to no avail.

CHAPTER
FOUR

Beams of sunlight hit the pages of my journal, sending long shadows across the length of the wooden table. My journal is open, my pen in hand. Only a few notes are written on the page I dated hours earlier, mainly names of forgotten Knights, or quirks about the realms that Professor Clara shared. Nothing particularly interesting, but just enough random information to use as embellishments for a future essay if need be. Professor Clara drawls on in the background of my thoughts, her voice fluctuating with excitement at the material.

"Omnis' central placement in the perfectly symmetrical system that is The Realms of Infinity, makes it so that its magical signature pulls the realms to it. This keeps the realms bound as one. And that my students, is why Omnis is the binder of the realms and the keeper of The

Book of the Bound. A shift in this infinite order can be catastrophic to all in the realms." The energy in the room is nonexistent. Professor Clara, seeming to finally take the hint, quickly wraps up the class.

"Now. No readings for our next class but please review your notes and turn in your papers if you have not done so already. Please put forth your best effort today in battle simulation, Lord Acastus will not be the *only* one watching." Professor Clara winks at me, and I allow myself to crack a smile. The lecture hall fills with the shuffling of papers and textbooks. "Have a good few days, everyone. I will see you at our next lecture!" Conversation erupts from the mouths of twenty soldiers.

I quickly shove my things into my leather satchel, with no regards for organization. Nova and I stand, and as we walk up the risers to the door out of the lecture hall, I remember Professor Clara and what she said at the beginning of class. When I get to the door I turn around and find her at her desk.

"Thanks for the lesson, Professor. I appreciate it."

Professor Clara looks up at me, a mixture of pleasure and surprise painting her face. "Of course, Miss Yamanu. Any time. Though don't go interrupting the Knights of the realms for fun now." She pushes out those last words with as much sternness as she can muster, but they still come out playfully.

"Whatever you say, Professor. Thanks again." I reply. I walk out of the doorway and Nova is waiting for me down the hall, so I pick up my pace and walk to her.

"Do you have any idea what time it is?" I ask Nova. There are no clocks in the fourth-floor lecture hall and by the stiffness plaguing my body, Professor Clara's lesson must have gone on for hours.

"Um… *twelve hundred hours?* Maybe thirteen?" Nova says, unsure.

My stomach growls. *How long was that lesson?* Long enough to have given my body time to digest my breakfast, though the adrenaline from this morning, and my encounter with Fay could have sped that up. My stomach gurgles in response to my theory. On our walk back to the sleeping chamber, I pass by a window that has the perfect view of The Castle of Lex and The Wall. To my surprise, snow is falling over the realm. I backtrack a few steps and stop in front of the window.

"What are you doing?" Nova asks with an air of curiosity to her tone.

"Look—snow." My voice is full of wonder as I point outside, touching the glass with my index finger. "Lex *can* be pretty sometimes." The bright sun and dark landscape, the all-encompassing wall, and the towering castle. They are a sight, the light fluff of snow making it all the more beautiful. As desolate as Lex is, it has its moments. This is one of them. I look out and see the battlefield below us, stretching into the boundaries of the first camps of foot soldiers.

"I guess it *is* kind of nice. In a bitter way. But—" Nova pauses. "I could say the same thing about you."

I turn to meet her face and chuckle softly. "Yeah, yeah. Thank you Nova, for the wonderful insight." I say sarcastically and bump her shoulder lightly. "Come on, it's cold," I usher Nova on. I pick up my steps, suddenly remembering the warmth that awaits me in the sleeping chamber. My stomach growls again—I also remember the snacks that Nova keeps in her trunk.

When Nova and I finally arrive at the sleeping chamber, it is completely empty. I assume that most of the girls are probably attending extra lessons or trying to make snowballs out of the flurries of snow outside. I place my bets on the latter. Practically jumping to the fireplace, I choose to sit on the warm stone in front of it rather than stand next to it. I pull the hood of my cloak down and delight in the heat. Nova is behind me digging through her trunk. I look at the clock above the fireplace, *1238*.

"Professor Clara's lecture really lasted three hours?" My tone is blunt. *The women knows how to talk.*

Nova laughs. "Yeah, I guess it did." She pauses and I hear the opening of her trunk. "Hungry? I heard the growling of your stomach echoing through the halls on the way down here." I turn around and make a mocking face. Nova holds up a bag of dried fruits and roasted almonds. I try to hold off, but with another growl of my stomach, I relent.

"Fine," I say. Nova throws the bag to me and I catch it easily. "Thank you."

I turn around to face the fireplace and tear into the bag of snacks pulling out pieces of dried fruit and shoving them into my mouth to try and hush the roar of my stomach. After I eat a few pieces, the grumbling subsides, but I continue to snack. Nova is rearranging her trunk behind me.

"Who else do you think will be watching us at battle simulation?" I ask, mouth full of food.

"You mean other than Lord Acastus?" Nova replies, continuing to dig through her trunk.

"Yeah." I pop some almonds into my mouth, the crunch echoing in my ears.

"Well Professor Clara hinted that she would be there. I wouldn't put it past Madam Alessia." Nova replies, only half invested in the conversation.

"General Aldera?" I wonder.

"Why do you want to know Sol? So, you can see who you are replacing?" Nova taunts.

"Maybe. Honestly, I'm just curious. He must be close to The Flight if he really is retiring."

The Flight is how the immortals of the realms leave their lives behind and go through The Door of the Dusk in Entis as spirits once more. When they feel as if they have lived as long as they wish to, at the end of the year they can let go of their physical bodies and leave this world. Some of the immortals take part in The Flight earlier than others. Legend says that some immortals don't take part in The Flight at all, instead living out their utterly infinite lives in isolation, away from anyone who doesn't understand what it means to truly live *forever.* Traditionally, a royal immortal would wait until they have abdicated their crown to their first-born heir before The Flight, but that *is* only a suggestion.

"He *is* ancient—ah-ha!" Nova exclaims loudly.

I startle, turning to see what she possibly could have found. "What's up with you?" I ask in a distressed tone, actively trying to bring my heart rate down. Nova is half-way inside of her trunk, many of her items scattered around the ground.

"My gloves!" Nova holds up a three fingered glove. Alma made them for her to use in battle, to protect her fingers from the tough strings and arrows when she uses her bow.

"I'm glad you found them." I let out a smile. She *has* been looking for them for star cycles. I pull out the last piece of dried fruit from the bag, shake the remaining almonds into my hand, and pop everything into my mouth, crumbling the bag into a ball.

"Thanks for the snack, Nov." I throw the bag into the trash can in the corner of the room.

"No problem." Nova replies while putting her things back in her trunk. I stand up with my satchel and walk away from my warm spot near the fireplace. I'm pleasantly surprised when I find that the rest of the room is warm too.

I open my trunk and throw my satchel into it, then dig for my fingerless gloves, moving them to the top of the pile. I pull my dagger out of its scabbard at my thigh and rub at the smudges from my encounter with Fay. I huff at a particularly stubborn smudge.

This dagger is one of my most prized possessions, a gift from Alma the day I left the Lost in The Castle of Lex.

I recall when she gave it to me. I had just finished collecting the last of my things—mainly books and the few clothing items I collected over the years—when Alma came to me with the beautiful dagger, sharp and spotless. I forgot how to breathe.

Daggers are expensive, and one of this caliber can feed an entire blockhouse of Lex's soldiers for a star cycle.

To be gifted one at such a young age was something that doesn't even happen to children in Omnis.

Alma studied at The School of the Unfading when she was my age. And yet, after studying magic and aesthetics in the warm Castle of Ingenium, she returned to Lex to bring knowledge and love to this bitter corner of the realms.

Her voice was unsteady when she spoke to me. "For you, my sun," she told me. "For being the light in my darkness. For opening yourself to the knowledge I had to offer. *Go light up the world Soleil.*" She paused and added, "and don't forget to visit *tribulatio.*"

Trouble, in the language of the world's past. I stared at the dagger then, allowing myself to make peace with my past before stepping forward into my new life as a light in the darkness of Lex. I know Alma meant well, but sometimes I see her words only as another burden to my Infinity-blessed life. Just another thing to earn.

Things aren't so bad in The Academy, though. Training is brutal and I have the scars and bruises to show for all my mistakes in battle, but each one reminds me to be *perfect*. In The Academy perfection means power, it means getting to lead when you leave. It means getting to earn my name.

I have always felt pulled to battle, to the metallic clang of steel on steel—simplicity and beauty in its own regard. I want nothing more than to lead, to send an army to battle and come out victorious, to strategize and plan, allocate and fight. All of this so that I might one day earn my name, earn the hand that was dealt to me. But now I might have the chance to do so, and I am terrified.

I close my trunk and walk to my bed, plopping into it face first.

In the dark of my own mind, I realize how tired I am—how drained. My thoughts have been a nonstop swirl all day and I haven't had a chance to let myself take everything in. The realization of what I have done is finally hitting me and it burns to the core.

I spoke directly to the Lord of Lex. I *interrupted* him and changed the course of my own life in the process. I held a knife to a girl's throat and I contemplated letting it slice—

As the feelings come, I retreat deeper into myself in an attempt to quell the emotion. I ache for numbness but can find no solace from the thoughts that occupy my mind.

"What are my odds of getting out of this?" I laugh humorlessly into my blanket.

"Don't mope, Sol. Seriously. Battle simulation is in a few hours and you have to be ready if you want Lord Acastus to remember you." Nova responds, hopeful.

"I don't think he will *ever* forget me." I say, my words muffled into my blanket. "Maybe he *was* planning on executing me on the spot. I bet that he is just trying to draw it out. Make me feel it—assassination maybe?" I ramble on, having a conversation with only myself. I feel Nova sit on the bed beside me. I continue, spiraling. "Or maybe he will just throw a soldier into battle simulation today, with the sole job of killing me." I laugh again. "That would be a way to go. Imagine my cause of death being my own big mouth—figures."

I feel tears begin to well up in my eyes. I try to stop them, but it makes no difference. I have trapped myself in my head all morning, not allowing my feelings to manifest, and now they are coming out with a vengeance. I shove my face deeper into my blanket trying to stop the flow of tears, but they persist. Nova puts a comforting hand on my back. She says nothing, her silence is enough. I shake, sobbing audibly.

I can't do this.

This is the opportunity I have searched for every day. Every day since I learned the gravity of the rumors that have milled about since I was found as a baby. But now that I found it, now that I see the way to show everyone that my blessing is *not* a waste, I look out and find only a looming darkness. When I investigate that darkness, I see the worst version of myself. All of the fears I have pushed away—every inadequacy that I hide from, every horrible thing I have been called—is staring back at me. I am afraid—afraid of myself and all the horrible things I can be. The temptation for power emerges from the darkness and I don't know how to face it. But for now, Nova's hand rubbing my back, her constant presence—it is enough.

I rattle with each wave of tears, heavier and heavier, as the dam that I held tight for so long, finally bursts. More and more power with every tear, I welcome the release. When the emotions subside, and the shaking stops, I sit up and Nova is still next to me, sadness in her eyes. Her face is glossy, she must have cried as well. I choose not to mention it. As I reach to wipe my face, Nova is the first to speak.

"Hungry?" She asks me with a slight smile. I let myself smile back; she knows how to get to me.

"Honestly, yeah. But I think I am actually in the mood to bother Arche. He must be in his room by now." I respond, trying to come up with something to do *other* than think about my life.

"Fine, we bother Arche. Then get lunch." Nova says with a sad smile.

"Deal," I say, satisfied with myself. I get up and walk across the room to the mirror on the far wall. My face is puffy from the tears and my eyes are red, partially from sleep deprivation I assume. My dreams have not been kind to me as of late. I fix my eyebrows with my fingers, smoothing the out of place hairs. I adjust my hair ensuring that it all falls to the front of my body and I flip the hood of my cloak up over my head.

I examine my body in the mirror for a moment. My blood red cape and white thermal set, and then my long hair, shadowed face, and hooded head. I look at the scabbard around my left thigh and just for a moment—I feel like someone who *can* be a general in The Undying Army. I look into my own eyes and see, for the first time, a second in command staring back at me.

I look at Nova who is placing the rest of her things into her trunk. I remember the day when I got my acceptance to The Academy and how, for a moment, I saw a future without her. I feel myself slipping back into that future, one where I leave Nova behind. I knew how I could hold on to her then, but this time I don't. So, when she puts the last of her objects into her trunk and stands up to face me, I walk over and loop my arm into hers. And we walk out of the sleeping chamber *together*.

Desperation and horror washes over me at the idea that I might soon lose Nova. I take a breath and make a mental promise to Infinity that I will stay by her side from now until we can be together no longer.

SNOW CONTINUES TO FALL STEADILY OVER LEX. I SEE THE battlefield covered in an even layer of the bright white fluff as I pass by a window in The Fortress' hallways. Nova and I are still arm in arm as we walk to Male Sleeping Chamber 7G, our pace much slower, and our alertness much lower, than what is usual for us. We haven't spoken—not a single word—since I took her arm and we left Female Sleeping Chamber G. But our silence—the feeling of our arms linked—is conversation enough.

Nova and I have always had an unspoken agreement. Growing up together, we realized that we don't need to fill every moment with words. We have lived through everything together since before we can remember, so our relationship doesn't rely on conversation. Nova was always much better at that than I was. Always the talker, I usually feel the need to fill the silence. But Nova quickly taught me that sometimes, simply being together is perfect. Sometimes, it is better than all the best conversations that the realms have to offer, combined.

As we walk down the halls, I try to feel the ebb and flow of my emotions. I focus on my breathing, in sync with every other step that Nova and I take. Somewhere during the course of the walk, I feel better. I recognize what I have done, and now I must attempt to learn to live with it.

Finally, we arrive at the male wing of The Fortress. Stretching forever, and four levels high, it is so much bigger than the female wing. We take a shortcut, cutting between floors and through different stairwells so that when we arrive on the third floor of the male wing, we simply walk past Male Sleeping Chambers 1G through 6G to get to Arche's room. The male wing is loud, so much louder than the female wing ever is. The clang of metal on metal comes from one sleeping chamber, a screaming match from a different one, and fits of laughter from another.

When Nova and I reach Male Sleeping Chamber 7G, the door is closed and locked. I unhook myself from Nova's arm to bang loudly on the wooden door.

"Arche, we know you're in there." I yell, my mouth against the door. I smack the door again, and soon Nova joins me. I hear footsteps from inside the sleeping chamber and Arche opens the door, just a crack. His hair is messy and his eyes are red. He yawns and it becomes clear that he has been asleep.

"What were you doing in there? It's lunchtime." Nova says as I push the door open the rest of the way.

"Since when do you two care about lunchtime, shouldn't you be studying? *I* was taking a nap." Arche says between yawns and stretches, he moves away from the door and backs up until he hits his bunk.

"Can't do that when we have battle simulation in a few hours. Like you said, *power of the realms in my hands.* Best not to waste it." My tone is taunting. I pause and continue. "Did you eat already?"

Arche replies casually. "No. I usually don't." He rubs his eyes.

He doesn't eat lunch?

Nova and I never eat lunch, but we fill up on breakfast and usually have extra lessons during lunchtime—Arche never does.

"Why not?" Nova asks for me.

Arche turns around to her, sitting on his bunk. "Well, you guys don't and I spend *enough* time with the guys in my squad. I usually lock the door and take a nap after lessons. I keep some food in my trunk if I'm ever hungry." I always assumed that he went to lunch without Nova and I. Every time we told him we *were* going to eat, he was there.

I think for a moment but chose to respond with indifference. "Well, where is the rest of your squadron now?" I look around the sleeping chamber.

"Well, I saw them in history lessons and afterwards they were making plans for some sword fighting practice. What time is it? They are probably at lunch by now." His words are almost incoherent.

Nova seems to understand though. "It's about *thirteen hundred hours.* I would assume that your squad is at the dining hall considering it *is* peak lunch time." She says pointedly while he digs through his trunk. I walk over to the fireplace—drawn to the heat—and sit myself next to it.

"What have you two been up to?" Arche asks, still rummaging through his trunk.

"You know, plotting my scheme to become second in command, calculating the probability of being executed—the usual." My words come out casually.

Arche laughs. "Yeah? And how is that going for you?" He pauses his search to look at me, his stone eyes full of humor. I crack a smile at him.

"Pretty well thank you very much," I pause, then question. "What *are* you looking for?"

"My cloak." Arche replies.

"That one?" I point to a black heap on the ground a few bunks over.

Arche turns, delight filling his face when he sees it. "Yes! Thanks Sol."

"Anytime Arch." I turn to face the fire, soaking up the warmth that is so rare in The Fortress. Nova and Arche chat quietly behind me as I relish in the snap and pop of the warm fire. When Arche is ready to go, he taps my shoulder. I get up and turn to him, finding the boy in complete disarray.

"No. You are not leaving the chamber like *that*." His emerald-colored shirt is untucked from his pants and his cloak is shifted to one side of his body with his hood down over his shoulders.

"What do you mean?" He questions.

I glare at him. "Look at you! You are an absolute mess, Arch. Tuck your shirt please. I'll take care of the rest."

He obeys. Whether he is too tired to argue, or he realizes that I am *right,* I have no idea. I shift his cloak so that it hangs evenly around his body and I lift the hood up over his head, smoothing it so that it falls properly. I walk around him and smooth the wrinkles out of the back of his cloak, draping it so that it falls symmetrically. When I am done, I walk in front of him and admire my work. I made only minor changes, but power *is* in the details. Especially for a fellow *Infinitely blessed.*

"See? So much better, you look like you actually care now." I say, looking up at him.

"What—ever." Arche responds sarcastically.

"Sol is definitely right. You look much more put to-gether." Nova adds.

"I am the best." I say, spinning around to exit the sleeping chamber.

When the three of us arrive at the dining hall it is packed full of people, the far clocks read *1330*. Peak lunchtime for everyone who has just gotten out of lessons.

Lessons usually rotate in The Academy. Everyone has a mandatory history lesson either after breakfast or after lunch and in the opposite time slot are various other lessons that are switched in and out. With our other lessons canceled, most have just gotten out of their history lessons like Nova and I, or their first session of battle simulation with Lord Acastus.

From the feel of the room, it is about an even split. The red noses and sweat slicked hair of some students are clear indicators of battle simulation, while the bored faces of others become the indicator of history lessons.

We weave silently through the crowds and I am care-ful to keep my hood down. My cloak may be a dead give-away as to who I am, but there are always people who sat so far away that they couldn't have seen it very well. I think it's best to play it safe, if they don't know me by cloak color, they can put the name and the face together quick enough.

The three of us walk to the food stations, collecting our trays and utensils. As we walk down the line, I pile my plate, surprised by the lunch options. This is the first time in star cycles that Nova and I have gotten lunch. If I wasn't so hungry, I would have skipped it and gone to Professor Clara's office to speak with her, or to another one of our superiors' offices for private lessons—but today, my stomach wins out.

From the food line I get a cold turkey sandwich piled with meat, stacked high with vegetables, and made with dark grain bread. Then, a bowl of fruit, a steaming bowl of chicken soup, and a small cup of creamy yogurt. The lunch options are light enough that I won't feel weighed down after I eat, but I will have the energy for battle simulation later.

Eventually, Nova, Arche and I make our way to an empty stone table and settle into our spots. The three of us eat slowly, taking deliberate bites and becoming enveloped in the roaring conversation around us until we can no longer hear ourselves think.

CHAPTER
FIVE

After finally releasing my emotions from the tight bonds I held them in, my mind is utterly clear. I can finally think without the crushing weight of my conversation with Lord Acastus caving in on me.

Lunch is over quickly—the dining hall so loud that no conversation between Nova, Arche, and I ever takes place. When we finish eating, we silently rise and walk our trays to the bins at the doors of the hall. We walk out, finding reprieve in the quiet but being hit by the frosty air all the same. As I let my ears adjust to the silence, Arche is the first one to speak. He peeks his head into the entrance of the dining hall.

"It's about *fourteen hundred hours*; we have time before battle simulation. Do you need me for anything? I want to meet with Commander Alexander for history."

"Go ahead, we'll figure out something to do." I respond for Nova and I.

"Maybe I'll stop by the armory. I haven't assembled any new arrows in a while. Running low during the *sim* would be a bad idea." Nova adds, using the shorthand for battle simulation.

"Are you sure you will be okay by yourself Sol?" Arche asks me honestly.

I look up at him and nod my head. "Yeah, I'm okay. I haven't seen Alma in a while, she would enjoy it if I stopped by," I pause and turn to Nova. "Meet you at the battlefield?"

"Yeah. Sounds good. See you then Sol." She makes a kissy face at me as I wave goodbye and turn away to walk towards the exit of The Fortress. Feeling bare without Nova beside me, I adjust my hood so it falls lower on my head and I continue to keep my arms loose, remembering that my dagger is at my thigh if I need it.

I am in the central part of The Fortress now, the area that I usually avoid, and for good reason. Soldiers move in and out for their daily rotation from the morning shift to the evening shift. Superiors go to their homes in The Castle of Lex for the day. Lieutenants and commanders of The Undying Army order squadrons of soldiers around.

The entry room of The Fortress always flows with people. It's cavernous with huge arching ceilings and grand staircases. The entry room is not decorated in any way, consistent with the rest of The Fortress, and the doors are always left wide open for the constant waves of people and the cold air, both relentless in their passage. I shift my gaze to the ground and soundlessly move through the crowd. I'm not stopped on my way.

The Castle of Lex—home to Lord Acastus among other highly ranked nobles—has extremely strict security protocols. As children of the Lost, Nova and I would often get scolded for wandering too deep into the expansive castle. The Castle is at least four times as big as The Fortress, and just as confusing, with even more hallways that lead nowhere and twisting staircases to take you to the most obscure of places.

Nova and I had the map to The Castle memorized, as we do now with The Fortress, but it took us quite a while to get to that point.

Only a year or two before we moved into The Academy, the two of us unknowingly made it to the war room. I faintly recall feeling pulled to it, pulled to the power behind that door. The thrumming and pulsing of cold, dark energy. We were found by guards and escorted back to the Lost wing of The Castle, but I will never forget the pure power behind the door—the promise of more.

As soon as the cold hits me, this time without even the barrier of The Fortress to provide relief, I wish for the warmth of my sleeping chamber. I imagine the fireplace that I was sitting at only a few hours earlier and grit my teeth against the wind. I walk quickly, taking big strides against the relentless air as I cross The Bridge to The Castle of Lex.

The Bridge is made of the same crumbling stone as the rest of Lex. As it is the primary artery of passage between the main sectors of Lex, it's used constantly. I stride past a horse leading a wagon of wood, probably freshly imported from the realm of Tellus. I see a squadron of soldiers taking an afternoon run, and a few superiors I recognize from The Academy. In the distance, on the land to the right of, and below the bridge where I walk, is the battlefield. I avert my gaze before I can take in too many of its details.

My boots click on the stone and I pray to Infinity that this bridge will hold for another hundred millennia. As I approach The Castle of Lex I am hit with the feeling of home. I lived here for so long. These walls—so similar yet so different from the ones in The Fortress—were once *mine.*

I walk up the grand stairs of The Castle and crane my neck to admire its beauty. It is incredibly tall, scraping the sky with its height. The walls of the castle are sleek and shiny, still stone, but so smooth that they are as reflective as glass. The stone itself is jet black creating a jarring contrast to today's blue sky. I am only a few steps from the doors to The Castle, when I am stopped by a guard who sticks out a sword my path.

"Watch it!" He huffs.

"What is this about?" I ask, annoyed by the sword in my face.

"What is your business at The Castle?"

I look up at the guard, a familiar face from my time living here. I am sure that he will recognize me. I pull my hood off my head and look him in the eyes. "Soldier Soleil Yamanu, I am here to see Alma Zuri of The Women of the Lost." I evoke a force in my voice that I save only for talking with soldiers as they usually do not react well to a timid manner.

The guard's eyes light with recognition, but he keeps the same gruff expression. "*Soleil Yamanu*—" he stretches the syllables of my name. "Madame Zuri is in the Lost wing; you should know how to get there."

My face remains stoic. "Thank you." I wait for his sword to drop, but it doesn't. I look back at the guard.

"Welcome back to The Castle, *Soldier Yamanu*." He finally lowers the sword and I step into the now open doors of The Castle of Lex. I am immediately met with a bustling receiving room. Servants and soldiers walk back and forth bracing themselves from the cold. They carry weapons, books, laundry, meals, fresh linens, and ingredients for the kitchens. I weave through the ocean of people, up to the grand staircase at the back of the receiving room.

I lift my hood back up over my head to block out any unwanted attention—not that it is needed to keep me warm any longer. I walk through the halls of The Castle, thankful for the constant heat. Despite the relatively short walk and the rare sunlight, Lex remains absolutely frozen, and so am I. I rub my hands together, working feeling into my fingers. By the time I arrive at the Lost wing, I am pretty warm. I still, however, long for Alma's fireplace. I reach the door to the wing and am stopped by a guard once again, this time a female and another familiar face.

"What is your business here?" She asks. I pull my hood down again and she smiles at me, recognizing my face from previous visits.

"Ah—Soleil Yamanu. Here to see Madame Zuri?" She asks.

"Yes, I am. Is she here?"

"Right inside, I think she is taking lunch in her room." The guard replies.

"Thank you." I say, as she opens the door for me. The Lost wing is just as I remember it, wood slats cover the stone walls and mismatched rugs cover the ground. I tiptoe past the sleeping chambers that are near the entrance, remaining quiet in case children are taking their afternoon naps. I hear voices coming from the common room at the end of the hall.

The common room is a beautiful place with windows that have a perfect view of The Fortress on one end, and rows and rows of bookshelves on the other. The floor is covered with more of the same carpets that line the rest of the wing. The fireplace is roaring, and a group of women surround it, sitting on the various pillows, blankets, and mattresses that are scattered on the floor. I walk into the room and joy lights the faces of the various Women of Lost as they exclaim just how excited they are to have a visitor.

"Hello everyone!" I speak. They welcome me in, but I scan the room for Alma, and she is not there. "No, I can't, I was just looking for Alma."

The red-haired caretaker replies to me. "She is in her room Hun, knock twice!" I smile at the woman. A new member of The Women of the Lost, I assume, for I don't recognize her.

"I did hear that from the guard out front. I just wanted to double check. Thank you all." They respond in a collective "*Your welcome!*" as I leave the common room. I walk across the hall to Alma's room and knock twice on the wooden door.

"Come in!" Alma responds from inside. I walk in and see her sitting at one of the big fluffy chairs in front of the windows. She turns around to face me and smiles widely, her eyes creasing.

"My tribulatio! You haven't visited in so long!" She gets up and walks swiftly towards me, taking me in a long and tight embrace. Alma is just a bit taller than me, so my head tucks into her body perfectly as we hug. She pulls my hood down all the way and kisses the top of my head, then releases me.

I look around at her room, utterly unchanged. There are two big armchairs near the window, her bed, an armoire, and a bedside table are against the opposite wall, and bookshelves cover almost every other space. Books of every height and width fill the overflowing stacks and I smile at the sight.

"Let me see you! Let me see you!" Alma says. She always does this. No matter how frequent our visits, she insists that I have changed so much that she has to *inspect* me so she won't forget who I am. I humor her.

"Yes, yes, well fed as usual," Alma laughs. "You and Nova need to *eat*! You two are growing young women."

I chuckle. "Alma, I think we have grown as much as we are going to."

"They work you too hard at The Academy, Soleil. Food is fuel!" She fusses. "Make sure to tell Nova to eat a bit more, that girl is a stick!" I always *was* the curvier between the two of us.

"Your hair! It looks wonderful Soleil!" She exclaims, focusing on the soft curls. I am glad to have reprieve from the talk of my body. I like the way I look, *as I am.*

Alma touches my hair, "I assume you are back for more shampoo and conditioner? I have a few bottles reserved."

Growing up in The Castle of Lex with the rest of the Lost, I was the only one to have hair so dense and curly. None of the other caretakers knew how to manage it, so Alma quickly found a solution. Mixing herbs and oils, soaps and scents, she created a shampoo and conditioner that protected my hair. It allowed my hair to grow long and strong, each coil beautifully defined and healthy despite the dry air of Lex. When Nova and I left the Lost, Alma sent me with huge bottles of the stuff, and a promise that whenever I need more, I simply have to make my way to The Castle and ask for some.

So now, every few star cycles, in my allotted free time from The Academy, I visit the Lost to see Alma for more shampoo and conditioner. We talk for hours. Alma takes a break from her role as caretaker, and I shrug off the title of *Soldier* and just become *Soleil*.

My favorite days, though, are the ones without the need to fill space with sounds. The ones where we don't talk, and we simply find comfort in each other's presences.

"Actually, I was hoping for some lotion." I smile.

"Yes, the air *is* getting quite dry." Alma agrees, turning around to the storage trunk where she keeps her homemade products.

"I was also hoping for some conversation. If you have time of course." I speak quickly, afraid that I have come at the wrong moment.

"I will always have time for you, tribulatio. I was planning on taking the afternoon off anyway. Sit, sit. I will get some coca for us."

"Oh Alma, I don't want to interrupt your lunch." I respond, sitting on the chair next to hers.

"No, no. I was just done with it." Alma picks up her tray of food and whisks out the door before I can say another word. Moments later she returns with two huge ceramic mugs of thick and steaming coca. I shiver at the sight and wrap my fingers around the mug.

"Thank you, Alma." I say gratefully.

"Of course, Soleil." Alma sits on her chair next to mine. "Now, what is it that you wanted to talk about?"

I shift in my seat, "I don't know." I need a moment to collect my thoughts. It feels best to let Alma lead the conversation for now.

"Is it about Arche?"

My neck snaps to her, eyes widening in disbelief. "What? No."

"Are you two finally together?"

I cannot believe this. "Alma…" I shake my head. *She always loved Arche.*

"You know I approve. You don't even have to tell me. I already know." She smiles devilishly.

"I am not *with* Arche Inconnu." My voice comes out with conviction. Thankfully this is one part of my life that is *not* a grey area.

"Sure…"

"He is my best friend Alma. Truly. And besides, Nova is in love with him." I roll my eyes and turn back to the window.

"That is news to me." I hear Alma take a sip of her coca.

"Yeah. It was quite obvious honestly; I guessed a while ago." I pause, then add pointedly. "She *did* tell me not to tell anyone."

"I am no one."

"Sure, sure." I smile and take another sip of coca.

"I know Nova is your sister Soleil, but you don't have to do that."

"Do what?" This is not what I came here to discuss, but it *is* giving me a moment to breathe, nonetheless.

"Sacrifice your feelings for the boy—"

"I am not *sacrificing* anything Alma." I say defensively.

"I do quite like him. I always thought you *could* do better. However, considering you didn't attend The School, he will have to do." Alma says begrudgingly.

"For Nova. He will have to do for *Nova*."

"Soleil, face your feelings," Alma begs.

"I do not see Arche in that way, Alma. He is my best friend and that is all. I could never love him like that." I lock eyes with Alma as I speak, willing her to understand. My life may be in shambles, but this will remain true.

"Truly?" She asks.

"Truly. My *person* is not at The Academy, I can tell you that."

I have always thought about that—love and marriage—but I know that I can't find anyone I love at The Academy any more than my dagger.

"Ah-ha! So, there is someone? Is he in The Castle?" Alma fusses.

"No Alma." I calm her down. "I love you. But there is no one."

"Well, you better find someone soon."

"Why?" I grow concerned.

"I need some grandbabies, tribulatio. The clock is ticking!" Alma laughs.

I take a sip of coca before replying. "Well, you can keep waiting. Maybe Nova will deliver on that request."

"Hmph." Alma crosses her arms, feigning anger. I chuckle and look out the window again. We sit in silence, drinking our coca to the dregs.

"Alma, I do need to talk to you about something."

"Yes?" She lifts an eyebrow in concern.

"Well Lord Acastus came to speak to us this morning."

"I did hear about that. The Castle has been in constant gossip. He hasn't spoken to The Academy in years," her tone remains casual.

"Mmhm. Yeah, General Aldera is officially stepping down. Lord Acastus is looking for a new second in command." I fix my stare at the window, watching the tiny figures on the bridge move back and forth.

"Oh! I am so sorry, Soleil. I knew it. The Castle has been abuzz since we found out that he is only considering the tenth year. I know you have always wanted an opportunity like this. I am so sorry that you won't be considered." She believes that I came here to be comforted over a lost opportunity. I pray to Infinity that this conversation will go smoothly.

"Alma——" I begin.

She continues to talk over me. "Maybe it's for the best. You and Nova can stay in the top of your class until graduation and become lieutenants *together.* That is what you wanted. Infinity knows you have to see the best in things—"

"Alma." I speak up, cutting her off.

"Yes?" Her tone changes again, more serious than before. I brace for impact.

"Lord Acastus *will* be considering me." I do not let myself stumble over the words. They come out slowly, each syllable enunciated to perfection.

"Excuse me?" I hear her set her mug down on the side table.

"During his speech. I stood up—"

Alma cuts me off. "Soleil."

"I don't know why I did it. I was angry, it felt right. He was curious and I—" I ramble, losing control.

"Do not tell me this." Alma stands up, walking away from where I sit. She has a hand over her heart.

"I interrupted Lord Acastus. I told him that what he was doing was not right, that there are so many talented soldiers in The Academy that will be overlooked because of his decision." I evoke my voice of power, too afraid of what Alma will say next to judge how it sounds.

"Soleil Yamanu."

I shrink away from my name on her tongue.

"He changed his mind, Alma. I did that—me. I made the Lord of Lex change his mind. He is considering students in their seventh, eighth, ninth, and tenth years. I won that myself." I try to fight back, but my words are brittle, the last remnants of the power they usually hold.

"Do not believe that! *Do not.* This is not a game, Soleil. Lord Acastus may have changed his mind, but you did not *win* anything. You should have been smarter than to put yourself on the Knight's watch." Each of Alma's words strike me like a stone. I feel utterly naked as her voice penetrates my skin.

"Trust me, I know that." I can't even look at her.

"No, you don't. You spoke out of turn once. You do not know *anything.* Lord Acastus has a history of ending people's stories before they begin. Infinity... Soleil. I do not need yours to end the same." I shake with that. I know what she means; she doesn't have to remind me.

"I won't. I *will* get this job." My eyes remain fixed on the carpet.

"It is not just a job anymore Soleil. It is your life at stake. Remember this. Being second in command has a reputation, people kill for it. And with your *shadow...*"

I know. I know. I know. She doesn't understand that I know what I have done. That the reason I did it is because of the rumors that have swirled around me since I was born. *Undeserving, unfit, out of place.* I have come to peace with my decision—with the risk—and Alma has too as well.

"I am not sorry." I find her eyes as I speak, regaining my confidence.

"You should be! This decision could very well end your life Soleil! Whether or not you get the job, every day that you live, Lord Acastus will remember. You were lucky to escape his gaze once. Lucky that the rumors of your *blessings* were not enough to put you on notice from the hour you were found. Your actions Soleil, put more than just yourself at risk."

"Nova." My voice quivers and my heart sinks. I have been so worried about leaving her behind, I never realized that she could be right there next to me if I am to be punished. Everyone I love, Nova, Arche, even Alma herself. My breaths come rapidly. The air does nothing to satiate the burn of my lungs. I can risk myself, but to have everyone else pay for my mistake is unthinkable. The world flips and I can't hold on.

My legs are weak and I slide to the ground, heaving, gasping for air. *It is done. It is done. It is done.* I can't fix it. I tuck my head in between my knees. I shut my eyes, in an attempt to escape the mess I've made. For a moment I see the blue eyes from my dreams. A sick joke. Just another thing to send me into panic and hold me there. I hear footsteps come towards me and I shy away from them while trying to hold on to the fraying pieces of myself.

"My tribulatio, shhh. Calm, please. Everything is alright. I am so, so sorry." Alma sits next to me and takes my head in her lap. She brushes my hair with her fingers as I sob. My throat tightens, the horrible sounds escape my mouth, but the tears never come.

"I don't know why I did it, Alma. I couldn't control myself. When my voice came out, I was afraid. I forgot who I was for a moment. I felt powerful and I liked it. *I liked the power.*" I close my eyes tightly, remembering what it felt like to have all eyes on me.

"Power is an intoxicating thing Soleil. Believe me, but we have to remember ourselves even in the face of it." She pauses, "please, please don't forget who you are. Don't lose that light, my sun. Do not be afraid of yourself, Soleil."

"How do I continue? If it's like what you said, how do I stop him from—" I can't continue.

"Do as you are doing. Simply play along." Alma's voice is stern yet comforting, I still can't see past the pain of putting my family in danger.

"I can't." I say softly.

"You *can.*"

CHAPTER
SIX

The freezing air of Lex whips me as I walk from The Castle of Lex, back to The Fortress. I clutch a bottle of Alma's homemade lotion to my chest, along with some shampoo and conditioner that she insisted I take as well. She must be encouraging my independence for the bottle of lotion is large enough to get me through the winter, and I now have shampoo and conditioner to get me through the next six-star cycles. I have no need to go back and see her for quite some time. I laugh at Alma's conspicuousness. *You can do this yourself, tribulatio,* I hear her say in my mind.

I am oddly grateful to see The Fortress when I return. It is a respite from the flood of feeling that came with being in The Castle. I enter through the front doors and am not stopped by any guards as I pass. The entry room of The Fortress still flows with people, so I keep my head down and quickly walk into the back hallway.

Down hallways and up flights of stairs, I finally make it to the female wing. I pass Sleeping Chambers J, I, and H, before arriving at Female Sleeping Chamber G. The door is just cracked open and I am able to push it the rest of the way with my hip, still holding onto the bottles of product in my arms. To my delight, the sleeping chamber is empty.

The fire is crackling as I walk in, the room beautifully warm. I quickly shut the door to keep it that way. I unfasten my cloak and pull it off, enjoying the freedom of my movements. The clock on the far wall of the room reads *1610*. I have less than an hour before the battle simulation begins.

Quickly, I open my trunk and arrange the bottles of product at the bottom of it, rotating them so that the oldest ones are up front. I was well stocked on shampoo and conditioner before going to see Alma, but I had no lotion at all. I pump some of it out onto my hands and rub it into the cracking skin, sighing in relief at the velvety feeling.

I pull my gloves on before relacing my boots. With a flex of my ankles, my feet adjust under the pressure of the tighter laces. I finish off by walking to the mirror. I stop for a moment to study my body. The powerful curves of my thighs, my broad shoulders, the slight dip at my hips, the soft bump of my stomach and the light hump of my biceps. Utterly mortal by all accounts, imperfect in every way. But this body has done *everything* for me, if that means having fuller curves that most people, than that is a trade I will accept. Taking one more quick glance at myself, I read the clock on the wall next to me, *1632. Plenty of time to get to the battlefield.* I think. I fasten my cloak at the neck, tighten the scabbard at my thigh, and lift my hood over my head.

Despite the hesitation in my mind, I can't help but admit that I am the vision of power. Striking is the contrast between my all-white thermals and boots and my deep red cloak. My scabbard shines lightly at my thigh, the whorls of gold sticking out along my waist and around my leg.

Deep breaths, Soleil. I spin around and open the door to the sleeping chamber, stepping into the cool hallway. With each step of my boots, I imagine myself as pure power sending a wave of dominance to echo through The Fortress.

DESPITE THE BITTER AIR, THE BATTLEFIELD IS PACKED WITH people. As I arrive, a group is clearing the space, removing the weapons that litter the ground. The arrows stuck in the dirt and the spare bits of armor that must have been pulled off during combat. On the side of the battlefield that juts up against The Castle and The Fortress, is the seating area for spectators. Sitting on a wood stage, at least ten feet off the ground, is Lord Acastus. I am able to recognize him easily, I pray to Infinity that he can say the same about me.

I cross the center of the battlefield, making my way to the makeshift armory at the end of it. There is an incredibly wide array of weapons available for the *sim*, shocking as traditionally the trainers would hand all the students participating, the same weapon, whether it be a sword, a bow, or a set of daggers. Today however, is special I guess. The armory, a glorified wooden shack with racks and racks of weapons, is bustling with people. I hear the metallic ring of swords being sharpened and cleaned, and students are putting their used, but still clean, weapons back on the rack to be used by the next groups. I stroll the racks until I find the swords. I pick up one to test the hilt, too slippery for my liking.

"Sol?" A voice calls out. I let go of the sword and turn around, it's Nova, with Arche just a few steps behind her.

"Hey." I smile. Nova already has a bow strung around her body, and a full quiver of freshly assembled arrows around her back. She wears no cloak, only her thickest pair of black thermals and a shining silver breastplate. Her silver bow, quiver, and dagger slice her body into clean sections.

"How was Alma? Did you tell her I said hi?" Nova asks. Arche leans casually against a rack of swords.

"She's good, and yes, I told her you said hi. She said you have to gain some weight." I laugh.

Nova feigns offense. "Hmph. Whatever—this is one hundred percent muscle." She hits her thigh for emphasis.

I nod my head. "Oh yeah, you tell her."

"Did she ask about me?" Arche asks. I look at him and he smiles boldly. Arche is a big fan of Alma, and the feeling is clearly mutual between the two of them. For the simulation, he wears his black thermals as well with a black breastplate that blends in perfectly, an unobtrusive back sword is sheathed at his waist.

"Yeah, she told you to calm down on the gall during battle simulation." I reply sarcastically.

Arche combs his hair back with his fingers, the shining silver strands and moonlight pale of his skin, a striking contrast against the black of his ensemble. "Sure, sure. By the end of the sim, I will make sure that *you* are the one begging me to calm down on the gall."

I stick my tongue out at him and turn around, returning to the selection of swords in front of me. I stroke the hilts of multiple swords. It isn't until my fingers graze one with a long, solid gold blade, that I make my decision. The sword also has a simple hilt wrapped with white leather for a comfortable grip. It's well made and clean, and it also matches my outfit. *If I'm going for dramatics…*

I pull the sword off the rack and walk it over to the counter where a few weapons masters sit. I walk up to one of them, a man with deep brown skin and dark hair.

"Just this, and can I get the matching sheath?" I ask coolly.

"Yes, and for armor?" He asks, meeting my eyes. His are brown too, but lighter. Like pure honey the way they catch the sun.

"Got anything gold?" I smile. He chuckles lightly, his voice deep and hearty.

"Yeah, yeah I do. Give me a minute." The man ducks behind a curtain of fabric and returns moments later with a white scabbard—one to match my dagger's perfectly—and a simple gold breastplate with matching gauntlets. My smile widens.

"All for me?" I ask, looking up at the man.

"I think you can pull it off." He responds slyly. I raise an eyebrow at him as he drops the supplies on the wood table separating us. "Will you be able to get it on alright?" He cracks a smile. I watch as his eyes scan my body, slowly. As if he is savoring everything he sees. All of a sudden, my skin feels too tight, too warm.

"Yeah, I can take it from here." I manage to get out. Thank Infinity, he retreats behind the curtain before things grow any more awkward.

Suddenly very ready to leave, I quickly pull the hood down from my cloak and unfasten it at the neck. I slide myself into the gold breastplate, delighted to find that it fits perfectly. The gold gauntlets go on next and I fasten them with the white leather straps. Then I tighten the sheath for the sword around my waist, sitting it on top of the scabbard that holds my dagger. I push the sword into the sheath and check that it is secure before putting my cloak back on, I leave the hood down over my shoulders. When it is fastened around my neck, I pull a thin strap of leather that I keep wrapped around my scabbard and I bunch my hair up to tie it back, high on my head.

When everything is secure, I walk away from the counter. The man who gave me the armor never returned but I shrug it off. The way he looked at me—it's for the best. When I eventually meet my squadron, they are standing at the edge of the battlefield, silent and staring at Lord Acastus. I shoulder Nova and smile at her when she turns to me.

"Ready?" She asks cunningly.

"Of course." I reply smoothly, turning to the battle-field in front of us as adrenaline builds in my core. Never-theless, my limbs remain loose and my head clear.

I focus on the terrain of the battlefield; rocky and un-stable ground. Large boulders scatter around the expanse of the battlefield, good for long distance attacks for Nova, but better for gaining the high ground during a sword-fight. Unstable ground means that we will be slowed while fleeing from battle. But it also means that when attacking, we can count on our opponents being slowed as well. I dig my boot into the ground, it is hard and slick from the cold. I grow worried for a moment, but it seems like the day's activities on the battlefield itself kicked up enough dust to give us some traction.

Slowly, I evoke the power that I know I have. *Infinitely blessed.* I remind myself. But that doesn't matter now, not when it is *my* training and *my* work that has made me the best. I feel the strength in my veins and remind myself why I stood during Lord Acastus' speech. This is it.

All eyes remained fixed on Lord Acastus, still seated in his throne. The last few students make it to the edge of the battlefield, lined up directly in front of the Lord himself. In front of us, in the far distance, we can see the bridge and The Castle of Lex, to our left, lies The Fortress, to our right, more of The Castle, and a small section of The Wall. Far ahead, we can see a few military blockhouses and camps and the opposite side of The Wall. I train my gaze on Lord Acastus, statuesque on his throne.

Lord Acastus finally rises and the air stills in response. He walks with the command of a thousand years. Wisdom flows from him, and his dominance echoes with each calculated movement. Simply by rising, he is in control. But I know that even when he sits back down on his throne, the authority will remain. When Lord Acastus speaks, his voice booms across the battlefield, echoing with pure, unbridled power, and he embodies it.

"Soldiers, you are here today to prove yourselves. Each of you has something unique to show me, and for the next twenty-eight days you will all have the chance to offer it up. Do not hold back in your efforts. One of you may very well be my next second in command and a general of The Undying Army. *I will be watching.*" He pauses and I have the burning feeling that his gaze is focused on me. I shake it off, returning to the composed and clear mindset I held previously. But it is hard to shake the feeling of his power, probing me, testing me. Trying to find a weakness, a way to defeat me. Therein lies the true power of the Knights of Lex, strategy.

"In traditional battle simulation, each of you would be given the same weapon. You would fight every man for themselves. Today however, you have all had the opportunity to choose the weapon that you are most comfortable with, ensuring that all of you have the chance to show off your skills. This is not the only rule change for my battle simulations." Two teams of soldiers walk out into the battlefield on either side, one carrying a black banner draped over a pole, the other a white banner. They stick the poles into the ground and walk off the battlefield.

"You will be divided, not by man, but by squadron. The job of second in command is not a lonely one. You will be expected not only to *lead* others, but to *work* with them as well. So today you will work in the squadrons you have lived with for the extent of your time at The Academy. Each team has been given a banner; it is their duty to protect it. If one team seizes the banner from the other, that team is declared the formal winners of this simulation. The title of *winner* is simply a formality, however the one who captures the banner will not be forgotten."

I hear the uncomfortable shuffling of boots. This is an unexpected turn of events; however, I know my squadron well. Nova will back me regardless, but after what Professor Clara told the rest of my squad, they will guard me with their lives. I have given them a chance, now I can lead them into taking it.

"Male Group 7G will protect the black banner, Female Group G will protect the white. Each team will have a few minutes to deliberate and strategize. When the war horn is blown for the first time, all soldiers are expected to get in position. When the horn is blown for the second time, the simulation begins. At the end of the hour, if neither team has acquired the banner, the war horn will be blown to announce the end of the simulation. If a soldier is able to obtain a banner before the hour is up, the war horn will be blown and the simulation will end." My body aches to move and my hand twitches, already longing for that black banner.

"Protect your banner. Any other rules of battle simulation remain. No fatal strikes; do not kick a downed soldier. Any rule breaking will be met with severe consequences. Now, you may make your way onto the battlefield to consult with your squadrons."

Nova and I walk silently to our right, towards the white banner. Arche walks towards the left, not even glancing in our direction. Alma was right, people will kill for this job and Arche has a shot at it.

I approach the bright white banner and zero in on strategy for the coming battle. The rest of Female Squadron G circles around the banner, watching me, waiting for me to speak. Nova is on my left and Lyra, to my surprise, attentively stands at my right. Around me, nineteen soldiers gather around an unwritten rule, *to wait for my command.*

I speak loudly, my voice clear and strong. I feel Nova's pride in me grow enough to swallow The Fortress whole. "I know how these boys work, they are going to attempt a strategy, but they will be drawn to the clang of metal and all end up in sword fights. Their craving for glory is going to win out and they will all try to make a break for the banner. But they won't do it together. I can count on Arche Inconnu to remain by the banner, he knows better than to abandon that post, but any of the other guys are fair game. I want us to spread out in half circles around the banner."

I look around and find two large boulders each about ten yards in opposite directions of the banner. I point to one of them as I speak. "Nova, I need you to go to that boulder, climb it and stay there taking your shots from afar, if anyone gets within a ten-yard perimeter from the banner… shoot." I turn to Lyra, the other archer in our group. She isn't as skilled as Nova, but she is a consistent shot. I point at the other boulder. "Lyra, I am going to need you to do the same but stay at that boulder." She nods.

"Now, I am going to need some of you to guard those boulders, two soldiers for each of them, four in total. Any volunteers?" Four hands rise, and my eyes light in excitement as my plan unfolds. Sage shoots a dark hand into the air, blue eyes lighting. Viola, Sylvia, and Alena all follow. All four of them are strong and competent with a sword, I am satisfied with this selection. I explain the plan and position Viola and Sylvia at Nova's boulder, and Sage and Alena at Lyra's boulder.

"Now I need Zya, Petra, and Iris to guard at the base of the banner, stay close and stay alert." The three of them are the best sword fighters the squadron besides myself, so I know that they can handle the task.

"Ingrid, Jade, Nola, the three of you will be joining me in attack, we will remain separate. If you have the opportunity to get the banner, go for it, do not wait up, do not go back to assist anyone else." The three of them always know how to hold their own in any situation, I can trust that if I don't get the banner, one of them will. After that, I am left with seven girls.

"As for the rest of you, spread yourselves in half circles around the banner, hold your positions, you *will* be the first to get provoked and you *will* bear the brunt of the attacks." I meet the stares of each girl. They all nod in agreement. And so, the plan is set.

"These boys want to play hero. They want this banner, but they do not know how to get it, much less how to protect their own. Hold your positions, humor them with your swords, play along and keep them busy. I will have that banner by the end of this." At my last word, the war horn blows for the first time.

"Positions!" I yell, my voice stirring the air. The girls obey. I glance at Nova who meets me with a quick smile. *Let's see what you can do,* I read in her face. I walk to my position at the head of the group, toes against the center dividing line in the battlefield.

I forget about the cold; I forget about everything as I focus on the black banner ahead. The men on the other side get into positions, ragged and arbitrary compared to the calculated and clean positions of my squadron. Arche remains at the base of the pole on the male side, sword out, guarding his banner. Exactly where I want him.

I reach for my sword, unsheathing it with a slice. No men meet me, they all stay at least five yards out from the dividing line. I spin my sword in my right hand, left arm loose.

The war horn sounds for a second time and the battle begins.

CHAPTER
SEVEN

The men yell as they run towards the dividing line on the battlefield, but my squad of female warriors refuses to give in. I don't have to look to know that they hold their positions, for the clang of steel is enough to tell me. The weak formations that the men held, break as soon as the war horn blows for the second time. I run straight towards the black banner, surprised at the ease of this direct route.

A dagger whizzes towards my left ear from behind, I narrowly avoid it with a slight tilt of my head. I spin around and find one of the soldiers from the male group, a lanky boy named Ollie, gearing up to throw another dagger at me. I begin charging towards him as he sends another dagger flying, I knock it off its path with the gold gauntlet around my left wrist. I drop to the ground to avoid his third dagger and pick up the one that I had knocked down previously.

Before Ollie can send a fourth my way, I throw the one I picked up back at him. It moves quickly and precisely through the air, meeting the skin of his thigh, and slicing the side of it deeply before falling behind him. Ollie's knees hit the ground and he cries out, dropping the dagger he held and moving to clutch his wound instead.

I stand quickly, spinning around to ensure that no one else is on my trail before continuing my run. I make it to a boulder and crouch behind it, taking account of myself. No wounds mark my body—none of Ollie's daggers seem to have made their mark. I sigh with relief, allowing myself to take a few breaths before I jump out from behind the boulder. I look across the battlefield and see my squadron fighting with everything in them.

Zya, Petra, and Iris circle the banner, alert, but clearly bored at the lack of action they are seeing. They will have to forgive me, for this is exactly what I want. If they are bored, the banner is safe. Nova is shining of course, as she launches arrow after arrow at the opposing team, dodging the ones shot at her in return.

Before I can register anything else, I see a flash of silver and dodge an incoming sword strike. I roll onto the ground to avoid the blade but get up on my feet quickly. I try to take a few gulps of air. An intense boy with dark eyes that I don't recognize, closes in on me, his sword pointed in my direction. I gesture at him, twirling my sword in invitation. He easily takes the bait, breaking into a sprint towards me.

He is much bigger than I am, brutish in his run, and I know that the momentum he is building is going to be hard to stop. The grip on his sword falters as he runs and at the last moment I dodge him, sticking my boot out to send him crashing into the ground and his sword flying in the opposite direction. I run to his sword and pick it up, raising it in the air along with my own and I bang the blades together as a symbol of victory. He sits up, watching me beat the swords, once, twice, three times, but he remains on the ground, nonetheless, accepting defeat.

I drop the other sword after that and sheathe my own at my waist. The metallic sound of steel is getting louder and I ache for just one more look at my squadron. I decide to scale the boulder that I was leaning against earlier, just for a peak at the other side. The climb is quick and when I find my footing on top of the boulder I smile brightly. My girls are running circles around Male Group 7G.

They are barely breaking a sweat while the men are in complete disarray. Nova is still taking shot after shot, never wavering in her attacks. No one makes it within ten yards of the banner. I turn around to try and find Arche, who I know will be my biggest competition. But I can't. I crane my neck to see him but he must know that I am looking, for he never shows his face. I know Arche well, he is my best friend after all, and I know that *he* will find *me* when the time comes.

As I am looking across the battlefield, an arrow narrowly misses my left arm. I realize quickly that I am an open target for the male archers. I jump off the rock and hit the cold ground hard. Pain radiates from my feet through my ankles and into my legs with the force of the seven-foot jump. I run on, sheathing my sword to allow me to sprint. Arrows continue to fly after me and, in my run, I finally see who is shooting them, a broad and muscular boy with flaming red hair. He has climbed onto a rock about five feet tall, probably looking for a better view now that I am back on the ground myself. He loads another arrow and I run towards him. I dodge three more but I feel my body slipping into clumsiness. I am only ten yards from him; an easy target.

He lets another arrow fly, quicker than any of the others before. Coupled with my clumsiness, it gets me straight in the thigh. I cry out in pain, clenching my teeth to regain control. My leg throbs, the arrow piercing through layers of skin, fat, and muscle. He is only twenty feet away now, drunk with the success of his easy shot. I see my opportunity and ache to take it. I reach for my dagger—Alma's dagger—that always sits at my thigh. It is perfectly balanced, the hilt already warm in my hand. I ready myself to throw it while the red-haired boy is still celebrating but an arrow hits him in the flesh of his bicep before I can let the dagger fly.

He grunts, dropping his bow as the arrow collides with his skin. Blood pours from the wound, and he yells out. I turn my head and see Nova staring at me from across the battlefield. I can just make out the wink she sends my way. I thank Infinity for my sister and sheath the dagger at my thigh once more.

With the red-haired boy taken care of, I allow myself a moment to deal with my thigh. I drag myself over to a boulder and sit, keeping my eyes on the battle ahead. I feel my heartbeat in the wound and finally allow myself to look down.

It isn't as bad as I expected, the arrow remains in the center of my thigh and it only went in about an inch or two. I thank Infinity that the clear shot didn't make its way *through* my leg. My white thermals are beyond help however, as they stain red with blood as more and more pours out. My heartbeat roars in my ears and the tinge of blood attacks my nose. I rip the bottom off my thermals and stretch out the fabric. Once it is long enough, I wrapped it tightly above the wound to slow the bleeding. I snap the arrow, leaving about three inches sticking into my thigh. It's the best I can do in the moment, but I will have to leave it until the end of the simulation. Pulling it out myself will do more damage than what it did going in, and if I go to the medics at the edge of the battlefield, I am forfeiting my spot in the sim. So, I have no choice but to deal with the pain.

A blood curdling scream rings out from the battlefield. A woman, I realize. I quickly look to where Nova stood only moments ago, and there she remains. I run into the battlefield and find Ingrid, sword to her throat, only a few yards away from me. She is pinned down on the ground by the same dark-haired man who I had taken down earlier. My heart pounds, as I run to her, remaining cautious of the ground that is slippery in patches. This goes against every promise we made, every promise to get the banner at whatever cost, but there are no guarantees that this man will abide by the rules of the battle simulation. He may as well get his revenge on *me* by seriously hurting Ingrid.

This time, I will not give him the benefit of a quick defeat. I unsheathe my sword and slice his back; he suddenly loosens his grip on Ingrid enough that she is able to get free. He cries out in fury and I feel that anger reverberate through my bones. He turns around to find me and I smile, keeping up the theatrics. I give a few spins of my sword and forget about the wound at my thigh all together. The man charges at me again, more controlled than before, but I am still able to slice his arm before our swords ever meet.

We dance, the man striking again and again. He is large and brutish, muscular but slow. I am smaller by far, but much quicker. I dodge every hit and match each strike of his sword with one of my own. I pull him in, further and further, allowing him to win. But I am playing my own game at the same time. He goes deeper, putting more power into his swings, but my golden sword is relentless. The clash of metal is music to my ears and as the man grunts, I smile. I see my window as he raises his sword. I pull into him, gliding past and behind his body. Before he can think, the backs of his thighs are sliced deeply and he is on the ground.

"Stay down," I growl at him. He obeys, not attempting to move from where he fell.

I turn to Ingrid who sits against a boulder, gasping for breath. I run to her, only a few feet, and crouch next to her. She has a deep gash on her cheek, another on her forearm, and a third on her thigh. Blood is streaming quick and I have to turn from the scene. Her usually rosy cheeks are devoid of color, her brown eyes glassy.

"Get up." I say sternly, tucking an arm around her and pulling her to her feet. The edge of the battlefield is only about fifty feet away. There, she will be out of the simulation, but able to receive medical attention.

I make the decision to take her there, even if we will be a woman short. She is smaller than I am, and skinner too, so it is an easy carry. The other girls must be covering us, for no daggers, arrows, or swords come our way. I grunt with each step towards the edge of the battlefield and Ingrid cries out. Eventually, we make it to the edge of the battlefield, a team of medics already waiting for her. They try to get me to go with them as well, to deal with the arrow sticking out of my thigh, but I refuse and sprint back into the battle.

The sun shines brightly in my eyes and I thank Infinity for the sign. *Soleil,* the sun, so rare in Lex but today it beams. I stop in the center of the battlefield and look up, letting the rays flood my face, a moment of reprieve from this draining battle.

I scan the battlefield. The men are occupied and each of the members of my squadron are fighting valiantly, but still, the girls look bored. I smile widely and turn to the direction of the black banner, metallic clangs ringing out in the distance. There are no men within a thirty-yard radius from me, and only a few boulders where they *could* be hiding.

The black banner belonging to the male group is unguarded. Beckoning me to go to it. It flows with each gust of wind, an all-encompassing black against the bright blue sky in the distance. It calls me, further and further in. My plan worked! The girls are keeping the entirety of the male group busy, and the banner is *mine.* So, I run to it, pumping my legs with everything in me.

A hundred yards, then fifty, twenty-five, and then ten. I am so close that I can feel the velvety black fabric in my fingers. I push my body, moving past the pain radiating from my thigh. A step, and another, and another, until I am only twenty feet from the banner. So, so close. Until something hits me hard from behind, square in the center of my back.

I am sent flying onto my face, my entire body crashing into the ground. Every bit of air is knocked out of me in a second. I can't move, can't breathe. I struggle, trying to fill my lungs. It is to no avail. The edges of my vision darken, and my thigh pulses, the piece of the arrow that once stuck out has lodged itself further into the muscle of my leg. Groaning, I remember what is at stake and will air back into my body. A few quick breaths later and I pull myself up from the ground, tears welling in my eyes. My back aches from where I was hit, and my thigh burns. Pain worse than I have ever felt before.

I stand, legs wobbling, and look down. Blood streams steadily out of my thigh despite the fabric wrapped above the wound. I cringe at the sight and draw my sword, turning to meet my enemy. On the ground behind me is a stone tipped spear, the end dulled out to a round knob. The pain branching out from the center of my back is quickly explained.

I look up but there is no one in sight. I hear a crunch behind me and spin quickly, sword at the ready. Arche Inconnu, with a clever smile, stands between me and the black banner. I had completely overlooked him in my race here and I curse myself for my ignorance. I draw a painful breath, calming my shocked expression.

I spin my sword and tilt my head, putting on a sly smile to match Arche's. "Have you been waiting for me all this time?"

"Maybe—it *was* quite the show." He looks down at me. His words are arrogant and cocky, he knows that he is the only match for me in all The Academy. "You never learned the biggest lesson, did you? Defeat your enemies, sure. But make sure they can't get back up." His voice turns gruff and he draws his sword. A long, black blade, impeccable and deadly sharp.

"I don't think that giving me that advice *now* is a good idea. Considering you might want to get back up after I finish you off." I taunt.

"It was odd though," Arche pauses. "You *never* go back to save anyone. In the seven years I have known you, Soleil, you have never played the hero." His voice is inquisitive.

"Maybe I'm not *playing*, Arch. Maybe being the hero is what I want." I try to drag out the conversation and settle back into myself, separating my mind from the pain that echoes through my bones.

"I highly doubt that, Soleil. You are simply being *dramatic.*" He knows then. What Lord Acastus wants; he must have put the pieces together after my outburst during breakfast. Arche may be my best friend, but I will not let him have this. He spins his sword—inviting me to battle—I spin mine in response—accepting. If it is dramatics Lord Acastus wants, it is dramatics he will get.

"Don't you dare let me win, Arche." I smile.

"I would never." He scoffs.

Arche lunges at me, so quick that I can barely avoid it. I drag my leg as I move. It is unresponsive, paralyzed with pain. I grit my teeth and bring my sword up to deflect Arche's next attack. I spin out of his hold and he comes at me again and again.

My arms shake with the weight of my sword, I feel blood continue to pour out of my leg and down into my boots. My lungs struggle to take in air, but still I persist. Arche never lets me get any closer to the banner, but I see my opportunity in front of me. I yell with each clash of our swords. The metal rings with each collision and sparks fly with the pressure of our strikes. Though Arche takes up the offensive, my defense does not let up. We dance, our movements fluid and the crashes of our swords, music enough.

My back aches with every strike and my vision darkens. My swings grow sloppy, and I begin missing Arche's blade, allowing him to slice the edge of my good thigh. I cry out, knees buckling, and Arche comes up for another strike. Out of sheer muscle memory, I bring my sword up with my arms, quivering, trying with all my might to block his hit. Our swords clash, the sound piercing my mind as tears stream freely down my face. Arche drives in on me, further and further.

He pushes down on me with all his weight and my knees give out. They crash to the ground, but my sword remains raised. I grunt with the effort to keep Arche away. I let myself look down for a moment and noticed that in his efforts, his legs are hyperextended. I shift my weight to my right thigh, the arrow fully lodged into it. I quickly free my left leg and swing it around to Arche's knees, knocking them in and sending him to the ground. He loosens his grip on his sword, so I drive mine up, letting go and sending both of them crashing to the ground.

Arche groans as his knees hit the ground and he falls into me. I quickly adjust and push him down so that his back hits the cold ground. I reach for my dagger quickly and straddle Arche's body. His eyes are wild with surprise and fear. I smile at him, a devilish grin, taking delight in my victory. I push my dagger up to Arche's throat, my knees pinning his arms, and my body holding him down.

"Congratulations." Arche smiles. His eyes glimmer despite my dagger at his throat.

"I am *not* done yet, Arch."

I bring my forearm to his throat and remove the dagger, moving it up to his hair that flows in the wind. I use the blade to cut a tuft of the icy strands, nothing too thick, just enough to annoy him. Arche's smile drops and a grimace replaces it. I take the tuft of hair and sprinkle the shining strands in his face. He spits, shaking his head in an effort to remove them.

I get off of Arche and he rises silently, weaponless and defeated. I walk to collect both of our swords from the ground, sheathing my dagger and then my own sword. When I pick up Arche's sword, the hilt still warm from his hands, I lazily spin it, humming to myself. It is only a few short steps to the banner, which still flows in the wind. I grab it, feeling the velvet fabric wrap around my hand, and I tug.

The banner comes off the pole. It is *mine.*

The war horn blows loudly and the clang of swords silences at once. The battle simulation is over, and I *won.* I look down at the velvet in my hand and throw Arche's sword to the side. I turn to him, meeting his eyes, and I give him a nod, he is still my best friend after all. He nods in return, gaze softening to the Arche I have always known. The war horn blows again and again in the distance and it is music to my still ringing ears.

I drag the banner behind me and walk to a nearby boulder. My dramatics are far from over. I climb the boulder, shaking with each movement. When I make it to the top, I stand, embodying the attitude of the future second in command of The Undying Army. As the war horn continues to blow, I know I have all eyes on me. I draw my sword and point it to the sky while lifting the banner in the air with my other hand. When I yell, my own battle cry, it is loud enough to shake all of Lex. Cheers echo from the female squadron on the other side of the battlefield and I continue to shake the banner in the air, my smile fierce. I look across the battlefield, making eye contact with all those who dare meet my gaze. I save Arche for last. He claps begrudgingly when I meet his stare. I wave the banner again and again, and I keep my sword pointed to the sky.

I won.

And finally, I look to the platform on the edge of the battlefield and spot Lord Acastus. I let the banner drop from my grasp and use both of my hands to point my sword at the Lord. A beam of sunlight, sent straight from Infinity, envelopes me and I smile brighter. I know I hold Lord Acastus' gaze and I don't back down.

In this moment, the power of the realms is contained in my eyes, and no one can deny it.

CHAPTER

EIGHT

When the war horn stops blowing and the cheering ebbs, Lord Acastus finally speaks. He breaks our connection first, his head turning to scan the rest of the battlefield. I sheathe my sword and sit down on the boulder, the banner cushioning my body. I take a few breaths in the silence that comes after the cheers and at last, I give myself leave to account for the state of my body.

The most obvious—and most painful—issue is the arrow lodged deep into my thigh. Blood still pours from the wound, but my vision is no longer dark, probably an effect of the adrenaline I am currently riding on. I cringe at the sight of the ghastly wound, my breaths growing shaky as I examine it. I probe the area with my finger, but gasp as the pain sends sparks into my vision. I pull away and look to the lower part of my left thigh, where the scabbard for my dagger, and the sheath of my sword meet. There lies a shallow cut where Arche sliced me during our fight. It's more like a scratch, a testament to my skills even while slightly incapacitated, I think smugly.

Pain continues to radiate from my back and I struggle to even sit up, breathing becomes taxing as the ache from the stone tipped spear roars in my body. The adrenaline subsides, the pain sets in, and I gasp for air, my lungs so abused that even my short, shallow breaths send sharp pains to my core.

My knees burn from the crash I took to the ground and pain flows from them when I move. Small scrapes adorn my fingers in the places the gloves don't cover. When I touch my face, blood stains my hands. I feel a particularly deep and stinging cut along my cheek—probably from my fall. My ankles are sore from my jump off one of the boulders, but I don't think that anything is broken.

From what I can tell, my cloak is unharmed, but my white thermal set is unsalvageable. The white leather of my boots is coated with my blood—still warm as it pours from my thigh—and it's clear that I will have to bring them to Alma to get cleaned. I take deep breaths to calm myself until my mind clears and the pain ebbs.

Lord Acastus finally speaks after long minutes of silence, his voice roaring across the battlefield. "The battle simulation is over. If you are in need of medical attention, please see the medics on the edge of the battlefield or make your way to the infirmary inside. Return your armor and weapons to the armory and remove all discarded weapons and arrows from the battlefield itself. Thank you for your participation, your bravery and finesse will be rewarded."

That's it? He spoke nothing of the battle itself and his voice was too calm—almost cautious.

I quickly disregard his words, as I am quite over this simulation, and this day as a whole. So, I grab the banner and slide—as cautiously as I can—off the boulder. Arche catches me before I hit the ground, preventing me from hurting myself further.

His hands—steady and warm—hold my waist as he gently lowers me to the cold ground. I am shocked that he has gotten over his defeat so easily. I know that if it went the other way and he won, I would not have been so forgiving. But he *was* always the charmer. I look up at him and smile. Wordlessly, he takes the banner from me and ties it around my neck, another cloak on top of the one I already wear. I laugh softly, shaking my head.

"Need any help getting to the infirmary?" He asks, concern edging his tone. He looks at the arrow wound on my right thigh. As much as I want to push his help away, the lightheadedness is returning, and I *do* need the assistance.

"Honestly, yeah I do." I quietly relent.

"Nova is on her way. We can both get you to the infirmary inside that way you can warm up."

I smile at that. My nose is probably bright red, and I can barely feel my fingertips.

"Sounds good." I say as Nova approaches. She runs to me and pulls me into a warm embrace. I grunt as her hand makes contact with my back.

"Sorry!" She steps back and gives me a once over. "You know what, all things considered. You don't look *that* bad," she chuckles. "Now, give me the weapons and armor you took out so we can get you to the medics."

"I was thinking the infirmary inside, she's freezing. Plus, the two of us can get her there easily." Arche replies.

Nova's cheeks flush with color, embarrassment maybe. "Of course! Here, let me help you out of the armor at least." Nova calls Jade over as she is the closest member of our squadron. She is unmarked and looks utterly bored as she strolls to us. Nova unfastens my cloak and the makeshift cape-banner and she gives them to Arche to hold. Then, she undoes the fastenings of my gold breastplate, my body aching with every movement. I grit my teeth against the pain as I put my hands up in the air and Nova lifts the golden metal off my body. She hands the breastplate to Jade and Arche throws my cloak back over me, tying the banner around my neck as well. Then Nova undoes the leather ties that hold my gauntlets around my wrists, letting them fall to the ground. And finally, she loosens the sheath that holds the gold sword I got from the armory.

I suddenly remember the man who gave me the armor and sword. Despite my injuries, I want to bring them back to *him.*

"Hey Jade, you can give that stuff back to me. I'll return it." I say quickly while reaching for the things. Jade obliges.

"What? No, Soleil you are not doing that. We have to get you to the infirmary." Nova's voice is authoritative and her eyes match the tone.

I don't know why, but I *have* to go back to that man, whoever he is. "I know what I'm doing. I'm fine, just wait for me here, and we can walk back to The Fortress together." My voice shakes with pain, but I pray that she can't detect it.

"Soleil, you can barely move. You need to go to the infirmary *now*. Arche, tell her." Nova looks to Arche whose gaze is trained on me. *He* knows that I will get my way regardless of the fight that may ensue.

"Nova, you can't win with her. We need to return our stuff anyway. We can go together and help her get there and back to The Fortress." I let out a breath of relief and meet Arche's eyes. A silent thanking.

"Okay, fine. But let's make this quick before you faint, Soleil." She *may* have been compliant, but she remains stern. I nod, taking a step, but I falter under the weight of my own body. Arche is there to scoop me up again before I hit the ground.

"Thank you." I whisper so quietly that even Nova can't hear. Nova comes over and takes my armor and sword, Arche wraps his arm around me to alleviate my struggle. I draw a breath and walk forward. My thigh screams and I feel the arrow move inside of the wound. Tears well in my eyes, but I continue to walk swiftly across the battlefield. Long minutes pass until we are finally at the armory. I walk in to find the next group of Academy students already getting their weapons for their own battles.

I spot the dark-haired man quickly and smile despite myself. He is shining a dagger when we arrive and Nova drops my things to go return her own. The man looks up at me and smiles brightly, I smile even brighter back, almost forgetting about the piercing pain from my thigh.

"It seems like the girl with an eye for style is also pretty good in battle." He puts the dagger down and stands to collect the things I'm returning.

"It seems—" I smile. "You were watching?" He is much taller than I am, broad shouldered and strong. Different from Arche though, for this man has none of the boyishness that Arche has.

"I couldn't take my eyes off of it. That was definitely the most interesting battle I've seen today." He is shining the breastplate as we speak and when he flips it over, he finds a large dent on the back. Exactly where Arche hit me. "He has quite the throw though." The man says, raising an eyebrow towards Arche. "You, okay?"

"He *does* have quite the throw. But yes, I'm fine. I think it looks worse than it is. The armor must have taken the brunt of it." *A lie.* My back is currently pounding with pain and it's only a matter of time before I collapse.

"Well, I'm glad. The sword looked great out there." He looks back at me.

"Yeah, it was really nice. Nothing like my own dagger though." I say, looking off to the side. Arche and Nova are a few stalls to my right, quickly returning their own items.

"Mind if I see it?" I turn back to the man, confused. "Your dagger, I mean."

"Oh yes. Of course." I unsheathe the dagger, careful not to mess with the cut on that thigh. The gold blade gleams in the slowly fading sunlight.

"It's rare that you see a blade like this around here. Most soldiers go for the simplest of weapons. But from what I can tell that is far from your style." He examines the dagger closely.

"It was a gift, but yes, I like to stand out. Weapons included." I crack a smile, pushing past the pain slowly enveloping my body.

"Well, when you're feeling up to it, come visit me in the armory, I can clean it up for you." He says as he returns my dagger. I sheathe it at my thigh and wince from the pain.

"Will do. Thanks again." I almost turn away but I remember my last question for him. "If you don't mind me asking, what's your name?" He looks surprised that I would ask that, but I keep my face open, welcoming an answer.

"Tor Warin." He smiles, flashing his teeth. "I put together that you are Soleil Yamanu. Everyone was talking today and after seeing you fight, it became pretty obvious that it was you." I do my best to play off my clear anxiety.

"Yup. That's me. Thanks for everything, Tor. I'll visit the armory; I think my dagger needs a good cleaning anyway." He doesn't say anything else. So, I turn and see Nova and Arche walking towards me.

"Ready?" Nova looks me up and down as my knees wobble. I look up at Arche whose brows furrow in discontent. I would ask what is wrong, but the pain is free flowing once again and I can barely stand.

"Yes." I say, an air of impatience in my voice. Arche comes around to my side and wraps his arm around me tightly. Nova takes my other side and together, the three of us walk back to The Fortress.

Conquered and Conquerors as one.

As my adrenaline continues to dwindle, my vision gets darker and my body heavier until I can no longer hold myself up. Arche and Nova, to their credit, do not falter as they bear the brunt of my body weight. I barely hold onto consciousness as we walk into The Fortress and through its winding halls to the infirmary. My mind spins with each tap of my own blood on the pristine white floors.

The infirmary is a large white room with giant windows on every wall. It smells of antiseptic and latex, and nurses in all white walk back and forth throughout the space. It is extremely well lit from today's rare sun and a grand fireplace in the back of the room provides a delightful heat to the place.

I shiver when the heat from the roaring fire reaches me at last, grateful for the warmth after being in the cold of the battlefield for so long. Arche and Nova essentially carry me to the front desk of the infirmary where a pale faced nurse sits. She is writing something in a journal.

"Name?" She looks up and her eyes widen at the sight of me. I didn't think I looked *that* bad considering the circumstances, but I also haven't been near a mirror since well before the battle. "Battle simulation?" The nurse asks, walking around the desk to get a better look at me.

"Yeah." Nova responds.

"Soleil Yamanu." Arche says after.

"Okay Soleil Yamanu, let's get you to a bed and we can take a look." Considering the arrow lodged in my thigh, and her wide eyes, the nurse's words are calmer than I expected. Arche and Nova continue to carry me, but I feel my body shutting down. My vision goes dark and my eyelids droop.

"Soleil? Soleil, stay awake. Don't close your eyes yet." Arche's voice is frantic, and his hand is on my cheek, urging me to stay awake. But I am tired, *so tired*, and the pain is all encompassing. I only find reprieve from it in the darkness of my own mind.

So, I let myself drift far away—from Arche, from Nova, and even further from Lord Acastus himself.

A stone table.
Seven ornate goblets.
Seven gilded thrones.
Seven shining Knights.
A pair of piercing blue eyes.
    "I will find a way."
One goblet lifted.
Six goblets rose in unison

I WAKE SLOWLY, THE IMAGES OF MY DREAM RETREATING UNtil I am left with only darkness, a steady beeping sound and gentle hum of voices in the background. Forever engraved in my mind, the blue eyes are far from gone though. I attempt to push them away, but nothing works until I force open my eyes—clearly crusted shut.

I am lying flat on my back on a bed with a thin mattress in a room that is not my own sleeping chamber. I take deep breaths to steady myself, it isn't until my spike in heart rate makes the beeping faster, that I realize where I am.

The infirmary is quiet, but voices mull in the background. It's definitely nighttime, but I have no way of knowing just how late. Flat darkness envelopes every window in the infirmary, and I sadden at the fact that I have missed the end of one of Lex's few sunny days. Arche and Nova are nowhere to be found in my small, ten by ten, curtained room.

I slowly sit up, expecting pain that never comes. I take a deep breath and my back doesn't ache with the effort. Looking down at my hands, there are no marks or scratches left from my fall on the battlefield. I pull the sterile blanket off my body and my arms don't scream with pain.

I am wearing a thin, paper-like gown and am able to roll it up to expose my thighs. On my left thigh, there is nothing. Not a single sign of the shallow slice Arche had given me during the battle. On my right thigh, there is only a circular splotch of a scar, another one to add to the already existing collection on my leg. The scar itself is thick and the edges of it jagged.

I rotate my joints, bending my knees and moving my ankles to test them out. Everything feels in good order. My mind is thoroughly clear and I relish in the absence of pain. I time my breaths to the beeping of the heart rate monitor next to me. There is a wrap around my left forearm and a needle in the vein of my right arm. The needle is attached to a tube which connects to a bag hanging on a metal pole. When I quiet my breathing enough, I can hear the dripping of the medicine in the bag.

Long minutes pass and I delight in the silence, until my stomach growls loudly. The last time I ate must have been at lunch before the battle simulation. Food becomes the only thing on my mind as I undo the wrap on my left arm and carefully remove the needle from the vein on my right arm. I slip out of the bed, my bare feet hitting the stone floor, which thankfully, is warm. On a chair in the corner of the room lies my red cloak with a note sitting on top of it.

SOL,

ARCHE AND I STAYED BY YOUR SIDE UNTIL WE WERE FALLING ASLEEP OURSELVES. YOU WERE IN AND OUT OF CONSCIOUSNESS, BUT YOUR INJURIES WEREN'T TOO SEVERE CONSIDERING WHAT THEY USUALLY SEE HERE. A FRACTURED RIB, A COLLAPSED LUNG, AND YOU LOST A LOT OF BLOOD FROM THE LEG WOUND. THE NURSES USED ALL THEIR SPECIAL TRICKS TO HEAL YOU QUICKLY—YOU KNOW HOW THEY ARE WITH TELLUS' TECHNOLOGY. BUT YOU SHOULD BE IN GREAT SHAPE AND READY FOR TOMORROW'S SIM WHEN YOU WAKE. YOUR THERMALS WERE UNSALVAGEABLE, BUT I MADE A QUICK RUN TO THE TAILOR AND PUT IN AN ORDER FOR A NEW SET. IT WILL BE READY JUST BEFORE TOMORROW'S BATTLE SIMULATION AS WELL. I LEFT YOUR CLOAK SINCE IT WAS STILL IN GOOD SHAPE. I HAD TO CLEAN IT, BUT IT SHOULD BE DRY WHEN YOU WAKE. THERE IS A STRAP OF LEATHER IN THE POCKET SO YOU CAN TIE YOUR HAIR UP AND A PAIR OF SOCKS, SO YOU DON'T HAVE TO GO BAREFOOT. I ALSO TOOK YOUR BOOTS TO THE CASTLE; ALMA WILL HAVE THEM CLEAN BY MORNING. YOUR DAGGER IS WAITING FOR YOU IN OUR SLEEPING CHAMBER. ALSO, ARCHE TOLD ME TO TELL YOU THAT YOU DID GREAT TODAY AND THAT HE IS SORRY HE THREW THE SPEAR AT YOU SO HARD.

WE LOVE YOU!
NOU AND ARCH

Warmth spreads through my core as I read the note and I thank Infinity for my almost-siblings. I am shocked at the extent of my internal injuries, and even more surprised at how long I lasted considering the fractured rib and collapsed lung. On top of the blood loss, I am lucky that my own competitiveness didn't kill me. I don't regret it though; I'm fine now. Plus, if I saw the medics when I brought Ingrid to them, they wouldn't have let me reenter the battle, and I wouldn't have won.

I throw the cloak over my shoulders and dig through the inner pocket to find the leather strap. I quickly tie my hair up and dig around the other pockets until I find the pair of socks Nova left for me. I slide them on too, thankful for the soft fabric. Tip toeing out of the makeshift room, I walk to the nurses that sit on a couch near the fire, taking notes, reading, and talking, while their patients sleep.

"Excuse me?" I say quietly when I approach the nurses, my best attempt at not waking or startling anyone. The nurses look at me and the pale one from earlier speaks.

"Oh good! You're awake. Your friends were worried." She sounds relieved and I wonder how much Arche and Nova must have pestered her. "How are you feeling?"

"I'm okay. No pain anywhere. I am hungry though." I say quietly, embarrassed that food is my biggest concern. But my stomach aches and I don't intend on starving.

"Oh of course! You must be, let me fix you something. If you are feeling up to it, you can join us here. Otherwise, you can eat in your room, we won't get hurt." The woman smiles.

"Thank you. But I can eat in my room, I wouldn't want to bother any of you." I long to be near the fire, but I don't want to impose.

"Honey, you won't be bothering anyone! Sit, sit, there are some books on the shelf over there if you need something to do." The nurse turns and walks away.

"Thank you." I call out to her. She doesn't respond. Curious, I go to the bookshelves near the fireplace. It isn't anything expansive—nothing like Alma's personal library—but I enjoy the sentiment.

I pick up a random book, small and well-worn with a paper cover. I look at the cover and shutter with horror when I discover that it's a romance. I quickly put it back into the shelf and find a book on sword care and maintenance. While I don't own a sword myself, I plan on getting one eventually and at the very least, the book will be mind numbing and impersonal.

Walking back to the fireplace, I do a quick scan of the open seating. I settle on a fluffy white armchair. For a while I don't read, I simply sit and stare at the fire. I allow myself to become transfixed by the bright flame and subtle crack and pop of the wood. When the kind nurse comes back, I still have not opened the book.

"You alright sweetie?" The nurse asks, handing me a tray of food.

"I'm fine," I reply quickly.

"*You* had a day if the rumors are true. Eat a bit and go back to bed, you need your strength if you plan on fighting in the simulation tomorrow." The nurse says warmly.

"I *do* plan on fighting." I respond with a more defensiveness than I intended. "Thank you for the food, and the care. I appreciate it." I add.

"Of course! Now, if you need anything, ask. I'll just be over there."

"Actually, I do need one more thing—what time is it?" I ask.

The nurse checks the watch at her wrist and looks back up at me. "About *oh two hundred hours.* Your friends left around *twenty-three hundred hours* if you were wondering. They were half asleep by the time they walked out of here. That girl especially, she walked to The Castle and back in only a few minutes." The nurse winks at me and walks back to her seat. I remove the metal lid from the plate of food and am delighted when I see a large plate of pasta in a creamy white sauce. Small pieces of chicken are dispersed throughout the noodles and a large piece of toasted bread is on the side. A tall glass of ice water is also on the tray. I thank Infinity for the nurse's kindness and begin eating.

I down the plate in only a few minutes. When I'm done, the kind nurse takes my tray from me and disappears into a back room of the infirmary. Warm, comfortable, and content, I clutch the book that I grabbed earlier, close to my chest and stare into the light of the fire, transfixed by its power. Finally, I find myself alone with my thoughts once more.

CHAPTER
NINE

Lex's winter continues to beat down on me but this time there is no sun in the sky to offer reprieve. After my night in the infirmary, I walked back to my sleeping chamber, wearing a pair of black sleeping thermals that the nurses gave me, with disposable black slippers to match. My cloak was wrapped tightly over my body with my hood pulled down over my head and I crossed my arms as I walked down the halls of The Fortress. I moved quickly that morning, the absence of my dagger at my thigh jarring, however I knew it awaited me in the sleeping chamber.

It was extremely early in the day, earlier than even Nova would usually wake, but I was far from tired. I opened the door of the sleeping chamber slowly, careful not to make any sounds. I walked to Nova's bunk and woke her up with a smile. Her eyes lit when she realized that I was okay.

Arche had a similar reaction when he saw me that morning. He had picked me up and spun me around in the middle of the dining hall, cheering and giddy with happiness. Even when he set me back down on the ground, he didn't let me go. Instead, he pulled me into a long hug. He didn't need to speak to tell me that he regretted what he did, and he didn't need to ask for my forgiveness either. I held no grudge against him, I would have done something similar if the situation was flipped. While I *did* take a moment to explain that to him, he laid on the apologies anyway.

After getting my new thermals from the tailor, my freshly cleaned boots from Alma, and my dagger back from Nova, the next days went by much like the first—however the lack of sun was unfortunate. The weather got worse as each day passed, and eventually the flurries of snow finally stuck. The battles only got more intense as we not only had to fight each other, but brave the elements as well. Some students of The Academy sat out of battles on occasion when the weather got too intense, but my squadron of female soldiers never let up.

I was more careful after the first day of battle simulation and, thank Infinity, I did not earn myself another trip to the infirmary. We fought fourteen different squadrons and defeated them all. I called a rotating set of formations ensuring that each squad we fought was thrown off guard. Every single day I caught the other teams' banners, and every single night, I hung them on the wall of our sleeping chamber. The girls and I grew closer with each passing day and we began spending hours training in the mornings before battle, and in the evenings after.

The word got around that Female Squadron G was undefeated during the battle simulations. We have a perfect record now, *14-0*, and the other squadrons curse Infinity when they are paired up with us. Our group was eventually coined *The Undying Squadron*, once we had beat ten squads in a row. The only people who could come close to matching me in battle are Nova and Arche, and considering that Nova is on my team, and I have already beaten Arche, the wins came easily.

Slowly, we began to look like a proper army squadron and not just a group of soldiers in training. Every time I grabbed the banner off the opposing team's post, I raised it high into the air, though my muscles ached for respite. However, I didn't point my sword at Lord Acastus again. I had to keep his attention and curiosity while remaining civil, and so that became the compromise. Lord Acastus couldn't know that while he was orchestrating the battle simulations, I was playing a game of my own.

After fourteen straight days of battle, it was announced that the fifteenth day of the star cycle would be an off day for all squadrons as Lord Acastus had his meeting with The Infinite Knight Court. While my squadron is on a great streak, we are all looking forward to a break.

Waking up at *1200*, all twenty of us rush to the bathing chambers before heading to the dining hall for lunch. We travel like a pack, our formation unbreaking even though battle simulation is not in session. When we arrive at the dining hall my face lights up the moment I see Arche. He runs over to Nova and I, pulling us into a tight hug.

"My two favorite warriors," he smiles. "How are the most fearless women in The Academy doing on this fine afternoon?" He winks at us on the word *afternoon.*

"We are doing just fine, thank you very much." Nova says, glaring at Arche.

"Fine, but hungry." I add.

"Well, let's get you two some food then." Arche replies, walking us over to the food stations.

"Wait a minute, aren't you usually sleeping at this time?" I glare, remembering how we found him during lunchtime on the day of the first battle simulation.

"I'm a changed man, Soleil. Plus, you two have been going to lunch every day since the battle simulations became a daily occurrence, so it's a habit now. I was also hoping that you two would be here considering your absence at breakfast." I nudge him with my shoulder, hard enough to show my discontent, but not hard enough to really hurt. "Okay, okay—she is quite the ball of anger when she's hungry huh?" Arche asks Nova.

"Tell me about it. I've long since resorted to keeping snacks in my trunk." Nova muses.

"How else am I supposed to build muscle? Especially now that we train twice a day." I glare. Nova and Arche laugh as I stack my plate high with food.

The three of us eat slowly, constantly distracted by conversation. Our meals for the last few weeks have been quick as we shovel food down our throats in between history lessons, training sessions, and rounds of battle simulation. For the first time all star cycle, we are able to simply enjoy each other's company.

We finally finish our food almost an hour later and we discard our trays at the bins near the doors of the dining hall. Nova and I quickly say goodbye to Arche before heading down to our history lesson.

When we arrive at the fourth-floor lecture hall, all the other girls in our squadron are already there. Nova and I's seats in the front row are empty—clearly reserved for us—so we make our way down to them. Professor Clara has not yet arrived.

"Any idea what we're doing for training today? The battlefield will probably be empty considering the sim is canceled. We could run formation drills into the night, there are still fourteen more battles and we won't get another chance to create new formations. I would rather not reuse any of them, people are studying us enough as it is." Nova speaks quickly, words tumbling out and her eyes glimmering. Since the first battle simulation, she has gotten progressively more excited about them, slowly taking on more responsibility for strategy until now, where the two of us have an equal split.

"Yeah, that sounds great, we can tell everyone after the lesson. I want to try a star formation with archers at each of the points. Ingrid has been itching to use a bow during simulation and I want to give her the chance." I respond coolly, twirling my pen between my fingers.

"She *has* been practicing a lot lately. I finally got around to adjusting her form the other day, she is a clean shot now." Nova says, gaze trained on the blackboard in front of us.

"Can we make winning any easier?"

"Let's try being humble for once." Nova chuckles with the words, knowing full well that she is having just as much fun as I am.

Finally, Professor Clara walks into the lecture hall, the heels of her boots clacking on the wooden floor. Today she wears a royal blue dress and her flowing silver hair is parted in the middle and tied back with a strap of leather, low on her head. She looks magical as always.

"Good afternoon class. I hope you are all enjoying your short rest from battle simulation. You have all fought valiantly these last few weeks and I am extremely impressed. Now, onto the lesson." I tune out there, already knowing that she will go on a tangent about the state of the realms. I am not missing anything, for I have already done the textbook reading *with* her annotations. Fixing my gaze on Professor Clara, I let myself think about the star formation that I will introduce to my squadron today.

The history lesson is over quickly and Professor Clara wraps up by assigning a few more chapters of textbook readings. By the time the lesson is done, I have perfectly planned the star formation and am extremely excited to begin training. As Nova and I pack up our satchels, Professor Clara walks over to our table.

"Soleil, I actually want you to stay for a while." She tells me, staring at me with her jet-black eyes. Her pearlescent skin shines beautifully in the fading light. I look over to Nova who shrugs.

"Okay, that's fine Professor," I respond. I turn to Nova. "Nov, can you just get the girls warmed up and start running the new formation ideas you had. I want to see at least a few of them in action by the time I arrive."

"I can do that. See you, Sol." Nova packs up the rest of her things and walks out of the lecture hall, shutting the door behind her. Professor Clara walks back to the blackboard and I sit down at the wooden table again. I take my journal out of my satchel, preparing to take notes, but Professor Clara stops me.

"You don't need that Soleil. I don't want you to take notes on what I am about to tell you." Her voice is serious. "You have to understand that this information is for your own benefit, but you *cannot* repeat it to anyone. Not even to Nova." Professor Clara evokes a voice I have never heard her use before and I can't help but nod my head in assent.

"Very well. The history I wish to discuss with you today, is that of our own realm," Professor Clara begins. "Legend says—*and history proves*—that the legions of soldiers in The Undying Army were always a force to be reckoned with. At one point, Lex held dominance over the realms in a way even beyond the power of Omnis. The Undying Army gained strength and numbers beyond anything ever seen before and fear spread throughout the seven realms." I have no idea where she could possibly be going, but I listen anyway, Professor Clara's voice smooth like the greatest of all storytellers.

"Ten millennia ago, the *then* Knight of Lex—one who has been erased from our history—rapidly expanded his legions. This Knight was Duncan Lex, a distant ancestor to our own Acastus Lex. Duncan Lex was incredibly gifted in the magical arts, as were those who came before him. His army grew beyond the capacity of The Fortress, The Castle of Lex, and The Wall as well. Soon, he began using it to attack other realms, sending out squadrons of soldiers to keep the citizens of the realms—and their Knights—in line." My eyes widen at what Professor Clara is telling me. She continues on despite my clear bewilderment.

"Omnis—the jewel of The Realms of Infinity—however, did not relent so easily. They held on, but barely. Eventually, Duncan Lex's own son, Marcellus Lex, *young warrior,* in the languages of the past world, escaped to Omnis. With the permission of the *then* Knight of Omnis, Marcellus used The Book of the Bound to siphon off small amounts of power from The Book of Law, thereby syphoning power from his father." This story is so different from the ones Alma once told me. So much darker, so much more detailed. And yet I don't doubt that what Professor Clara is saying, is true.

"By the time the tyrannical Lord Duncan Lex finally realized that his power was getting weaker, it was too late. Marcellus Lex and the six remaining Knights of Infinity marched on our realm, with nothing but their wit and quickly draining magic, to protect them. Lord Duncan, managed to kill off all six of the Knights in a battle that was said to have decimated Lex, making it the desolate wasteland we see it as today. Marcellus was drained, for he had only a portion of the power that Lord Duncan held, so when Lord Duncan took a dagger and slit the throat of his own son, Marcellus did the last thing he could. He pulled power from The Book of Law and with his blood as the cost, forged an unbreakable law. A law that not only killed Lord Duncan as he had killed his own son, but also cursed the bloodline of the royals of Lex. The curse said that from that point on, each of the immortals in Lex's royal bloodline would be born with less and less of the magic that they originally had held so well. This would occur until the newborn Knights of Lex held only a whisper." Suddenly I can't breathe.

Every bit of history I learned for the last seven years, every story of negotiation and peace treaties—they were lies. The weakening power of the royals of Lex, is not simply coincidence, not a byproduct of a peaceful realm where the power of an army isn't needed. It was cursed into the bloodline… by a member of it.

"With all seven of the Knights of Infinity dead, it seemed at the time that all was lost in the realms. However, young Marcellus married and had a daughter when he snuck away to Omnis to escape his father's rule. And so, each of the realms rebuilt with the new heirs to their respective thrones taking the mantles of their parents. Decades later, with the memories of the great war still fresh, the new heirs, including Lord Marcellus' daughter, Lady Myla Knight of Lex, forged a new law. All the Knights of Infinity, present and future, save for the royal bloodline of Omnis, would give up their powers in the magical arts, to prevent any future Knights from starting another war. The royal bloodline of Omnis would become the high rulers of The Realms of Infinity and bind the realms for the better." I can't imagine a time where the Knights of Infinity were so consenting, especially now, when their disagreements are common news.

"A stipulation in this agreement was that all of the immortals that were not of direct royal blood, save for a few extremely special ones, would be sentenced to The Flight at the end of the century. This would allow them to live the lifespan of a normal mortal, and then pass through The Door of the Dusk when it was complete. The law was forged and today there are very few immortals that are not of royal blood. And today, only Lord Eric, and the royal bloodline of Omnis, hold any magical abilities. The other Knights and bloodlines have certain *powers* per say, but Marcellus' curse remained, and Lex's royal bloodline knows nothing of those powers, even if the law were to be broken."

I shiver at the image. One bloodline with generations to expand their magic while every other bloodline had none. I can't imagine the power Lord Eric must have, but I wonder why he has not yet used it. There must be a reason why he hasn't already deployed his strength to control all the realms. But then I realize, Omnis already holds binding power in the realms, there is no point to do anymore when his realm is already most powerful.

"Why are you telling me all of this?" I ask Professor Clara, my voice shaking as I speak.

"Soleil, it is clear that you are in the running for second in command of The Undying Army. However, you must understand the magnitude of the world you will be entering. You will not simply be second in command of The Undying Army; you will be Lord Acastus' second as well. Those duties go beyond the army and you have to know what is at stake." Professor Clara locks eyes with me and I shiver as her words hit me. I want power, and again, and again I choose it despite the costs that lie in front of me. I realize though, that I will still choose it, despite my new knowledge.

"I know what is at stake Professor. I appreciate you telling me all of this and I won't forget it, but I am not going to change my mind. I *will* get that job, at whatever cost." I stand quickly, grabbing my satchel and I walk towards the exit of the lecture hall.

"That is where you are wrong, Soleil." I turn back to Professor Clara. "There *is* a cost—one that you won't be able to pay. You won't know it until you see it, but when it crosses your path, you will do anything to run from it. Lord Acastus is planning something and I hope that what I just told you can help you spot it. You are in a precarious situation girl, think twice before you make a move." My blood runs cold, but I nod at Professor Clara before turning away.

As I walk through the halls of The Fortress, I can't help but think about everything Professor Clara told me. It isn't the history that scares me, the idea that Lord Acastus is planning something, or the cost that Professor Clara said I will have to pay one day. It is her certainty that I *won't* be able to pay it that shakes me most. Still, in the face of everything Professor Clara told me, I continue on my path, choosing power again.

CHAPTER

TEN

The history of Lex echoes through my mind every day. Along with my recurring dreams, and the piercing blue eyes that follow me everywhere, I begin seeing who could only be Duncan Lex. In my dreams, he is simply an older, gruffer, version of Lord Acastus, and he shakes the realms with his power. I do my best to push those images out of my mind, and while I am mostly successful, my other dream persists.

A stone table.

Seven ornate goblets.

Seven gilded thrones.

Seven shining Knights.

A pair of piercing blue eyes.

"I will find a way."

One goblet lifted.

Six goblets rose in unison

Again, and again, and again, the dream chases me. Each time I wake with the rising of the six goblets, the blue eyes brand themselves into my eyelids. I can't escape the dream, and now more than ever—*I have to.*

It's becoming more realistic as the days pass, my reactions to them growing stronger as well. I often wake in a fit, sweating, screaming, out of breath. Some nights I even wake the other girls in my panic. If it was any other way, I know that I would deprive myself from sleep, simply to avoid those eyes—I tried to do so. But at the end of each day, after training, lessons, and simulation, I crash onto my bed with no choice but to be roped into endless oblivion.

The next thirteen days of battle simulation go much like the first. Female Squadron G now has a *27-0* win streak. We are the most talked about squadron to ever pass through The Academy. Out of the last twenty-seven rounds of battle simulation, only Arche's group offered us any challenge. Even the older groups were not a problem. Each time a squadron believed that they knew our formation, small changes were always made to throw them off.

Nova's strategic thinking has gotten better as well, and once we realized that we wouldn't be going up against Arche again, we began enlisting his help. Having nothing better to do, Arche began joining us for early morning and late-night training sessions. He quickly became the twenty-first member of *The Undying Squadron.* All the girls enjoyed his company, appreciating a male view on things. Many times, when Nova and I believed that we had something that the men of another team would fall for, we would run the formation with Arche to be sure. Usually we got it down, but on occasion, large cracks in our defense would show through, even against one person.

Arche glowed in the opportunity to loosen his muscles against us. His team was doing decent at a *20-7*, win-loss ratio, but there is nothing like fighting with the winning squadron. Arche didn't ask for anything in exchange for helping us out, and he never told a single person about our formations. As thanks, Nova and I would spend time during meals discussing formations that he could try with Male Squadron 7G. As a result, his team began winning more and they hadn't lost a single simulation since the middle of the star cycle.

The clang of steel became music to my ears as I danced the days away, relishing in the feeling of battle. Arche and I often sparred and it was always a sight to see as people from all over The Academy circled us to get a look. I won every sword fight against Arche. I accused him of letting me win on more than one occasion but since I was often down in the dirt by the end of our fights, I assumed that he wasn't feigning his losses.

Lex's weather remained abhorrent, the snow sticking for only a few days, before melting and refreezing into a solid sheet of ice on the battlefield. Those few rounds of battle simulation, against Female Squadron E, and Male squadron 10G, were the worst. The students of the Academy eventually banded together to scratch up the surface of the ice on the battlefield in an attempt to give it some grip. Thankfully it worked until the ice melted and fresh snow covered the battlefield again.

The walls of Female Sleeping Chamber G were absolutely covered with the crushed velvet banners of our enemies, turning our sleeping chamber into a patchwork of rich colors. I had captured all of them, but the black banner from Arche's squadron remains my favorite as it was the one that I fought the hardest to get.

The morning of the twenty-ninth day of the star cycle arrives quickly, my dreams following me through the night as always. Last night, my squadron stayed out extremely late to nail down the star formation that I had been planning. It took two weeks to figure it out, but in perfect timing, for the last day of the star cycle and final round of battle simulation is upon us.

I wake at *0500*, before anyone else. Even Nova still sleeps as I promised my squadron that if we nailed the formation, we could skip morning training. To my relief they did, but I have no intention of sleeping in. I shower and change quickly, putting on my white battle thermals and boots, strapping my dagger to my right thigh, and wrapping my blood red cloak around my body with the hood low over my head.

I sneak out of the sleeping chamber, gritting my teeth against the chill air. No matter how much time I spend outside, nothing will allow me to get used to Lex's weather. As I close the door, I scan the schedule, looking for today's battle simulation assignment. The bottom of the schedule reads *Battle Simulation with Female Group J / 1700-1800*. I smile at the words. Battle simulation with Fay Enyo... *How much more dramatic can it get?* All lessons are canceled for the day too. Maybe all of our superiors will be at the final rounds of battle simulation. Wonderful. The perfect chance to have all of the eyes in the realm on me.

As I close the door, I feel the need to write Nova a note so she won't be worried in my absence. I walk back into the room, go to my trunk, and rip a page out of my journal.

> NOV,
> I WOKE EARLY TO TIE UP SOME LOOSE ENDS. DON'T WAIT UP. LESSONS ARE CANCELED FOR THE DAY, SO MAKE SURE THE GIRLS ARE COMPLETELY READY FOR BATTLE. TAKE THEM DOWN FOR BREAKFAST (OR LUNCH, DEPENDING ON WHEN YOU WAKE) AND HEAD STRAIGHT DOWN TO THE BATTLEFIELD. WE ARE BATTLING FAY'S SQUADRON AT 1600, BUT I WANT EVERYONE DOWN THERE ALL DAY. I WILL MEET YOU AS SOON AS I CAN. I WANT ALL OF THE GIRLS IN ARMOR—WEAPONS READY. NO SITTING WHILE YOU WATCH, BUT FEEL FREE TO RUN WARMUPS—SAVE THE FORMATIONS FOR THE BATTLE ITSELF. DON'T WORRY ABOUT ME, IT'S NOT A BIG DEAL, I JUST WANT TO VISIT SOMEONE.
> SOL

I fold the note in half, write *Nov* on the front of it and place it on my bunk. Then I quietly slip out of the sleeping chamber before anyone can wake. While I *had* no intentions of getting breakfast, the growling of my stomach says otherwise. I curse Infinity for my lack of a proper eating schedule and adjust my path to the dining hall. When I arrive at about *0630* the hall is empty save for the soldiers making breakfast at the stations and a few students that happen to be early risers. Sun peaks in through the stained-glass mural at the back of the dining hall, distorting the image of the forgotten Knight of Lex and his legions of men behind him.

I warm at the thought of a sunny day. Two in a single star cycle is unheard of, but the sun making an entrance on the first *and* last days of battle simulation would be a blessing straight from Infinity. Making my way to the food stations, my stomach grumbles at the smell. I walk down the line, piling my plate up with food. Large servings of scrambled eggs, fried potatoes, and thin cakes smothered in syrup and strawberry preserves, make it onto my tray.

About halfway through my breakfast, I am startled when someone wraps their arms gently around my waist and sits down to my left. I shake in fear and almost throw my fork at the unknown person. I calm when I turn and realize that it's just Arche. *Infinity—he knows how to startle me.* His hair is wild from sleep, but his face is clear and refreshed. He smiles at me.

"Good morning, Soleil. Where *is* the rest of your squad?" He asks, looking around.

"Asleep," I reply indifferently. I shift to get out of Arche's hold, but he tightens it. I shoot him a look and he lets go.

"Are you—" he stops, quieting. "*Sneaking out?*" Arche whispers, wiggling his eyebrows suggestively.

"Is it sneaking out if you leave a note?" I respond coolly, turning back to my breakfast.

"Depends, did you tell Nov exactly where you're going?"

"No," I say.

"Well then you have your answer." He pauses. "So, what are you up to anyway? I don't think I've ever seen you get up this early of your own accord."

He's right, but I still won't tell him where I am going. "I'm running errands—tying up some loose ends before today's battle. We're going up against Fay's squad and I need to make some preparations." I take a bite of food and chew it slowly.

"You see—I *would* believe you, but you couldn't have known that you were facing Fay until this morning, *and* you would have had to be awake pretty early anyway to be here now. Which means that you weren't awake because of the battle with Fay, you were already up, and now that's just your excuse." He replies smoothly, taking one of the thin cakes off my plate and biting into it.

"Arche, I said I have errands to run, can you please just leave it alone." I roll my eyes at him.

"Sure, sure. I know that you are going to visit Alma for a gossip session. You could have just said so." My face floods red, but it's not from embarrassment as Arche would assume, it's from relief at his assurance in a false theory.

"You got me. Fine. But before you ask, no you cannot join." I say quickly, attempting to enhance my false embarrassment.

"We both know Alma likes me more than you." Arche says, "but I will respect your wishes. Do you have any idea what your squadron is going to do without you?" He asks, taking another thin cake from my plate.

"I told them that after they wake and clean up, they can grab some food and head down to the battlefield. They should be there all day, so you guys can run drills to warm up. I want them to watch every battle today." I pause, "what time is your battle?"

"*Fourteen hundred hours,* I think. We are going against Male Squad 9 from our year. I think it will be an easy win with that spiral formation you and Nova came up with." He responds, focusing on the thin cake he stole from my plate.

"You guys should be fine." Realizing that I am plenty full, I slide my tray over to Arche and stand up to leave. "If I don't see you before the battle, good luck Arch. You'll do fine, and if I miss the battle, I want a full play by play when I see you next. Keep an eye on the girls for me and tell Nov I said hi." I begin walking away but Arche grabs my hand before I can leave.

"Thanks Sol, and of course." He smiles, and lets go of my hand, turning back to the tray of food I left for him.

And so, I set out to The Fortress' armory to visit Tor Warin—and to get my dagger cleaned of course. I don't visit the armory often as I keep my dagger in good condition and have no need for a sword of my own, so it takes me a moment to orient myself in The Fortress and find it.

On the third floor of The Fortress, at the end of a series of winding hallways, lies the student armory. The room is large and filled with people, even at this early hour. Students and soldiers alike talk, work, and forge in the steaming chamber. I walk over to the front desk where a man sits, his arms covered in scars.

"Yes?" He says his voice deep and crackling.

"I'm looking for Tor Warin, he told me I could find him here." I say with as much force I can muster this early in the morning.

"I don't recognize the name." The man hesitates, looking up at me. "Where *did* you meet this man?"

"At the makeshift armory by the battlefield during my first simulation of the star cycle. He told me I could find him at the armory so here I am." I respond calmly.

"Well, if it was during a simulation then he must have come from The Castle's armory. Lord Acastus completely took over this simulation's planning. Which includes getting members of The Castle's armory to manage weapons." The man sounds slightly resentful. "If this *Tor Warin* is a real person, you should be able to find him in The Castle's armory." I feel extremely stupid for bothering this man, but I say my thanks and leave before I can waste any more of his time.

With my new information I walk through the halls of The Fortress and out of its main doors, into the bitter land of Lex.

My walk to The Castle of Lex is a swift one. Either the guards recognize me, or they are simply feeling lenient, but I am not stopped on my way in. I wander The Castle for what seems like an hour, before relenting to ask someone for directions.

"Do you know where I can find the armory?" I ask civilly, keeping composure in the face of a fully trained soldier. She was the first person I found and if I wasn't so desperate after wandering for so long, her cold look would have been enough to keep me from even making eye contact with her.

"Upstairs, in the north hall, the room is clearly labeled. Good luck getting in there though." The woman replies, looking me up and down. I simply nod my head and move on.

I find the nearest set of spiral stairs and go up one level, then I make my way to the marked *north hallway* and walk down it. I eventually make it to a guarded room with people flowing in and out. From what I can see, this armory looks a lot like the one in The Fortress but on a much larger scale. When I reach the guards, they begin questioning me immediately. I remove my hood to allow them to see my face.

"I'm looking for Tor Warin. He told me I could find him here, I'm a friend." I smile at the guard choosing benevolence over cool civility.

"Stay here, I'll go find Mr. Warin and he can decide whether or not you enter." The guard says, switching out with another soldier. I am filled with relief when the guard recognizes his name and after a few moments of waiting, the guard returns with Tor trailing him. I can't help but smile.

"She's with me." Tor gestures for me to follow him and I step into the sweltering hot room that is The Castle's armory. I follow Tor into a small office which—thank Infinity—is much cooler. Tor is the first to speak.

"It's been a while…" His voice trails off as he turns away from me. It *has* been a while. After the first battle simulation I haven't seen him at all. However, the same gold breastplate, gauntlets, sword, and sheath that he gave me on the first day of the star cycle are always ready for me before my daily simulation. Every time I ask for armor and a sword, that set is brought out for me, a card with my name on it attached.

"I thought that I made you up." I say keeping my voice casual. "A man with an eye for steel *and* style? Impossible," I scoff. Today Tor wears a brown long sleeved shirt that is laced in the front with a strap of leather. He has on a leather belt that hangs low on his waist, as well as black trousers. His shirt is not tucked into them. His black boots and cloak are well worn but they look taken care of.

"Not exactly impossible." He says, turning around to face me. "Improbable? Maybe. But how could it be impossible when I am right here." He chuckles and walks towards me.

"Good to know that you are real." I crack a smile. "I actually came here for you to fulfill that promise you made me."

"What promise?"

"*Come visit me at the armory and I will clean that dagger for you.*" I say mockingly, lowering my voice for full effect. "You know I made a complete fool of myself when I went to the wrong armory today."

"The wrong armory?" Tor's face floods with amusement.

"Yes! There are two, if you didn't know. The Fortress has one as well." I fake annoyance.

"So, you went to the one in The Fortress first?" I nod. "Sorry, I should have clarified." Tor reaches his hand up to comb his hair and I notice the grime on his face, probably coal dust from the forge. "Now, to make it up to you. I will clean your dagger *and* let you watch."

"Oh, what an honor!" I put on a show, "gracious Tor Warin, my eyes would be blessed to see your craft in action." I muse, laughter punctuating my words.

"Okay, enough playing around. Come on." He gestures for me to follow him and we go back into the armory. I follow him through a door, and then into another, until we are in a large stone room lined with weapons. I gasp at the sight of the beautiful swords, bows, daggers, and spears.

"So, I can blame your absence at the battle simulation on… this?" I joke.

"Well, *this* is my job," he replies. "But *I* made the decision not to see you during the simulations. I didn't want to distract you, considering you got hurt last time."

I fill with anger at his words, at the allegation that his mere presence distracted me and got me hurt during the first battle simulation.

"If you think that I got hurt because *you* were there, you are dead wrong." I huff.

"Well, you did come back to return the armor while you were halfway to The Door of The Dusk." Tor responds.

"As common courtesy! Infinity—you know what? I think I'm just going to head back to The Fortress." Tor catches my hand before I can leave.

"I'm kidding, Soleil. You were incredible out there." I glare at him. "I was there—every day—just watching though. How else could I leave your armor and sword for you? Perfectly shined and sharpened as well." He winks. "To be honest, you really impressed me. I didn't want you to only see me as the person who forged the weapons when you were the one putting them to incredible use."

"If I intimidate you, *Tor Warin*, just say so." I smile.

He laughs. "*Soleil Yamanu*, you intimidate me."

"Very well. Now about my dagger—" I pull it from my sheath and hand it to Tor. "I usually take pretty good care of it, but since the daily battles, it's been getting more use than usual. A few days ago, it took a tumble during a particularly nasty one-on-one with a girl a few years older than me—"

He cuts me off before I can continue, still analyzing my dagger. "I saw that. You won, but she stepped on the blade, shoving it into the ground before you could knock her out with a stone." I am silent for long seconds after he speaks, completely bewildered at the fact that he remembers. "I told you I was watching." He looks up at me and smiles widely, clearly content with himself.

"Yeah, well now it's all scratched up, *and* there is a slight bend. It doesn't throw as cleanly anymore." I say, recalling yesterday's simulation when my missed dagger throw almost cost me the banner.

"I can take care of it, don't worry. It should only take me an hour or so. I want to make sure that I get it completely smooth and balanced again. You don't have to stay; I was joking about you having to watch me." He says casually, walking to the bench at the other end of the room.

"Well, I actually want to stay." He turns back around, a smile on his face. "It looks like you could use some company."

"Take a seat, Soleil." He gestures to a leather chair near the bench.

"Sol. You can call me Sol." Tor nods, surprise painting his face. I wink in response.

He begins fixing my dagger, the scraping of metal music to my ears. His fingers work quickly and nimbly and the two of us become equally transfixed by the process

TOR WORKS DILIGENTLY FOR WELL OVER AN HOUR. BY THE time he is finished, my dagger looks exactly the way it did when Alma first gave it to me. I didn't realize how bad the blade and handle alike, have gotten over the last seven years until he hands it back to me. I gasp in shock when I see it, shining even in the dim light of Tor's weapons room.

"Tor—this is incredible!" I am giddy with excitement as I examine the golden blade.

"It's nothing, Sol. Anytime." He tries to underplay the beauty of his work.

"It is *everything* Tor." I look up at him. He is clearly shocked by my reaction. I flip the dagger to its other side and notice that he missed a spot. A deep scratch from the fight that messed up the rest of the dagger remains embedded in the handle. I run my thumb over it, it's oddly smooth.

"You missed a spot." I look up at him.

"It was intentional. They say that the best warriors keep certain *battle scars* on their weapons, even after getting them cleaned. The point is to remind them of the battles they won *and* those they lost." Tor speaks smoothly, his voice deep.

"Well, I haven't lost."

"I can see that, *Miss Yamanu*," he responds coolly. The deep smoothness of his voice caresses my spine, flooding me with a warmth that I never knew I was missing. His eyes glimmer in the warm light.

"Well thank you for—" I hold the dagger up. "This," I smile and tuck the dagger into the scabbard at my thigh.

I turn around to finally examine the weapons lined up floor to ceiling on the walls of this room. Mainly attempting to shake the feeling that has welled up in my core. "So, you made *all* of these?" I ask, mesmerized by the detail of a steel tipped wooden spear.

"Yeah, everyone needs a hobby I guess." Tor says from behind me. Even at this distance, the warmth of his tone affects me.

"I think this is more than a hobby." I reach for the wooden spear. "Do you mind if I?" I gesture to the weapon, turning back to face Tor.

"Yes of course," he nods. I grab the wooden shaft and lift it off the hooks that hold it to the wall. It's so much heavier than it looks and I almost drop it out of pure shock.

"Why is it so heavy?" I ask, finally adjusting to the weight.

"It has a steel core. Not traditional by any means, but for the right person—in the right battle. It might prove useful."

I nod in assent as he talks. His gaze is trained, not on the weapon, but on my hands caressing its wooden shaft. Wisdom and warmth that I will never truly be able to describe, flow behind his irises. Beyond what anyone in this world—anyone save for Tor himself—will ever be able to see.

"It has some weight to it though." I say, spinning the spear around, I point it at Tor and laugh. Spears break all the time in battle, to have one with the feel of wood, but the durability of steel is unheard of.

"Yes, it does, it would probably take quite a bit of training to get used to." I place the spear back on the hooks and examine the room again. Rows of ornate bows, shining swords, elegantly crafted daggers, and hand carved spears meet my gaze. I walk to a workbench pushed against a wall of swords and my eyes widen at the sight.

It is just a hilt, too big for a dagger, too small for a longsword. Probably for an arming sword if I have to guess. The base wood of the hilt is black and there are beautiful waves of gold pushed deep into the wood. The waves of gold metal flow up to form the cross guard which looks as fluid and interconnected as a spider's web, the various pieces of gold trapping a beautiful red stone in the center. The red stone is shimmering and heart-shaped and for a moment, I see it beating. Embedded in the waves of gold are pearls of various sizes and tones. There is no blade, but I am confident that this will be the most beautiful sword to ever exist.

"What is this?" I ask, the beauty of the hilt knocking the wind out of me.

"Just something I've been working on. It's going to be a sword of course. I was commissioned to make it." Tor's words are casual and I am bewildered. How can one talk of such beauty in a casual manner?

"So, it's spoken for?" I query, pulling my gaze from the hilt.

"Yes. It is meant to be one of a kind." I let out a sigh—mostly of relief. If this sword was *not* spoken for... I have no idea the lengths I would go to make it my own. I don't allow myself another look at the hilt.

"Too bad—" I say longingly. "It's quite beautiful." I smile at him quickly, suddenly remembering that I haven't eaten in a few hours. "Do you happen to know anywhere to eat around here?" I ask sarcastically. I know *exactly* where to eat in this castle.

Tor ponders for a moment. "Is the dining hall alright? Or is that too simple for your *exquisite* taste."

"My taste *is* exquisite, isn't it? But yes, the dining hall sounds great."

"Come on then." Tor begins walking to the door and I follow, sneaking one last look at the hilt that glimmers on the workbench. I envy the person who will get the incredible sword once it is finished, and I know that I will never forget its beauty as long as I live.

"Do you have any idea what time it is?" I ask Tor as we walk out of the armory and into The Castle's hallways.

"*Ten hundred hours* on the mark." Tor replies, slowing his pace to match my own. "Got anywhere to be?"

"Battle simulation at *seventeen hundred hours*. But I'm fine for now." I respond, looking up at him. My shoulder brushes his as we walk through The Castle and towards the dining hall, sending a jolt of energy through my body. *What is wrong with me?* Am I so touch deprived that a brush of fabric sends me into a spiral? I would continue my mental interrogation of myself, except for the fact that when we arrive at the dining hall, Tor continues to walk.

"Tor? Where are you going?" I call after him. He spins around and begins walking backwards.

"Just trust me," he calls out. Something about the way he carries himself, the tuft of brown hair that has spilled onto his forehead... I quicken my pace to meet him without question. We go up a flight of stairs and down a hallway marked *south* until we come upon a room with a wooden door.

"What *is* this?" I ask curiously as Tor pulls a set of keys out of his pocket. He shoves a black one into the lock.

"A surprise." He replies, opening the door.

It takes a moment for my eyes to adjust to the room. Three of the four walls are made entirely out of glass, the ceiling as well. It's gorgeous, *and* it has a perfect view of Lex. Another door, leading to Infinity knows where, is next to the one that Tor and I came through.

"You seem to have this castle on lock, Tor." I say in amazement.

"Well, when you are head bladesmith, you get your way." He says slyly.

"I don't see any food though," I add, disappointed. Just then, there is a knock on the door and Tor opens it. In comes a servant dressed in all white, leading a cart full of metal trays with domed lids.

"Thank you, sir." Tor says, handing the man a few coins before closing the door behind him. "You didn't think I would leave you hungry, did you?"

Eagerly I make my way to the cart and begin lifting the domed lids. I find roast chicken, grilled fish, seared steaks, stir fried vegetables, fluffy mashed potatoes, crispy bread, and a beautiful chocolate brownie with vanilla ice cream for dessert.

"It looks wonderful." I sigh graciously.

While I was one of the Lost in the castle, the caretakers cooked for us. We never got to eat what the servants cooked as that is only for nobles, the royal family, or highly ranked soldiers. This is the first time that I have ever eaten food this decadent.

"Ready to dig in?" Tor asks me.

I nod and he begins unrolling a rug that was propped up in a log against the stone wall. He lays the rug on the stone floor and starts placing trays on top of it. I help, carrying a few at a time until the cart is empty. Tor grabs the last few items off the cart—a pair of ceramic plates, two sets of cutlery, and a pair of metal goblets—and sets them down on the rug as well. I sit down and pour a bubbly soda into the goblets for both of us and Tor sits across from me.

The two of us begin piling food onto our plates and I make a point to get a small amount of everything. I am especially excited when I find small bowls of soup that I missed previously. I take one of each kind. One a bright orange, and the other a creamy tan. The two of us eat in silence and I am grateful for the rich foods considering I gave Arche my breakfast this morning. When we finish, Tor slides the dessert tray in between us and offers me the first bite. The brownie is fudgy and warm, a perfect contrast against the cool vanilla ice cream.

"So…" I begin. "Head bladesmith?"

"Mmhm." Tor responds, a bite of brownie in his mouth.

"How did that one come to be?"

Tor swallows the bite. "Well, I am a *School* dropout. I was originally from Ingenium anyway." That explains the warmth that flows from him. It has nothing to do with my apparent *touch deprivation,* I tell myself. "Over there they suck you in with the *magic* of knowledge. They make this place seem cold and unforgiving, and while it is—"

"Tell me about it." I interrupt, smiling.

"The simplicity is something you can't get anywhere else." He says, smiling back at me. "So, I studied at the school for three years, learning as much as I could about sword and armor making and then I dropped out. I took the first portal here and begged the old head bladesmith to give me a chance. He passed away two years ago and by that time I was already doing better work than people thrice my age. So, I took over, I've been head bladesmith ever since."

"What is it?" I ask.

"What?"

"Your age," I clarify, then take a bite from the brownie.

"Nineteen—and a few star cycles." He pauses. "Would it be crossing a line to ask yours?"

"Why would it be?"

"You know what they say about never asking a woman her age."

"I don't," I hesitate. "Eighteen."

"You are very accomplished for an eighteen-year-old." Tor responds.

"You know nothing of my accomplishments, Tor. And I am a year younger than you, not a child."

"Then tell me *Miss Yamanu*. About your accomplishments. What brought you here?" He asks, curiosity lighting his brown eyes.

I think for a moment about exactly how much I wish to tell him. I settle on the simple story. "I was an orphan here on Lex, I grew up in this castle actually." I avoid the topic of my supposed *blessings*. "My caretaker always told me stories about her time at The School, and she assumed I would go too. But when it came down to it, I couldn't walk away from the steel, no matter how cold it may be. So here I am, one of the few girls at The Academy." I keep my voice casual, pulling the emotion out of my own life story.

"The *fiercest* girl at The Academy. Might I add."

"Person." I respond, taking a sip from my goblet.

"Hm?" Tor puzzles.

"I am the fiercest *person* at The Academy."

CHAPTER
ELEVEN

Snow begins to fall on Lex, but in the glass room, Tor and I never feel it. For hours we eat, drink, and talk. He tells me of his time in Ingenium, and how he learned to craft swords without ever touching a forge. I tell him about my life growing up in The Castle of Lex and all the trouble Nova and I got ourselves into. By the time we each walk as far down memory lane as we dare, we are exhausted from conversation. I'm laying down on the plush rug, staring through the glass ceiling and watching the snow fall when Tor speaks.

"Hey Sol, it's a little past *thirteen hundred hours.* I think we both should get down to the battlefield." His voice is warm and gravely. My chest flutters. *Only the magic of Inge-nium,* I remind myself.

I sit up and stretch my body, wincing at the crack of my back. "Good idea. If I stay here any longer, I'm afraid I won't leave."

"I wouldn't want you to become trapped in the glass castle." Tor laughs gently.

"Is that what you call this place?" I smile at him, watching his brown eyes glimmer in the soft light.

"Yeah, it was an abandoned room when I got here, I took it upon myself to clean it out and now—"

I cut him off. "Is it your *hiding place?*" I muse, my eyes widening.

"If you want to call it that, sure. You must admit it has a killer view though." He turns to look out of the glass.

"Even better that you can't see the battlefield," I mutter.

"That bad?"

"No, not really." I pause, unsure of how to continue. "Being in battle makes me feel alive, but the battlefield itself isn't the most relaxing of views." I say, my voice coming out more hesitant than I intend it to. Tor nods though, absorbing each of my words. "Well, I better get down to there."

"Let me walk you, I'm going anyway." Before I can answer, he continues. "I also want to hand deliver your armor and sword to you today. As—good luck." Tor stands but he holds an uncertain expression on his face.

I stand as well and look up at him. "Sounds good to me. Not that I need luck though." I wink.

"Oh of course, *Miss Yamanu.*" Tor says, barely holding back his gentle laughter. He holds his arm out and I loop my own through it. I shiver gently at the connection, at the warmth that comes from this one touch and brands itself into my skin.

We don't speak as we walk, arm-in-arm, down The Castle's halls. Our steps are in sync, and I know that we are a striking image.

The rose and the bladesmith.

I laugh at the idea of anyone thinking me a rose. But with my red cloak, the thorns *are* well hidden.

We stride out into Lex, the snow falling harder than before, I wince at the cold and unconsciously tuck myself into Tor's arm. He doesn't say a word as he guides me along the bridge. My teeth chatter and I quickly come to the conclusion that today's battles will have the worst conditions of any. For the few moments I dare to pull my face away from Tor's body I can't see five feet in front of me, I shudder at the thought of facing Fay blindly.

"You alright?" Tor asks, concerned.

"Just fine."

"You are *not* a fan of the cold, are you?"

"Can you tell?" I reply sarcastically.

"She hates the cold and yet she won't leave Lex." Tor jokes. I nudge him with my shoulder, but he doesn't budge, he just laughs. I pull myself closer to him. The warm feeling is accompanied by the reminder that at one point, *I will have to let go.*

I slowly peak my head out and find that we are only yards away from the battlefield. Despite the weather, everyone remains outside, watching the current battle; a six-way competition between the younger male groups. People cheer when they get even a glimpse of what is going on as the wind and snow has made the visibility nonexistent.

Tor guides me to the armory tent—flaps down and stakes in the ground to block out the snow and wind. We walk in between the rows of weapons and beat to death armor until we get to the back of the tent. He takes me past the tent flaps and we are in a small back room, tables, and tables of used armor, broken weapons, and damaged pieces of both lining the walls of it. I finally unhook myself from Tor knowing that if I wait any longer, I will refuse to do so. He doesn't say anything in response, but I immediately feel the effect of the lack of his presence at my side.

He walks to a back table and returns to me with the golden sword I have used every day in battle, and the gold armor that matches. The blade is so simple, but perfectly balanced and completely unmarked.

"Do you mind if I help you into your armor today?" Tor asks. There is a certain vulnerability to his voice that I haven't heard before. I like it.

"Not at all." I brace myself and pull my cloak off my body, shivering as the ruthless wind lashes at me. The white battle thermals offer no reprieve from the winds, and I can do nothing but attempt to get the armor on. Tor—to his credit—quickly slips the breastplate over my head and fastens it at the sides.

His hands make quick work of the gauntlets, as well as my cloak. Each brush of his fingers on my skin, sends a shock to my bones. How badly I want to hold his hands to my wrists, my arms, my waist. I shake the thought out of my head.

After the armor is secure, he holds out the white leather sheath and I step into it. Tor works around my cloak, tightening the straps around my thigh and waist, ensuring that the sword sheath sits above the one for my dagger. I feel his fingers linger at the small of my back. Just for a moment too long, as if he is having a hard time letting go, too.

Tor hands me the beautiful gold sword and I am transfixed by the beauty of the blade; so simple but absolutely perfect. With a slice, I tuck it safely into the sheath. Digging into the pockets of my cloak, I find my white leather battle gloves and slide them on. I finish off by tying my hair back.

When I'm done, Tor pulls my hood back over my head. "Now you *look* just as fierce as you are."

"Don't I always?" I loop my arm back through his, as if in muscle memory, and lead us out into Lex's harsh winds. I don't tuck myself into Tor, however. Lord Acastus is always watching, I will not seem weak.

"Do you need to go?" I ask softly.

"Do you need me to stay?"

"I should find my squadron; they've been out here all day."

"Of course." Tor pulls away and stand in front of me. "Good luck, Sol." He walks away without another word, back into the armory tent with its relative barrier from the wind.

I can't see five feet in front of me and I dread the battle that lies ahead. I huff, searching for Nova, but the war horn sounds before I can find her. People rush off and onto the battlefield and I remember the time. It must be *1400* by now, which means that Arche will be going up for battle. As the thoughts come to me, someone runs up from behind and picks me up by my waist.

"Hey Sol." Arche says into my ear before I can back my head into his nose. I relax my body and hang from his arms like a rag doll, utterly annoyed at how easily he can lift me. I am far from small, and Arche is not *that* muscular, but he can still pick me up without problem.

"Put me down please." I say, the snow smacking my face with no remorse. Arche sets me down and I turn around to face him, getting close to his chest to find sanctuary from the wind. "Thank you," I say graciously. "Are you ready?"

Nervousness that I have never seen before paints Arche's face. "We'll see."

I reach up and pull the black hood of his cloak far over his head. "We *will*. And you are going to do great, it's an easy win remember? Just do the rotating formation exactly how Nova and I taught you in practice." I say sternly.

"We won't be able to see out there, Soleil." Arche responds.

"You don't need to *see* to run the formation. The whole point is that every area is always covered anyway. Tell your squad to remember the steps and *do not* break." I look at him in his grey eyes which are darker than usual. "The other team can't see either and *they* don't have the advantage of a rotating formation. They're going to make a break for the banner, I know it. When you hear the steel, make a run and the banner will be *yours*." Arche nods in reply. "Do you have any idea where Nova is?" I ask, trying to shift his focus from the battle ahead.

"She and the rest of your squad have been lined up at the center mark of the battlefield since *oh nine hundred hours.*" He says, confidence returning to his voice.

"Perfect," I pause and grab his hands. "Good luck Arch. Remember; you are second *only* to me." I muse. He laughs in response and pulls me in for a tight, but brief embrace. By the time he pulls away, he is practically sprinting onto the battlefield, disappearing into the snow and wind.

Arche's battle is extremely quick. Less that fifteen minutes after the war horn blows to signal the start of the simulation, it sounds for a third time to signal the end.

"Male Squadron 7G, has won the battle. They will be ending with a standing of 21-7." Lord Acastus announces.

Nova and I cheer at the news. The two of us hear Arche running at us before we see him. A green velvet banner is wrapped around his neck like a cape and he scoops Nova and I up into his arms, planting friendly kisses on our foreheads.

"Congratulations Arch." Nova says, eyes glittering.

"I wouldn't have won without the two of you." Arche replies.

"Keep that in mind the next time we ask you for a favor." I add.

"Sure, you might need one when I am chosen as second in command." He laughs.

Lord Acastus speaks again before we can continue. "There will be no more battles until our final one at *seventeen hundred hours.* You may all take lunch in The Fortress' dining hall." Lord Acastus' voice reverberates across the battlefield.

"We have the final battle?" I question no one in particular.

"I guess—" Nova answers, voice trailing off.

"Well, I wouldn't mind some food." Arche adds.

"Let's get you out of this armor and return your sword Arch, then we can go eat. It's not even *fifteen hundred hours* yet." I reply. Arche nods in assent.

The three of us march into the almost empty armory and Nova and I begin helping Arche out of his breastplate and gauntlets. I struggle to untie the gauntlets that he fastened so sloppily, until I hear a voice from behind.

"Need any help with that?" I turn around and find Tor towering over me. *Thank Infinity.*

"Please?" I relent, handing him Arche's left arm. Tor quickly undoes the knots and slides the gauntlets off. "Thank you." I say gratefully, turning back to Nova and Arche who are clearly confused.

"Oh!" I exclaim. "Nova, Arche, this is Tor Warin. He is the head bladesmith at the armory."

"I am *always* in the armory and I have never seen you." Nova hisses.

"I work in The Castle's armory, a common mistake." Tor explains, looking only at me as he speaks. I can't help but crack a smile.

"And you two are—" Arche begins.

"Friends." I cut him off with a pointed look before he can say any more. "Tor, do you want to join us for lunch?"

"I mean we already ate lunch, but I wouldn't mind a snack." He says casually. *No, no, no!* I curse Infinity for Tor's innocence. With a sharp intake of breath, I prepare to speak, but Arche beats me to it.

"Well then, considering the two of you ate already, you are welcome to join Soleil in a *snack*." Arche says, stretching out his words. I glare at him, but he doesn't let up.

"Sounds great, I just want to put these things in the back." Tor tells Arche, holding his ground. *Well thank Infinity for that.* "Meet me there?"

I try to reply but this time Nova goes first. "That sounds great, just follow the crowd and you'll hit the dining hall." Nova says bitterly.

I look at Tor apologetically and he nods in understanding before collecting the armor and sword and walking to the back room of the armory.

When Tor turns his back, I storm out of the tent, no longer caring about the weather. I huff, hearing *them* run after me. Arche grabs my arm and I pull away. Nova tries to do the same, but they are both wise enough to let me go.

"What was that about Soleil?" Nova yells.

"What were you doing in there?" Arche adds. "Is that who you snuck away to see today?" I continue walking, quickening my pace.

"Soleil. Stop!" Nova calls.

Fine, I will. "What do you want?"

"You sneak off to spend the day with *Mister Sword-Maker* and don't even bother to tell me?" Nova yells.

"Why should I Nov? Every decision I make, you scorn me for. When I convinced Lord Acastus to consider us, you yell. When I get an arrow in my leg and still win the simulation, you yell. And now? I go to someone to get my dagger cleaned after a bad battle, we happen to become friendly in the process, and you yell *again*." I pause, taking a breath. "I met him the day of the first battle simulation. He promised me that if I ever needed my dagger cleaned, he would do it. A few days ago, when I got into it with that girl from squad H, she stepped on it and it got shoved into the rocks. It was all bent up and almost cost us the sim yesterday. So yes, I woke up early to get it fixed by him. And yes, we had lunch together but that was *it.*" I stop there. Arche's face pales at the information and Nova holds a look of guilt.

"Sol—" Nova begins.

I don't want or need an apology from her. "All I want is for you to trust me. That is it, every decision I make is one that I feel is right. Can you just trust that? I get enough from Alma about my choices, I do not need that from my sister, too." Nova runs to me, pulling me into a fierce hug, Arche joins, encompassing both of us in his arms.

"You two are absolutely insane." Arche laughs.

"I'm sorry, Sol." Nova says.

I press my forehead to hers. "No apology necessary. Just give me a break, *please.* Tor is great, I promise."

"Okay." Nova replies.

"Count me in on that too," Arche adds.

"You guys are the worst." I chuckle, feeling safe in my own personal galaxy.

THE DINING HALL IS PACKED WITH PEOPLE, SO, AS ARCHE AND Nova go to stack their trays with food, I search for a spot. After long minutes of wandering, I find four spots in a square formation and quickly take a seat. Moments later, Nova and Arche make it to the table, choosing to sit in the two seats across from me. Nova slides me a plate of veggies, with a small bowl of white dip and Arche passes over a plate fruit. They also hands me two forks and I smile at them.

"Mind if I sit?" A voice asks me from behind. *Such a nice voice…* I turn around and find Tor.

"Of course." I say, turning to Nova and Arche. "Compliments of these two." I add, sliding the plates to Tor. "*A snack.*"

"Looks great." Tor smiles at Arche and Nova who remain civil. I hand Tor a fork and we dig into the spread.

"So, you're the head bladesmith? That is a big honor, especially in The Castle." Nova starts.

"Yeah, I dropped out of The School in Ingenium and came here." Tor responds between bites of fruit.

"You willingly left Ingenium to come here?" Arche asks, dumbfounded.

"I have the same question." Nova adds.

"Yeah, I did." Tor laughs.

"Well, you two are perfect for each other." Nova says suggestively, taking a sip of water from her cup. Arche glowers when she speaks and I look at him questioningly.

"Absolutely *perfect.*" Arche adds, holding onto *some* air of civility in his voice.

"Nova, Sol tells me that you're a pretty good archer." Tor changes the subject.

"I like to think so." Nova replies.

"You should stop by The Castle's armory with Sol sometime. I can show you some bows I've been working on," Tor responds genuinely. I smile at his acceptance of my friends despite their initial hostility.

"I would love that. Thank you." Nova replies kindly.

"What are you into Arche?" Tor askes.

"Whatever I can use to slice a throat." Arche growls. I kick him under the table in warning and he quickly straightens up his attitude. "Sword," he huffs.

"Well, you have some competition there." Tor chuckles. "I don't think anyone could best Sol in a swordfight."

"You're right on that Tor, but Arche *is* a close second." I stick my tongue out at Arche in mocking and he finally cracks a smile.

"Did she tell you about the time I *accidentally* sliced her hair in battle?" Arche teases.

"It was far from an accident." I say coldly, glaring at Arche.

"No, she didn't." Tor responds.

"Well, it's a wonderful story. Do you want to hear it?" Arche queries excitedly.

"Of course." Tor says, curiosity lighting his face. "Wait, does this have anything to do with Sol cutting your hair during that first battle simulation?" Tor asks.

"It has *everything* to do with it, *Mister Warin*." Arche says, his fingers rising to the still-too-short lock of hair that I trimmed at the beginning of the star cycle.

Arche tells the story, and a few more after that. Tor listens, eyes widening at every twist and turn. Nova laughs at Arche's words, engrossed by the way he speaks. And I watch lovingly, mesmerized as my personal galaxy grows just a bit bigger.

CHAPTER TWELVE

Completely taken by conversation, I'm shocked when Tor tells me that it's already *1615*. Arche is in the middle of telling Tor the story of when he first met Nova and I, and how we fought him in battle simulation until he was on his knees. Tor's eyes widen as Arche speaks. On more than one occasion, he stole looks at me for confirmation when Arche's words seemed too unbelievable.

All slightly disappointed that Arche's stories have to end, we dispose of our trays and plates and begin walking back to the battlefield.

My limbs ache for movement and my hands long for the sword currently sheathed at my hip. I am so ready for the battle and am absolutely delighted when we step outside and find that the snow has stopped falling. There is still a bit of wind, but the cloudy sky and whipping snow has been replaced by bright sunlight. I smile at the sign from Infinity. I know now that this is meant to be. My particular blessings may just be whispers, rumors, folk tales, but *this.* This is a sign. While Arche *is* also high in the running for second in command, I'm not worried. If the job goes to someone else, I can only hope that it will be him.

"Are you ready?" Tor asks, looping his arm through mine as we step onto the bridge. This gesture, the connection between us, feels as natural and inevitable as my rise to second in command. *Infinitely blessed…*

"Absolutely."

"Should I be offering any words of encouragement?" He smiles.

"Knowing that you are watching will be encouragement enough."

"Time to be intimidated again." Tor jokes.

"You better get used to it." I chuckle. A beam of sunlight hits me directly as I speak. I lift my face towards the sky and let my hood fall so I can feel it. In times like this, it's hard not to ignore the rumors. Still, that only encourages me to work harder to earn them.

When we arrive at the battlefield, it's empty. The girls from my squadron, however, are already warming up on an empty patch of land near the field. I smile at Nova, proud of her leadership ability for the day.

"Well. This is where I leave you, Tor." I say awkwardly, not knowing how to release my hold on him. I slowly slide my arm out of his, once more jarred by the lack of his presence.

"Good luck Soleil. I will see you after the battle so I can *personally* help you out of that armor." He winks, suggestively. *Infinity*—I gulp.

"Sure, sure." I nod. "Don't get *too* intimidated while you watch."

"I'll try."

"It'll take more than that." I smile before turning away from him. Nova and Arche follow me and, for a moment, I watch. The battlefield is deathly still and all too inviting. I ache to get on it. I press my hand into the hilt of my sword to calm my growing anxiousness.

I begin running one-on-one rotating sword battles with our squadron, the clash of steel fills the battlefield. Nova and the other archers do some shooting practice and they send arrow after arrow flying at wooden targets. Eventually, Arche joins in, battling me repeatedly until he complains of a *sore arm*. It feels good to finally unsheathe my sword and let my body settle into the flow of battle. I relish in the feeling of the fight and take down my own team members quickly. They put up a good effort, flawlessly executing the maneuvers we have been practicing, however, only Arche comes close to challenging me.

Slowly, people make their way out of The Fortress and start either lining up around the battlefield or squeezing themselves into the small spectator's area. I see a glimmer of excitement in my squadron by the time Lord Acastus takes a seat on his stone throne.

"That's enough practice." I say, voice filled with command.

"I'm going to find a spot. Good luck." Arche says to Nova and I. We each reply with curt nods as he walks away. Now is not the time for sweeping declarations of friendship. Not when the chance of a millennium is upon us.

The girls line up in a formation behind Nova and I. We sheath our swords and the archers swing their bows across their bodies. We take deep breaths and stand completely still—a striking image—*the perfect soldiers*. We wait to be called onto the battlefield, but—nothing.

Fay Enyo and her squadron are nowhere to be found. We wait, and I watch Lord Acastus scan the area until his eyes lock onto the bridge, clearly seeing something with his blessed immortal vision that no one else can make out. Only a few moments before *1700*, Fay and her squadron sprint off the bridge and onto the land around the battlefield, disheveled and on the verge of being tardy. I smile at the development, nudging Nova out of pure satisfaction.

All eyes are on Fay's squadron as they attempt to catch their breath and look slightly more put together than they are. *At the very least they already have armor and weapons.*

Eventually Lord Acastus stands which is enough to make the battlefield fall silent. "I have watched many a battle in the last star cycle and I have seen a number of promising soldiers. On this last day of the star cycle, I am pleased to announce that I am far from disappointed by your performance thus far. I look forward to seeing what this last group of soldiers has to offer and hope that they follow suit." I feel each of Lord Acastus' words penetrate my body and ring in my ears. His words are for me. I know they are.

"Tomorrow morning at exactly *oh eight hundred hours* I will announce my new second in command in The

Fortress' dining hall. I expect my decision to be honored without hassle and with full respect and faith for my new second in command." *Me. Me. Me. Me. Me. Me.* The word rings out like a prayer in my mind.

"Now, for the rules. At the end of my speech, I will invite you onto the field for deliberations. At the first blow of the war horn all soldiers must get in position, at the second, the battle begins. The third blow of the war horn will mark the end of the battle, either by a team acquiring the opposite banner, or by the end of the one-hour block—whichever comes first. Protect your banner, and all other rules remain. No fatal strikes and medics are at the far side of the battlefield if you are in need of assistance. Rule breaking will be cause for extreme consequence." Lord Acastus pauses and two teams of soldiers carry banners onto the field. On our side is a banner of pure white—the same color we began with—on the other is a banner of blood red.

Fay's banner is the same color as my cloak—Lord Acastus is toying with me. The realization comes suddenly as I glare at the velvet fabric. *Mine.*

Lord Acastus continues. "Both teams are welcome onto the battlefield for their deliberations."

I keep my hood down over my shoulders and bathe in the sunlight. When I win this battle, Lord Acastus will *see* me. Nova and I begin walking, our steps in sync, crunching on the snow beneath us. Our squadron follows, lining up their steps with ours. The people lining the edge of the battlefield split without a word to let us through. As a unit, we make it to our white banner and form an even circle around it. Nova to my left, and Ingrid to my right.

I speak loudly, my voice filled with power. "Infinity has blessed us with sun and clarity for our battle despite the harsh conditions of the morning. There are no excuses. We *will* be perfect, and we *will* win." Now that the weather has improved, we can continue our plan of the star formation. I wish to run through it once more. "Nova, Lyra, Ingrid, Evelyn, and Petra. The five of you will make bases on each of the five large boulders. If anyone gets past our star—you shoot." The girls nod at me and I see anticipation flowing in their veins.

"Alora, Kienna, I need you two covering Nova's base. Lorelei and Alena, you two will defend Lyra. Zya, Viola, I need you by Ingrid. Ivy and Iris, I want you to take care of Evelyn. Sylvia and Cora, you will guard Petra." This formation is one that we have nailed down, but I still need to know that each girl understands what to do.

"Elise and Sage, you stay at the banner. *Do not leave.* Jade and Nola, we're on the offensive, cover me and I will get the banner." Everyone nods in assent. I turn to Nova who beams at me. "Fay's group is arrogant and unorganized. They are going to scramble when they hear that horn go off, but they won't *all* be coming at us. We have seen them fight; they all attempt to do everything at once but that does not work. Stay in your positions, do as we practiced and this one is ours. They don't call us *The Undying Squadron* for nothing." I wink at them as the first war horn blows, but my squadron remains still, awaiting *my* command.

"Positions!" I yell, and they disperse quickly. I give Nova a quick look and we nod at each other before finding our own spots. Jade and Nola flank me on either side as we walk to the centerline of the battlefield. Fay's squadron stumbles to their positions but no one meets us in the middle. The war horn sounds for the second time and I smile brightly as the battle begins.

THE SOUND OF THE WAR HORN ECHOES IN MY EARS AS I unsheathe my pristine gold sword and begin running. One foot in front of the other, I pump my legs, going straight for the banner. As much as I want to enjoy beating Fay, I don't want this battle going a moment longer than it has to. For a moment, I delight at the thought of a quick victory. Until an arrow whizzes past my ear.

I make a dive to the ground, rolling behind a boulder in an attempt to find cover. As I sheathe my sword, the arrows continue to come, relentless in their pursuit. The shots themselves are off, but still filled with power. With this in mind, I know that I can take the risk to stand and search for the archer. The arrows continue to fly and I am able to knock a few away with my gauntlets, though I feel the force of their impact radiate through my wrists.

I make quick work of finding the archer in question. A tall and broad-shouldered woman with her hair pulled back into a knot on the top of her head. She wears a black cloak and battle thermals. Not having any other option for long distance attack, I pull out my dagger, praying to Infinity that Tor's work performs as well as it looks. Knowing that I am a clean shot, I throw with all the force I have. The seconds stretch as I wait for impact. Before she can realize, my dagger lodges itself deep within the woman's upper thigh. She cries out and her knees make contact with the hard ground.

Once she hits the ground, I sprint to her and pull my dagger clean out of her thigh. She screams again but I have no remorse. With the way her arrows were flying at me, she would have relished the opportunity to rip them out of my skin.

My dagger is drenched in blood and I reel as I feel the warm liquid. Not knowing what else to do, I stick the dagger in the snow in an attempt to clean it and dry it off with the woman's cloak. She still screams in pain. I roll my eyes, remembering the arrow in my thigh only a few weeks earlier.

The battlefield shines brightly in the sunlight and after leaving the woman behind and finding a safe spot near a boulder, I allow myself a moment to enjoy it. I un-sheathe my sword again, watching it twinkle in the light and I smile at it, letting my mind stray to Tor. The clang of steel pulls me from my lull and I snap my head to the other side of the battlefield. The star formation is working wonderfully and the girls guarding the banner, are bored out of their minds. They remain watchful though, circling the banner like beasts on the prowl.

I watch my archers in amazement, their bodies flu-id as they aim and fire arrow after arrow, never missing their marks, and never hitting a fatal shot. The rest of my squadron—swords in hand—move like the wind. No one gets past them either.

I pull myself back into the battle and come out from behind the boulder. Running, I smile at the sight of the un-guarded flag, but it doesn't last long as another girl comes out from behind a rock. She is short and slight, her face distant as she pulls a dagger from her belt. Quickly realizing that it is not going to be a sword fight, I unsheathe my dagger as well. My thumb finds home in the deep scratch that Tor kept and I smile at the memory. Not of the battle I won—*but of Tor himself.*

The girl begins running towards me and I realize that while she is small and quick, her movements repeat like a pattern. I can anticipate her blows and use my own strength against her. The girl lunges towards me in a blur. Barely dodging it, I end up on the ground. Again, she comes at me, this time joining me on the ground too. The snow begins melting on my thermals, leaving an uncomfortable coolness in its wake. After dodging her, the pattern in her swift strikes grows clearer and I grab her wrist before she can make another.

I flip her over—using the slickness of the snow to kick her off balance—and am able to slice her upper arm. I can't hold her to the ground though, so I choose to use the time to get up on my feet instead. I continue to pick out patterns in her actions while randomizing my own and am able to slice her repeatedly. She has not hit me once and her movements are growing sloppy with fatigue as mine only grow stronger with confidence.

In a clear moment of weakness, the girl leaves her face unguarded and swings too wide. I dodge her strike easily but take my chance slicing her forehead and pulling away before she can react. Blood immediately begins streaming down to her eyes and she drops her weapon to clutch her face. I kick her dagger away and when I turn back, it's clear that she can't see a thing.

I sheathe my dagger and continue my sprint. To my left, Jade and Nola fight off three girls, using their spears to keep them away from the banner. I believe that I have an open chance, until I notice Fay circling the banner pole, her movements animalistic. It's clear that she has been watching and waiting for me, but I smile anyway at her lack of strategy. At the very least, Arche was able to completely draw me in to the banner and get a few good hits on me before ultimately losing. Fay on the other hand, clearly has no experience in the skill of going unnoticed.

I slow to a walk, beckoning Fay to meet me in the middle. Making the obvious choice to keep me as far away from the banner as possible, she walks towards me. I unsheathe my golden sword and take my walk in large and powerful strides. My red cloak flows behind me and my hood remains down. *Everyone* will see who I am today.

The rose who strikes again.

Fay approaches me, unsheathing her own sword. "I am not going to let you win this time." Fay yells; her voice filled with unbridled rage.

"You know, I really thought you would have gotten over that by now. For Infinity's sake, it happened almost a star cycle ago. " I retort, putting on a show for the audience.

"Seven years and you couldn't even *slice*." Fay replies, venom gilding her words.

"Now where would we be if I did?" I spin my sword in invitation and tilt my head slightly, feigning innocence. Fay begins moving and I do too, until we are walking in a large circle, sizing each other up. I know that I can jump into the fight and win, but I have to play the game for a moment. This needs to be dramatic, or Lord Acastus will simply forget.

Eventually, Fay lunges at me. I dodge her strike quickly. She slides to the ground, losing footing on the layer of snow coating the battlefield. She returns to her feet and begins striking repeatedly. I take her blows and match them with my own blocks, not yet needing to make moves of my own. Fay will obviously lose this, but the audience can't know that yet. I continue to block, allowing Fay to become a pawn in a game she doesn't know she is playing.

After a particularly hard strike from Fay, I spin out of my block to collect myself, but am filled with shock when she chooses to strike again. I'm too late to turn and I hear the clean slice as she takes a chunk off my hair. There is no chance for me to recover, only deflect once more as I try to shake myself from the only true shock I have felt this whole simulation.

In an effort to regain control, I speak as Fay drives repeatedly. "I always knew you were jealous of my hair."

Fay yells in response, driving down on me. I manage to pull her into the same position I had Arche in on the day of the first battle simulation. It's easy enough to swing my leg around and kick her knees in. In her jolt, she loosens her grip on the sword and I knock it away, keeping hold of my own. She is still able to get up quickly, running to take cover behind a boulder.

I begin moving towards her sword which lays in the fine snow, but am stopped when Fay returns from the boulder with a spear in her hands. *Are you kidding me?* I take a deep breath and spin my sword at Fay again. She twirls her spear in response, pointing it directly at me. *What is she playing at?* I roll my eyes at her theatrics and we fight again. I am skilled in spear fighting myself and am able to deflect Fay's strikes, while getting a few hits of my own. However, using my sword against her spear… I ache for a matching weapon. In my mind's absence, Fay knocks the sword out of my hand, and I have no choice but to duck behind a boulder as well.

I hear Fay's heavy breathing and know that she will use this moment to collect herself rather than attack again. Only fifteen feet away from me, Nola takes down a brutish girl and smiles as she does it. I yell out to her, asking for her spear. She obliges and throws it directly at me, the shaft twirling perfectly. I stand and catch it, shocked by its weight in my hands. *Infinity, what is this thing made of?* With no time left to think, I come back out from behind the boulder to find Fay crouched over, using the spear to hold herself up.

"Too much to handle?" I ask her with a devilish smile creeping across my face. Fay straightens slowly at my words and points her spear at me. I spin my spear, allowing the anticipation to build as I walk back to her. Our weapons clash and Fay remains on the offensive, her spear beating down on me. I feign weakness, but still manage to hit her arms and legs, watching her precision crumble. Readying to block another one of Fey's strikes, I stick my spear straight out and Fay smacks her own down on it. I wince, anticipating the snapping of my own weapon, but it's Fay's spear that breaks instead.

Suddenly, the weight of my own weapon makes sense. It's a steel core spear, the same type that Tor has in his workshop. I smile as Fay stands frozen in shock at the loss of her weapon. I know that this time, she has no back-up plan. Using Fay's surprise to my advantage, I hold my spear tightly and whip it around, hitting Fay in the back and knocking her towards me. Before she can hit me, I discard my own spear and grab her by the shoulders, slamming her down into the ground.

Fay struggles for breath as I pin her to the ground, only a few feet away from the blood red banner. In this moment, *she is mine.* My knees dig into her arms, holding her in place and the rest of my body weight keeps her there.

"This is it, Fay." I growl in her face, ensuring that my voice is loud enough for all the worlds to hear. I unsheathe my dagger from my thigh and set it on Fay's cheek in taunting. "I am done with you." My voice is raw with power—addicting. I press my dagger to Fay's throat and her eyes are feral, pupils dilating to the point that they are entirely black. Her skin is whiter than the snow she is pinned against and with my dagger at her throat, I can feel the pulsing of her heart.

"I told you what would happen if you messed with me again Fay." I taunt as she shakes beneath me. "No, no." I coo, mimicking the exact tone I used on her at the beginning of the star cycle. Fay thrashes and attempts to scream, but no sound comes out.

I am sick of her, sick of toying with my meal. So, I push my dagger into her throat and slice. It's just enough to bleed, not enough to be fatal, but by the way Fay reacts, anyone might think that I truly did kill her.

"Stay down, or next time it won't be a gentle slice." Fay obeys, ceasing her struggle. She goes limp under me.

I fill with satisfaction at the sight, at how compliant she is. I *could* end this story here… if I wanted to.

Standing up with my dagger in hand, I watch to make sure that Fay remains still—she does—so I walk to the banner that flows tauntingly in the wind. I reach up and viciously tug on the banner, making it mine for the twenty-eighth time. The war horn blows and the simulation is over.

Cheers ring out from every corner of the battlefield, from every squadron of soldiers in The Academy. I ache to climb a boulder and celebrate with them. Before I can though, I walk to my golden sword—still shimmering in the snow—and pick it up, sheathing it at my side before climbing the largest boulder I can find. Once I find my footing, I look around the battlefield and the land beyond to find *everyone* cheering. I raise the banner high into the air and the cheers grow even louder than before. I smile brightly, turning to the other side of the battlefield where Nova celebrates, still standing on a rock of her own. I raise the banner a little higher, letting it catch and wave in the wind.

Twenty-eight rounds of battle simulation and I won them all. The cheers are deafening, and the power is intoxicating. Despite my better judgement, I unsheathe my sword and point it straight at Lord Acastus, choosing to end the star cycle as I began it. I relish in the dominance as a ray of sunlight straight from Infinity, swallows me whole. I can only imagine the power that radiates off me.

I see the image in my mind's eye, my blood red cloak flowing in the wind and my gold armor shining. I see my sword glimmering and the banner—the same color as my cloak—waving behind me. I see my white battle thermals, the same shade as the snow coating the battlefield. And lastly, I see my eyes, brown that swallows the light, beckoning Lord Acastus to meet my stare. While he does, it's clear that nothing can ever compare to the power I hold as Infinity's rays encompass me. All of a sudden, the whispers make sense. Who wouldn't believe that I am *Infinitely blessed?* And who wouldn't believe that I deserve it?

The power of the realms is in my eyes, my hands, and my soul. I feel utterly *infinite.*

CHAPTER THIRTEEN

As the cheering fades away, I lower my sword, reminding myself not to outshine Lord Acastus. The battlefield goes silent with anticipation and my sunlight abates as Lord Acastus stands from his stone throne and walks to the edge of the wooden platform.

He speaks, voice reaching even the furthest parts of the battlefield, it never falters. "The battle simulation has come to an end. If you are in need of medical attention, please see the medics, or make your way to the infirmary according to the state of your injury. Return all weapons and armor to the armory and remove all abandoned weapons and items from the battlefield itself. Thank you for your participation." With that, he sits back down on the throne, resuming his statue-like position.

Despite my slight annoyance at the lack of recognition from the Lord, I sheathe my sword and tie the banner around my neck in a cape as Arche did for me at the beginning of the star cycle. I sit on the boulder and slide down, catching myself before I stumble. Beginning my walk to the armory to return my weapons, I take account of my body again. I have no visible cuts or scrapes, just some soreness in my wrists where the gauntlets sit. My knees and arms are aching as well, but after a battle as intense as the one I just had, I'm far from surprised. I almost forgot the situation with my hair but as soon as I remember it, I push it away, not willing to have a breakdown over something that trivial when I just won the last of Lord Acastus' battle simulations.

Though the pain in my knees radiates up through my body, I continue to take my steps in a powerful stride knowing that Lord Acastus is still watching. Finally coming across the solid line of spectators surrounding the battlefield, I set my jaw and, without a word, they part to let me through. Everyone's eyes are on me as I walk past, but they remain silent at Lord Acastus' dismissal. I trudge through the snow right into the armory. Tor runs to me the moment I walk in, with a true smile creeping across his face. He picks me up, encompassing me in a tight embrace that melts away every pain and worry that plagues my tired mind.

"Hey." I say softly.

"Hey? After all of that—*hey*?" He mocks. "You are incredible! What you did out there was amazing Soleil. The sword, and the dagger throw—"

I cut him off there. "Thank you for the praise but I really don't need it. I only got the dagger throw right because *you* fixed it for me. Otherwise, I probably would have been shot or I would have had to take my chances with my sword which I was not thrilled to do." I say slowly, giving him time to calm down.

"Do not give me credit for that amazing throw. My bet is that even if I didn't fix your dagger, you still would have been able to make it." I roll my eyes in response as I hear Nova and Arche walk through the tent flaps. By the sounds of their voices, they are giddy.

Arche comes up from behind me and grabs my waist, pulling me into a tight hug. "I always knew you had *something* in you Sol." He says slyly into my ear, I elbow him in the stomach, but his grip holds.

"It took you this long to figure out?" I respond; my words punctuated with laughter. A weight has been lifted off of me, and for the first-time all-star cycle I am truly happy.

"*I* have *always* known you were special." Nova jokes, gently shoving Arche away so that she can pull me to her.

"Do not undersell yourself, Nova. Our formation would not have held without you at the point of the star. *You* are incredible." She hugs me tighter and we hold each other for long moments until Arche speaks.

"Enough of that—how can we celebrate?" He says from behind me.

"I don't need to celebrate." I respond, completely content with this moment in time.

"Yeah, that's great and all—" Nova hesitates from beside me. "But we worked ourselves to the Door of the

Dusk and back for the last star cycle. I really need to do something fun, Soleil."

I laugh at her words. "Let's give the girls the night off so they can do whatever they want." Nova nods and I turn to look up at Tor. "Tor, do you have anything fun we can do?" I ask with a smile.

"I have some ideas." He responds, checking the watch on his wrist. "It's just about *eighteen hundred hours*; the sun should be setting soon. Do you need any time to recover?" He asks. I think for a moment and feel that a shower and a change of clothes would be wonderful, so I nod my head. "Okay, is two hours enough?"

"Yeah, that's fine. What do you have planned?" I ask skeptically.

"Arche, do you need any time to yourself or are you okay?" Tor queries, disregarding my question. I glare at him.

"No, I'm fine. What's up?" Arche replies.

"Okay, so you two take whatever time you need and meet me at The Fortress's dining hall no earlier than *twenty hundred hours*." He speaks directly to me, so I nod in affirmation. Tor turns back to Arche. "You can come with me until then."

"Sounds cool." Arche shrugs.

"Okay... let me get out of this armor and I can get out of your way." I say, unsure of Tor's plan.

"Yes of course, let me help you." Tor says apologetically. Nova and Arche walk to the weapons racks. "Shall we?" Tor ask, gesturing awkwardly to the back room of the armory tent. "I want to make sure you're comfortable."

I smile at him and nod, following him to the back room.

When we make it, Tor unties the makeshift cape at my neck and unfastens my cloak, I shiver—not at the cold hitting me, but at the gentleness in Tor's touch. *Infinity*—I want that touch forever.

"Sorry." Tor says apologetically, quickening his pace. Little does he know that my shiver has nothing to do with the absence of my cloak.

"It's fine," I pause. "Thank you for keeping my armor clean for the last star cycle. It means a lot." I say, in an attempt to distract myself from his nearness.

"You don't have to thank me, it *is* my job, I have to do it." He says as he loosens my breastplate. His fingers work deftly at the ties on my waist.

"*This* isn't your job." I stop him, grabbing his hands. "You did not *have* to keep the same armor and sword in perfect condition battle after battle. You did not *have* to mark it with my name. You did not *have* to watch every battle simulation I was in. You did not *have* to fix my dagger. And you certainly do not *have* to help me out of my armor." I say, pulling the breastplate off myself with a grunt. My arms shake with the effort.

Tor gently takes the armor from me, his eyes growing vulnerable. "You're right." He agrees, his voice going low and smooth. "But you're misguided in your thinking. Sure, I don't *have* to do any of this. But I *want* to." His eyes sparkle and his movements are slow as he reaches to undo the leather ties on my gauntlets. I don't pull away as he does it. To my delight, he takes great care not to disturb my wrists with the movements.

"Let me thank you." I say quietly.

"Let me praise you." He retorts, eyes not moving from my wrists.

The words penetrate the darkest parts of me, they erase my inadequacies and fill them with all of the things that I won't let him say. This perfect person believes me worthy of praise. I attempt to speak but I have nothing to say.

Tor quickly gets me out of the rest of my battle gear, including the sword sheath at my hip. As he undoes one side of the sheath, he lets his palm rest on the other side, flat on my hip. My eyelids flutter closed for just a second, before I stop myself. *This is dangerous, he is dangerous.* Tor fastens my cloak at my neck again and even ties the banner back around me. When everything is done, we walk out of the back room, and he deftly hooks our arms together as we do so. I can't help but hold on.

Arche helps Nova out of her breastplate near one of the rows of weapons, as we approach them. They laugh as she slides out of the armor and I see the familiar glitter of her eyes. She notices that Tor and I are approaching and calls out.

"Hey!" She says brightly and I can't help but feel that brightness in return. "Let's get going, because I *need* to wash up." I nod and look up at Tor who begrudgingly unhooks his arm from mine.

"*Twenty hundred hours.* Don't forget." Tor says as I walk to Nova's side.

"I got it." I say casually. "We'll see you later."

When Nova and I walk out of the armory, very few people are left on the battlefield. I notice some of Fay's squadron is at the medic tent and I smile out of satisfaction. The wooden platform, and Lord Acastus' stone throne, are both empty. Almost all the spectators have cleared out.

In the center of the battlefield itself—having an intense snowball fight—is my squadron. Nova and I look at each other and laugh before making our way to them. On our approach they promptly halt their fight and circle up immediately.

"Thank you all for your work these last few weeks. We won *twenty-eight* rounds of battle simulation. Now you guys get the evening to do as you please. Depending on tomorrow's events—" I stop for a moment, reminding myself that this feeling—the pure happiness—won't last. "Tomorrow we'll regroup but enjoy yourselves tonight. Be proud. You've earned it." The girls all beam back at me, each one of them full of joy at our success.

Upon arrival at Female Sleeping Chamber G, I immediately collect my things for a shower and pull off the banner, my cloak, boots, gloves, and scabbard. I slide on a pair of slippers and run out of the sleeping chamber. I beat Nova to the bathing chamber which is completely empty when I arrive.

I pick a bathing room and lock the door, quickly undressing. I almost jump into the steaming water and groan as the warmth hits my skin and loosens my sore muscles. I had forgotten to pull the leather strap out of my hair and I gasp when I run my fingers through it. Realization floods through me as I comb through my—now short—hair. I tremble at the unevenness in the cut, and the length—so much shorter than I am used to.

Attempting to calm myself, I use Alma's shampoo and conditioner to wash my hair, and some soap to scrub the sweat and grime from my skin. Once I shut the water off, I smooth lotion across my body and wrap towels around myself. I collect my things and sit at the benches near the roaring fireplace to warm up and dry off. Only minutes later, Nova comes out of her bathing room and sits next to me.

"How bad?" She asks softly.

I stare into the fire. "Shorter, uneven maybe. I don't know, I haven't taken it out of the towel." I reply in defeat.

I won twenty-eight of Lord Acastus' battle simulations and yet, Fay's petty move stings the most. I remember how Alma used to spend hours raking products through my hair, brushing it and braiding it to keep it safe from the cold. I remember how careful she was when she trimmed it and how excited we both were when she came up with the perfect shampoo and conditioner formulas. "Hair grows back." I sigh.

"It does." Nova replies. "You know, I cut my own hair all of the time. I could fix whatever is uneven and save everything I can. It'll probably be a bit shorter, but Alma can mix up something to help it grow." I pull my eyes from the fire and turn to Nova. There is a look of concern in her eyes. It breaks my heart to remember that she won't *always* be here—be next to me.

I decide to let her help. It's the best bet I have as I can't even think about the state of my hair without tearing up. "Okay." I tell her.

"Okay." Nova repeats, rising. She walks around the bench until she is standing behind me. I feel her gently pull the towel off my head to reveal my hair. She rakes her fingers through it, adjusting my head to get a better look. Nova finally makes the first cut and I shudder at the noise. She stops and rests a hand on my shoulder.

"It's okay. I'm going to take care of this." Nova says warmly. I have no doubt that she will.

After lots of small snips and once my hair dries completely, Nova announces that she is done. I quietly collect my clothes and walk into the changing room. I pull on a thick sweater and matching pants, reveling in the feel of the soft fabric. I throw an old cloak of mine on, a thick and fuzzy black, so old and worn that I barely use it anymore.

I walk out of the changing room and go directly to the mirrors lined up near the door to the bathing chamber itself. I brace myself and look at my reflection. Relief floods me when I realize that it is not a *horrible* look. Nova did a wonderful job and the cut itself looks intentional. My hair, which once teased my hips, now makes it only a few inches past my collarbone. I take a few deep breaths and slowly get used to the look.

"How do you like it?" Nova asks as she walks out of her changing room.

"I think it's growing on me." I reply with a smile.

"It suits you. It makes you look—*powerful.*"

I chuckle at those words and turn around to face her. "Maybe I should thank Fay for the haircut then."

"I would love to see the look on her face if you did." Nova says mischievously.

I shake my head. "Let's get out of here before we're late."

By the time Nova and I arrive at the dining hall, Arche and Tor are already waiting joking and laughing. Tor's eyes light up when he sees me. Before I can say anything, he pulls me into a hug and I am glad to be enveloped by the warmth of his strong body. This, this is my wish. That I can just stay here for all of Infinity and never have to leave. But my blessings seem to only go so far. When Tor pulls away his face puzzles and then recognition sets in.

"It's my hair, isn't it?" I ask.

"It looks perfect." Tor says sweetly. "I had just forgotten—"

"That it wasn't long anymore?" I cut him off.

He reaches out and grabs a curl, twirling it with his fingers. The gesture warms my bones. "It's beautiful." He says after long second's pass. I smile in return and Tor releases the curl, letting it spring back into place.

"Cool hair." Arche says, throwing an arm around my shoulder. I chuckle and elbow him as he strokes the fabric of my black cloak. "You are so soft. This cloak is like a blanket. Why don't you wear this more often?" Arche demands.

"Because I like my red one." I reply slowly.

"Well, you should wear this more often." Arche says, leaning into me. I shrug out of his grasp and bump right into Tor who pulls me to him.

"He's right. You *are* soft." Tor says, laughing. His hands start at my shoulders before moving up and down my arms, I breathe deeply to steady myself.

"Not you too!" I say, feigning defeat. Tor loops his arm through mine and I allow myself to curl into his body as we walk with Nova and Arche behind us.

"What exactly did you two do?" I ask, remembering the reason that Nova and I came down here anyway.

"We prepared the celebration." Tor responds playfully. I laugh and shake my head, just slightly tightening my grip onto him.

After a brief walk through The Fortress, we arrive at The Fortress' common room. The doors of the common room are closed and no voices come from inside.

"What are we doing here?" I ask skeptically. "This place must be filled with people celebrating."

"Just wait." Tor says, pushing open the wooden doors.

The Fortress' common room is a beautiful stone room with arched ceilings. It has a large fireplace on the back wall, sofas, chairs, pillows, blankets, carpets, and mattresses scattered along the wooden floor, and tall windows along the other walls. I sigh at the warmth that radiates from the room and am shocked to find that no one is inside.

"You get certain *perks* as head bladesmith." Tor says, clearly satisfied with himself. "And while I don't usually take advantage of them, I figured that a special occasion like this is as good a reason as any." He smiles at me and I beam. This is *perfect*. Tor leads me inside of the common room and we sit on a sofa near the fireplace.

"I have never seen this place so empty." Nova says, wonder in her voice. "Seriously, I have been here for seven years, and it is always *filled* with people."

"Trust me, I was very shocked when all we had to do was take a walk to The Castle. He just told some guy that he wanted the common room of The Fortress cleared out for the evening and it was empty by the time we arrived." Arche adds, words spilling out in amazement.

I look at Tor who sits next to me, smiling innocently.

"Thank you. This is perfect." I shake my head, gaze fixed on Tor.

"I think we need to play a game." Arche says.

I raise an eyebrow at him curiously. "A—game?"

"Yeah!" Arche replies enthusiastically. "They always keep stuff over there." He gestures to the cabinets and shelves on the far wall.

"Go check it out then." Nova says.

After a few moments of shuffling and digging—while Nova and I can't help but laugh—Arche finds what he was searching for.

"Ah-ha!" He blurts. I crane my neck to look at him and he is holding up a crumbling white box. He walks back to us and sits on the ground. "I heard about this card game, it's something that the children in Omnis's play. According to Ollie, it was popular in the old world and was passed on from The Book of Wit." Arche pauses for dramatic effect but I cut it short.

"If it's from The Book of Wit, then why do children in *Omnis* play it?" I ask skeptically.

"You know what Soleil, just humor me for a moment." Arche responds, getting slightly agitated.

"Continue." I say, gesturing to him and his deck of cards. Nova chuckles and I wink at her.

"Well, you need at least two players to start."

"Check." Tor says from next to me. Arche shoots him a look of annoyance and I giggle.

"To set up, everyone gets five cards. The rest of them go in the middle of the players—face down. Then, we start playing. One player can ask anyone for a certain card number, if they have it, they give it to them, if they don't, they tell them to *go swim*. Then, that player takes a card from the pile in the middle—that is called the lake—and if they get the card number they wanted, they can ask another player for cards and they keep going until they don't get another one. Then it goes to the next person and they do the same thing."

"What exactly is the point?" Nova asks playfully, smiling at Arche.

"Well, there are thirteen different sets to collect, ace through ten, and then king, queen, and jack. The goal is to collect as many sets of four as you can, and we keep playing until they have all been collected. The person with the most sets becomes the fish and they win."

"What's this game called?" Tor queries, stifling a laugh. I nudge him with my elbow.

"Go swim in the lake and become the fish." Arche responds seriously.

I can't help myself and I burst out laughing, despite my warning to Tor. Tor and Nova follow suit and we laugh until our stomachs hurt and laugh some more. Eventually we end up on the floor. The game sounds great, but the name—I can't take Arche seriously. Once the three of us calm down—and Arche stops looking at us as if we're insane—we sit down on the ground in front of the fireplace.

"You said five cards each?" I ask as Arche deals them out to us.

"Mmhm." He hums, silently counting out the cards. When he's done, the remaining ones are set in the middle.

"This is the *lake*." Nova points out, holding back a laugh.

Arche shoots her a look and she smiles innocently in response. "Okay. I'm going to start." We nod at him. "Soleil, do you have any sixes?" He asks me.

I look down at my five cards, a three of clubs, a five of hearts, an ace of diamonds, a two of hearts, and a ten of spades. "Nope."

"Are you sure?" Arche queries.

"Very sure. You can go swimming." I say with a smile.

"It is *go swim*."

"That is what I said." I retort as Arche picks a card from the lake.

"Okay Soleil, it's your turn."

I look at my cards and then look to Nova. "Nova, do you have any aces?"

"Here you go." Nova responds, handing me an ace of hearts.

"Do I go again?" I ask Arche. He nods. "Arche, do *you* have any aces?" He begrudgingly hands me an ace of clubs, not saying a word as he does. "How about you Tor? Any aces?"

"Yeah, I do." Tor hands me the ace of spades—the final one I need for my set.

"Now what do I do? I have a full set, does that make me the fish?" I ask.

"No one is the fish until the game is finished. Just put all four cards in the set on the ground, face up." Arche replies. I do as he tells me, very satisfied with myself for getting the first set of the game.

The game goes on for long minutes as Tor, Arche, Nova, and I collect the various sets of cards. Once every set has been collected, I am delighted to find that I won with five of the thirteen sets. Tor jokingly places the ace of spades he gave me at the beginning of the game, on my head and he says the word *"fish."* After that game is over, we play many more rounds, each one more intense than the last. I win a few more, but Nova beats us all after she wins her sixth game out of the twelve we played.

It's nearly *2200* when someone knocks on the door of the common room. Tor gets up to answer it. When he opens the door, a silver cart full of food is wheeled into the room. I delight at the sight and quickly walk over to the cart. The four of us begin placing the various trays and plates on the floor and we uncover them to find a wide array of food. Roasted meats, crispy breads with butters and jams, sauteed vegetables, colorful salads, pastas in creamy sauces, warm soups, and a variety of small, bite sized desserts are spread out in front of us.

Ravenous, we immediately begin eating, only stopping to take sips of water from silver goblets. The food is delicious and, from what I can tell, it was brought in from The Castle itself. No one speaks as we gorge ourselves on the rich cooking. Once we're done, we lounge lazily on the couches and chairs around the fireplace.

For the next few hours, we tell stories of our lives, some more embarrassing than others. We take turns, Nova beginning by telling the group how we used to get in trouble for sneaking away from the Lost wing of The Castle when we were young. Arche goes next, telling an awful story about how he sleepwalked through The Fortress and ended up alone in the dining hall on his first night. Tor talks about his time in Ingenium and how The Boundless Library goes on forever and ever. I end by reenacting my first training session with a sword, and how, despite the sword being made of wood, I still ended up sending my instructor to the infirmary.

Nova is just gearing up to tell another story when someone knocks on the door again. This time, Tor looks as confused as the rest of us and I know that this is not a part of his plan for the evening. When he pulls the door open, a male soldier in full black battle armor stands on the other side.

"Yes?" Tor asks the soldier curiously.

"Your presence is required in The Castle immediately." The soldier responds. I shift in my seat at his tone.

"I made it clear that I'm busy this evening." Tor replies sternly.

"Yes, however these are matters above either of us. You are required at The Castle *now*. I will give you a moment to say your farewells for the night, and then you must come with me." The soldier says, voice stoic.

"Very well. I will be out in a moment." Tor closes the door again. I stand up, grabbing his cloak from the sofa, and walk it to him.

"Thank you for tonight." I say warmly.

"I'm sorry I have to leave."

"It's fine, it must be midnight by now. It's probably for the best. I want to be awake early for Lord Acastus' announcement tomorrow." I play off my clear disappointment.

"Right, I almost forgot about the announcement. I will be there. *I promise.*" Tor says, taking his cloak from me and wrapping it around his shoulders. "Good luck."

"Thanks."

"See you guys later." Tor adds to Nova and Arche. He winks at me before walking out of the common room doors.

"I wonder what that was all about." Arche yawns after a beat of silence passes.

"He *is* head bladesmith." I reply with a sigh.

"And tomorrow you will be second in command of The Undying Army. You two *are* perfect for each other." Nova teases. I throw a pillow at her in response. "What? I'm just looking on the bright side." She adds after the pillow hits her in the face. I sigh again, not knowing what else to say.

"How about we turn in for the night?" Arche says, understanding my need to be alone with my thoughts. "I can walk both of you to your sleeping chamber and we can call it a day." I look up at him and nod.

"Yeah, I'm tired anyway."

"The quicker we get to sleep, the quicker we find out who the new second is." Nova jokes.

"I *will* throw another pillow at you." I say, with a pointed look. She puts her hands up innocently.

"Let's get the two of you to bed—preferably *unharmed.*" Arche adds.

And so, the three of us walk out of the common room to Female Sleeping Chamber G, and my mind slowly fills with the clacking of three pairs of boots on the stone floors.

206

CHAPTER FOURTEEN

A stone table.
Seven ornate goblets.
Seven gilded thrones.
Seven shining Knights.
A pair of piercing blue eyes.
"I will find a way."
One goblet lifted.
Six goblets rose in unison

I do not wake at the rising of the goblets. Instead, I am pushed through the worlds—through time itself—until I am on the battlefield.

I have Fay pinned down in the snow, my knees digging into her arms to hold her in place, the weight of my body keeping her there. My dagger is pressed against her throat, its golden blade glistening. I am *so close* to the banner; I don't have to move my body from its position to reach up and pull the banner down. The war horn sounds and the battle is over. *I won.* But I don't stop. I can only watch as I slice Fay's neck and smile as it runs red, her eyes rolling back and her skin growing cold under me. Her blood, warm and thick, coats my hands, and my smile only grows wider at the sight.

I shake awake, throwing the blanket off my body and I slide to the stone floor below. On my knees, I heave as my stomach rolls and my head spins. My breaths are shallow and quick, and none of them bring me any relief from the burning within. I rub my hands raw on the stone floors, attempting to find reprieve from the feeling of Fay's blood that still lingers. When that does nothing, I clutch myself and tears streams quickly down my face. I try to scream, but my throat is dry, and no sound comes from it.

Minutes, hours, or days pass, and as the cold slowly penetrates my skin, I am brought back to reality. In an instant, my eyes focus on my surroundings. I am on the floor of Female Sleeping Chamber G, my thermal blanket is crumpled on my bunk and light is beginning to peek in from the windows. The fireplace is unlit—it's still early. My breaths slow and I take satisfying gulps of the cold air, listening to the beat of my heart slow to a resting pace. I sit for a while, staring into the empty fireplace as if I can light it with a thought.

Eventually, I build up the courage to look at my hands, horrified at what I might find. They are red and littered with scratches which—from what I can tell—had bled and clotted quickly. However, Fay's blood is nowhere to be found. I let out a sigh of relief, letting my shoulders drop, grateful to have real evidence that everything was just another dream. Using my thermals, I rub at the pinpricks of blood on my hands, wincing at the stinging sensation.

I force myself to think about the dream that had shaken me awake to come to terms with what I saw. It was simply a nightmare. I know that the battle simulation is over already, I know that I won, and I know that Fay lives for she is probably sound asleep in her chamber right now. Though, the feeling of her blood on my hands remains and I am disgusted by myself. The idea that I could even *dream* about something so horrific, appalls me.

But it's knowing that I could have done it, that scares me most.

My mind moves from that dream to the one that came before. I've seen it a thousand times over, but tonight I did not wake as the goblets rose. After more time sitting on the stone floor, I realize just how cold I have gotten. Between my thin sleeping thermals, lack of a blanket, and the unlit fire, my fingers are still from the icy air. I stand up to shake the stiffness from my muscles and squint at the clock above the fireplace—*0400*.

I grab my red cloak, dry after spending the night hung up on Nova and I's bunk, and I wrap it tightly around myself. I climb the ladder at the end of the bunk frame and begin poking Nova to wake her up.

"Nov. It's time to get up." I say gently.

"Did they light the fire yet?" Nova groans.

"No."

"Then wake me when they light the fire."

"I'm not doing that. Get up. I bet it is super warm in the bathing chamber anyway." At that, Nova opens her eyes and stretches. "Good morning."

"What are you doing up?" She asks me uncertainty.

"Bad dream." I say while climbing down the ladder, hands still stinging from my altercation with the stone floor.

"I'm sorry about that." Nova says between yawns.

"It's fine, I want to be at the dining hall early." I respond, rummaging through my trunk to find something to wear. I settle on a white shirt and trousers to wear over black thermals, anything to keep me warm.

"Wear something nice." Nova replies, stretching her limbs.

"Already on it." I slide into my slippers. "Let's get going."

Nova nods before climbing down the ladder. After a few minutes of her deciding what to wear, we walk out into the halls of The Fortress, and to the perfectly warm bathing chamber. The fire roars in the grand white marble room and the crack and pop of the wood sends shivers through my body. I delight at the heat and make my way to a bathing room.

After my shower, I brush my teeth and scrub my face. I then sit at the stone benches in front of the fireplace and apply lotion to my arms and legs, cringing at the cuts on my palms. Nova comes out of her bathing room, wrapped in a towel, and sits next to me, her eyes widening at the sight of my hands.

"What happened Sol?" She asks gently, taking one of my hands in hers.

"Bad dream." I reply coolly.

"Was it that horrible?"

"*This* isn't the half of it." I say as she opens a black pouch, pulling out a salve and roll of gauze.

"Let me fix it and then you can put your gloves on." I nod my head and she begins wiping the area with a small piece of gauze. Then she slathers the eucalyptus scented ointment on each of my hands, finishing by carefully wrapped my hands in more of the gauze. She ties the thin fabric in small knots and helps me pull my gloves on. The fit is snug, but my palms no longer hurt and with the gloves, on no one will be able to tell.

When she finishes, we both sit on the benches in silence, transfixed by the light and warmth of the fireplace. Eventually, we make our way to changing rooms where I pull on my black thermals as well as the white shirt and trousers I picked out. I wrap my crimson cloak around my body and pull the hood up over my head.

When Nova and I arrive back at the sleeping chamber, the door is open, the fire lit, and the room warm. The clock above the fireplace reads *0615* so Nova and I quickly arrange our things back into our trunks. I put on a pair of black socks and slide on my battle boots since they match my outfit more than my usual black pair. I scoff at the absurdity of the situation—anything for the dramatics I suppose.

After digging through my trunk for my dagger, I loosen the scabbard and fasten it tightly around my waist and thigh. I then slide the dagger itself in place. Before we wake any of the other girls, Nova and I tip-toe out of the room, shutting the door as we leave.

My heart beats quickly and my stomach flips at what might lie ahead. I swiftly hook my arm through Nova's, holding onto her tightly. Neither of us say a word as we walk in sync along the stone hallways.

For the last star cycle, I have dreaded the thought of leaving Nova's side, and emotion fills me at the fact that today—I may have to. She shifts and pulls me a bit tighter and I know that she is coming to the same realization. I steady my breath and do my best to hold an expressionless mask over my face. I am not willing to break down during breakfast.

Nova and I arrive at the dining hall as crowds of people are filing in. I spot Arche at a table by himself and point him out to Nova. Nova fills her tray with food from the food stations, however I settle for a piece of crispy bread with a thin layer of butter and a mug of herbal tea. My stomach churns with nervousness, so the light breakfast is welcome. By the time Nova and I arrive at the table, Arche is already stuffing his face with food, his eyes light up when he sees us.

"Morning." He says, mouth full.

"Hey." Nova responds, taking her seat next to him. I sit down across from them and begin taking sips of the scalding tea and small bites of the crisp bread. My heartbeat quickens with each passing minute and it never slows. Eventually I push my breakfast to the side altogether, choosing to zone out to the hum of voices instead.

"Soleil." Arche says, bringing me back to reality.

"Yes?" I ask, annoyed that he has interrupted my inner worry.

"Why aren't you eating?" He queries, concern in his tone.

"Not in the mood." I respond, turning from him. He grabs my gloved hand from across the table.

"Listen to me. You will be fine. This job is yours and you know it. I won't force you to eat, but at least finish your tea. It might help settle you." Arche say each word with conviction and while I do not want to, I pick up my mug of tea and take a few gulps. I feel the hot liquid move down my throat and—as Arche said—it settles me.

"Thank you." I reply.

Arche smiles and speaks again. "So, what's going to happen when you become second? I know Fay will have meltdown, but what then?"

I glare at him before realizing that I truly have no idea what will happen next. I simply shrug my shoulders in response and pull my hand away from his.

"Whatever it is, she will be *fine*." Nova responds for me. I send her a grateful look.

Before Arche could speak his retort, Tor takes a seat next to me and grabs my hand under the table. When I look at him, he gives it a squeeze and I smile gently. I am immediately settled by his mere presence.

"Did I miss anything?" He asks me.

"No, we are just discussing my future as if I am not here." I reply and take a moment to glare at Arche again.

"Sounds interesting." Tor says, eyebrows raising skeptically.

"*Very.*" I respond, then add. "How was your night? What did the people at The Castle need you for?"

"The usual—last minute forging duties. I *was* awake until *oh three hundred hours* getting it finished. But the work is done." It's just about *0730* so I assume that Tor is running on very few hours of sleep. So are Nova and I, but we usually elect for that. Plus, I doubt that I would have been able to sleep again after the dream I had, even if I tried.

"I'm glad. Sorry we kept you, if I knew that you would have been needed, we would have called the whole evening off." I say sincerely.

"It was a sudden thing." He pauses. "Last night was the most fun I've had in a while. I'm glad we did it." I smile at that and so do Nova and Arche. I pick up my mug to take another gulp of tea and Tor begins eating his breakfast. But our hands remain linked under the table. Whatever words fail to pass through our mouths, whatever feelings we do not dare share aloud, they pass through us in this simple gesture.

For the next thirty minutes, only idle conversation passes between the four of us. I don't register much of it as I retreat further and further into my own mind, attempting to hide from the panic that wells in me. My breaths remain controlled and my face shows no emotion, but my mind swells with thoughts. The dining hall crowds with people as they fill any available space and conversation reaches a roar so loud that even my thoughts are drowned out.

Two pounds of a staff on the ground and both the room, and my mind, go silent. Two more pounds and the hoods of our cloaks come down, Tor and I unlinking our hands to complete the action. I place my hands firmly in my lap, pulling myself away from him now, rather than later. Another two pounds and our eyes are on the stage. Two final pounds—a total of eight—and we know that Lord Acastus is finally ready to speak.

The clacking of boots on stone fills the dining hall as the Lord walks to the front and center of the stone stage. Today he wears a black gambeson with leather buckles, black pants, and black boots. He looks striking as usual and I can see the shine in his grey eyes from where I sit. Ever handsome, ever perfect, no matter how unsettling that immortal perfection may be.

"For twenty-eight days I have watched, evaluated, and truly experienced numerous rounds of battle simulations." Lord Acastus begins, voice booming across the dining hall. "All of you have shown me skill beyond your years and I am content to say that I have found my second in command." Blood roars in my ears. I take deep breaths, keeping my gaze trained on Lord Acastus.

I am the picture of grace and power.

"This decision was not taken lightly and much deliberation has gone into the choice. I ask all of you to respect my wishes and by extension, the wishes of my crown, throne, and The Book of Law itself. I will not tolerate *any* outrage or offense directed at myself or the newly announced second in command. Harsh consequences will be dealt to those who disobey my command." The dining hall remains silent and I know that regardless of who is picked, *no one* will question Lord Acastus' decision.

"On this, the first day of the ninth star cycle in the nine hundred and ninety-ninth year of the ninety-ninth millennium. I announce that my new second in command of The Undying Army is *Soldier Soleil Yamanu*." My breath comes out in shaky relief.

It's me. The job is mine.

Despite the mix of emotions beginning to fill my body, I rise—my stance perfect—and walk with the power of the worlds as I approach the stage. I feels thousands of eyes on me and I send a silent prayer to Infinity that I will have the strength to do this.

Taking each step slowly and deliberately, I feel the Infinity evoked dominance course through my veins. My face remains emotionless, that of a soldier who has known all along that this job is hers. When I climb the stairs and make it onto the stage, I find that Lord Acastus has stepped aside. He holds his hand out for me. Making my way to the Lord, I take his hand—ice cold, yet soft in a way I hadn't expected—and he leads me to the proper spot. I look out to the thousands of people that have crowded into the dining hall.

I take a deep breath, settling into my new position. *Above them all.*

Lord Acastus stands beside me and I do my best to hold my head up high and strong, ensuring that I will not be overshadowed by the power that flows effortlessly from him. And it does… In this close proximity to the Lord of Lex, it is hard to believe that he has no real power, it is hard to believe that Professor Clara's stories are true. Still, I do not dare move as Lord Acastus turns around and retrieves something from a nobleman who waits near the back of the stage.

"Soleil Yamanu," he says. "Do you vow to protect and defend The Realms of Infinity for as long as you live?" Lord Acastus asks.

I evoke the strength of Infinity as I reply. "I do." Something cold and heavy is placed on my head and Lord Acastus quietly orders me to put my hands out. I obey as I will obey him for as long as I live.

"Soleil Yamanu, do you promise to use your sword for the betterment of this realm, of your *home*, and all of The Realms of Infinity?" Lord Acastus asks.

"I do." I reply, my voice solid and strong as Lord Acastus places a sword in my hands. The sword is a perfect—beautifully balanced—the hilt and the blade are already warm.

"I present to you *General Soleil Yamanu, Second in Command of The Undying Army.*" The crowd claps respectfully. I find Nova, Arche, and Tor, rising as I look to them. Following suit, the rest of the crowd stands, and the dining hall is enveloped in the sound of applause. My face remains stoic, unaffected by my new position or the acclaim that has followed.

I am second in command of The Undying Army and this moment is beneath me.

PART II

THE GENERAL

CHAPTER
FIFTEEN

Once the applause fades away, it is just Lord Acastus and I in front of the entire Academy of The Undying Army. I finally give myself leave to look down at the sword that is in my hands, doing my best to keep my head up so the item atop my head—a diadem I presume—won't move. I take one quick glance at Tor in the audience, his gaze trained on me, and then my eyes travel down. My heart skips when I see exactly what I am holding.

The incredible hilt that I saw in Tor's workshop only the day before is resting in my hands. My knees tremble and I do everything I can to remain standing as I examine the beautiful craftsmanship. I swear that the heart shaped, blood red, stone beats in my palms. I pull my eyes away from the hilt to look at the blade and I am shocked to find that it is *my blade.* The blade I used in battle for the last star cycle has been attached to this hilt. It looks slightly different however, as the waves of gold from the hilt flow seamlessly into it.

I inspect the rest of the shining blade and find slight whorls engraved into the metal. They are the same as the ones on the dagger that is currently strapped to my thigh. Beautiful swirls that climb the length of the sword, but are so fine and subtle that I can only see them in certain light. My breath hitches when I see my name hidden amongst the engravings, tucked closely near the hilt. It's gorgeous, the perfect complement to my own dagger, and I know that Tor has created it especially for me. When I look up, Tor is smiling brightly and I can't help but smile back, unable to believe that this sword is mine.

Long moments of silence pass before Lord Acastus speaks again. His voice continues to penetrate every corner of the dining hall. I pull my eyes from Tor and resume my stoic expression, reminding myself who I have just become.

"You are dismissed."

All at once, everyone stands and leaves the dining hall, even Nova, Arche, and Tor. The hall is clear only moments later and the only people left are Lord Acastus and I. I finally move, turning to see the Lord who stands just behind me.

As if looking at a snake, I set my face in determination and stare into the cold grey eyes of Lord Acastus.

"Let me take the sword, it must be awfully uncomfortable to hold like that." He says, his voice strong and commanding, though his words are casual.

"Yes, thank you." I hand him the sword by the hilt and his cold fingers brush my own. I shiver at the sensation.

Lord Acastus walks to the back of the wooden stage and picks up a white leather sheath embossed with gold to match the one currently at my thigh. He sheathes the sword and walks back to me. "It was made for you—the sword and all—a token of my *generosity*." The Lord says. Lord Acastus hands the sheath to me and I relish in the feeling of the supple leather in my hands.

"I am pleased with your confidence, my Lord." I respond coolly.

"Very well. You may pack your things and meet me here in one hour, no later." Lord Acastus says. Bewilderment spreads through me. *Why would I need to pack my things?*

"My Lord, I'm sorry, but I don't understand. I am a student of The Academy and I live in The Fortress." I keep my composure despite my confusion.

"You *were* a student of The Academy and you *lived* in The Fortress." Lord Acastus clarifies. "From the moment you took your vows, you officially graduated from The Academy. Your high rank necessitates that you move to The Castle and your rooms are being prepared for you as we speak."

Despite the swirl of questions in my mind, I reply concisely. "Thank you my Lord, I appreciate your forethought and preparation."

"You are dismissed." Lord Acastus says casually.

Clutching my sword, I leave and quickly make my way out of the dining hall. Taking the most obscure hallways of The Fortress to avoid crowds, I quickly make it to Female Sleeping Chamber G. Inside, I find not my squadron of soldiers, but Nova, Arche, and Tor. The moment my eyes meet Tor's I run to him and he pulls me into a tight embrace, my crown presses up against his chest.

"It was for me?"

"The whole time, Soleil." He responds, lifting the crown off my head. I pull him closer and I don't let go for long moments. When I finally pull away, I ask him another question.

"Was this what you were called away to work on last night?" I ask, holding up the sheathed sword. Tor nods in response and I shake my head. He hands me the diadem and I examine it in amazement. The crown itself looks like two thin swords connected by their hilts. Their blades curve around and cross at the front where they rest on my forehead. It's the perfect crown for a General.

"So, what now?" Nova asks.

"I am to pack my things and move to The Castle." I reply. Nova's eyes widen.

"You are only in your seventh year." Arche says, shocked.

"*Was.*" I correct. "When I made my vows, I graduated." No one speaks for long seconds.

It is Tor that finally breaks the silence. "Let's get you packed." His words are gentle.

"What's its name?" I ask Tor.

"The sword?"

"Yes." I insist.

"*Fate.*" The name rings out in my mind the moment it passes Tor's lips.

Fate, Fate, Fate, Fate, Fate.

"It's perfect." I respond. I take a moment before moving to my trunk to begin packing.

When the shock wears off, Nova and Arche begin helping too. We sort my things into various leather bags. Once everything is packed, Tor helps me into the sheath of my new sword, his fingers deftly working to secure it. The sheath sits perfectly on my thigh, just above my dagger. When I sheathe Fate at my hip, it feels perfectly natural in its new home.

Tor quickly zips my leather bags and begins slinging them over his shoulders.

"What are you doing?" I ask, grabbing for the bags.

"I'm helping." Tor replies simply.

"You need to go home, not with me to The Castle." I say, beginning to pull the bags from his shoulders.

"Soleil, where do you think I'm going? I *live* in The Castle."

I step back and laugh. "Well let me take some of the bags then."

"There is no need for that." Tor says, laughing through his words. I sigh in defeat and turn to Nova and Arche who lean against a set of bunks. I pull Nova into a tight hug first. Tears stream from her eyes and she shakes as soon as we touch. Neither of us speak and I hold her until she pulls away first. When she does, I rub her face with my hand and look into her eyes. She nods and that is enough for me to know that she will be okay.

Arche is waiting for me when I turn to him and he grabs me by the waist to pull me into a deep hug. He wraps his arms tightly around my body as if he wishes to protect me from the world. His face digs into the spot between my neck and shoulder and he begins speaking so softly that only I can hear.

"You are going to be okay right?" He rasps.

"Yes."

"You will come back to visit." He states. Not a question, a fact.

"Or you can come visit me," I joke. Arche pulls away and presses our foreheads together.

"You are the best warrior I have ever seen, Sol. Remember yourself when you are with Lord Acastus." His hands rise to frame my face and I pull him back to me.

"Thank you, Arch. Take care of Nov." I beg.

"Everyday."

Once I pull away from Arche I look up to Tor and nod. He walks to me and places the crown back on my head before taking my hand in his. After taking one more look at Arche and Nova, the two of us walk out of Female Sleeping Chamber G.

"I have to meet Lord Acastus in the dining hall." I tell Tor as we walk.

"I will go with you." He replies, looking down to meet my gaze. The two of us continue our walk to the dining hall, hand in hand.

The rose and the bladesmith once more.

My red cloak flows behind me and the new sword at my thigh is a welcome feeling. Oddly enough, no one is in the halls of The Fortress, but when I pass the windows that overlook the battlefield, I see why.

I stop dead in my tracks and begin walking to the windows. Every student in the entire Academy must be out there. The battlefield is filled and each person has a sword. They are running drill after drill—a sight that I have never seen—I look to Tor for clarification.

"What is this?" I ask softly.

"Academy-wide mandatory training. Trainers stopped by each sleeping chamber while you were still in the dining hall. Everyone is there by order of Lord Acastus himself." I let out a breath and pull my gaze away from the battlefield below.

"Let's go." I say curtly.

When we arrive at the dining hall, Lord Acastus is already waiting for me, though I know that my hour is far from being up.

Lord Acastus' face puzzles, then lights in recognition when he see Tor. "My favorite bladesmith." Lord Acastus says warmly, putting a hand out for Tor to shake.

Tor unlinks his fingers from mine to shake the Lord's hand. "Hello, my Lord." Tor says courteously.

"You did say that you know Miss—excuse me—*General* Yamanu."

"I do." Tor responds.

"Wonderful. Now let us get to The Castle, there is much to do I am afraid." Lord Acastus gestures for me to lead the way. "General—today *is* your day." I nod and begin walking to the entrance of The Fortress, leading Lord Acastus, Tor, and a squadron of guards.

The walk across the bridge to The Castle is quiet, however the cold wind whipping at my body never lets up. I walk quickly, hearing my boots click on the stone bridge. While I wish to, I do not wrap my cloak around myself, opting instead to put my hood up and keep my arms loose at my sides. The Infinity evoked power from earlier still flows through my veins and I keep my chin high.

Without a word from Lord Acastus or the guards outside of The Castle of Lex, the doors open for us. Still leading the group as we enter The Castle, I begin to settle into the idea of this being a permanent position. In the very few times that I have seen Lord Acastus with my own eyes, prior to this past star cycle, General Aldera was *always* ahead of him, a safety precaution I was sure, however it now has an air of something else.

One would think that leading the group would put *you* in the position of power, however I feel as if I am being stripped of it. It is so different from walking arm in arm with Nova or Arche. Here, at the front of the group, I could never know if the Lord is secretly planning to stick a dagger in my back. I may be leading the Lord, but he has all of the power.

When we make it to the back halls of The Castle, memories of my past life flood through me. For years The Castle was all I knew and then I moved to The Fortress and I saw firsthand the beauty of calculated battle. I have always imagined that after my time in The Academy, I would move back into The Castle as a highly ranked member of The Undying Army. I never thought that it would come so soon.

As I lead our group down the halls, I hear the clacking of heels coming from afar. Remembering my position not only as the second in command of The Undying Army, but as Lord Acastus' second as well, I know that if faced with a threat I will have to protect him at any cost. General Aldera was famous for being extremely protective of the Knights he served; I mustn't be any different.

Loosening my arms, I account for the weight of my sword and dagger on my left side. My posture remains commanding, so I simply give into the senses I have sharpened as blade these last seven years. I continue to walk forward, vigilant in case of threat. It takes only moments for the sharp heel clacks to grow louder and then reach us at last. My breath hitches when I see who it is. Alma, hair bound in a tight bun, a deep purple cloak wrapped loosely around her, and her face soft as always, greets us as we turn the corner.

"Soleil?" Alma asks—as shocked as I am.

I give her a sharp look, probably too intense for what the situation calls for. But before I can continue on as if nothing happened, Lord Acastus speaks.

"General Yamanu, you may stop." I cringe at Lord Acastus' words and the pure force that comes from them. Even if I wanted to continue walking—after his words— I'm not sure that I can.

"Yes, my Lord." I say calmly, quickly growing accustomed to the title that a Knight of Infinity demands. I turn around to face the rest of the group. The small squadron of soldiers that I assumed still follow us, are no longer present and I feel totally sightless in the observation.

Are my senses that dull compared to those of fully trained soldiers?

"What business do you have with the second in command of The Undying Army?" The Lord asks Alma.

Alma's pales as she struggles for a response. "Sol—"

I stop her there, taking a gamble by speaking out of turn. "My Lord, this is Alma Zuri. She is the head caretaker of The Women of the Lost as you may know." My voice is soft out of respect; however, it contains power enough to deal with the Lord.

"I am not dull, General Yamanu." Lord Acastus spits. It takes all of my control not to back away. "I would like to know what *her* business is with *you*."

"My Lord, Alma was my caretaker for many years as I was formerly of the Lost." This time, I choose not to shy away from the power inherent in my voice. I use it to its capacity while remaining benevolent.

After a moment, the Lord responds. "Ah… I see. Madame Zuri, we are out on official business for The Undying Army and I must get my second in command to her new quarters as soon as possible. If you have a grievance with General Yamanu, I can ensure that you receive a copy of her schedule as soon as it is formed. Thank you, and I bid you a good day." Lord Acastus speaks with false chivalry, courtesy disguising resentment.

Alma looks at me, her face still pale, and I soften my gaze enough to let her know that everything is okay. She calms slightly and I nod my head at her before turning back to Lord Acastus. Tor remains beside him, head down as a sign of respect for the private conversation taking place.

"Thank you, My Lord." Alma replies, voice quivering. She put her head down as well.

More and more respect.

"Very well. General Yamanu you may continue—up the next staircase please." At his words I turn around and pick up my pace again, attempting to push the last few moments out of my mind. Lord Acastus *cannot* see me as weak, not after I spent the last star cycle convincing him otherwise.

I hold my head up high and—for the first time—rest my hand on Fate's hilt.

"Down this hall." Lord Acastus says from behind me.

"Yes, my Lord," I reply dutifully.

"You may stop." Lord Acastus says after a few more paces. I turn to my right and a beautifully carved wooden door meets my gaze. Carved into the dark wood are figures and stories that I promise myself I will dedicate an entire day to deciphering. I turn to Lord Acastus who is holding a well-worn skeleton key out to me, I take it without another word.

Giddy on the inside, and completely composed on the surface, I walk to the wooden door, insert the key, and twist. With a nervous breath I push the door in, letting my fingers graze and linger on the ornate carvings. The room inside is completely dark. It isn't until Lord Acastus comes from next to me and pulls a metal lever down, that light fills the room.

Immediately, I feel at home. The stone walls are covered in more of the dark wood of the door. The floors are stone by feel, but they are covered in layers of the same mismatched carpets that cover every inch of the Lost wing. We step into what must be a living room, but I am shocked to find that there is no furniture in it. Not a single sofa, chair, mattress, or table fills the space, the only thing of substance is an unlit fireplace. I turn to Lord Acastus; an eyebrow raised despite myself.

"The room is completely bare, only the essentials were moved in prior to your arrival. There is a bed in the sleeping room, and your closet is fully stocked with appropriate clothing. If you simply write a list of anything you need, the handmaidens will give it to the appropriate party, and you will have all that you request."

I am still looking around at the living space. I can easily imagine bookshelves lining every wall. Tor is setting my leather bags down near the door while I do my inspection.

"Do you mind if I give you a tour? It will be brief." Lord Acastus asks with the most sincerity I have heard from him thus far.

"Yes, thank you my Lord."

Lord Acastus turns to Tor who has just set down the rest of my bags. "You are excused, thank you for your services." Tor quickly looks at me and before I can say a word, bows his head and leaves. Cold washes over me at the lack of his presence, however Lord Acastus ushers me into the tour of my quarters.

"If you enter through this door—" he says, pushing a sliding door away. It stays put and I enjoy the openness of the space. "This is your sleeping chamber."

A beautiful room with the same dark wood meets me, in the center of the back wall is a four-poster bed with blood red curtains draped on it. "I took some *liberty* with the decoration I am afraid. I hope you don't mind, General Yamanu."

"Thank you, my Lord." I walk to the bed and caress the carvings on the wood, and then the velvet curtains— the same fabric that the banners were made of during the battle simulations.

"The door on the left is your bathing chambers, on the right, your closet. As I said, it has been stocked with all the necessary clothing for a second in command. However, The Castle's tailor makes rounds at the beginning of every star cycle. I believe he is arriving within the next few days. If there is anything you need, let him know and you will have it right away."

I turn to the Lord and nod, allowing myself to crack a gracious smile. "How do I go about payment?" I ask. Students at The Fortress receive a stipend to use each year for weapons, clothing, thermals, shoes, and anything else we may need.

"General Yamanu—I do not think that you understand. No one, save for me, outranks you. You are the second in command of The Undying Army. The Castle covers all your living expenses, including furniture, clothing, food, and all else you may need *or* want. If you wish for something, simply say it and it's yours. As for your salary, a sum will be deposited into an account for you each star cycle. It is yours if you wish, however you needn't use it here in Lex." Lord Acastus' words are jarring. My new status stretches so far beyond a title and duty.

I outrank everyone.

"You said that I don't need my funds here in Lex. Where else would I use them?" My mental question escapes from my mouth instead.

"In any of the other realms I suppose. As second in command of The Undying Army, you have complete access to the portals. I would appreciate a moment's notice before any inter-realm travel, however it's not required. Please see The Castle's banker if you need access to any funds from your account or otherwise. A deposit has already been made in your name for your work this last star cycle." So many privileges, more than I ever imagined, beyond even the most highly ranked officials of The Undying army. Though, I suppose, I *am* one.

"Thank you for your generosity my Lord." I respond graciously. This is all wonderful but I wish for nothing more than to collapse into the bed behind me.

"Of course, General Yamanu, please get some rest. You will receive your first assignment tomorrow." I stare into the icy grey eyes of Lord Acastus, just as intimidating as ever. But still, he seems so—mortal up close. I nod deeply, bowing my head in respect for the Lord. By the time I look up again, he is gone and I am alone.

With the events of the day spinning in my mind and my lack of sleep from the night before still weighing on me, I quickly unlace my boots and strip my cloak, shirt, trousers, sword, and dagger, from my body, folding them neatly on the floor near my bed. I top off my pile of clothes with the golden crown. There is no clock in my room yet, but it can't be past noon.

After an entire star cycle of rigorous training and strict schedules, I finally relent and listen to my body. I lock the wooden door to my rooms and draw the curtains of the four-poster bed closed. Tucking myself under the thick covers, I relish in the quiet.

It takes only a moment before I realize that this is the first time I am sleeping in a room that is mine alone.

CHAPTER
SIXTEEN

Calm washes over my body like waves in the sea and I delight in each crashing of the surf. I finally wake and find my body stiff from sleep. No light meets my eyes. I pull the curtain of the four poster bed away to find that my room is as dark as it was when I went to sleep. I walk to the window and pull back the curtains to find a soft light setting into the sky.

Did I really sleep all day *and* through the night? Despite the stiffness in my body, which I promptly shake out, my mind is clear and refreshed. Smiling to myself, I realize that my usual dream did not plague me in my slumber. Opening the curtain of the large window and letting the light flood the room, I think of the last time that I had a night without the dreams—I never have.

I look out the window. From the look of the dreary sky, it's clear that today will not be a sunny day, however the soft light is satisfying enough. A light powder of snow coats the parts of The Castle that I can see from my window and I quickly realize that I'm far from cold.

I turn my head to examine my chamber and am startled when I find that the fireplace in my living room is already lit. I double check the lock on my door, then realize that the handmaidens must have keys of their own. It must be incredibly early considering the sun is just coming up, but this *is* The Castle, and fires are usually roaring at all hours.

Walking back into my sleeping room I examine the doors on the opposite side of the window. Lord Acastus told me that one door is my closet and the other is a bathing room. Aching for a shower, I choose the bathing room and find a large space with elegant tiling. There is a shower and a beautiful ceramic tub with gold feet, the vanity is shining with a huge spotless mirror. Fluffy white towels hang from racks and there is a large storage cabinet near the vanity as well. I walk to the door of my room and dig through the leather bags until I find my shower things.

After a quick and refreshing shower, I walk into the door of my closet and pull the metal lever down to turn on the lights. The air is pulled from my lungs. Racks and racks of clothing line every wall. After pulling a few out, I find that they are all in my size as well. There are simple dresses made for everyday wear, thermals in every color, two more blood red cloaks, one with fabric much thicker, and the other with fabric much thinner, than my current one.

I find many pairs of shoes, including thick and fluffy slippers that I slide on right away. There is a selection of boots in both black and white. A whole rack of clothing is dedicated to lounging thermals which is a welcome sight. And right near the door—an immediate favorite— lies hooks for my sword and dagger. For today, I choose to wear a white dress with a black gored overskirt. The dress even has a slit on the left side for easy access to my dagger. I find a pair of simple black boots with shiny leather, and lastly I pull out the thicker version of my own red cloak.

I bring all the clothing pieces into my bedroom and shut the door of the closet behind me before I become too overwhelmed. After sitting in front of the fire and allowing my hair to dry off, I change into the clothing and fasten my scabbards and cloak around myself. As I adjust my cloak in front of the vanity mirror, I hear a knock on my door.

Cautiously, I walk to the door of my room and crack it open. Two girls in black robes are on the other side. My handmaidens, I presume.

"Good morning." I'm unsure of the way to treat them considering my title.

My title? I scoff at my own thought. They are just normal people; my *title* does not make them any less deserving of respect. I soften my gaze at them and shove the pretentious idea out of my mind.

"Hello General Yamanu." They say in sync. "We are here to wake you and receive your order for breakfast. Lord Acastus wishes to see you at *ten hundred hours.*"

"Sounds great. I'm plenty awake, thank you. As for breakfast…" I trail off, not knowing what to say. "Feel free to bring me whatever is available, I am not picky in the slightest." The girls look at each other, utterly confused at my words.

"Of course, ma'am." One of them responds unsurely. "We will return with your breakfast soon." I nod and smile at the girls who quickly retreat down the hall.

After shutting and locking the door, I slide on my new pair of black boots. These, unlike my usual pair, do not have laces. I flex my foot and find that the leather molds to my feet nicely.

I search through the leather bags containing my things, finally finding the notebook that I previously used for history lessons. I flip through the already used pages and take a seat on the floor in front of the fireplace, before writing a list of the things I want for my rooms:

- *Bookshelves covering every wall of the living room*
- *A selection of books to fill said bookshelves*
- *A sofa*
- *A few soft chairs*
- *A dining table with chairs*
- *A small table next to my bed*
- *A clock*

Satisfied with my list, there is another knock at my door and a cart of food—much more than I could ever eat—is wheeled into my living room.

"Sorry for the wait Miss, we wanted to ensure that you got everything that was available." I realize the error in my wording very quickly.

"Thank you both." I say graciously anyway. At least they will know that their effort is appreciated. "Lord Acastus told me that I could write a list of the things that I need." One of the girls eagerly grabs my piece of paper.

"Of course, General Yamanu. Please enjoy your breakfast. We will return to clean your room when you have left for your meeting with Lord Acastus."

"Where exactly am I meeting him?" I ask before they can leave.

"His formal office in the north wing on the second floor of The Castle, it is clearly marked." The other girl responds. With their hoods drawn so far down their faces, the two of them are indistinguishable. Before I can speak again, they leave in a blur of black robes. With a sigh, I close the door and move to open the trays of food. I find eggs, meats, yogurt with fresh berries, a platter of fruit, fluffy thin cakes with all of the toppings, vegetables, a variety of juices, crispy breads with jams and butters, and toast battered in cinnamon and sugar. I take a bit of everything, and pour myself a drink from a metal pot, delighted to find that it is filled with steaming coca.

Savoring the warmth of my personal fireplace, I take my time on breakfast. By the time I finish the last few bites from my plate, I find that the coca I poured has grown cold. I drink it to the dregs anyway and do my best to clean the mess I made.

When I am finally done with breakfast, I insert both my dagger and Fate into their respective scabbards. Before sheathing Fate, I admire it in the soft light of my bedroom, smiling at Tor's skill. Each etching into the gold blade, a testament to his skill. The flawless—and deadly sharp—metal, proof of the hours that must have gone into creating the weapon. I imagine his hands, strong and sure, as they worked deftly to create this weapon for *me*. Only those hands could create something so perfect.

After checking my appearance thrice in the bathroom mirror—while also thinking of Tor, and Tor's hands, and his eyes... *Infinity*—I walk out of my room and into the halls of The Castle. It doesn't take long for me to find Lord Acastus' office. When I arrive, I push the wooden doors open to meet the sound of a crackling fire.

The Lord's office is bare, a wooden desk, two simple wooden chairs, and a large fireplace are of the only items of substance. Lord Acastus looks up at me, grey eyes cold as ever, and silently gestures for me to sit. I obey quickly and wait for the Lord to speak. He is reading something out of a large leather-bound book with tiny words—I cannot make out any of them from where I sit.

Long moments pass in silence, the only thing filling the air, the sound of the crackling fire. Heat wafts towards me, warming the gooseflesh that appeared on my skin the moment I walked into the Knight's office. Finally, Lord Acastus sticks a thin piece of fabric in his book and shuts it, sliding it to the side of the desk. When his eyes rise to look at me, mine are already prepared to meet them. I see curiosity bubble behind his grey irises, but it's quickly shadowed by seriousness. My gaze remains relentless, however.

"General Yamanu—" he draws out the syllables of my name unnervingly.

"Yes, my Lord?"

"You have created quite the stir in The Fortress."

It has been little more than a day since I was announced as second in command and I have been here in

The Castle for most of it. "I am afraid I don't understand what you mean."

"It isn't you per say," he says more casually than before. "It is more the fact that *I* chose you as second in command."

"Is that a problem?" My voice is commanding, but I work to imitate some of his own nonchalance.

"What isn't?" He says, brushing my concerns away.

"Isn't it my job to take care of them? To take care of those *problems…*" I ask simply.

"It is, but after being without a second for more than a star cycle, I find myself becoming used to them."

"A dangerous game."

"What isn't?" He repeats.

"My Lord, I do not understand the point." If there are problems in The Fortress, they would be far below the Lord's radar. I can't imagine why he would care.

"The point is that you must remain vigilant. This job has put a mark on your back." He pauses, letting his words settle. "Don't forget to look over your shoulder." This is far from the first time someone has told me that. "I would not want to have to search for another second in command so soon. You *mortals,* are just so fragile it seems."

I don't allow any shock to paint my face, instead I begin. "My Lord—" I am quickly cut off.

"Do not disappoint me, General. That is all." His voice is stone cold, but I don't soften.

If Lord Acastus is going to be ice, I will become fire.

"Never, my Lord." I pull power into my voice despite my words of complete submission.

"Very well," he pauses for a moment. "As you may already know I called you here so we can discuss your first assignment."

"Yes."

"Everything that I am about to explain to you is confidential. The state of the realms depends on you keeping this information to yourself. Do you understand?" The same power that I heard in his voice earlier, comes out again through this question. Whatever my answer is, I know it will be binding.

"Yes, my Lord." *Complete submission.*

"The realms are in disarray. Lex—thank Infinity—has been spared, however something must be done. The end of the millennium is fast approaching, and while it is an already fickle time, past events have made it even more so." Lord Acastus speaks each word deliberately, his speech slow and precise. There will be no misunderstanding.

"Past events?" I ask.

"I believe that I speak on behalf of *all* the Knights of Infinity when I say that we haven't been the most harmonious as of late."

Typical political argument. "History says that the relationships between the Knights have *always* been capricious." I say, thinking back to Professor Clara's lesson. I have not given headspace to her *stories* in weeks, they are far from what I have known all my life and I can't deal with that revelation now.

"There are multiple sides to every history depending on your point of view." Lord Acastus replies indifferently.

"And if mine is second in command of The Undying Army?"

"Then I require something of you, General Yamanu." His eyes darken.

"What do you need me to do, my Lord?" This is it; I will prove myself with this task, or he will see that he has chosen the wrong second. I will not let that happen.

"In order to fix what is happening, to last the realms, I need information. I need *wit*." He speaks gravely.

"My Lord—" I begin, but his hand goes up. I hold my tongue.

"The Book of Wit in Ingenium is endless, new information is added to it at every moment. Because of this, the earliest Knights of Ingenium made copies of the information in the book, splitting it into smaller books which make up The Boundless Library. Magic from Infinity-knows-where, keeps the information in the books up to date and linked perfectly with The Book of Wit itself. Theoretically, a person would need only one of the books to have a direct connection to that slice of information for all time."

Another history lesson—it takes everything in me not to roll my eyes. "I am well versed in the history and knowledge of the realms, my Lord." I say smugly.

"You don't know everything General Yamanu and I advise you to keep your ears open. You never know when you will hear something new." The Lord spits. I quickly realize that he is keeping my ego in check, whether consciously or not.

I pull back on my tone, much too pompous for speech with the Knight of Lex. Promising myself I will be more conscious of my words, I respond. "My apologies my Lord I did not wish to act arrogantly. What can I do?" My words are as compliant as ever.

"You must go to the realm of Ingenium and convince the Lady Fable to allow you access into The Boundless Library. There, I will need you to locate The Book of Infinite Prophecy and bring it to me without Lady Fable knowing." Mentally, I scoff at the ask. Lady Fable is known for *knowledge*. To do something without her knowing is an oxymoron in itself.

"Lady Fable is *all knowing* my Lord. This is an impossible task—it's suicide. There is no way for me to smuggle an entire book between the realms." I lose the calculated control on my tone and pray to Infinity that Lord Acastus does not register the slip.

"General Yamanu—I would never send you on a fool's mission. The book is small enough for it to go undetected, but I have this for you as well." Lord Acastus opens a drawer and pulls out a small rectangle of black cloth. It can't be more than a few inches on any side. Upon further inspection… it's a pocket.

"What is it?" I ask curiously.

"An *endless* pocket—a relic to sew into your cloak when you go to Ingenium. The book is small enough to fit and will remain undetectable once it is inserted. Even if a guard were to stick their hands into the pocket to search you, they will not feel the book. Only I can retrieve it from inside." Professor Clara's story about how the Knights—other than that of Omins—don't have magic, rings like a bell in my mind.

"How is that possible?" I ask feigning amazement in the item, when really, I long for clarification about the magic itself.

"A bit of ancestral ingenuity, if you will." *So, no magic then?* "You will do it?" Lord Acastus asks, a command disguised as a question.

"I will." I say firmly, then add. "I crave a boon, however."

"Yes?" He responds, curiosity winning out. It seems that if something piques the Lord's interest enough, it can slide. I make a mental note of this particular quirk before replying.

"Tor Warin must come with me. He studied at The School in Ingenium and knows Lady Fable personally. I will not be able to distract the Lady without him." I say, not having much faith in a relic that I don't fully understand myself.

Lord Acastus takes a moment to think before replying. "I will grant your *boon*," he says. "But you may not tell him any of what I told you. Tor Warin cannot know the true goal of this mission. You may tell him only enough, but he can never see or know the book you are retrieving. And believe me, I *will* know if you choose to tell him and the consequences will be harsh." I believe him with every bone in my body, but there is still one thing I am unsure of.

"Why me? *You* are the Knight of Lex and you must know Lady Fable personally." I say despite myself.

"Very true General Yamanu, however the Lady and I have not been on good terms these last few decades." *Decades?* I chill. I remind myself that Lord Acastus is of the immortals, he isn't tied to age as I am—as us *mortals* are.

"Any particular reason why?" I ask in an attempt to shield my surprise at such a trivial fact. I know that Lord Acastus is an immortal of course however, in conversation, he seems so normal. It must have slipped my mind.

"Nothing that you need to concern yourself with." His response is quick and there is a sort of finality to his tone. I choose not to push my luck.

"When do I go?" I ask, returning to the topic at hand.

A rare smile creeps across Lord Acastus' face. "When I decide that you are ready. I am afraid that my second in command is in need of some sharpening."

CHAPTER
SEVENTEEN

I become a sword, sharpened in both mind and body, with power beyond any mortal, as Lord Acastus pushes me to a fault. For two weeks I know nothing but the sound of his voice, impossible not to obey, and the thick gleam of sweat on my body. I keep the softness in the parts of my body that I loved. The curves of my thighs, the slight swell of my stomach, the contour of my arms—but when I flex my muscles, the definition shows through. I look entirely the same, but the muscle hides underneath, disguised by a delicate facade. Lord Acastus trains me personally—he the bladesmith and I the blade—and slowly I take shape.

The Lord is blessed with gifts that no mortal could dream of. His senses are fine-tuned, and he can hear even the faintest of sounds. He trained me to discern the beats of different shoes, then the differences in the ways that various groups walk—soldiers, trainers, nobles, servants—and finally I learn the footsteps of specific people. I simply have to clear my mind and *listen* to understand.

To work on my strength, Lord Acastus set up obstacle courses in The Castle's training room. I was to carry additional weights and complete the courses under certain time restrictions. I failed constantly.

Then my legs began to grow stronger, and I grew able to do the course thrice without fail. My body was the perfect canvas for the shaping that Lord Acastus had planned. For seven years I built up strength and power, all he had to do was polish the skills.

Despite the Lord's harsh words and stern tone, the look in eyes told me that he is pleased, and I know that slowly, he grew to trust me. In between training sessions, we dined together in his formal office. At first, we were stoic—only saying the bare minimum to each other outside of official business—and then our conversation grew. Past the walls of Lex and into the rest of The Realms of Infinity, we discuss history and magic, strategy, and politics.

Lord Acastus' history lessons were often brief, but they aligned with everything I have been taught for my entire life. Professor Clara's story—her *warnings*—stray further and further from my thoughts until they are nonexistent, drowned out by Lord Acastus' words instead. His words are familiar and well understood to be true—they are *comfortable.*

I remain at Lord Acastus' side even outside of training and meals, only departing him to go to my rooms for the evening. The Lord brings me to meetings of strategy for The Undying Army itself, and slowly I begin speaking during them too. The highly ranked soldiers don't falter in their obedience to me, for I outrank them tenfold. My wishes are unbreakable law in their eyes, and by the end of the two-week period, I begin attending meetings *without* Lord Acastus. He brings me into the depths of the army blockhouses and camps, teaches me the jargon of the military, and introduces me to every lieutenant, commander, and superior in The Undying Army.

The space between The Wall and The Castle and Fortress, has always intimidated me. Maybe it's because I was orphaned there—how my parents could be within the confines of The Wall itself—that scares me. Maybe it's the whispers that mill about, of my *blessing*, of my curse. But I do not let that stop me from making rounds with the Lord.

I don't see Tor very much, except for in passing, and I still have not told him of his trip to Ingenium at the beginning of the next star cycle. Our interactions are brief as Lord Acastus is always with me or awaiting me, and at nightfall I'm always so drained that I fall into bed fully clothed. Alma stays away thankfully; I do not need her to get involved with the Lord as well. But I know that I will have to see her eventually. I continue to push away both of those visits indefinitely.

The items that I requested for my rooms are delivered promptly and I delight at my overflowing bookshelves each time I walk into my rooms. I don't have much time to read, but when I manage to stay awake for a few minutes before bed, it' usually spent doing so.

Not able to leave The Castle due to my tightly packed schedule, I'm not able to see Nova or Arche at all. Not a word comes from them either. It doesn't bother me as I barely have time to breathe, much less write back, and by the end of the first week, I almost forget about it.

Eventually, the fifteenth day of the ninth star cycle arrives and Lord Acastus is to go to Omnis for his meeting with The Infinite Knight Court. After an intense day of training and meetings, he departs late in the night without a word of goodbye. A note is slid under my door though. It leaves me very few instructions, simply stating that I am well prepared to run the realm for the day.

My only formal command is to attend The Undying Army's strategy meeting this morning. While I had gone to strategy meetings alone before, Lord Acastus was always nearby in case of dispute. This time I am alone and my anxiety builds through the morning. The meeting itself, however, goes on without fault and I am delighted at the outcome. Left with an entire day to myself, I decide to make my rounds to those I've been ignoring these last two weeks.

Zoning out to the musical *click-clack* of my new black boots, I walk down the halls of The Castle to the armory. I have become accustomed to the layout of The Castle in these last weeks, slowly making my way around as Nova and I once did as children. The memory sends a pang through my chest. One that I promptly shake off.

My walk to the armory is swift, my red cape flowing behind me. Today I wear a simple black dress with tight, long sleeves. Fate, and my dagger are both strapped to my hip. When I arrive at the armory, I walk straight into the doors, passing the guards without a word.

No one stops me now, not for anything.

Heat radiates through the armory and the sounds of metal banging on forges fills the air. I remember where Tor's workshop is, and I weave through the various workstations in the main room of the armory. Eventually, I make it to the workshop and knock twice on the already open door before stepping inside.

"Hello?" I say, unsure. When I look to the left, Tor is sitting on the worktable, the same one I found Fate's hilt on only two weeks earlier. He spins around in his chair and stands up when he sees me.

"Soleil?" He asks, surprise in his voice. "What are you doing here? Don't you have training?"

"Lord Acastus has taken his trip to The Knight Court, so I am running the place alone for the day." I say, smiling.

"Well, you should get going then, I'm sure this place would fall apart without you running it." He says with clear sarcasm in his voice.

"You're joking."

"Absolutely not." He laughs.

"I think I have a pretty good grip on the realm. I needed to run some errands." I say casually.

"So, I am just an item to cross off of a list then?" Tor replies, feigning hurt.

"If you want to think about it that way—then sure. But it might please you to know that you are the *first* item on that list." I respond, playing his game.

"What an honor."

"A blessing straight from Infinity I suppose." *A lot like me…* I turn to look at the weapons lining his walls.

Tor comes up from behind me and pulls me into a hug. "How are you?" He asks me, his voice gravelly. My heartbeat flutters as I feel his breath, warm, on my ear. *This. This is what I have missed.* I relish in the feeling of his body against mine. It feels warm, it feels like home.

"I'm good." I say, pulling away enough that I can see his face.

"The Lord hasn't been working you too hard, has he?" Tor says, pulling me back to his chest gently. He must miss me too, more than he lets on. But the gentle *thump* of his heart gives him away.

I laugh. "Hard enough that I collapse on my bed every night. Hard enough that I haven't seen you in two weeks."

"I've been keeping myself busy. And I get it, it's an interesting transition."

"You could say that again." He looks good—healthy and not too tired. Something in me worried that his association with me would be bad for his relationship with Lord Acastus, but he seems to be okay.

"But other than that, are you adjusting well? People have been talking, they are surprised at how well you seem to be handling it." His words are casual, as if common knowledge.

"I feel so closed off. Being at Lord Acastus' side means that I don't hear *anything*—it's *all* below his radar. Too trivial for his concern." I whine. I shift my tone again before speaking. "I'm glad that everyone believes that I'm adjusting well."

"That sounds awfully sarcastic, Soleil." I must not have adjusted my tone well enough then. I do not respond to Tor's words. I let my gaze wander away from him. "Soleil? I need you to talk to me." That *voice*. The vulnerability in it…

Wonderful. I have no choice but to tell him about what I did, the end of the star cycle is fast approaching, and he has to know. "I have something to tell you. I don't want you to get angry." My words are as jumbled as my thoughts.

"Tell me. Whatever it is, we'll figure it out together." When I look at Tor, his face is as grave as his voice is—unnecessary considering what I did isn't *that* bad.

"It isn't that serious."

"I don't believe you." *Probably for the best.*

"I have an assignment from Lord Acastus, I must travel to Ingenium to complete it." My voice is clearer now, and I speak each word deliberately.

"What do you have to do?"

"You are on a need-to-know basis." I reply, remembering Lord Acastus' orders.

"Then what do I *need to know?*"

"I need Lady Fable to give me access to The Boundless Library so I can find a book for Lord Acastus." The information spills out quickly and I curse Infinity for my lack of control.

"That shouldn't be too hard. Do you need me to prepare you to talk to the Lady?" *Oh, his innocence.*

"No, not exactly."

"Soleil." Tor's voice is grave once more. I can't do this. I can't drag him further into my business with the Lord and I never should have told Lord Acastus that I need Tor with me. It is my own selfishness, my own ache for Tor at my side, that urged me to do it. But if this is how I have to repent, then so be it. I look into his warm eyes and prepare for them to turn cold.

"I told Lord Acastus that I need you to go with me to Ingenium." I thank Infinity for my directness, but Tor's eyes widen at my words. His eyes remain warm though.

"Why would you do that?" He is in a clear state of bewilderment, but the volume of his voice doesn't increase. *Thank Infinity.*

"You studied there!" My voice raises in defensiveness. Completely unnecessary considering Tor has done nothing to warrant it.

"I practically got myself kicked out. I'm a traitor in Ingenium." I had not thought about that... Tor remains patient.

"I am sure it's not that bad."

"I doubt that my presence will help your case," he pauses. "Why can't the Lord do it himself?" *If only Tor knew my thoughts.*

"Lord Acastus and Lady Fable are not on good terms at the moment, I'm afraid." I respond courtly.

"So, you *have* to do this?" Tor sighs.

"I *am* his second in command."

"Believe me, I won't forget it." Tor mutters.

"And I would *love* it if you were there with me." I continue, smiling and batting my eyelashes for effect.

"How is that going to work? What do we tell her?" Tor asks, finally relenting.

"I have an idea..." I start. "She will already know that I am Lord Acastus' second in command—common knowledge among the Knights at this point, especially since they are meeting today." I have thought about this plan since Lord Acastus told me of my mission, and I know that it will work perfectly.

"Yes." Tor sighs, gesturing for me to continue.

"So, I will introduce myself as second in command, and you as my bladesmith—which is true anyway—" I am cut off before I can continue.

"Technically."

"What?" I question.

"I am, *head* blade smith. Not *your* bladesmith." He says slyly, a smile creeping onto his face.

I glare at him in response. "I outrank you. A hundred times over." Tor doesn't drop his stare. "Fine, second in command and *head bladesmith*." I say, emphasizing the last part.

"Much better."

I roll my eyes. "We will tell Lady Fable that you raved to me about the wonders of The Boundless Library, and how I have been struggling with battle strategy recently. I will tell her that the small libraries in Lex are not enough to allow me to expand my knowledge of strategy and battle, and that I need more. That is where you step in and tell the Lady that you explained how expansive The Boundless Library is, and how it would be the perfect place for me to go for research." I pause and Tor nods along. "Do you think she will believe it?"

"Lady Fable has a soft spot for the sharing of information—it should work." Tor replies after taking a moment to think.

"Great. Then I get the book for Lord Acastus and we get out." I say, satisfied by my idea.

"She will never let you leave with it." Tor responds in warning.

"I have that part covered." I say impishly, allowing myself to crack a slight smile.

"Whatever you say, *General Yamanu.*" Tor bows deeply. I scoff at his dramatics.

"Will you, do it?" I look up to meet his eyes.

"Do I have a choice, Soleil?" He says in resignation. Something in me breaks. *Have I lost his trust so soon?* Still, I am second in command and he is my soldier.

"No. Not at all."

AFTER MY CONVERSATION WITH TOR, WE SAY CURT GOOD-byes and I promise to see him again before we are to leave for Ingenium. I feel good that I have finally seen him after so many days, and even better now that he knows about the mission—mostly. Still, the resignation in his tone, the look in his eyes. They'll haunt me for a while. After I leave the armory, I immediately start walking to the Lost wing of the castle to see Alma. I have nothing to tell her, but I believe that she deserves a visit, nonetheless.

I arrive at the wing and the door is opened for me without a word. Heat radiates towards me. I delight in the memories that always come forward, while taking a moment to relish in the feeling of *home*. Alma's door is open and I stand in the doorframe, knocking twice before walking in.

"Alma? Are you there?" I ask loud enough to fill the entire room.

"Soleil, is that you?" I smile at Alma's voice, warm as ever. She walks out of the small bathroom and I wave at her.

"Yes, it is." Her face fills with emotion and she walks over to hug me. I hold her tightly and we don't speak until she pulls away.

"Come here let me fix you something to eat. You are much too skinny!" She says, half pushing me to a seat near her window.

"Alma, I actually don't have much time." I respond. It's nothing but the truth.

"You should always have time for meals." She says, brushing me off.

Not knowing how else to explain to her that I *can't* stay, I say the first thing that comes to mind. "I am running the realm today, Alma."

"Excuse me?" She stops pushing me at once and I turn around to find her face painted in shock.

"Lord Acastus is in Omnis for a meeting with The Infinite Knight Court. I was left in charge." I talk slowly in an attempt to calm her.

"Then what are you doing here, tribulatio?"

"Alma it's fine, I have a moment. Besides, I had to come see you, it has been quite a while." My words come out with conviction.

"It has," she pauses. "I watched your games, you know." She adds matter-of-factly.

"You did?"

"Yes. There was an indoor viewing room here in The Castle. You were wonderful, Soleil." I swear that I see a glimmer of pride in her eyes, but it leaves quickly. Alma is usually so expressive I'm shocked by the clear repression of her emotions today.

"Thank you." I respond curtly.

"Congratulations on your promotion." Alma's words feel *off*. I can't put my finger on the tone, however.

"I *am* proud of you Soleil." Alma says with a sigh. "I do worry though." *Not again.* I can't deal with other people worrying about me, not when I have so much to worry about myself.

"Alma, there is no need to *worry*."

"Have you seen Nova and Arche since you moved here?" She asks offhandedly.

"No—" She cuts me off before I can continue.

"Soleil, you must go see them."

"I will, I was going to visit The Fortress today, I swear to Infinity." I feel as if I'm pleading for my life.

"Soleil, this is more than an old woman's worries. I don't need you to lose yourself." Those last words are piercing and I burn as she speaks them.

"I am right here! Alma, I am right here. I have not changed. I am not *losing myself*. I am the same person I have always been!" No tears fill my eyes, I may be fire, but I know how to let my flames burn cold.

"With more power." Alma reminds me, discipline in her voice. I feel like a child.

"With a higher position." I correct her. "Power is in the name, not the thing itself. I hold a powerful position." My voice does not waver, I will not let it.

"Does that not mean that you are inherently *powerful?*" Her words are taunting, but I refuse to let them diminish me. They are cruel and cold, everything that Alma is not.

"No."

"The fact that you say that shows that you are drunk with power already."

My breath hitches. "Bold words Alma, truly. You have shut me down every time I talk about moving up the ranks, telling me not to *lose myself.*" My words come fast, but my tone remains powerful. I am second in command of The Undying Army and I will not be belittled by my ex-caretaker.

"I will not deny it." Alma turns away from me.

"I never understood why. Never understood why you felt the need to tie me down when I can be so much more. I *do* have power and it feels *good*. It feels incredible. I can make changes that were never possible before. No one— in the entire realm—outranks me, besides Lord Acastus himself. So, tell me why you never believed I could handle it!" Despite my efforts, I scream the last words. Alma has caged me in for so long and despite her love for me, I have had enough.

"I know you are strong tribulatio—" her words are simple enough, but she keeps the same condescending pitch.

"Stop calling me that! I am not a child; I am not *trouble.*" My voice is raw and my throat tightens with emotion. *I will not cry.*

"Soleil. You are strong and powerful. You always have been. I have seen many take the dark path, climbing the ranks of power, and getting poisoned by it in the end.

They lose themselves; I do not need that to happen to you." As if she can stop it, even if it did. I resent her, resent her words.

"I am not everyone else. I am more and I do not need you to tell me not to lose myself when I am right here." My voice is barely more than a gasp.

"Your cloak. It is different." Alma says casually.

"What does that matter?" I ask coldly.

"You are deep in Lord Acastus' trap." She scans my body.

"Believe me Alma, I am playing a game of my own." I swallow my emotions and push the words out.

"But you are losing."

"You are so blind to my potential that you can't even fathom that *I* may come out on top." My words bite like the cold winter air of Lex. *I want them to.*

"He has you trapped so well, tribulatio. I hope you remember my words." Alma warns.

"I do not need to." I speak. I hope that my words cut through the air, I hope that she feels what I do.

Pulling my hood up over my head, I spin around and walk straight out of Alma's room, past the Lost wing of The Castle, and out of the main castle doors as well.

MY WALK ACROSS THE BRIDGE—FUELED PURELY BY RAGE—IS unnervingly brief. Before I realize that I left The Castle in a fury, my legs carry me to The Fortress. I want nothing more than to collapse into Nova and Arche's arms.

I walk up the stairs and to the doors of The Fortress, which open without a word from me. I am surprised at that, considering that my hood is pulled far over my head, but I realize that they must recognize the color. My surprise continues when I am not met with heat radiating from every corner of the stone fortress. In the last two weeks, I have grown so used to the warmth that I forgot about the constant cold I lived in for seven years.

Quickening my pace, I eventually make it to Female Sleeping Chamber G. I knock twice but no one answers. The door is unlocked so I push it open and find no one inside. The fireplace is unlit and the banners that adorned our walls in a beautiful patchwork, are all taken down. The beds are pristinely made and none of the trunks are left open. It's eerily quiet. I keep my hand on Fate's hilt.

Frantic, I am out of breath by the time I check the dining hall, common room, battlefield, and Arche's old sleeping chamber. Utterly confused, I begin walking aimlessly down the halls, trying to find any sign of Arche and Nova. Very few people are in The Fortress at all. In my fruitless search, I bump into Professor Clara, her flowing silver hair undone.

Her black eyes widen at the sight of me. She looks… dull. "Soleil is that you?"

"Yes, hello Professor." I can't help but notice that her skin—usually pearlescent and glowing—is grey and sagging.

"How are you my dear." Professor Clara asks genuinely.

"Good. Thank you." I say briskly. Despite my worry for her wellbeing, I want only to ask her about Nova and Arche.

"Adjusting well to the new job?"

"Yes, thank you. I have a question actually." I reply.

"I may have an answer—what is it?" She says, understanding the urgency in my tone. I pray to Infinity for forgiveness, for not really caring about Professor Clara right now.

"Nova Ignotus and Arche Inconnu. They were both in my year, Nova was in my squadron. I can't seem to find them and I have searched the entirety of The Fortress." My tone grows frenzied as I speak and my words tumble out.

"My dear," she speaks slowly. "Nova Ignotus and Arche Inconnu have been graduated from The Academy."

"Excuse me?" I say more rudely than I anticipate.

"I thought you knew. It was a big event here in The Academy. As Lord Acastus' second in command, you *should* have known." Professor Clara is skeptical as she talks, but I believe her—it *does* explain the disappearance of my two best friends. I take a moment and scan the woman. *Infinitely blessed, my—*

"I am sure the Lord simply forgot to tell me." I reply coolly. So much news has been filtered out from my radar recently that I honestly don't care.

"Two days after you left, Lord Acastus announced that seventh through tenth years in The Academy will be graduated at once." Professor Clara says as if it is obvious information—it is I suppose. To everyone except for me.

"Excuse me, Professor." I say before running past her and to The Fortress' doors. My feet carry me quickly and my dress does not betray me as I run out of The Fortress and across the bridge to the military blockhouses and camps. My voice is raw as I scream their names against the cold. No one answers though, I am simply met with the stares of countless soldiers as I run from camp to camp. I am near the edge of The Wall, its stature imposing and all-encompassing as I get closer. I call out Nova and Arche's names again and, for the first time, I hear mine in return.

"Sol!" A female voice calls from behind me.

"Soleil!" A male voice follows.

I turn around to find Nova and Arche, frail, tired, and their clothes in rags behind me. I run to them, colliding with their bodies. When we pull away, the two of them lead me to a large camp and we sit near a fire.

"Please, tell me everything." I say first, exasperated by the struggle it was to find them.

"Co-lieutenants." Nova says smugly.

"The day after you were crowned second in command, Lord Acastus returned to The Fortress. He called us to the dining hall and told us that four years worth of students will be graduated immediately." Arche fills in the rest.

I see the picture in my mind. That was the same day that Lord Acastus gave me my mission. After a quick tour around The Castle, he left, and I didn't see him for the rest of the day.

"Our ranks stood and, once you left, Arche and I were tied for first." Nova continues, satisfied with herself.

"We were named Lieutenants of adjoining squadrons."

I turn back to Nova after Arche finishes speaking. "Our squadron?" I ask, struggling.

"And 7G of course." Nova responds. I sit for a moment; my mind clouded by thoughts. I can do nothing but stare into the depths of the bonfire.

"You didn't know." Arche says.

"No."

"How come? You *are* second in command." Nova asks curiously.

"Lord Acastus is incredibly busy and I was in training myself. It must have been too trivial a concern to tell me." The truth is that I have no idea why the Lord didn't tell me.

"Too *trivial?*" Arche muses.

"When I barely had time for meals these last few weeks, breathing became trivial, Arch. I don't care much, the only thing that bothers me is that I haven't heard from you in two weeks." I reply coldly.

"We are still on probation—no letters and no visiting The Castle or The Fortress." It makes sense. They *are* seventh year lieutenants. I doubt they will get full privileges for quite some time.

"If you weren't Second in Command of this entire army, you would probably be escorted off of the premises right now." I laugh at Arche's addition.

"So, you two have been living in tents for the last two weeks?" I joke.

"And for two more." Nova's tone is begrudging and I can't help but chuckle.

"Mandatory training." Arche adds bitterly.

"Then what? Lieutenants move to The Castle, right?" I see a better future ahead, one where all three of us live in The Castle—Generals and Lieutenants in our own re-spects.

"Not exactly," Arche says. "They graduated so many of us that they aren't doing that. We have a set of block-houses with our names on them. The rest of the squadron remains in the camp. People are complaining about space as it is."

"What do you mean they are *complaining about space?*" I ask.

"We are packed in the tents. They are pushing mul-tiple squadrons into camps only made for one. Too many of us too quickly." She pauses and lowers her voice. "There was talk—people want to move beyond The Wall. It makes sense—why stay within it when the magic made to keep the weather out doesn't work anyway?" Nova's words ring in my mind. *Move beyond The Wall?* That is im-possible, no one has ever gone beyond Lex's walls.

I recall Professor Clara's lesson for a moment. She told me that the battle between Marcellus Lex and Dun-can Lex decimated the realm, making Lex the wasteland that we currently know. But if The Wall was built by the first Knight of Lex—*before* Lex was turned bitter, then why was The Wall built in the first place? *Did its construction have anything to do with the weather at all?*

"I will see what I can do." I say, shifting the subject to something less rebellious. If I talk to Lord Acastus, I'm sure that Nova and Arche can get rooms in The Castle. I imagine the life I can have with my two best friends living with me once more.

"Don't—" Nova replies quickly. "We want to remain with our units. In the spring we are planning on moving back into the actual camps too. I *would* stay here now, but I can't exactly lead when my limbs are frozen."

"Are you sure?" I ask them both.

"Positive. This is what we have always dreamt of, remember?" Arche answers. Emotion floods me when I realize that I can't have this dream anymore.

"I do." The three of us go silent at my words.

Nova eventually breaks the lull. "How have you been, *General Yamanu?*"

"Good. Tired and overworked, but good."

"Welcome to the club." Arche laughs.

"Can you stay for a while? We were just going to have a meal." Nova asks, smiling in invitation.

"I can't." I say quickly.

"I'm sure the Lord can give you a moment's rest—"

I cut Arche off before he can continue. "The Lord isn't here. He's taking a visit to Omnis for his Knight Court meeting. I am running the realm myself today."

"Perfect, then you can—" Nova stands.

"I really can't. I have taken too much time to myself already. If Lord Acastus returns to the realm and new problems have arisen, it will be me on the execution block." Nova's smile drops from her face and she sits back down.

"Does he really do that?" Arche asks.

"What?" I reply.

"Execute people."

I scoff at his words. "Goodbye Arche." I stand and Nova and Arche follow. The three of us hug tightly.

"Stay safe." Nova mumbles.

"You too. I'll see you guys at The Eternal Dance, right?" I ask, still pressed up against Arche's chest.

"Of course, I'm going to get fitted for a suit as soon as we can visit The Castle." He replies.

"Come and visit me when you do." I say, pulling away from my two best friends.

"We will." Nova assures me.

"I love you both."

I walk away from the camp and make my way back to The Castle; back to *my* home.

CHAPTER

EIGHTEEN

Lord Acastus remains relentless in his training—as intense as Lex's biting cold. Two more weeks pass and the Lord continues to beat down on me with his words. After his visit to The Infinite Knight Court, he grew flighty and tense and I feel it every day.

Since my talk with Nova and Arche, I wonder why they are not in The Undying Army's battle strategy meetings that I have been attending. But I quickly realize that their probationary period must be preventing them from attending. I keep my distance, not wishing to harm their progress or give the superiors reason to punish them. I keep my distance from Tor as well. After telling him about our trip to Ingenium, I worried that I overburdened him. My relationship with Alma remains the same, however I do not feel guilty about what happened between the two of us.

When Lord Acastus returns from Omnis, we immediately get back to work. The two of us work on sword training and I find that I put up a good fight against the Lord. He wins, every time, but that is to be expected by an immortal, and one born in steel especially. I push my body and mind to the limits during those fights—my arms shaking and my legs burning after each one—but I never relent.

In between sword fighting lessons, Lord Acastus makes me pick up a bow. I was never the best at archery and I didn't care for Nova was always behind me, taking out enemies from afar while I fought them up close. I learned how to use a bow very generally while at The Academy, but once I made it clear that I preferred a sword, the superiors left me to my own devices. Lord Acastus explained however, that a *soldier* can be skilled in one thing, but a *general* must be skilled in everything. So, with Lord Acastus standing behind me, adjusting my grip on the bow, fixing my stance, and guiding me to a proper shot—I learn how to shoot. Turns out, I am a pretty good shot to begin with. After some tinkering with my position and after learning how to aim properly, my shots are clean and consistent, full of power even at long distances.

By the end of the star cycle, I no longer *look* like the perfect general, I *am* one. My body feels more powerful than ever before, fine-tuned to battle and sharpened to perfection. My mind follows suit as I learn to see every outcome of a battle even before it happens. I am flawless. I revel in the feeling.

On the last day of the ninth star cycle, Lord Acastus declares that my training is complete. He calls the end of our training session at *0200* after eight hours of evaluations, leaving me with the directions to meet him in his office at *0700* for dinner. And so we can prepare for my mission.

Tomorrow, I will travel to Ingenium, arm-in-arm with Tor Warin. I will complete my first official assignment for the Knight of Lex, finally proving myself as second in command of The Undying Army.

I glance at the clock on top of the fireplace, it reads *0615*. I will have to leave soon to make it to Lord Acastus' office in time, I think, while sitting on the large and fluffy sofa in front of the fireplace. I am reading a book off the shelves that surround me. Today, it is a simple one on sword care, which, oddly enough, is much different than dagger care. I take a sip of my tea—hot and sweetened with extra honey—and savor the warmth of the fire. With a sigh, I set the tea down and tuck a slip of paper into the book to mark my page before walking it back to its spot on the shelves. I smile at the sight, the sheer number of texts to explore.

I am already dressed for the meeting with the Lord. I wear a simple white dress with a corseted, bloodred overskirt. The dress is thick and warm, so I have no need for my cloak—especially when The Castle is so warm already. My red cloak has become somewhat of an identifier for the citizens of Lex. A way to spot their second in command at a distance. So, even when I am not wearing my cloak, I try to include red somewhere else in my clothing.

That task became easy enough once I realized that Lord Acastus stocked my closet with items in that very shade.

Already missing my spot in front of the fire, I walk into my bedroom, then to my closet where I find a pair of black, lace-less boots. They have a slight heel to them and are reinforced at the toe.

Grabbing for the scabbard of my dagger, I cringe when my hand grazes my crown instead. I still have not gotten used to wearing it. I only do so if it's absolutely mandatory. So far it has only been required of me when Lord Acastus made an announcement to The Undying Army about an adjustment in training schedules. The event was trivial enough that I didn't mind, but I refuse to even look at the crown now, afraid that I will enjoy it too much if I do. Sometimes I put it on, staring at myself in the mirror for only a moment before tossing it out of sight. I feel *powerful* in it, as if my power is not simply in my title. *As if I am powerful myself.*

It feels good—and that terrifies me.

I quickly fasten the scabbard of my dagger around my waist, not bothering to grab Fate, as this is a simple dinner. I walk out of my closet and into the bathroom to check my appearance in the mirror. My skin is glowing, a combination of a higher quality diet, and being shielded from Lex's dry air in The Castle. My hair looks wonderful, the curls thriving in the warmth. I am finally used to—and I even enjoy—the new length.

When I am satisfied with my appearance, I turn off the lights and walk back into the living room. There, I clean up the remnants of the snack I ordered earlier, putting the plate, teapot, and mug near the door for the handmaidens to collect later. Taking account of myself and ensuring that my scabbard is secure, and my corset properly laced, I walk out of my room.

The walk to Lord Acastus' office is brief. After living in The Castle for a star cycle, I have it mapped the way I once did as a child, this time with the added benefit of having no area restricted to me. My strides are powerful and I keep my head up as I walk. Though my limbs are loose—ready to grab my dagger if necessary—my status ensures that it won't be. Even if I didn't hold the most powerful position—besides that of the Knight—in all of Lex, most people saw my battle simulations, or the ruthless training that followed. I can only assume that *anyone* would stay away, even if I was a foot soldier.

When I arrive at Lord Acastus' office, I knock twice on the door that is already cracked open.

"Come in." The Lord speaks coolly. I walk into his office without a second thought and he lets out a slight smile when he sees me. "My second in command, looking as lovely as ever."

"Thank you, my Lord." His eyes trail me with each step, an icy intensity behind them. It caresses my arms, the exposed skin of my chest.

"General Yamanu," he begins. "I am pleased with your performance thus far." He sounds genuine and I am filled with relief at his words.

"I appreciate it my Lord, but it is your training that has improved my performance." I smile despite my better judgement.

"Only an incredibly skilled soldier—excuse me—*general*, could have kept up with my training as you have."

I take my seat at the desk in front of him. "Ah, General Yamanu, you needn't sit. We will be going somewhere else for dinner this evening." I puzzle at his words.

"Anywhere I know?" I ask, confused.

"Quite the opposite actually." He smiles, a true smile, flashing his perfectly white teeth. His beauty is unnerving. The way he looks no older that I am… It is only the endless wisdom and years behind those eyes that stirs something in my mortal soul. Something that marks him as a predator, and me as prey. I stand quickly and walk back to the door.

"Very well. Are you ready my Lord?" I ask civilly.

"Yes, General Yamanu. I am." He rises from his seat and walks towards me. I reach for the door, but he stops me. "That is not necessary, I can get the door myself." He is so *close*. I take a step back, dazed by his presence. Lord Acastus pushes open the door and I swiftly walk through, not wishing to get close to him again.

"Lead the way my Lord." I gesture to him. He nods and walks next to me, holding his arm out for me to take. I shudder at the thought of being led so intimately, but he *is* the Knight of Lex, and I am his second. I take his arm gingerly and we walk into the halls of The Castle.

The walk itself is not very long and eventually we make it to a secluded wing of The Castle. Lord Acastus' pace is steady and I do not struggle to keep up with him. Our arms remain linked the whole time. It's dizzying, being so close to the Lord. I attribute it to the pure power that radiates from him—the grace of an immortal—that he handles so impeccably. Despite my training, despite becoming *the perfect general,* I am a stumbling fool beside him. My mortal curse.

Once we reach the end of the wing, Lord Acastus finally releases my arm. I relish in the respite that comes with no longer being attached to the Lord, but I am confused as to why we are standing in front of a wall.

"General Yamanu, do we have any visitors?" He asks me. A simple enough request. I take a moment to listen for footsteps, the rustle of clothing, the slice of metal. No sound disrupts the air.

"No, my Lord." I respond curtly.

"Very well General." Lord Acastus pushes in on one of the stones of the wall and—to my surprise—it gives. The stone moves at least four inches into the wall, and then a larger section of stone in front of me, taller than Lord Acastus and at least twice as wide, moves as well. I gasp in shock as the stone swings open and reveals a room.

"Is this—" I begin, my voice soft from shock.

"My chambers, yes." Lord Acastus finishes. He loops his arm through mine and leads me inside. *Infinity*—Lord Acastus' personal chambers. Ice runs through my veins.

The room itself is extremely simple, a fireplace roars and ornately carved stone—different than that of the rest of The Castle—makes up the walls. In this room, there is nothing but a rug, a small sofa, a dining table with two chairs, and another door, which if his chambers are anything like my own, goes on to a bedroom, bathroom, and closet.

On the dining table lies an assortment of steaming foods. The scents mix and fill the space. My head spins at the strong smells and my stomach began to growl. I curse

Infinity for my appetite as Lord Acastus walks me to the table. He releases my arm and pulls out a chair, gesturing for me to sit. He pushes me into the table gently and then goes to the chair across from my own.

The table holds an entire roast chicken with vegetables adorning it. There is a basket of assorted breads, some chopped from a larger loaf, others small rolls. Small plates of various butters surround the basket. There is a large bowl of pasta in a creamy white sauce and I know that it is the one that has become my favorite while living in The Castle. The final bowl holds a hearty salad with mixed greens, nuts, seeds, and a white dressing.

"What is this for, my Lord?" I ask, looking up at him.

"It is a congratulations of sorts. For completing your initial training." He replies, meeting my gaze. His eyes remain filled with force, but after spending so many days staring into them, I have learned how to fight the urge to shy away. Instead, I look deeper.

"This is far from necessary, my Lord. I am simply doing my job."

"General Yamanu, you are doing *more*." I warm at his words. His tone is so authentic that for a moment, it feels as if he is not an immortal. Until his power creeps up on me, tendrils of icy air that work their way into my hair, my skin. Forceful by nature.

"You may call me Soleil, Lord Acastus. At least outside of official business. I believe we have both earned that." I crack a small smile.

"As you wish, Soleil." He winks. *He winks…* "Enough with the, *my Lord* as well. At least outside of official business," a smile then. "Please call me Acastus, very few people do."

"I am afraid that's not proper, my Lord." I say as respectfully as possible.

"Of course." He replies, voice resigned. "Let us eat then." I nod and stand to serve him as I always do but he gestures for me to sit. "Tonight, Soleil, I serve you." His voice is thick and velvety. It reaches out and coats my skin as thoroughly as his flowing magic. I sit back down slowly and nod once more, taking a deep breath for confidence.

Lord Acastus carves the chicken and places some on my plate, adding servings of pasta, salad, vegetables, and a roll. I am uncomfortable at the actions, the opposite of what is normal between the two of us. But I remain still until Lord Acastus has served himself as well.

He reaches for an ornate silver jug on the side of the table. "A drink? It's wine, only the finest from Omnis itself."

"I don't drink my Lord." I never have. So many soldiers die each year—*drunk* out of their minds—impaling themselves on their own swords. I will not be one of them.

"Just a sip. In celebration." Lord Acastus urges.

"No disrespect my Lord, but I do not wish for a drink. Thank you for your offer." I say more sternly.

Lord Acastus nods in resignation and reaches for another jug, this one made of glass and filled with water. "Is this alright then?"

"Yes, that is fine." I nod. The Lord reaches for my goblet and fills it with water, then his own with wine.

"A toast. To my second in command, General Soleil Yamanu." He speaks. I grow uncomfortable by the way he phrases it, as if a crowd of people surrounds us. I tap my goblet to his and take a sip of the water. After that, we eat in silence.

Once the meal is over, I begin cleaning up the plates, stacking them and organizing the table for the maids to clean once we left. My heart beats quickly and I know that Lord Acastus is watching my every move.

"*Soleil?*" He asks, stretching out the syllables of my name.

"Yes, my Lord?" I respond, turning to him.

"You can stop now." I am puzzled at his reaction to my cleaning, the exact thing that I do after each of our meals.

"My Lord—" I begin.

"Soleil. You are a *General*. My *second in command*, you must stop doing jobs that are beneath you." I feel my face flush red with embarrassment. He is right. *Who am I to make a maid's job easier?*

"Of course, my Lord. I am sorry for my error." I say, turning away. He stands with a sigh and walks in front of me. His hand rises to grip my chin and he gently tilts my head upwards to meet his eyes. There is nothing, *nothing*, between us now. Not an inch between his magic, his power, and me.

"Soleil, you are *my* second in command. You are *mine*. As long as you live, you will be bathed in luxury and power. You needn't belittle yourself." My breath is shaky as I look into the eyes of the Knight of Lex. I remind myself repeatedly that he is not a mortal as I am. It takes everything in me to reply.

"I will keep that in mind, Lord Acastus." I say with all the courage I can muster.

His hand drops from my chin. He loop his arm through mine and leads me out of his hidden chambers and back into The Castle's halls. I have no idea where we are going. Clearly not to my chambers, as they are in the opposite direction, and on a completely different floor. Not to the armory or the training rooms either, since it is the wrong floor as well. We finally make it to a simple wooden door, and Lord Acastus knocks thrice.

Tor Warin opens the door and I flood with happiness. I can't stop the smile from spreading on my face when I meet his eyes. But that smile begins to dissipate when I realize that I am arm-in-arm with the Knight of Lex. *What am I doing?*

"My Lord." Tor says with a curt nod. "My General." He adds, his eyes flashing to meet mine for a moment. I despise that title on his tongue. I miss the way he says my name. With all of the warmth and light the realms have to offer.

Tor steps aside and holds the door open, gesturing for us to come inside. His chambers are quaint. Simple stone walls, a desk, an armoire, and a workbench. On the far wall, something has a curtain thrown over it. I can't make out the shape beneath.

Lord Acastus releases my arm and goes to shake Tor's hand. "Is it complete?" The Lord asks Tor.

"I have never missed a deadline, my Lord." Tor replies, resigned.

"Let us see then." I have no idea what they are talking about, but Tor gestures to the covered shape and I walk closer to it.

On Lord Acastus' nod, Tor rips the curtain off to reveal two mannequins. The larger one—clearly meant for a man—wears a tight fitting, and well made, set of black pants and a long-sleeved shirt. Over top is a black breastplate that almost blends into the fabric. There are also matching cuisses on the thighs, grieves on the calves, and gauntlets around the wrists. Straps of black leather cross over the breastplate and I assume that there are two sword sheaths on the back. There is a black leather belt as well, with room for multiple daggers. The entire thing is covered by a thick black cloak that wraps asymmetrically, covering most of the mannequin's body. It is simple and unassuming, good for stealth.

It is the smaller of the two mannequins however, that steals my attention. This mannequin has on a matching set of white—battle thermals, I conclude after inspecting the fabric. They are thicker and of much higher quality than my old ones from my time in The Academy.

Over the thermals lies a gold breastplate. I let out a gasp when I realize that it is the same one I wore during the battle simulations. It is engraved with the whorls that adorn Fate and my dagger. The gauntlets, grieves, and cuisses are matching too, all engraved with the tiny swirls that you can only see from up close. Over the mannequin is another blood red cloak, this one thick and sturdy. I finger the fabric and it is clear that it is made for battle. On the ground is a pair of white leather lace up boots, clearly enforced with steel at the toe box.

"What is this?" I ask, looking up to Lord Acastus.

"You have a very important mission tomorrow. I cannot let *my* General leave this realm if she is not perfectly dressed." He says simply. The emphasis on the word *my* sends a chill down my spine. As if his magic is possessively tracing the sensitive skin of my back.

"It's mine?" I ask, bewilderment in my voice.

"Of course, General." The Lord replies.

"What about the other one?" I query.

"That one is mine." Tor smiles, the first unguarded expression I have seen from him this evening. "While you will clearly outshine me—I need to at least *look* as if I am on your level." I let out a gentle laugh. My hands move to the golden breastplate.

"It's perfect. Thank you." I say to both Tor and Lord Acastus.

"The endless pocket has already been sewn into the cloak. Once your mission is complete, it will be removed." Lord Acastus adds sternly.

"Of course, my Lord."

"Tomorrow, I need both of you to meet at my office at *oh eight hundred hours.* Please be fully suited." He turns to me. "General Yamanu, I need you to have your sword and dagger sheathed at your thigh," a pause. "And your crown atop your head. Your handmaidens will arrive at your chambers at *oh five hundred hours* to prepare you." I do not understand why I will need to be *prepared* for tomorrow, or why my handmaidens will be required to help me, but I nod anyway.

"As you wish my Lord."

"Very well. Get some rest, and I will see both of you in the morning." Lord Acastus leaves quickly after that, closing the door behind him. I practically fall into Tor's arms the moment the door closes.

"Are you alright Soleil?" He says, concern in his tone.

"Mmhm." I take a deep breath, lungs filling with the scent of a crackling fire. No, that is just Tor. He must have just left the armory.

"Do you like the armor? I didn't know if you would—"

I cut him off. "It's perfect." I say, pulling away to look up at him. "As always."

"I am glad you think so, those engravings were a pain." His hands move down to the small of my back, absentmindedly stroking.

I laugh and pull out of his arms. "I have pretty good taste. Thank Infinity that I have an incredible bladesmith to make my dreams reality."

Tor hugs me from behind. His arms wrap around my waist, and his chin rests on my head. "Yeah. Thank Infinity."

We stand there for long minutes, simply admiring the work. I notice small details that I hadn't before. Like how Tor's black breastplate has the same whorls engraved into it that mine does. I smile at the thought of Tor spending countess hours making the same markings in his breastplate as he did to mine. They seem to be perfect foils of each other in every way. I also notice how Tor's breathing has synced with my own. After the minutes pass, Tor is the first to break the silence.

"Let me pack everything for you so you can take it back to your rooms." He says, pulling away from me. I nod in response and sit on his bed.

I can't help but yield to my thoughts in the silence. Tomorrow I am going to leave the realm for the first time *ever.* I know nothing outside of The Wall, and suddenly I am going to travel space itself to leave. I shudder at the thought.

"Soleil?" Tor is kneeling in front of me. I feel wetness drip down my face—tears. I move to wipe them, ashamed at my unnecessary emotion.

"Soleil?" Tor repeats, more worried than before. He takes my hands in his, the callouses on his hands more pronounced that usual. "What is wrong?"

"I have never left the realm. My entire life has been lived in the confines of this castle, then The Fortress, and back to The Castle again. I know *nothing* beyond this stone." I hesitate in an attempt to calm myself. "And yet— tomorrow I am to leave. Tomorrow I am General Soleil Yamanu, second in command of The Undying Army. A fancy title for someone who has never stepped foot out of her realm."

"That doesn't matter." Tor begins. "I have been to Ingenium and back and I am confident that there is no one as powerful as you in *any of the realms.* Soleil, you are *it.*" His hands reach to cup my face, thumbs wiping the tears away. I raise my hands to cover his and my breaths begin to slow.

"It doesn't feel right—*leaving.*" I think of Nova and Arche and how they remain in the military camps right now. I think of how my dream was once to lead a squadron into battle with Nova at my side. My heart breaks. Once I leave the realm tomorrow, it will *never* happen.

"Sometimes we *have* to leave, that way we can return and see everything as if it is new once more." I calm at Tor's words. How he is able to quell my panic is beyond me. Eventually, he rises to finish packing my new battle gear.

"Thank you, Tor." I say as he hands me the white leather bag.

"Anytime, Soleil." He replies. "See you tomorrow, *General Yamanu.*"

CHAPTER
NINETEEN

A stone table.
Seven ornate goblets.
Seven gilded thrones.
Seven shining Knights.
A pair of piercing blue eyes.
"I will find a way."
One goblet lifted.
Six goblets rose in unison

Not again. Not again. I pull against the force of the dream, but it is relentless in its efforts to disturb me. I have no body, no way to pull myself out. I have no choice but to give in and wait for the rising of the six goblets. But even then, the dream holds me in its trap. I see nothing but the goblets rising again and again. I can't leave. A hand is on my arm, but I have no body. I shake and finally open my eyes.

A handmaiden looks down on me and I can't make out much of her face for it is obscured by the hood of her cloak. My breaths are shallow and burning, my covers thrown off my body. I watch my chest rise and fall quickly as I become accustomed to my body once more. That dream has not crossed my mind since the morning I was crowned as second in command. And today—it held me in its grasp, not even allowing me to find reprieve in waking.

The handmaiden still stares at me, completely still. "Are you alright Miss?"

"Yes." I respond curtly; the handmaiden leaves without a word. In the last star cycle, I have woken up of my own accord every morning, my brain hardwired to my routine of early waking from life in The Academy. Today though, the handmaidens wake me to prepare me for my mission in Ingenium. With a sigh, I rise from my bed and make my way directly to the bathing chamber which—to my delight—is already prepared for me.

My shower is quick and cold. I scrub my body raw with soap and a washcloth, and do the same with my scalp, holding my head under the stream of cold water to wake myself up. When I am thoroughly awake—and scrubbed to the bone—I shut the water off. A set of red lounging thermals are laid out for me on the counter, so I pull them on quickly and tie my hair in a towel.

Still dazed from my dream, I walk out of the bathing room and back into my bedroom. The handmaidens are bustling around my chambers, making my bed, clearing the clothing from my floors, and putting away the books strewn about my bedside tables. I rarely let them clean my rooms even when I am not inside—they work hard enough as is—but I know that even if I protest, they will not stop now. So, I leave them to their duties, secretly relieved that my room is finally getting a good cleaning.

I take a seat on the sofa in front of the already blazing fire. The heat is intoxicating as I reach for my plate of food and pull the metal lid from it. My plate is stacked high with my favorites that are rotated for me every morning. Today it is thin cakes with syrup and butter, as well as eggs, shredded potatoes, and fruit. To drink, I have a goblet of juice. I pull my hair from the towel before digging into my plate, shaking the curls out so they can dry evenly.

The two handmaidens—whose names I do not know—still scurry around the room. They are almost indistinguishable to me, their faces always concealed in shadow, however I know that they rotate daily. Each of them look slightly different in stature—some taller than others, some thinner—but they are never the exact same. Once I finish my breakfast, eating the last bites of the thin cakes and the remaining eggs, I set my plate down and become absorbed by the light of the fire.

"Are you ready for us to prepare you, Miss?" One of the handmaidens asks. Despite her soft voice, I am startled by the question. It takes me a moment to pull my eyes away from the fire and turn to her.

"Mmhm." I nod in reply, wrenching myself from the comfort of the sofa. The handmaiden—the shorter of the two that are here today—gestures to my bedroom and I follow obediently. A chair is placed in front of my bathroom vanity, so I sit. As soon as I do so, the taller hand-maiden begins removing small pots and tubes of product from a black bag. The shorter, walks a metal contraption out of the bathing chamber and into the living room.

The taller handmaiden begins putting small amounts of product onto a brush and I quickly realize that it is makeup.

Before it can hit my face, I stop her. "That is not necessary, thank you."

"Miss, the Lord himself requested it." My stomach lurches at her words and I know that I have no choice but to let it happen. I am still General though, so I use my position to my advantage.

"Keep it simple then. No face makeup, I despise it." I reply, my voice stronger. It is a similar tone to what I use during council meetings, and it seems to work, for the handmaiden puts down the brush that holds the flesh toned product. The shorter handmaiden returns after that, with the metal contraption nowhere to be found. She grabs a hairbrush from the bag and begins combing through my hair. I wince at the crunching sound that follows. Typically, if I wish to brush my hair, I would do it while wet. But my hair is now bone dry from sitting by the fire and it protests every pass of the Infinity forsaken tool.

After brushing my hair, she sprays a product that smells of lemon and rakes it through. My curls are lost to the motion of the hairbrush and my hair is puffed out. Knowing that I have pushed my luck on the makeup, I choose not to object. The shorter handmaiden leaves the bathroom once more.

The taller one continues on my makeup, allowing me to brush my eyebrows the way I like them before she applies a pomade. Then, she puts a black gel on my eyelashes, and finishes off with a lipstick of deep red, similar to the shade of my cloak.

The shorter handmaiden returns with the metal contraption. When she squeezes the handle and the clamps close, I realize what it is. I do not disagree when she takes small portions of my hair and presses them between the hot plates. My curls disappear entirely and are replaced with sections of pin straight hair. I can't help but cringe at the heat on my neck and the crackling of my hair. Once my hair is completely straight, the handmaiden parts it down the middle and touches up any areas that are unsatisfactory.

When the handmaidens announce that they are finished, I feel unrecognizable. Despite the changes being subtle, my features are almost elevated in a way I have never seen. I turn away from the mirror quickly, horrified at the fact that I don't see myself in the beautiful creature, at all.

I see the Second in Command of The Undying Army.

"Thank you for your work. It's wonderful." I say curtly, attempting to muster up as much authenticity as I can. The words still come out cold, despite my efforts.

"Your battle thermals are laid out in your closet, please don them and then we will help you into the rest of your gear." The shorter handmaiden says.

I rise from my seat in front of the vanity and walk quickly to the closet. I shut the door and before I can think about doing otherwise, I strip off the lounging thermals, careful not to ruin the hair or makeup, and slide into the pristine white battle thermals. They glide on perfectly and for a moment I can't tell where my skin stops and the thermals begin. I open the door and the handmaidens rush in.

Together, they help me into the white lace up boots, gold breastplate, gauntlets, grieves, and cuisses. I can't help but smile at Tor's work as everything fits me perfectly. Each piece of golden metal, formed perfectly over my curves, holding them graciously. As I imagine his hands would. I shiver at the thought.

I strap Alma's dagger—*my dagger*—I think, correcting myself. While I have never been one for naming weapons, now that my sword is named, my dagger needs one too. I pause for a moment and pull the dagger from its scabbard; one look and the name comes to me, as if it has been waiting for seven years.

Fury.

Fate and Fury. I smile at the names, so perfect for what my life had become. My smile continues as I strap Fury tightly to my thigh. Fate goes next, and I strap the empty sheath around my waist before sliding the magnificent sword in place. The two beautiful blades adorn my body with their lethal perfection.

Once my scabbards are secure, the handmaidens wrap my new cloak around my body. It is made from my usual blood red fabric, but it is asymmetrical, covering my entire back, but also going halfway over my body from the right side. The neck portion is a bit thicker than what I am used to, and it wraps—almost like a scarf—across my neck and chest. The endless pocket is on my right side and I notice just how easy it will be to slip the book in while remaining unnoticed. When the cloak is secure, my sword and dagger remain exposed on my left side. Everything becomes clear. Lord Acastus plans to use my weapons as the status symbol of a General.

There is a knock at my door. One handmaiden goes to answer it while the other works on draping the cloak perfectly over my armor. She touches up my hair, smoothing down any out of place strands, as I hear the footsteps of the visitor approach.

"Leave us." Lord Acastus says with a swipe of his hand. The handmaidens obey immediately. I do not know what to say as I stare into the grey eyes of Lord Acastus. *"My General."*

"My Lord." I nod deeply. When I lift my head Lord Acastus is holding my golden crown out to me, the crossing swords of my diadem glimmering in the light. The crown that I have avoided for the last star cycle. He places the crown atop my head and his fingers linger over my hair. I shiver at the weight, at his proximity.

The Lord remains only a breath away. My eyes are locked into his for long moments. It takes three breaths to move. One to steady myself, a second to breathe in his scent—evergreen, cool and refreshing—and a third before he takes my arm and walks me out of my room. My breaths are shallow as we walk through the halls of The Castle. Filling with both that distinct scent, and his magic. The feeling of his deft fingers as they placed the crown on my head—I push the thought out of my mind. The two of us walk down the stairs of The Castle and I realize that we are not going in the direction of his office.

"My Lord, where are we going?" I ask softly, my voice a mere whisper. All I can muster when he is this close.

"Change of plans," he begins. "I thought it would be more—*prudent* of me to walk you to the portal room considering it is your first time."

"That is not necessary my Lord, I could have walked with Tor." I add, maintaining my respect. I was expecting Tor, not the Lord, to walk me to the portal room. To be at my side in my last moments before my life changes, for Infinity.

"Yes, but I wanted to walk you *alone,*" he insists. "You look lovely," he pauses. "As lovely as a rose, Soleil. One bathed in light." *Or one covered with thorns.* I think smugly. His eyes scan over my body, predatory and possessive. Phantom hands roam over my body. I feel his magic twine around my waist, around my upper thigh, around my neck.

"I appreciate that, my Lord." I say, on the verge of exasperation. Lord Acastus stops walking and, with his immortal strength, I have no choice but to stop as well. He uses my arm to make me face him and I look up into his eyes.

"Soleil," his voice is almost gravely. This time, it is his actual hands that move down my arms, testing me, claiming me. "You are the best decision I have ever made." I feel his breath on my face, it smells of…mint. He is intoxicating. He is infinite. He turns and walks on though, not waiting for a comment at all.

Dizzy, lightheaded, and with my heartbeat roaring in my ears, I struggle to remain standing. *The way he looked at me.* I think of his eyes and the way his gaze is trained on me at all moments. Every day since the day of the first battle simulation. Between the dream I had for the first time in a star cycle, Lord Acastus' surprise visit, and the mission today—my anxiety rises steadily. Lost in thought, I am surprised when we make it to the portal room.

Deep in the core of The Castle of Lex, is the beating heart of our realm. The only proof, in all of Lex, that magic ever existed in our desolate wasteland. Guards are stationed at the stone entrance and my heart flutters when I see Tor, wearing his new battle gear with daggers strapped into his belt. He has his head bowed down and his legs apart, his arms are held behind his back. Despite being raised in Ingenium, despite being a blade smith, I see him only as the perfect soldier. No, he is my *bladesmith*.

As if sensing our arrival, he looks up. I smile as the Lord and I approach him. Before either of us can say a word however, Lord Acastus nods and the stone doors to the portal room open. As soon as the room is revealed, the wind is knocked out of me. I begin pulling myself gently from Lord Acastus' grip and he releases my arm as I walk forward into the portal room. Despite the stories I heard, this is more than I ever could have imagined.

All of this magic. Hidden in the core of The Castle. And I have known nothing of its true beauty. It pulses with power. The magic of each portal mixing and stirring through the air to create something new. Something golden and beautiful.

Six portals are equally spaced on the walls of the stone room. Each portal is made of the same stone archway, but it is the feeling that radiates from the portals that makes it obvious which ones lead to the different realms. The stone doors close and Tor, Lord Acastus, and I are the only people in the room. I begin walking around, examining each portal carefully.

The first is a portal of wind and flow. A soft blue glow comes from it and I know that it can only be the portal to Spiritus. My gaze softens in curiosity at the portal that comes after, one of life and purity. A green glow comes from this portal and I can almost smell the crisp air, it's clearly the portal to Tellus. My gaze dances to the third portal, one that glows purple and feels of space and time itself. When I squint my eyes, I can see stars in the deep purple and I know that this is the portal to Aetas.

The next portal glows orange and feels of warmth and knowing. I know that this is the one I will be taking today, this is the portal to Ingenium. I linger at it before moving to the next one, a portal of death and sorrow. An all-encompassing black, clearly Entis' portal.

The final portal pulls me to it and I can't resist. A portal of sun and light itself, it glows a golden yellow. I linger for a moment in front of the portal, mystified by the overwhelming feeling of everything and anything. *Omnis*, I think with a smile.

Pulling myself back to the portal to Ingenium, I hear Lord Acastus approach me from behind. He speak softly, his voice deep, but low enough that only I can hear. I feel his breath, hot on my ear. "*My General.*" He begins and I felt him pick up a few strands of my hair. "Come, let me prepare you." I let out a breath as he retreats and follow him to the center of the room where Tor stands, a wounded look on his face. *Tor*—I can't continue down that path of thoughts, not when Lord Acastus stands in front of me.

"Lady Fable is awaiting your arrival." The Lord begins, his voice filled with command. "Travel via a portal can be an *interesting* experience. However, it's painless and quick. It is different for everyone, but you will commonly see light and colors and feel as if you are being pushed through space—which you are. It will be over before you know it." I feel my hands begin to shake in nervousness at my sides, but I quickly ball them into fists.

"Once you arrive in Ingenium, I understand that you have your plan well figured out." I nod at that. "Lady Fable is not as intimidating as she has been made out to be." *Then why won't you go?* I think smugly. If in answer, cold magic crashes out of the Lord and places a hand at the small of my back. As if it knows my every thought. "However, she is protective of her library above all else. I need you to get in and out as quickly as possible. Tell Lady Fable that you are in a rush and you simply want to *see* what your bladesmith had been talking about." He added that bit to my plan when I told him about it a few days ago. I look to Tor quickly, who nods at the new addition.

"Do not disappoint me, General Yamanu—or you Mister Warin." I shudder at his words, the same ones he repeats to me time and time again. He continues to speak. "Now, I trust that you can figure out the proper portal. Remember, I will be expecting your prompt return." He looks at me again. "You know where to find me, General"

His chambers—I cringe at the idea of returning to the hidden room but nod anyway.

With a bow of his head, and one more caress of those phantom hands on my body, Lord Acastus leaves the portal room, leaving Tor and I alone. My eyes remain trained on the stone door until Tor breaks the silence.

"Well, you look great." Tor laughs, I glare at his nonchalance. "What?" He shrugs. "It's true. So does Fate."

"I think that Fury does as well." I smile, pulling him to me in a hug, not minding that the hilts of the daggers he wears dig into my torso. I breathe Tor's scent in, comforting and woodsy, like the crackling fires blaring through The Castle.

"Fury?" Tor asks.

"My dagger needed a matching name." I shrug, still in his arms. "It seemed fitting."

"Very." Tor replies.

"Thank you."

"For what?" He asks, holding me tightly.

"For being here. For agreeing to do this with me."

"Of course." He replies kindly. I hold, and hold, and hold and let Tor's warmth fill me. Let his hands move down my spine, let his breath tickle my ear. *Infinity*—if I could freeze a moment. I force myself to pull away from him eventually and walk to the portal to Ingenium.

"This is it." I say with a sigh. Tor walks next to me and takes my hand in his. His calloused fingers, worn from years of forging, envelop my own and his thumb rubs over our intertwined hands reassuringly.

"I'm right here." He says.

I am still staring at the portal, but his words, and his touch, they do something to me that nothing else in this world can. And so, together, the two of us step through the portal to Ingenium, into the warmth and knowing of a new realm.

CHAPTER TWENTY

I am dreaming—but I am not. I can't feel my body, just the faint pressure of Tor's hand holding my own, or where it *would* be. That is enough to ground my mind as total darkness fills my head. Then red streaks my vision, blood red—the color of my cloak—fills my sight as if I am swimming in the color. Then streaks of white make their appearance. White—purer, and brighter than anything I have ever seen before, until it glows like the sun itself. I bathe in the light, almost golden, until everything goes black all at once.

Then, my body returns to me and all I have to do is open my eyes.

I cannot lift my gaze from the stone floor. I am back in Lex's portal room. I must be. I look to my left where Tor stands, still holding my hand. He's looking down at me. The moment our gazes cross though, I know that we are in Ingenium. Pulling my stare from his, I'm startled to find that Lady Fable is standing in front of us, her eyes shimmering with curiosity. Dropping my hand from Tor's, I sink down into a deep bow. Clothing shuffles next to me and I know that Tor follows suit.

"You may rise." Lady Fable's voice is filled with the wisdom of a millennium. I know now why they called her the all-knowing. I rise quickly and finally meet her gaze.

She is perfection itself. I have only ever seen one other Knight of Infinity, and after spending so much time with Lord Acastus, he seems… *mortal*. But I know that no matter how much time I spend with Lady Fable, she will *always* be immortal. My blood chills as I look at her—*too perfect*. Her dark brown hair falls to exactly her shoulders, bouncing up in perfect coils. Her skin—a deep umber—is flawless, not a wrinkle or imperfection to be found.

She has an unnatural stillness to her. Whereas Lord Acastus clearly tries to shake that part of his immortality, Lady Fable seems to embrace it. I am staring into the eyes of a predator, one that not only can kill me in an infinite number of ways but can also recite those ways to me without hesitation. She would be wonderful on the battlefield, I know, and I envy the power, the *knowledge,* that radiates from her.

I crave it for myself.

It takes me a moment to speak once I rise from my bow. I send a silent prayer to Infinity to give me strength to challenge the marvel that stands before me.

"Lady Fable," I dip my head. "Thank you for allowing me entry into your realm. Your generosity is much appreciated." Lady Fable cocks her head slightly. My prayers must have worked then, for not only is my voice strong and clear, but I know that the Lady is now questioning my mortality—or lack thereof.

"Well, to have *the* Knight of Lex vouch so highly on your behalf is an incredible feat. But to be his second in command…" her voice trails off. "I must say that I was quite curious about you myself, and your needs of course." She smiles, revealing a set of perfect teeth. While the intention may be kindness… it comes off more predatory than anything.

"Believe me, I did not become so much of a wonder overnight." I reply humbly.

"I must disagree, General—" she pauses, waiting for me to fill in. A clear declaration of power. The *idea* of me is more interesting than the *reality* of me. I am so insignificant that even though I piqued her interest, she did not care to remember my name.

"Yamanu. General Soleil Yamanu." I clarify.

"Well then I must disagree, General *Yamanu*. According to Lord Acastus, you were quite the hidden—gem." She hesitates before the last word, but I know that it is only for effect, she has our conversation completed and stored in her mind, she is simply humoring me.

"I try not to think so highly of myself, my Lady." I thank Infinity for the confidence, so much of it in the face of a woman so intimidating.

"That is wise, General." Lady Fable says venomously.

"Thank you, my Lady."

"This must be your *bladesmith*?" She asks, shifting her gaze to Tor for a moment and then back to me. It is clear that Tor will not get any attention from the Lady, not as long as I am here.

"Yes, he is. Lady Fable I would like to introduce you to the head bladesmith of Lex, Tor Warin." No surprise marks the Lady's face when she hears the name. She was feigning ignorance and I missed it. Lady Fable knows exactly who Tor is, she was simply toying with me.

"We are well acquainted, thank you General." The Lady replies.

"My Lady." Tor bow his head slightly.

Lady Fable does not pull her stare from mine. "Lord Acastus was quite vague while sharing your reason for being here. Care to explain further?" Lady Fable asks, chin up as if in disgust.

"Of course, my Lady." I begin. "As you know, my bladesmith, Tor Warin, once studied under you at The School of The Unfading. And while we only met a mere two-star cycles ago, we have grown quite close. In my first month as Second in Command of The Undying Army I have learned very much, however my skills in strategy are *lacking.*" I pause for a moment. Simply for effect as I have this conversation prepared as well.

"The libraries in Lex are essentially nonexistent and I believe that I have read every book on battle strategy that exists in my realm. In the short time that I have known Tor Warin he has raved about The Boundless Library and its infinite collection of knowledge. While I am on quite the time crunch, I simply wish to see if he is right." Every word comes out smoothly and surely and I am delighted at the ease of my plan thus far.

"I understand that The Boundless Library is the work of millennia, and I offer it my utmost respect. However, I truly just want a peek at it. I just want to see, even a portion of what my bladesmith has been describing. I assure you that I do not need long, I simply wish for a look to fulfill my curiosity, so that one day I can return and truly explore."

Lady Fable's gaze has softened beyond anything I could have anticipated. She is silent for long seconds before responding. "General Yamanu, do you know of any other former students of mine?" She asks inquisitively.

Alma—I think, stifling a gasp. I refuse to let emotion show on my face. Lady Fable has no idea of the rift between Alma and I. I have to continue to play the game. "Yes. My caretaker, Alma Zuri." Relief washes over me at the clarity of my voice despite the feelings swelling in my mind.

Lady Fable smiles as Alma's name leaves my tongue. "Ah, Miss Zuri," the Lady says happily. "One of my brightest. Many questioned her decision to return to Lex after graduation—I never did." The Lady pauses. "Still, it seems that even indirectly she has led another to the knowledge of Ingenium." Lady Fable turns to Tor. "Even you, Mister Warin, though you never *did* make it to graduation, you still unknowingly spread the knowledge of Ingenium." Lady Fable smiles warmly and I know that we have won. "You are both welcome into The Boundless Library. Stay as long as you wish and return as often as you like."

I can't help but let a genuine grin spread across my face. "Thank you, my Lady. You are ever kind."

"Of course, General Yamanu. Please know however, that I have strict rules in relation to The Boundless Library. Generally, they are as any library; do not damage the texts, do not write in them, remain quiet within the library itself, and return books to their proper locations, or to book disposal boxes to be resorted. Above all, *do not remove any books from the library itself.*"

The last rule comes out as a hiss. "The Boundless Library is welcome to all and it is always open so there is no need to remove books from the library. Follow these rules and The Boundless Library is yours. Break any of them, and you will face severe consequence." I nod in understanding and from the corner of my eye, I can see Tor follow suit. "Very well, I will lead you to The Boundless Library myself. There, you may do as you wish."

LONG MINUTES PASS AS LADY FABLE LEADS TOR AND I TO The Boundless Library. To my dismay, we spend much of our time underground, weaving through hallways that look much like those of The Castle of Lex. It is not until we finally climb a set of spiral stairs, that I realize how different Ingenium truly is. I can't help but walk to one of the large windows lining the hallways, surprised to find that there is no glass filling the space.

Ingenium is a sight out of a picture book. Trees—*real trees*—fill the landscape over rolling hills as far as the eye can see. For a moment, before my eyes adjust, I believe that the realm is ablaze. The leaves of the trees are the most gorgeous shades of red, orange, yellow, and brown. The grass is bright green and I want nothing more than to lay in it endlessly. A gentle breeze caresses my face, it's warm and beautiful. I take big gulps of the air—sweet and fresh—full of life in the way that Lex's never is. The sky is a soft blue with fluffy clouds. The sun is out, letting a soft light hit the landscape. For the first time in my eighteen years, I do not cringe at the weather, I do not shy away from the wind.

Footsteps approach and Tor appears at my side. I look up at him and know that despite my best efforts, my eyes have welled up with tears. Tor takes my hand and, for a moment, I hesitate, remembering that Lady Fable must be behind us. However, I let him do it anyway.

"It's gorgeous." I say softly, attempting to keep the tears at bay.

"Yes, it is." Tor responds. He sounds… resigned. But there is something else, some other hidden feeling that I cannot put my finger on.

"You left this for Lex?" I say breathlessly.

"Yes. And I would do it all over again. For this, for *you.*" He squeezes my hand gently and my heart flutters. This perfect person… he would choose me over the beauty of this realm? Do I even deserve such a thing? No. I deserve the dark and cold of Lex, I deserve Lord Acastus' wandering magic, wandering hands. But that doesn't mean I will let go of Tor. If that makes me a horrible person, then so be it.

I linger for a few more moments at the window, trying to engrave this image into my mind before leaving. I force myself to take in every detail. The sound of the rustling trees, the exact shade of blue in the sky. The sweet scent of the air. I commit all of it to memory. Something bright to hold onto in the darkness of my home realm. Eventually, I pull myself away and apologetically nod at Lady Fable for the interruption. She simply raises her hand in courteous dismissal and continues to lead us to The Boundless Library. I see pity in her eyes though, pity at my situation? At what my home is? I will never know. I will never ask.

Everything in The Castle of Ingenium is different and it is odd to be in a place so full of warmth. Every step that I take has a particular glow to it, one that I can't place in this moment, but I know I will miss once I leave. The Castle is enormous, from the walk alone I can tell that it is much bigger than The Castle of Lex, and so much more beautiful. Everywhere I walk, the walls are lined with bookshelves crammed with texts, artwork made from words or books themselves, and people lounging on chairs and sofas. It takes quite some time to reach The Boundless Library, but it is unmistakable once we do.

Two gigantic mahogany doors mark the entrance of The Boundless Library and guards are stationed at either side. My eyes widen as we approach. The library goes up for levels beyond what I can see, and down for even more. Each level is neatly organized with rows and rows of mahogany bookshelves. From where I stand at the entrance, it is clear that they are in impeccable condition. The center of each floor is carved out and a wooden staircase spirals up through the space.

It is incredible.

It is magical.

It feels like home.

Lady Fable speaks to the guards quickly, explaining that Tor and I are guests from Lex and that we are welcome for as long as we wish. The guards make a reach for Fate strapped at my hip and I step back defensively.

"That is not necessary. These two have full security clearance, including weapons privileges." Lady Fable says with a wink at me. I smile in return.

"This is where I leave you," The Lady says. "Please make yourselves at home, take as much time as you need. When you are done, one of the guards will escort you back to the portal room. I am afraid that I will not be able to see you off, so this is my goodbye as well." Tor and I bow deeply.

"Thank you, my Lady. This library is beyond my wildest dreams and I appreciate your generosity in letting me explore." I reply with as much graciousness as I can muster.

"Of course, General Yamanu. I hope to see more of you in the future." She dips her head slightly in a show of respect and I crack a smile. After that, Lady Fable turns and walks back into the halls of The Castle of Ingenium, disappearing behind a corner.

Tor and I walk into The Boundless Library then, and I am mesmerized by the sheer beauty of the space. It is dead quiet except for the occasional page flipping, shuffling of clothing, or near silent whisper. I lead Tor up the center stairs to the next level as I begin scouting out the area. We find a row of shelves that is empty and for a moment, I just look around.

This place is enormous and I curse myself for not asking Lady Fable how to locate specific books. Then I realize that I am holding the hand of a former student of The School of the Unfading. A living map to the library.

"You wouldn't know how to find your way around this place, would you?" I ask, my voice barely more than a whisper.

"I may have dropped out of The School, but believe me, I spent quite a bit of time in this library. What do you need?"

I smile at him slyly. "Prophecy. Bring me to the books on prophecy."

"This place is an alphabet. There are twenty-six levels, each one corresponding to a letter. We are on the level for letter—" he pauses, craning his neck. "M, which means we are on level thirteen. The level for letter P would be level sixteen." I nod along. I peek over my shoulder and find books on music as far as the eye can see, confirming Tor's instruction.

"Okay, so three levels down?" I ask.

"Yes. And then we find the rows on prophecy." He replies. A guard passes by us and nods before continuing.

No, no, no. I was not expecting that. Lord Acastus never mentioned guards. I calm myself, remembering my endless pocket and how small this book is supposed to be. All I have to do is slip it into my pocket and all will be well, I reassure myself.

"Let's go then." I say with determination, pulling Tor's hand back to the spiral staircase in the center of the library. I curse Infinity for the lack of time that I have in this place. It is perfect. It is everything I have ever dreamt of, and I can't stay to explore. Finally releasing myself from Tor's grasp I begin taking the stairs quicker, he struggles to keep up with me.

"Soleil, you *can* slow down."

"I have to find this book Tor." I reply, barely more than a whisper.

When we finally make it to level sixteen, I let out a small sigh of relief and begin scanning the floor for guards. There are three that I can see at the moment, but I have no way of telling how many more there will be.

"I see four." Tor says from behind me. Somehow, even in this ever serious situation, his voice manages to fill me with warmth.

But four guards? There are only three, I see them clear as day. "There are only three, Tor."

"Look." Tor says, standing behind me, using his hands to guide my head. "One, two, three—" he shifts my head a final time. "Four." He is right. A fourth guard stands, back to us, behind a bookshelf. I can barely make out his arm and the faint outline of his bow and quiver. An odd choice for a weapon in a place like this...

I turn around to face Tor. "You might have me out of a job if you keep this up."

"I'm a quick learner." He teases.

"Come on, let's find that book." I grab his hand and drag him into the nearest bookstacks. The books in this section are all about philosophy. I glare at the titles and shake my head gently at the simplicity of those from the old world.

"Philosophy, philosophy of the old worlds, philosophy of politics, philosophy of the new worlds." Tor begins to read. I turn back at him and glare. "We are clearly not in the right section."

"I hadn't realized that Tor. Please, take me to the *right* one." I reply, with more cheek than I intended.

Tor feigns hurt and then laughs it off. "Let me lead then." He says while moving in front of me. This time he drags me behind him while we look through rows and rows of books on physics, psychology, politics, performance, painting, and palaces. For hours we search for the section on prophecy, but it is nowhere to be found. The floor is extensive, but taking it in sections, Tor and I are able to search through the entire place.

I am going through some shelves on policy—a smaller section compared to most—but it still has five rows of shelves dedicated to it. The shelves are in the back corner of the sixteenth floor. It is utterly silent. I can't help but look over my shoulder however, just in case a guard is near.

Angry, confused, and exhausted, I stop for a moment and let myself slide down to the floor. I have been in this library for *hours* and still found nothing. My stomach growls and I sigh in defeat. Standing once more—despite my mental state—I continue to walk on, confused when I see a single stone bookshelf tucked in the very corner of the sixteenth floor.

I approach it nervously and my heart pounds in my chest. There is no reason for me to be afraid, but the shelf feels *off*. As if it is pulsing with the beat of my own heart. I clutch Fate's hilt at my side. Taking deep breaths, I continue to walk to the stone shelf. When I arrive, I find it completely empty. With a sigh, I hit the floor again, anger returning. This is useless. The book doesn't exist and Lord Acastus will just have to deal with that. I scan the area around me one final time. A bit of green peaks out from under the empty stone bookshelf.

Jamming my finger into the small gap between the floor and the bottom of the shelf, I struggle to get the item out. I take a few looks over my shoulder to ensure that no one is nearby. In this obscure area of The Boundless Library, no one is. Finally, after long minutes of struggling, I pull a small, green, leather-bound book out from under the shelf. The gold letters stamped into the book read *The Book of Infinite Prophecy.* I gasp in shock, nearly tossing the book out of my hands. In an effort to remain inconspicuous, I stand slowly, holding onto the book with all the power in me.

When I rise, I take a closer look at the small text. It is incredibly simple. Other than the title, the book has no other markings. With a deep breath and one more look around the library, I quickly stuff the book into the endless pocket sewn into my cloak. The book slips in without a sound, disappearing into the curious relic. Moving swiftly though the aisles, I waste no time searching for Tor.

It takes a while, but he is searching in the opposite end of the library between the shelves on photography and pets. I shake my head at the arbitrary organization system and run to Tor, pulling him into a tight hug.

"I did it." I whisper into his ear.

"Good. Where is it?" He asks.

"I took care of it, it's fine." I reply, almost sagging into his arms with relief.

He wraps his arms around me even tighter than before, holding up almost all of my weight. "Are you ready to get out of here?" He asks softly. His voice soothes my roughness, my worries.

I am, I truly am. Until I think about what I will be leaving behind. This realm, so unlike Lex, so unlike my home, it feel *right*. The moment I pull away from Tor and meet his eyes, I realize why. The warmth that flows from him is Ingenium itself. I saw it in his dark brown hair the moment I met him, I see it in the way his eyes catch the light, and I hear it in his voice, strong and deep. Tor is a living piece of Ingenium and I relished in that long before I had known the realm itself.

"Yes." I nod, knowing that even as I leave this incredible place behind, Tor will remain at my side. A living, breathing piece of the realm I have come to love.

A GUARD IN BLACK ROBES—A BOW STRUNG OVER HIS SHOULDER, and a quiver of arrows on his back—walks us back to the portal room. Having full security clearance must mean something, for Tor and I are not questioned, nor patted down before leaving The Boundless Library, as many others are. I attempt to hold on to Ingenium with every step that I take towards the portal room. While I know that Tor will remain with me, leaving the beauty of this realm will be difficult. It is easy to believe that I don't want *more* while I am in Lex. But it is only because I never knew what *more*, truly was. Deep in my core, I dread returning to the barren wasteland that is my home. However, I am second in command of The Undying Army, and I will do what is required of me.

I linger at the same window that I stopped at before. The sun is setting, casting the most beautiful orange hues across the sky. I sigh in longing, aching to see this every day. The trees sway gently in the warm breeze and as it passes, it caresses my face once more, carrying more of its sweet scent. A tear slides down my cheek at the sight. I do not stop it. How miserable I must be to cry at a sunset. But sunsets like these don't happen in Lex. Lex's sky doesn't get painted in a cascade of warmth when the sun dips down low over the horizon. No, Lex's sun leaves without ever saying goodbye.

Tor stands next to me, still holding my hand. He squeezes it tighter as the tear falls. It is all I need to know that he is there. That even in the dark and cold of my home, *our home*, he will remain at my side. I do not dare move until the sun dips low, beyond the rolling hills, and the once orange sky is painted black with night. Before I lose the will, I turn my head from the window and walk silently behind the guard, resuming our trek to the portal room.

I can't help but examine the guard in front of us. I realize that he looks *different*. Lex is the military force of the realms which means that soldiers from The Undying Army are dispersed across the lands to act as guards for this very purpose.

"Excuse me?" I ask, my voice soft.

"Yes?" The guard replies, walking along.

"Are you from Lex?"

"No. I was born, raised, and schooled here in Ingenium. Why do you ask?" The guard responds coldly.

"I am second in command of The Undying Army." I say with more power than before.

"I know who you are." The guard sneers.

"Well, aren't all guards and security forces in the realms supposed to come from The Undying Army?" I ask, returning his insincerity.

"Sure, but the Knights of each realm can choose *not* to use your squadrons in certain areas. The Boundless Library is sacred and it needs specially trained forces to protect it." It takes everything in me not to chuckle at his arrogance. Especially since a book from his *sacred* library is currently in my pocket, well on its way back to my realm.

"Very well." I reply indifferently. The rest of the walk goes on without another word from anyone and we reach the portal room quickly. Somehow, my cloak feels heavier than before, as if the weight of that tiny book is bearing down on me. I know that it isn't, it is just my mind playing tricks, but it feels real enough. The portal room in Ingenium is unguarded from the outside, something I hadn't noticed before.

"Where is the security?" I ask offhandedly.

"What security?" The guard sneers.

I am puzzled at his response. "The security that you keep around the portal room. To prevent people from leaving the realm."

The guard looks at me as if I am insane. "General, why would we keep people from leaving Ingenium? Travel via portal is without restrictions. Citizens who live in Ingenium that wish to travel to the other realms know the risks of each and make decisions on where to travel based off of that."

How is that possible? For someone to travel via portal in Lex, they need special security clearance, Lord Acastus himself has to sign off on it.

I shake my head and smile at the guard, attempting to rectify the mess I have just made. "Of course. We have a surplus of guards in need of training on Lex, keeping them stationed near our portal room has become second nature." I laugh lightly.

The guard turns back around, opening the doors to let Tor and I back into the portal room.

"You two have a safe trip." The guard says.

Tor and I give curt nods in response and the stone door closes behind us. I sigh in relief and begin scanning the room for the portal to Lex. My eyes linger on the golden portal to Omnis for a moment and I long to step inside. I pull my gaze from the golden glow and track down a portal that glows stone-grey. I shake my head at the irony and approach the portal, an overwhelming feeling of dread rising in me.

"Are you ready?" Tor asks from beside me.

"Mmhm." I reply softly. Even though I am anything but ready.

Together, we take a step into the cold and unwelcoming portal. Back home and back to Lex.

THE PORTAL TO LEX IS JUST AS UNPLEASANT AS THE PORTAL to Ingenium. The same blood red streaks my vision until it is overpowered by a bright white, and then black as I make it home. Cold immediately penetrates my skin and I know that during my hours in Ingenium, I have grown too used to the all-encompassing warmth. Even the heat of The Castle of Lex cannot compare.

I drop Tor's hand and walk swiftly out of the portal room and into the halls of The Castle.

"I have to get this book to Lord Acastus." I say, unable to meet Tor's eyes.

"I can go with you—" he begins.

"No. I need to do this myself." I reply softly. "Thank you for going with me." I reach for his hand and give it a slight squeeze, all of the affection that I can muster right now. I shift my gaze to meet his own. My heart skips when I look into his eyes and I see Ingenium's warmth flow from him.

"Let me join you." He insists. *Oh, how I want him to.* I am undeserving of him, of his care, his compassion.

I shake my head and acceptance paints his face. I begin walking away, holding onto his hand for as long as I can. My fingers are on the verge of slipping from his before he grabs my hand and pulls me back to him in a tight embrace.

"My General." He says softly. For the first time, I do not cringe away from those words.

"My bladesmith." I laugh as he releases me.

I pull my hood up and set my jaw in determination before making my way to Lord Acastus' chambers.

I recall the path to the Lord's chambers perfectly, thanking Infinity for my attention to detail. The walk is quick and eventually I make it to the empty wall at the end of the hallway. It takes a moment, but I am able to find the brick that Lord Acastus pushed in, and the stone door opens for me in response. After a deep breath, I walk into Lord Acastus' chambers and find him sitting at his dining table—sipping from a goblet—with an entire meal laid out for him.

I approach the Lord slowly and he does not acknowledge my presence for long seconds. I sneak a look at the clock above his fireplace and find that it reads *0847. Tor and I were in Ingenium for close to twelve hours.* The Lord's gaze is awaiting my own, his eyes are lit in an icy blaze that sends a shiver down my spine. Without a word, he gestures to the empty seat at the other end of the dining table.

My plate is already filled with food. Steak, vegetables, pasta, and salad are all neatly arranged. I take my seat without breaking eye contact with the Lord. I feel a chill in my bones at his cold stare. For a moment, we sit in silence until Lord Acastus finally speaks.

"Eat," a command. This is a test.

He sent me to Ingenium—to another realm—unsupervised. And now, he wishes to see how I am reacting to returning. He is testing my loyalty. My strength.

I pick up the fork and spear a few pasta noodles before putting them in my mouth, almost sighing in relief at the delicious food after all these hours. In an attempt to prove my loyalty to the Lord, I continue eating without a word. And soon, Lord Acastus begins as well. The meal is quick and, in my hunger, I get seconds of the pasta and steak. When Lord Acastus and I are both done, I make no move to clean up the mess, recalling what he told me before.

The Lord stands and gestures for me to follow. My heart thuds in my chest as he nears, but I do not shy away from the ice in his eyes, willing myself to become fire in return. Lord Acastus is a breath away when he reaches his hand out and into my cloak. Using all my control not to shake in response, I realize that he is reaching for the endless pocket. But his hand grazes my stomach, then my waist in the process. I feel his phantom hands, the ones made of pure power and ice, they caress me too. Much more confident and possessive than Lord Acastus' true form. He finally removes his hand—both literally and magically—and pulls out the green book, smiling in satisfaction.

"My General," he hisses. "You have done it." He says as if in disbelief. I cringe at his words; at the way he says *my General* as if he owns me. "Thank you."

"Of course, my Lord. Is there anything else you require of me?" I ask, my voice strong despite the feelings within. I thank Infinity for the clarity as I await Lord Acastus' answer.

"No, General Yamanu. You may return to your chambers and get some rest. Thank you for your work today." He smiles brightly, as if he was not testing me at all. "I will see you tomorrow."

But that is a lie, for I do not see him the next day, or the day after that, or the one after that.

CHAPTER
TWENTY—ONE

I have not seen Lord Acastus for almost two weeks. The end of the star cycle is fast approaching, preparations are being made for The Eternal Dance and I have to make decisions alone. I see no one for those two weeks. Days go by, and I don't not even see Tor in passing. My time is filled with strategy meetings for The Undying Army, where I become the leader due to Lord Acastus' absence. Then there are meetings for The Eternal Dance's preparations where I have to choose decorations and create seating arrangements for the grand ballroom. I have no idea what to do for most of it, delegating the work to some of Lord Acastus' closest advisors instead. Once the work is done, I check it and sign off without another thought.

I am getting anxious, at Lord Acastus' absence—at the lack of instruction—but I do the best I can, and the realm works as smoothly as ever. Most have no idea that the Lord is even *gone* as I chose to keep that information close, creating false stories to explain his whereabouts. At times I tell the lieutenants during strategy meetings that I have specific instruction from the Lord himself to complete certain tasks. This at least, solidifies my power for the time being, and allows me to rule the realm without question.

When the anxiety rises to fill my body, I make my way to The Castle's training room with Fate in hand and beat the feeling out of myself until my arms ache for reprieve. I do not see Nova or Arche during this time, they never make it to the strategy meetings, and I never question it. While I am second in command of The Undying Army, I have much to learn about the way it operates. I receive word on the second day of the star cycle, after I returned from Ingenium, that the Lieutenants in training—Arche and Nova included—have been successfully moved into their blockhouses. That is enough for me to know that they are okay.

As for Alma, I continue to remain as far away from the Lost wing of The Castle as I can, not willing to apologize myself, or receive an apology from her. I spend days in isolation, moving from meeting to meeting. I am surrounded by people, but more alone than ever.

The fourteenth day of the star cycle arrives before I know it. I sit up in my bed, the plush covers virtually untouched after my deep and unmoving sleep. I walk over to my window and pull the curtains open so that my room can flood with the soft morning light. I sigh—as I often have since returning from Ingenium—at the unwelcoming stiffness of my home.

After making my bed and checking that my fireplace is lit—it is—I bathe quickly and move to the sofa in front of the fire to dry off. I twirl my hair around my fingers, still straight, as it has been for the last two weeks. Every few days I wash it but the handmaidens always return to straighten it once more. I do not object, assuming that it is Lord Acastus' expressed instruction that ensures their return. It seems as if he has given everyone instruction for his absence—except for me. With my hair already dry and straight, my body dries and warms quickly and I am able to go into my closet to change after only a few minutes.

My freshly washed battle gear is already laid out for me, the breastplate shining in the light. I have worn it every day since Tor revealed it to me, usually without the gauntlets, grieves, and cuisses as they are awfully uncomfortable for everyday wear. Each night I strip the gear and every morning I wake to them freshly washed, shined, and laid out for the day by my handmaidens. The endless pocket was removed by the time I woke up on the second morning of the star cycle and not even the stitches from where it was sewn in remained.

I lace up my white boots, tighten the gold breastplate around myself, and fasten Fate and Fury to my leg. I finish off by wrapping my blood red cloak around my body and I place my golden crown on my head.

In my bathing chamber, I adjust my appearance, straightening my crown and shifting my cloak so that Fate and Fury gleam in the morning light. My hair is flawless, not a strand out of place. When I walk out of the bathing chamber, my handmaidens are waiting for me in the living room.

"Good morning." I say civilly.

"Good morning General Yamanu." They reply. "Your breakfast is on the table. We will begin cleaning if you don't need anything else from us."

"Thank you. I do not require anything else of you." I gesture to the room and they begin scurrying around, dusting, shining, and organizing my chamber while I eat.

For breakfast I have an egg scramble with potatoes, cheese, meat, mushrooms, and vegetables. There is some crispy bread, with butter and strawberry jam, and a goblet filled with orange juice. I eat quickly, enjoying the light and the cracks of the fire. When I am done, I place my plates and goblet on the table beside my sofa and leave my room without another word.

The clacking of my sturdy leather boots echoes through the halls. I take the main hallways, not shying away from the crowds of people who, as soon as they see the red of my cloak, bow as I pass. At first, I stopped them and let them know that it was unnecessary. But now I let it happen, embracing my position. It satisfies me in a way— the feeling of power—but I have to remind myself that the dominance I hold is in my title alone.

Still, I let them bow.

Down the south wing of the fourth floor of The Castle, I make my way to the war room. The room has stone walls and a large mahogany table with matching chairs that take up most of the space. Traditionally, Lord Acastus sits on one end of the table, and the second in command on the other. Now that Lord Acastus is on a *leave of absence*, I take his spot and my old one remains empty.

When I arrive at the room, every seat is filled by commanders and lieutenants of The Undying Army. Only the most skilled and seasoned leaders of The Army are allowed in strategy meetings. Even though we are not in active war, there are many items to discuss and many decisions to be made. I take my seat at the head of the long meeting table and the eyes of every leader in The Undying Army are trained on me.

Pulling my hood down and laying it gently over my shoulders, I make eye contact with each lieutenant and commander, ensuring that they remember their positions in this army—and who leads them. I sit in the wood chair and let silence fill the council room.

I send my usual prayer to Infinity for strength during the meeting and begin. "Good morning, everyone. Today is the fourteenth day of the tenth star cycle in the nine hundred and ninety-ninth year of the ninety-ninth millennium. I thank you for your prompt arrival. Let's begin."

"General Yamanu, we wish to bring to your attention a *grievance*." An ancient Lieutenant—Lewis Gunther—speaks. His voice is gravelly and almost nervous. I know right away that whatever his *grievance* is, it will not be good.

"Yes, Lieutenant Gunther? Infinity knows that I do not have all day." I drawl.

The man sinks into his chair. "General Yamanu, after Lord Acastus' order to graduate four years' worth of students from The Academy, our army has grown beyond the capacity of The Wall."

I knew this was coming. I felt it the moment that Nova and Arche brought it up to me just a star cycle ago. "What do you want, Lieutenant?"

"We ask for permission to move *beyond* The Wall. The Wall's magic that kept Lex's harsh weather out, is no longer, so we wish to create camps and blockhouses outside of its perimeter." I listen to his words carefully.

The problem is that I agree with him. If I am to believe the traditional history of Lex and not the twisted version that Professor Clara shared with me almost two-star cycles ago, then it makes sense to move beyond The Wall. However, this is not a decision that I can make alone.

"No. I will not authorize this. The Wall has been the perimeter of The Undying Army for nearly one hundred millennia. This established practice will not be overridden simply because our soldiers are *uncomfortable*. I will authorize an organization and relocation plan, as well as the creation of new blockhouses, considering the fact that they hold nearly twice the soldiers that traditional camps do. This, coupled with a complete reorganization of the soldiers will make them much more *comfortable*." I pause, allowing my words to sink in. Everyone nods. Whether they truly agree with me, or they are simply afraid, I do not care.

"Lieutenant Gunther, please draft this plan and return it to me for confirmation and signing no later than three days from today." The Lieutenant nods slowly. I know that regardless of his feelings towards the plan, he will draft the proposal. At the very least, it will satisfy the leaders for now, until Lord Acastus decides to end his sabbatical.

"General Yamanu, we also have decisions to make regarding The Eternal Dance." A blonde haired, green eyed, Lieutenant speaks. He is tall and lanky, always good to lighten the mood. We are not particularly close, but I know that if I became a Lieutenant myself, we would have been.

"Please share them." I say, cooling my tone.

"To begin, we would like to discuss the presence of the soldiers at The Eternal Dance itself. Traditionally, when the dance has been held in other realms, soldiers from The Undying Army are only sent as security forces, not able to attend the dance themselves. When the dance is held here in Lex, the same pattern follows. However, Lord Acastus himself has never presided over The Eternal Dance before so we ask you what the protocol will be for the soldiers' attendance." Lieutenant Liam Kane's green eyes light as he speaks.

For a moment I want to play it safe, to agree to precedent. But it does not feel right, to enjoy myself at The Eternal Dance while Nova and Arche are denied entry except as guards. I recall when Lord Acastus announced The Eternal Dance only a few star cycles ago, and exactly what he said.

"When Lord Acastus announced The Eternal Dance to everyone—over two star cycles ago—he stated that *everyone* is invited as representatives of The Academy or The Army." I say, giving time for Lieutenant Kane to correct me if I am wrong.

"He made that incredibly clear. So, with his words in mind, I have some requests of you, Lieutenant Kane." He gestures for me to continue. "First, I need you to go to every squadron and get a list of soldiers who will volunteer as guards for The Eternal Dance. I believe that the most updated security plans require only five hundred guards to cover the whole castle that night." I look around for confirmation and the Lieutenants nod in answer, so I continue.

"That should be easy enough to get considering our numbers. Tell the soldiers that if they volunteer, they will get special consideration for promotions in the future—I don't really care just tell them *something.* If we don't have the five hundred soldiers we need, pick from the bottom of the ranks, only the lowest of foot soldiers. Only use that as a last resort, I do not wish for our entire security protocol to rely on our *lesser* soldiers." I look back to Lieutenant Kane. "Draft this proposal and bring it to me within three days."

"Very well, General Yamanu." Lieutenant Kane nods.

"Can I get a status update on the invitations?" I ask no one in particular. A red haired and gruff man, Commander Callan Alvaro, answers me quickly.

"They were sent out on the first day of the star cycle, General Yamanu. We have received word from every realm save for Omnis, but that is to be expected." The room fills with laughter.

"Enough." I say, my voice loud enough to shake the room. "I will not tolerate *laughter* on a matter such as this." The room silences at once. "Send another invitation immediately and if we do not get a response then consider their silence to be acceptance." No one replies. "Is that clear?" I add, my voice loud enough to penetrate their skin. I receive a curt *yes* from every Commander and Lieu-

tenant in the war council room. "Are there any other orders of business for us to attend to today?" I ask coldly.

"Just one." Commander Alvaro says, clearly attempting to rectify his mistake. "There are rumors of subversive
behavior at The Academy. It is simply talk for now; however, we want to ensure—" I cut him off.

"Commander Alvaro, you have not brought to my attention one item of substance during this meeting. I suggest that you stop talking immediately. Now that I know
that there are *no* consequential items to discuss, this meeting has come to a close. I will see all of you in two days'
time." With that, I stand, pull my hood over my head, and
walk out of the council room before anyone else can speak.

Utterly annoyed at the outcome of the council meeting, I set my course back to my chambers to cool down. I
need Lord Acastus, need his instruction, need his advice. I
have been Second in Command of The Undying Army
for little more than a star cycle, and now I am running the
realm as if it is my own.

I don't know what to do.

WITH A SIGH OF RELIEF, I SHOVE MY KEY INTO THE DOOR OF
my chamber, lingering for a moment at the intricate carvings. My relief is short-lived, for when I open the door, I
find fabrics lining every surface of my living room, and a
tall, dark-haired man standing near my fireplace.

"Excuse me?" I ask. I do not having the patience to
deal with this.

The man turns around to face me, his dark skin catching the soft glow of the fire. "General Yamanu," he smiles.

"I am Nelio Journee, The Castle's tailor." He puts a hand out and I shake.

"Mister Journee—"

"Please call me Nelio." He cuts me off. I smile politely and continue.

"Nelio, what exactly are you doing in my chambers?" I ask, as civilly as I can.

"Well General, Lord Acastus gave me a specific date to come see you. We must make decisions regarding your gown for The Eternal Dance."

Excuse me? Everyone seems to have Lord Acastus' expressed instructions except for the person that needs it most. Anger bubbles inside of me, but I allow myself to take a moment and cool down. I *do* need a gown for the dance. I may as well get it over with.

"Yes of course." I say cordially. "I apologize, Nelio. I just finished with a meeting."

"No rush General Yamanu, you are the last person on my list." He says with a sip from his goblet.

I puzzle at his response. "Is there any particular reason that I am last?"

"Only the most obvious, General Yamanu. Lord Acastus himself said that your dress must be made last, this way no one can steal your design. Your gown will be completely unique!" Nelio is unmoving as he speaks. It is almost eerie—the level of his stillness, in stark contrast to the emotion and expression in his words,.

"You made the clothing in my closet?" It is less of a question and more of a realization.

"With the express direction of Lord Acastus of course. He was very particular about your wardrobe. Something about the color red…" his voice trails off.

"I wore a red cloak for the seven years that I studied at The Academy." I reply faintly.

"Well, it has become quite the signature color, General Yamanu. Speaking of red, let me show you the designs that the Lord and I came up with." He walks over to my dining table and gestures for me to follow. Nelio begins flipping through a portfolio, laying out various sketches and drawings of me. Each of them wears a dress that look almost the exact same, but with some minor modification.

Every dress is the same blood red of my cloak.

"They are incredible." I gasp.

"Thank you, General. But these are simply the concept sketches," he pauses and pulls out one last paper, placing it in front of me. "*This* is the final design."

It is gorgeous, everything about it is pure perfection. The dress has a square neckline that comes up over the shoulders to make two long and puffy tulle sleeves that cinch at the wrists. The bodice has exposed boning, colored a slightly deeper shade than the rest of the dress. The skirt is long and full, but not puffy, and even in the drawing it looks full of movement. The entire thing is the most gorgeous shade of blood red I have ever seen.

"It's exquisite." I say breathlessly.

"Do you have any changes you would like me to make?" He asks.

I continue to stare at the drawing, imagining every possible outcome, everything I will need in the dress for that night. I imagine Fate and Fury strapped to my leg—

that's it. Fate can go around my waist no problem, but I am most comfortable with Fury at my thigh. If I do that, I will have no way to access my dagger.

"I need a slit, down the left leg." I point to that portion of the skirt on the drawing and drag my finger down. "I have to have my dagger on me at all times and it must be accessible at my thigh."

Nelio nods. "Yes, I can do that. Anything else, General?"

I think for another few seconds. The dress is beautiful, but it's missing something else. I imagine my gold crown on the head of the girl—me—in the drawing. It needs something gold.

"Can we get rid of the exposed boning?" I ask. "I want a gold corset instead. It can hit the exact points that the boning would have and stop just before the skirt as well."

"I will have to bring in fabric samples—" Nelio begins.

"No. Not fabric. I want it made of metal. The exact same as my breastplate." I point to the shimmering gold on my chest.

"General Yamanu, that is well beyond my skill set." Nelio replies.

"I understand that. But if you go to the armory here in The Castle and ask for Tor Warin, you can show him the sketches and tell him the plan. He will make it for you. He made this breastplate for me. He makes all of my armor. He made me my sword. Tor Warin can do the engravings as well and he has my measurements already."

Nelio ponders for a moment. I know that if I was anyone else it would be a clear *no*. However, I am second in command of The Undying Army, and no one will deny me. "I can make that happen." Nelio says hesitantly. He pick up a notepad from the table and begins writing things down.

"Okay. Changes that will be made include a slit along the *left* leg for dagger access." I nod in confirmation. "No exposed boning on the torso of the dress," another nod. "And a corset—in the exact style of your current breast-plate—made by Tor Warin of The Castle's armory."

"That is all," I pause, then add. "I want the top of the corset to be a point, tell Tor that I do not want it squared or rounded."

"General, you will kill yourself with a metal point so close to your chest." Nelio replies.

"Tor Warin knows what to do, I trust him with my life." I say, matter-of-factly.

"Very well." Nelio replies, his tone resigned. "As for the fabric," he gestures to the room around us. "Take your pick, General." I began scanning the room, touching the various tulles and examining the shades in different lights. I settle on one that is draped over my sofa. It is incredibly soft and almost velvety. The color is spot on to my own blood red cloak.

"This one is perfect." I say, holding the bolt of fabric up to show Nelio.

His face lights with happiness. "Yes, yes, yes." He says, merrily walking towards me to collect the material. "This *is* perfect."

"Is that all?" I ask as he walks away.

"Almost, General. Do you have a shoe preference?"

"Do you?" I lift an eyebrow.

"Gold. Gold is good." He responds quickly.

"Then gold it is."

Nelio takes some more notes, scribbles on the original drawing, and then gestures for me to return to the table. The drawing is the same, but this time the shoes are roughly colored in gold, there is a line on the left leg where the slit is to be, and a gold under bust corset is hastily drawn in as well. Though it's a concept, I know that it will be gorgeous when complete.

"So?" Nelio asks.

I turn to him and his features are set in a self-satisfied way. "It is *perfect*, Nelio. I appreciate it."

"Wonderful! Your dress will be delivered on the morning of The Eternal Dance. Thank you for your time, General Yamanu." I can't help but smile at Nelio, the man who has been making my clothing for the last two and a half star cycles.

"Thank *you*, Nelio. For this, *and* my other clothing."

With a smile and a humble nod, Nelio collects his things and loads them onto a cart before leaving without another word.

After Neilo leaves my chambers, I pull off my cloak and armor, unfasten Fate and Fury from my leg, place my crown on the table beside my bed, and unlace my boots. I walk into the bathing chamber and splash cold water on my face to cool myself down. When I am thoroughly refreshed, I walk into my living room and pick a book off the shelves; it is a collection of short stories. Tucking myself into my bed and ruining the perfection of the covers, I crack open the book and begin reading.

The ticking of my clock on the wall in front of me is unnerving. Every few moments I pause my reading to check the time. *1043... 1044... 1045...* Eventually I become so engrossed in the stories that I completely tune it out. When I next check the time, it reads *0127*. I have finished every short story in the book and am incredibly satisfied when I realize that I did so in less than three hours. Stretching widely to shake out my stiff muscles, I ponder on what else I can do today.

I am covered when it comes to General duties as I have already attended today's meeting, and just yesterday I visited the army camps, dutifully avoiding the blockhouses that Arche and Nova are stationed in. Lord Acastus still has not shown face in days and I am getting sick of his absence. I have done everything that he asked of me. I went to Ingenium and back for him. I trained endlessly for him. I destroyed my relationship with Alma, *defending* him. I haven't seen Arche or Nova in weeks because of him. And Tor—I don't let myself finish that thought. All of this and he just *left*.

Fed up with the Lord's silence at one of the most unstable times of the millennium, I pull on my armor, cloak, boots, and crown, finishing by strapping Fate and Fury to my leg as well.

If Lord Acastus refuses to see me, I will go see him myself. I walk out of my rooms and straight to Lord Acastus' hidden chambers. I attempt to calm myself, but my vision is tinted red. My mind keeps returning to our last conversation, the way he pulled The Book of Infinite Prophecy from my cloak and told me that he would see me the next day. The way his hands grazed the sensitive skin of my waist. And then? Nothing. I set my jaw in determination and am at the empty wall in minutes.

After a few moments of pressing in on various bricks, I finally find the one that gives and press it in with all of my strength. The stone door opens for me in response and I hear the gentle crackle of a fire. The servants would not keep the fire going if Lord Acastus wasn't in the realm. At the very least I know that he will return soon. *If he is not already in the chamber.* I remind myself. I walk in slowly. My breath hitches when I behold the state of the room.

What happened?

The fireplace is the only light source in the room as the previous lights in the ceilings are smashed, littering the chamber with shards of glass. The walls and floors are covered with paper. Sheets of all different sizes are plastered over the—previously bare—stone walls. The papers are covered in unintelligible scrawls, some in black ink, others in a blood red. The walls are much neater than the floors, for there, the paper is crumpled and torn. Pages torn from books, parchment covered in scrawls that I cannot decipher, and leather bound books with their covers ripped off. I glare at the dining table, the only clean surface in the entire chamber. Careful not to make a sound—a trick that Lord Acastus himself taught me—I walk over to the table.

Three sheets of pristine white paper are laid out. They each have something written on them, all in perfect calligraphy that is so unlike the scratches on the walls. Calligraphy that is much more *Knight-like.* The energy in the room thrums. Not Lord Acastus' rolling magic. No.

This is the unmistakable power of The Seven Books of Infinity. The power than roars in the portal room. The words seem to… glow. No. That is impossible. I leave the papers where they are and begin reading in an attempt to grasp at the reason for Lord Acastus' absence. I begin with the paper on the left.

> THE CONVERGENCE OF THE BOOKS OF INFINITY
>
> AT THE CLOSE OF EACH MILLENNIUM, THE KNIGHTS OF INFINITY MUST PERFORM THE CONVERGENCE TO AID IN THE ALIGNMENT OF THE SEVEN REALMS. TO PERFORM THE CONVERGENCE, THE BOOKS OF INFINITY MUST BE PLACED IN A CIRCULAR FORMATION FOLLOWING THE INFINITE ORDER, WITH THE BOOK OF THE BOUND TAKING THE CENTER POSITION. IN THE SEVEN MINUTES FOLLOWING THE STROKE OF MIDNIGHT ON THE FIRST DAY OF THE NEW MILLENNIUM, THE KNIGHTS OF INFINITY MUST JOIN HANDS AND EACH MUST SPEAK THE NAME OF THEIR RESPECTIVE BOOK, FOLLOWING THE INFINITE ORDER ONCE MORE. THIS PROCESS WILL ENDURE THE REALMS FOR ANOTHER MILLENNIUM AND ALIGN THEM ONCE MORE IN INFINITE PERFECTION.

I know that it's not wise for me to be reading this. The moment I lay eyes on the title I know that it's not for me. Still, I *am* Lord Acastus' second in command and I *will* be seeing this exact process being performed soon enough. The Convergence of The Books of Infinity is a sacred process and while it is written down in numerous history books, the wording is always slightly different. This paper must be the true instructions for performing The Convergence. The instructions only for the eyes of the Knights. I hesitate for a moment, still looking at the first piece of text, before letting my eyes shift to the paper in the center of the table.

THE PROPHECY OF THE INVISIBLE
AT THE DAWN OF THE REALMS THE BOOKS OF
INFINITY WERE FORMED.
BOUND IN ETERNAL LIGHT THEY JOIN NAUGHT.
AT THE ALIGNMENT OF THE REALMS, ONE WILL SEEK TO
BIND THE BOOKS.
TO DESTROY AND REBUILD THE REALMS ANEW IN
UNDYING MAJESTY.
ONLY ONE IN INVISIBILITY CAN HALT THE DEMISE OF
THE SEVEN REALMS.
FORGED IN EVERLASTING LIGHT, THEY ALONE WILL HAVE
THE POWER TO LAST THE REALMS.
THE POWER TO BIND EXISTENCE FOR ETERNITY.

I tremble as I read the prophecy, swearing that it shimmers in the light as I do. My hand shoots up to cover my mouth, stifling a gasp. *What is this? What is this? What is this?* The question bounces in my mind repeatedly. *Infinity*—my eyes scan the paper, hoping for answers. *What is Lord Acastus planning to do?*

He can't—The Books of Infinity remain separate for good reason. *That much power, bound as one*—my body trembles uncontrollably as I think of the possible outcome. My eyes water when all I see is catastrophe. The power at the core of this castle, in the portal room. That power is suffocating enough. But to take *all* of the books, to bind them as one. *Impossible.* A prophecy… it must have come from the book that Lord Acastus sent me to retrieve from Ingenium. If the realms fall, will it be my fault? With that haunting idea in mind, I reluctantly pull my eyes to the final paper, loathing the idea of what I may find.

THE BINDING OF THE BOOKS OF INFINITY
AT THE ALIGNMENT OF THE REALMS, ONE WILL SEEK TO
BIND THE BOOKS—

TO BIND THE BOOKS OF INFINITY AS ONE, THEY MUST BE STACKED ACCORDING TO THE INFINITE ORDER, THE BOOK OF THE BOUND TAKING TOP POSITION, ENSURING THAT THEY MAY BECOME ONE. IN THE SEVEN MINUTES BEFORE THE STROKE OF MIDNIGHT ON THE LAST DAY OF THE MILLENNIUM, THE ONE WHO WISHES TO BIND THE BOOKS AS ONE MUST PLACE THEIR HANDS ON THE BOOK OF THE BOUND AND SPEAK THE NAMES OF EACH BOOK ACCORDING TO THE INFINITE ORDER.

This is how he will do it then, how he will claim all of the power in The Seven Realms of Infinity. Lord Acastus has no power of his own. Only the shadow of it. Forever bound, never to be released. For whatever reason, whether it be the history of Lex as he told me, just a byproduct of the peace in the realm, or Professor Clara's history, Lord Acastus cannot use his icy magic. But this? This could give him access, not only to the power of The Book of Law, but the power of *every* Book of Infinity.

But The Infinite Order... the words sound familiar. I recall one of Professor Clara's history lessons. One from long before I became second in command, long before I was trapped in the web of the grey-eyed Knight. The Infinite Order is the sequence in which The Books of Infinity were formed, thereby creating The Seven Realms of Infinity as we know them to be.

First came The Book of Life which created the wandering spirits that would one day live in the realms themselves. Then, The Book of Element which created the material lands of our realms—Spiritus, Tellus, Aetas, Ingenium, Lex, Entis, and Omnis—and gave the spirits a place to live. The Book of Age came next and tied the spirits and their lands to time. Then, The Book of Wit which gave the spirits knowledge of every world, not just our own. The Book of Law allowed the spirits—immortals as we now know them to be—to bind themselves to laws unbreakable by anyone. The Book of Death created the mortals, tying them to a shorter lifespan, giving them true *lives*. Finally, The Book of The Bound tied The Seven Realms of Infinity together and created magical connections between each of The Seven Books of Infinity that allow for The Convergence and The Alignment to take place.

I found The Book of Infinite Prophecy for Lord Acastus—*me*. And if Lord Acastus binds the books, the demise of the realms will forever be my fault. I hear Alma's voice in my head—*power is an intoxicating thing, Soleil*—she once told me. Now I will see it first-hand.

"Now you know." Lord Acastus' voice comes from behind me, nearly causing me to cry out from fear. I spin around, my right hand on Fate's hilt. *Fate*—oh, how I wish Tor was here with me right now.

I know that when I meet the Lord's icy stare, my eyes are welled with the tears of deception. "How could you?"

"Soleil—" He begins, walking towards me.

"Stay away!" I yell, trembling. "How could you send me to Ingenium to find a book that would *last the realms*—when truly you planned to destroy them?" He does not speak. "Tell me!" I beg, tears beginning to stream down my face. Lord Acastus looks utterly broken, as if he hasn't slept or eaten in the two weeks of his absence. I do not feel for him.

"Soleil, *please* let me explain." His voice comes out calm and controlled, it scares me, how cool he is, even as

I turn to ash. I remain silent, only because I cannot live without knowing his true intentions. Maybe if I know, I can stop him. I continue to stare, allowing the fire to rise within me.

"I sent you to Ingenium with a mission. To bring me The Book of Infinite Prophecy so that I could last the realms. Is this correct?" He asks, taking a step towards me.

"Yes—" I stop myself before I can say *my Lord* again. Never again.

"Did you read the prophecy?" He asks, taking another step.

"How could I have stopped myself?" I scoff.

"Recite it to me," he speaks. I make no move.

"Recite it to me, General Soleil Yamanu." He counters with a command.

I curse Infinity for my mortal weakness, my urge to obey. I pick up the paper and read the prophecy, my voice shaking as I do it. The words feel hot as the morning sun against my throat, but I persist until the end.

"This prophecy references more than one person, Soleil." He begins, taking another step to me. "*At the alignment of the realms, one will seek to bind the books.*" He repeats from the prophecy. "That is *one* person, the one who seeks infinite power. But there is another in that prophecy. *Only one in invisibility can halt the demise of the seven realms,*" he pauses for a moment. When I do not speak, he continues. "This person, the *one in invisibility* will stop the destruction of the realms."

"Why are you telling me this?" I rasp.

"Soleil, you are not seeing. Lord Eric Knight of Omnis, who has known nothing but power in his entire existence—he has the only other copy of this prophecy." *No,* I think desperately.

"Lord Eric wishes to bind the books on the evening of The Alignment. I am going to stop him." I remember Professor Clara's lesson, how she told me of Omnis' royal bloodline that has had generations to expand their magic. But Omnis is already the binder of the realms; they are already the high rulers of The Infinite Knight Court.

Power is an intoxicating thing Soleil. Alma's voice reminds me.

"The prophecy says that only *one in invisibility can halt the demise of the seven realms.*" My words come out in a struggle, each one grating against my already tight throat.

"Soleil—" Lord Acastus is only a breath away from me now and I slowly lower my hand from Fate's hilt. "Can't you *see? I* am the one in invisibility." He pleads with me as if I hold a dagger to his throat, as if my disbelief is killing the unkillable. Something in me breaks at that.

"Outcasted from The Infinite Knight Court for my entire rule, left to lead this *wasteland,* unable to travel between the realms myself, and wholly *alone.* I *am* the invisible, and I *will* stop Lord Eric." His words are little more than a whisper as he begs. His hand reaches up to my chin and I do not protest as he tilts my head up to look him in the eyes.

For only a moment, the space between the seconds themselves, I see Lord Acastus' eyes. A piercing blue, as vibrant as the best paints, as deep as the lowest oceans, as perfect as the night sky. I know that he is telling the truth, I know it in my core. It feels right, all of it. The dreams that I have had for *all of my life,* the blue eyes that are engraved into my mind, the shade of blue that I cannot not escape. It is him; it is Lord Acastus. The blue is gone as soon as it comes, and my tears stream more quickly when I finally speak.

"I believe you." My voice cracks and I reach my own hand up to cover his.

He breaks in a sob. The picture of a man who has just finally been seen. *"My General."*

"What do I need to do my Lord? How can I help?" This time I am begging, reaching my other hand to cup his face. He leans into it and I feel at *home.*

"When I bind the books, you will be my Queen, Soleil." The words are dizzying.

Queen? A word so rare amongst the realms as most male Knights refuse to bestow the title upon their wives. But for me to become one…

Lord Acastus begins talking quickly. "Lord Eric will attempt to bind the books himself in the seven minutes before midnight on the last day of the millennium. But this won't happen. Tor Warin is creating exact replicas of each of The Seven Books of Infinity. We will switch the real books out with the fakes and display the false books in the center of the ballroom during The Eternal Dance." *Tor?*

"How does Tor even know what they look like?" I ask skeptically. Tor is but a bladesmith, I doubt that he has even seen a Book of Infinity with his own eyes.

"Your bladesmith is more that you have come to realize, General Yamanu. Under my direction, he has seen and studied each of The Books of Infinity—last of which being The Book of Wit in Ingenium." I recall the hours that Tor and I spent apart while in The Boundless Library.

He had an assignment of his own. I feel a stabbing pain in my core, deception.

"But if he has only seen them once—" I protest.

"You recall how he replicated the carvings of your dagger, General Yamanu. *Fury.*" Lord Acastus' voice is a growl, deep and low.

The Castle has eyes. I know that it does, but I still feel vulnerable, knowing that Lord Acastus saw every moment that Tor and I shared. I recall the times Tor saw my dagger before creating Fate and before carving my armor. Only twice, once on the day of the first of Lord Acastus' battle simulations, and again on the day that the Lord went to Omnis during that star cycle, the day that he repaired Fury. *Fury*—Lord Acastus knows the name of my dagger as well. A name that I have only uttered once, *only* to Tor. I remember the blue of the Lord's eyes and calm at once.

"Yes. I remember."

"Then you understand that this, *project,* is in good hands." I nod in assent. "Lord Eric, unable to use his magic during The Alignment will attempt to stack the false books. *We,* will be waiting on the balcony with the true Books of Infinity already stacked in The Infinite Order."

"Won't Lord Eric know that the books are fake, the magic that radiates from them—"

Lord Acastus stops me in my speech. "The real books will be close by, Soleil. Having all seven of them so close to each other means that their magical signatures will fill the ballroom regardless of where they are placed. All of the Knights will feel the magic and simply believe that it is coming from the false books." I nod my head, choosing to take his word considering I have never even seen a Book of Infinity, nevertheless felt their power.

After a moment, the Lord continues, dropping his hands down and holding tightly to each of mine. "The Binding only takes a moment, so I will use part of the sacred seven minutes to tell the realms of Lord Eric's horrible plan." Lord Acastus pauses and unlaces his right hand from my left. He digs in his pocket, pulling out a simple gold ring. "I will announce you as my wife, as my *Queen*. And then I will bind the books. Together, we will rule *all*. And tomorrow, you will join me at the meeting of The Infinite Knight Court in Omnis." Before I can say another word, Lord Acastus slips the gold band on my left ring finger.

His wife.

I feel power course through me, thorough my very blood. The sheer idea of being Lord Acastus' Queen is power enough—but with him ruling *all* the realms? There is no hesitation in my voice when I speak next, for I know that it is right. That *this* is right. Years of dreaming of the most intense pair of blue eyes, years of wondering. All for this.

"I accept, my Lord."

The gold band burns hot on my finger where I know it will stay for *Infinity*.

CHAPTER TWENTY—TWO

The gold band weighs me down with each step—the physical embodiment of the power I now hold. After Lord Acastus slipped the golden band onto my finger, he walked me back to my chambers and gave me a kiss on my left hand—exactly where he placed the ring only moments earlier—and then he left without another word.

I stripped my armor, scabbards, and clothing off, sliding into a pair of sleeping thermals and tucking myself into bed before I could even begin to think about what had happened. The gold band remained on my left ring finger, almost warm to the touch, and I rubbed the warm metal as I was roped into infinite oblivion.

My handmaidens woke me early this morning. It took long seconds before my eyes adjusted to the morning light and even longer before I got out of bed. I almost forgot why my handmaidens even cared to wake me up today, until I remember Lord Acastus' words from the night before—until I feel the weight of the gold ring on my finger. Today, I will travel to Omnis. There, I will be the first mortal to witness the proceedings of The Infinite Knight Court.

My handmaidens work quickly to prepare me after my shower. They straighten my hair, and apply my make-up, in an almost routine fashion.

When I am thoroughly prepared, I slip into my—already washed—white thermals, and the handmaidens assist me in getting my full golden armor on my body. Fate and Fury are strapped to my leg and my cloak is draped perfectly across my back and shoulders. Before I can reach for my crown to place atop my head, there is a knock at the door. I smile at his perfect timing. I move to open the door, finding Lord Acastus, in his ceremonial Knight's armor that I have never seen him in before. The armor is silver and ornate, thick and well made—a clear sign of status. Over it he wears a cloak of slate grey, bringing out the hidden hues of his eyes. Atop his head sits a silver crown with a black gem embedded into the center point. I smile up at him and his eyes flicker to my left hand. He smiles when he sees the ring still there.

"Soleil." He whispers, kissing the ring. I love the sound of my name on his tongue.

"My Lord."

"Do you mind if I crown you?" He asks, then adds, "*my Queen.*" I gesture for him to come inside. Lord Acastus retrieves my crown from the plush red pillow on which it sits. Slowly, so painfully slow, he lowers the diadem onto my head. I can't help but stare at him. *Really* examine my husband. He is gorgeous. "Beautiful." The Lord murmurs, taking my chin in his hand. We stay there for a moment, frozen in time, as I take in his scent. The fresh mint of his breath, and the cool evergreen of *him*. He puts his arm out for me to take. I do so without command. Together, we walk into the halls of The Castle and back to its beating heart.

The portal room is utterly the same with the six portals evenly spaced around the stone chamber and the pulsing magic that makes me feel alive. Still, after coming here before, after *traveling here before*. It manages to take my breath away. I take a deep gulp of air as Lord Acastus and I walk into the room and towards the portal to Omnis. A golden glow emits from the portal. It is so perfect… the overwhelming feeling of *everything* returns as I stare into the glow, afraid that if I move, it will simply cease to exist. Even if I wanted to move, to turn away, I am not sure that I could.

"My Queen." Lord Acastus says from behind me, his voice deep. He places his hands on my shoulders and I lean into his touch. "Are you ready?" His hands move down my arms and rest at my stomach, guarded by my breastplate.

"Yes, my Lord."

Lord Acastus walks next to me and takes my hand in his before leading us into the golden glow of Omnis.

I am everything and nothing. My body ceases to exist as I am pushed through time and space, stretched and molded until I forget who I am. When the red stains my vision, all I can hold on to is the feeling of the gold ring on my finger. Then the white peeks through and not soon after—everything goes black. Feeling returns to my body at once and I open my eyes to find another portal room that looks the same as the one in Lex. No one is in the room, not a single soul is awaiting our arrival.

"Where is everyone?" Shouldn't there be a welcoming committee? This is a Knight of Infinity; he should be treated as such.

"Either they have not yet arrived—which is quite unlikely—or they received an earlier arrival time as usual." Lord Acastus' tone is resigned. I quickly begin to understand the depth of his *exile* amongst the other Knights of Infinity. How they could disregard and diminish the selfless immortal next to me… I could never understand.

"Then let's go before we are late." I reply, keeping my tone light. He gives my hand a gentle squeeze before guiding me out of the portal room and into the halls of The Castle of Omnis. I brace myself for the shock I know will come. But his presence, the presence of my husband, it is enough to settle me for a moment.

Unlike the underground halls of The Castle of Ingenium, those of The Castle of Omnis immediately feel different. Though we are clearly levels below the surface, the hallways are grander than any space I have ever stepped foot in.

The floors are made of a deep black cherry wood whose panels align seamlessly along the floor. The walls—a gorgeous white marble—are carved in baroque and moving swirls, each foiled with pure gold. Every single space of the ceilings has been meticulously painted with the most gorgeous of artwork. Each celling panel is slightly different, varying in style and composition, but they pull together to create a breathtaking sight. Every few feet, a small slit in the wall reveales a golden glow, diffused by a pane of frosted glass.

Lord Acastus does not make a sound next to me and it takes all of my control not to stop him to get a better look at the artwork on the ceilings, or to touch the golden swirls on the marble walls. I keep my chin up and do my best to match pace with the Lord whose legs are much longer than mine—*and* blessed with immortal composure. Our boots create a melody of clicks on the wood floor that echo along its length. Eventually, we reached a set of stairs made of the same wood, with walls of the same marble, that form the rest of the hall.

We climb and climb, Lord Acastus eventually releasing my hand and continuing the trek on his own. When we make it to the proper floor, Lord Acastus takes my arm and continues to lead me through The Castle of Omnis' beautiful halls. This hallway is somehow grander than the last; it has the same marble walls and wood floors, but the ceilings are so much higher, elegantly vaulted too. Each of the beams between vaults are foiled in the same gold that lines the swirls of the walls. Despite the paintings on the ceiling being much larger, they still fill every space, creating a patchwork of intricate stories.

Rather than thin slits in the walls where lights are, there are now large windows. I can't help myself from gasping when I see what is beyond The Castle's walls.

Great mountains line the horizon of Omnis, as if it is a living piece of art itself. Then comes its rolling hills full of greenery—true green that I have never seen before. I let go of Lord Acastus' arm and make my way to the window to get a closer look.

Below the castle is a charming village that stretches far to the edge of the rolling hills, and then beyond. The houses and buildings are quaint but full of color. The citizens dance and sing in one corner, daze, and relax in another, and in a city square, they sell and barter. The paths of the village are made of stone, clearly well loved by its citizens over the years. Flowers bloom in gardens and in fields, and then, in every nook and cranny that they can thrive. A winding river loops between the mountains and through the forest, catching and reflecting the light of the sun. The sky is perfectly blue, bright and flawless with fluffy and light clouds moving softly through the expanse. There is no glass in these windows—similar to The Castle of Ingenium—and a breeze passes through the space ruffling a few strands of my hair. I smile at the feeling; the air is neither warm nor cold, not dry nor humid. It is everything, it is *perfect*. The sun is cast high over the horizon, sending streams of perfect light over the land.

How can a place such as this exist in the same universe as Lex?

I feel Lord Acastus' hands on my hips, solid against my curves, as I admire Omnis' beauty. I feel as if I have fallen in love with its perfection and, in this moment, I know why the portal glows golden. Every inch of Omnis sparkles with magic, but my love dissipates when I remember who is behind it. Lord Eric, Knight of Omnis who has *everything*, who has all of this, yet still craves more. I turn my head abruptly from the perfection, fearful that if

I look for another second, I will become wholly entrapped by its beauty.

"Let's go." I beg Lord Acastus.

"Of course, my Queen." He says gravely, looping his arm through mine. I hold on to Lord Acastus' arm tighter than before and he slows his pace to accommodate. The windows and Omnis' perfect landscape beckon but I keep my gaze trained on the wood floor, reminding myself what—*who*—I am here for.

Eventually we make it to an unassuming stone door. Lord Acastus stops, knocks twice, and the door is opened for us. It reveals a simple stone antechamber, something that could easily belong in The Castle of Lex, or even in The Fortress. It isn't the room itself that piques my interest, but those who are inside.

Six Knights of Infinity—all in their finest armor— watch me with predatory interest.

My eyes dart around the room, too quick to register any one Knight. Some lounge on chairs or sofa's, others lean against walls, clearly in conversation. I find Lady Fable eventually, her eyes glowing with warmth when she meets mine. I look up at Lord Acastus who understands my want without me needing to ask. He unhooks his arm from mine so I can walk to the Lady.

When I am only a few feet from her, I give a deep nod which she returns civilly. Lady Fable wears a beautiful and formfitting gown of deep purple. Over her gown, she wears a perfectly shined breastplate—a deep copper—that almost glows with beauty. Her gauntlets match but it is a simple set—without any of the engravings that Lord Acastus' armor has—however it *is* gorgeous, nonetheless. Her hair is bound in an elegant updo, and her crown—copper as well, inlaid with purple stones—sits atop her head.

"General Yamanu," she says warmly, taking my hands in hers. "How are you?" I had almost forgotten about the reason I know Lady Fable in the first place.

"I am doing very well, thank you my Lady." She smiles in response. "And thank you for allowing me access into The Boundless Library."

"Ah—yes! How was your time there? Were you able to explore enough?" She asks genuinely.

"My time was brief. However, I was able to get the gist of what my bladesmith was talking about. I wish that I could have returned, however prior engagements have kept me tied down." My voice is smooth and sweet. I feel as if I have done this a thousand times before.

"Oh, I understand, a General's work is never done. Please remember that The Boundless Library is always open for you whenever you wish to visit." I grin in thanks. "This is your first-time meeting most of the Knights, is that correct?"

"Yes, I am afraid that I don't know anyone besides you, my Lady. And Lord Acastus of course." I reply, feigning nervousness. Infinity—you would think it would be easier to fool an immortal, a Knight of Infinity at that.

"Let me introduce you then!" The Lady exclaims. "Vale!" She calls.

A tall, lean, and angular man with bright green eyes and fluffy brown hair walks over to Lady Fable. His face is soft and kind, and he wears a dark bronze crown that looks to be made of branches, atop his head.

"Lord Vale." I bow deeply. When I rise, he smiles gently and gives a subtle nod. I barely notice when his hand wraps around Lady Fable's waist, pulling her to him.

"Vale, this is General Soleil Yamanu, second in command of The Undying Army. And General, this is my *husband,* Lord Vale, Knight of Tellus."

Husband? I stop my eyes before they widen. In all of the history lessons I have sat through, not once did Professor Clara mention that two of the Knights of Infinity are married. It takes me a moment before I can form the words to reply.

"Lord Vale, it's a pleasure." I say civilly, thanking Infinity for the strength in my tone despite my shock.

"Please, General Yamanu. The pleasure is mine." His voice is kind and pure. My smile grows wider despite myself.

"My love, let us introduce the General to the rest of our friends." Lady Fable says looking up at Lord Vale, her eyes sparkling as she speaks to him.

"Of course." Lord Vale nods. "Let me see—ah yes. She would be perfect. Lady Kala!" Lord Vale shouts. Before I can register, a slight woman with soft features and long black hair, stands in front of me.

"Lady Kala, this is General Soleil Yamanu—"

"Yes, yes. *Second in command of The Undying Army.* I have heard much about you, General." Lady Kala speaks, her voice almost lazy. She is the oldest of the Knights, a millennium old herself, she rules over the realm of Aetas.

"Lady Kala, it's an honor." I bow deep again. When I meet Lady Kala's eyes, I am startled. I swear that I see the stars themselves.

"Thank you General." The Lady replies curtly before walking back to her seat on a wooden chair.

I puzzle at her abruptness, but Lord Vale reassures me. "She is *always* like that. All of that time looking at the stars—she eventually lost patience with all of us." He chuckles.

"Anyway…" Lady Fable says, giving Lord Vale a pointed look. "Who else can I introduce you to? Vale, I am no longer in need of your services, you may go."

"Of course, *my Lady*." He replies before planting a kiss on Lady Fable's cheek.

Lady Fable takes my arm before walking me to a man and a woman who chat together in the corner of the room. The man has tan skin similar to my own. He is only an inch or two taller than me, with intense and almost shadowy features. He wears black armor and a black cloak as if he is a shadow himself. The woman he is talking to is much shorter than I am. She has fiery red hair and almost doll-like features. Her skin is covered in freckles and she wears shining white-gold armor, carved and inlaid with red stones. The man's crown is black and rugged, the woman's that same white-gold and fine as a spider's silk. I immediately recognize who they are—life and death incarnate.

"Lord Nasim, Lady Psyche, this is General Soleil Ya-manu, second in command of The Undying Army." I loosen myself from Lady Fable to give the Knights a deep bow of respect. When I rise, they are hand in hand. It becomes incredibly clear that Lord Vale and Lady Fable are not the only two Knights that are *together.*

"You're Acastus' girl, huh?" Lord Nasim Knight of Entis, asks nonchalantly.

"I am." I reply, maintaining my respect.

"How does it feel to be the first mortal second in command of The Undying Army?" Lady Psyche, Knight of Spiritus asks, her voice airy in the way it travels. It feels new and bright, even though the Lady must be hundreds of years old.

"It is quite the honor to serve under Lord Acastus and I am grateful for every moment." I reply, staring into the wide green eyes of the Lady. She smiles brightly.

"Well… *General Yamanu,* enjoy your time here. Please know that Lord Acastus had to pull—" Lady Psyche cuts Lord Nasim off before he can continue.

"Please, have a wonderful time General." After that, Lady Fable walks me away. Curious…

"Did I do something to offend Lord Nasim?" I ask Lady Fable quietly. I know however, that no matter how low my voice is, the immortal hearing of every Knight can pick it up.

"Oh no, General Yamanu. *You,* have nothing to worry about. Some of the Knights are a bit *cautious* at Lord Acastus' move. No mortal has ever witnessed The Infinite Knight Court in action, it is unprecedented. Naturally, some of us do not know how to react. I am afraid that Lord Nasim seems to be one of them." I nod in understanding. It makes sense—I am an outsider; I am *mortal.* To these infinite beings, my life is inconsequential. But to witness The Infinite Knight Court in action. That makes me important.

"I am missing someone, aren't I?" I ask, scanning the room. "Him." I jut my chin towards a man who leans casually against a table, taking deep sips from a goblet.

He is the most perfect man I have ever seen. His skin is pale, contrasting elegantly against the darkness of his flowing hair and perfect, thick eyebrows. He wears armor in a shade I have never seen before, a royal blue so deep that it is almost black. A matching blue cloak is effortlessly draped over his shoulders. A grand silver crown—inlaid with deep blue gems—sits just above his brow.

"Yes, you are. But I am afraid that my presence won't help you with him." I puzzle at her words. "Introduce yourself for the sake of respect, but do not be surprised if his manner is… *less than welcoming.*"

I nod my head even though I have not the slightest idea of what Lady Fable means. I walk over to the man anyway. *Infinity*—he is so much taller than I am. I remain a few steps away from the immortal so I can comfortably stare into the endless depths of his eyes. They are intense, a shade so dark it *is* simply black. My gaze intensifies when his eyes meet mine and I realize *exactly* who he is. I bow deeply, putting on a show for Lord Eric, Knight of Omnis.

"General Soleil Yamanu, second in command of The Undying Army." I say with a sly smile.

"*Yes,*" he hisses. "You are the mortal who somehow slithered her way up the ranks." He spits. As if he did not insult me at all, he sips from his goblet.

"I am, though I wouldn't say that I had to *slither up* the ranks. When you are the best, the title seems to *slither* its way to you." I am playing a dangerous game and I know it; Lord Eric is the only Knight to have true magic. The only Knight to be able to wield his Infinite gifts. He can kill me with half a thought and yet, I do not regret the tone of my reply.

"What did you say your name was?" He asks nonchalantly.

"Soleil Yamanu."

"Soleil—that is a word from the old world, yes?"

I nod, refusing to break his stare. He ponders, and for long seconds we stare at each other in silence. "If that is all Lord Eric, it was—*lovely* to meet you."

"Yes, yes. It was a pleasure to meet you as well *sunshine.*" The word slides smoothly off of his tongue and I fill with anger at it. *How dare he?* I have to steady the feeling burning within, reminding myself where I am, *and* who I am talking to.

"Thank you, my Lord." I reply curtly and walk away, until I met Lord Acastus once more. He takes my arm without a word. I loosen a breath and let my perfect posture crumble in the safety of my husband.

"Are you alright?" He asks.

"Yes, I simply made the acquaintance of the rest of the Knights." I say breathlessly.

"Tricky business." Lord Acastus murmurs into my ear, taming a stray piece of hair. The stone doors opposite the entrance to the antechamber open, revealing a stone table, surrounded by gilded thrones.

"The council meeting of The Infinite Knight Court may begin." Lord Eric announces.

Seven Knights and one General are seated at a round table, the air around us thick with magic—the power, and promise, of war.

I am seated between Lord Acastus and Lord Vale, who sneaks me a gentle smile as I take my throne. An ornate jug is placed in the center of the stone table, painted with beautiful depictions of battle and council throughout the history of the realms. In front of each throne sits a beautiful goblet filled to the brim with a plum-colored liquid that I immediately recognize as wine. My goblet will stay full, then.

As soon as everyone takes their seats, each Knight reaches up and pulls their crowns off their heads, placing them next to their goblets. Slightly delayed—I follow suit, placing my golden diadem in front of me.

My head snaps up when a wall of magic—encompassing all seven Knights of Infinity, myself, and the round table—goes up. It is almost black, but transparent enough to see the stone walls around us. It glimmers and moves like water. When I reached out to touch it, it molds around my hand. I look to Lord Eric who sits directly across from me on the stone table. This magic must be his doing. He glowers at me from the other side of the table and I can only wonder how *he* can rule a place so full of beauty and perfection.

I am disgusted by his craving for power, by his need to have more than he already does. He rules over the most perfect realm in all of existence. His people are happy. He is the high ruler of The Seven Realms of Infinity, and he still craves more power. As if being the sworn ruler of The Book of The Bound isn't enough, Lord Eric needs to rule them *all*, even if he destroys everything in the process. My gaze is fire enough to set the whole castle ablaze as Lord Eric finally speaks to begin the meeting.

"We have much to attend to today. So let us begin. All rise to state The Infinite Order." Everyone stands at his words and it is Lady Psyche who speaks first after that.

"Spirit." She says, and the magic swirling around us glows blue for a moment, before returning to its original color.

"Element." Lord Vale follows from next to me, turning the magic a deep green.

"Age." Lady Kala speaks, her voice proud as the magic turns a purple so dark it is almost black.

"Wit." Lady Fable says, giving me a smile as the swirl of magic glows a warm orange.

"Law." Lord Acastus says, his voice stone cold from my right. The magic turns a dull grey color, as cold as Lex itself. *Typical...*

"Death." Lord Nasim hisses. The magic turns an all-encompassing black.

"Bound." Lord Eric says, glaring at me from across the table. A chill creeps along my spine as the magic turns a gold as bright and beautiful as the sun itself. I can't help but gape at the whorls, so like the ones on my armor. The magic pulses for a moment before returning to the dark shade it held previously. We all take our seats after that.

"Very well, we shall begin. Our first order of business is in relation to The Eternal Dance that is but a short two weeks away," Lord Eric sends a pointed look to Lord

Acastus. "Lord Acastus, may we get a report on the status of the event?" Lord Eric's raises an eyebrow as if he is reeling in for an attack. He smirks like this entire meeting is below him.

"Preparations for The Eternal Dance are underway as far as my knowledge extends. It is my second in command who has been taking the lead on these preparations, however. I believe that she is the most qualified to speak on this topic."

Infinity—oh Infinity! My pulse quickens; not only am I the first mortal to *witness* the proceedings of The Infinite Knight Court, but I will also be the first mortal to speak during them as well. Sending a prayer to Infinity above, I brace for Lord Eric's reply.

"Good to know that the girl is not simply here for *decoration*, Lord Acastus." Lord Eric sneers; his eyes as black as the portal to Entis. "Okay *sunshine*, speak." He barks the command.

That is what he thinks of me then, a mere piece of decoration. *Of course*—to Lord Eric, I *am* merely a piece of decoration. I am mortal, but a speck of dirt, so inconsequential in the eyes of a man who has lived hundreds of years. I am *nothing* to him.

Choosing not to react however, I meet his gaze with the Infinity evoked intensity that I know I hold in my own eyes. "Preparations for The Eternal Dance are going wonderfully, Lord Eric. I thank you for your concern." My stare does not travel from his. "Decorations have been chosen, music has been selected, seating arrangements created, and the invitations have been sent out. Though you may not have known about that last part, my Lord, for we have sent you two invitations already and you have yet to respond. Do we need to send a third?"

My voice is clear and taunting. I will not allow myself to become prey in a room of predators, especially against one as arrogant as Lord Eric. I swear that the magic around the room ripples in response to my words. While Lord Eric remains as smug as before I said them, the magic is enough to tell me that I reach him.

"Big words for a mortal." Lord Eric replies after long seconds of silence. "Though, I suppose when your lifespan is so insignificant, one *would* feel untouchable—" Before he can continue, I cut him off not willing to be reprimanded by his words.

"Or, when you are a *mortal,* and your lifespan is so *insignificant,* you learn to pick things up much quicker than most. You learn that the man who growls at the prey without taking a bite—only does so because he is simply food himself." I cock my head to the side tauntingly, letting a sly smile spread across my face.

I am playing quite the dangerous game, but I know that if Lord Acastus is ostracized at this table, then I have *no* chance if I don't play for *my* spot.

A flicker of surprise travels across Lord Eric's face and, for a moment, his smile drops. The magic gives a few beats, as if my words have somehow interrupted its flow, but it persists, nonetheless. Lord Eric opens his mouth to speak but Lady Fable does so instead.

"General Yamanu, thank you for the report. We look forward to seeing the outcome of The Eternal Dance soon." She smiles at me, though it feels more like a reprimand than anything else. I turn to her and nod, choosing only to see authenticity in her features.

"Yes, General sunshine, we are all very excited to see what you have done." I burn hotter at his words. I know that he will never tire of them, never tire at even my most subtle reactions when he calls me—*that.* "I do have one question for you." I turn back to him, a chill running down my body as I meet his depthless eyes. How could they be so dark in a realm so full of light?

"I may have an answer, my Lord." I reply casually.

"What is it like being the first *mortal* second in command of The Undying Army. Especially when you are so filled with that, *mortal fragility* and people tend to…*kill* for the job." It isn't anything I haven't heard before, so his quip does not sting as intended. Still, he chuckles after he speaks, amused by his own cleverness.

"I hold the position well," I smile, in no attempt to be humble. "You may find that I am not as *fragile* as I seem."

"We shall see, *sunshine,*" he winks. After a pause he continues. "It seems that General sunshine's eagerness has crossed many an item off our list of discussion. There is one more article to converse upon, in regard to the realm of Lex." I hear Lord Acastus shuffle next to me and nervousness swells in my body once more.

"Whatever the matter of the item, my General and I will be pleased to discuss it." I wonder how a man such as Lord Acastus can be outcasted as he is in this court. Power flows from every word he says. His magic moves from his body in icy waves. Being near him is dizzying in itself. And yet—the power-hungry Knight in front of me still wins.

"I would prefer *you* to answer this one, Lord Acastus. We wouldn't want our entire council meeting to rest on the back of a simple mortal, would we?" The magic around us whorls more confidently than before. I wonder why Lord Eric puts it up anyway. It is a clear vulnerability, and I know that I am not the only being in this room to recognize the patterns. There has to be a reason behind it.

"Of course, Lord Eric. Though I wish that you would simply *speak*. It's much too childish to play silly games such as these, especially during council." I let myself crack a small smile as Lord Acastus speaks. Pride for the man I will soon rule beside flows through me. I watch as Lord Eric's magic continues to flow, though less sure now.

"Very well. There have been rumors, Lord Acastus, that your legions of soldiers in The Undying Army have been expanding at an alarming pace. While I am not often one to put stake into simple talk such as this, in relation to the royal bloodline of Lex—and its *history,* this cannot be ignored." Lord Eric goads Lord Acastus with every word, but I hang on to one of them in particular—*history.*

Professor Clara's lesson floods back to me. The way that she talked about Duncan Lex and how the tyrannical ruler expanded *his* legions in The Undying Army before nearly leading the realms to ruin. The way Professor Clara explained it to me, as if it wasn't another one of Alma's old tales from an Ingenium storybook. *As if it was real.* It can't be, Lord Eric is teasing. He is deceiving everyone at the table, his sworn companions. It is another one of his lies, I reassure myself.

"I can confirm that those rumors are indeed true, Lord Eric." Lord Acastus says simply.

I thank Infinity for his control, knowing full well that I would have lost my temper myself if faced with a question such as that.

"Care to elaborate, Lord Acastus?" The High Knight muses.

"The Undying Army's numbers have been slowly fading in these last years. We have lost an alarming number of men simply from exposure to Lex's harsh climate. The numbers when seen on a year-by-year basis do not seem of any consequence, however when we add them up, we have lost thousands of soldiers." That is news to me. I keep the shock from my face by reminding myself that I had been Second in Command for less than a star cycle and a half, I have much to learn.

"After seeing how well trained and skilled my own second in command is, despite her only being in the seventh year at The Academy of The Undying Army, I decided that now was a wonderful opportunity to graduate a few extra years' worth of The Academy's students. This way, The Army can make up for the losses that have slowly accumulated."

Suddenly, his decision does not seem so rash. Lord Acastus seems so mortal to me that I often forget that he is hundreds of years old, that he has been leading The Undying Army since long before I was even born. His decisions are always well thought out and calculated. I somehow miss that again and again.

"Yes, it seems incredibly wise to base a decision such as this on the fluke that is a single mortal student in her seventh year at The Academy." Lord Eric mocks. Before Lord Acastus can reply—I do.

"If you are questioning the integrity of these newly graduated soldiers, Lord Eric, I will gladly lead them into Omnis to… *clear up* any misunderstandings that you may have." I keep my features neutral, almost bored with confidence. The magic ripples and I crack a knowing smile at Lord Eric as it does.

"General sunshine, it seems that you don't know me well enough. If I wished to reassure myself of the *integrity* of a few soldiers, I would simply take a portal to Lex myself. The only thing preventing me from doing so right now, is the idea of taking a single step in that frozen wasteland you call home."

Fire roars in my eyes and I make no attempt to shield it. "One would think that you are quite familiar with the idea of a *frozen wasteland* considering that your soul seems to be one too." It is a low shot, but it does the job for Lord Eric's magic stops moving all together.

"Enough!" Lord Nasim growls; my heart thuds at the power of his voice. "I will not sit here and let a mortal disrespect The Infinite Knight Court any longer." Blood roars in ears. *I* am disrespectful? "And I will not allow a Knight of Infinity to be baited by a mortal, no matter the position she may hold."

I am nothing but a smudge on their pristine armor, nothing but an inconvenience in their overarching lives, nothing but a rustle of wind to shift a tuft of hair out of place. *I am nothing.* All of the power that I hold, it means nothing to them. Maybe I *should* just let Lord Eric destroy the realms—but the image of him kneeling before me as I am crowned Queen of The Seven Realms of Infinity is too enticing. The sheer idea of him groveling at my feet is too perfect for me to let go.

Without a word, I place my crown back on my head and stand, the scraping of my throne on the stone floor music to my ears. Nearly turning to walk right past the wall of magic, right out of the counsel room, I decide that I am not done yet. I roughly grab my—still full—goblet of wine from the table. After staring at the shimmering liquid for a moment, I throw it directly at Lord Eric.

My aim is true, and the entire goblet of purple liquid splashes and covers Lord Eric. It coats his hair and face, and seeps into his cloak. I know I truly surprised him, as the magic around us is left in tatters. I bow to all of the Knights, feigning respect as I meet their stares. Each of them looks at me with shock—more emotion than I have ever seen on the faces of the immortals. Everyone except for Lord Acastus, for he simply seems *content*.

I put my hand out to the tattered remains of the magic wall and find that it no longer forms around my hand. At that, I walk past the magic, out of the door to the council room, and through the antechamber until I am back in The Castle of Omnis' pristine hallways.

They disgust me. The marble walls, the gold foiling, the artwork that covers every inch of the vaulted ceilings. I despise the perfection of the landscape beyond the castle. I crave my home—*my Lex*—instead.

A click, clack of boots on stone echoes from the antechamber and my trained ears know it is Lord Acastus as soon as the first step hits. He will not reprimand me, nor shun me for my actions. But my pulse still quickens as he nears. The stone door opens and Lord Acastus walks out, his face perfectly calm.

"I want to go home." I plead.

"Of course, Soleil." Lord Acastus reaches his right hand out to me and I take it in my left, grateful for the presence of my husband. When he has my hand in his, he gently caresses the golden ring on my finger as we walk through The Castle of Omnis, and back to *our home.*

CHAPTER TWENTY—THREE

A stone table.
Seven ornate goblets.
Seven gilded thrones.
Seven shining Knights.
A pair of piercing blue eyes.
"I will find a way."
One goblet lifted.
Six goblets rose in unison

The dream does not alarm me any longer. It has not plagued me in weeks—not since the morning Tor and I went to Ingenium. Even as it pulls me into its depths, I find solace, rather than fear, in the piercing blue eyes. When the six goblets finally rise and I am able to pry myself from the dream's grasp, I do not wake with anxiety filling my mind. Instead, an overwhelming feeling of calm. The blue eyes—Lord Acastus' eyes—remain engraved in my mind, but I do not shy away from them any longer. They are the eyes of my husband and if they are to follow me for Infinity, then so be it.

The clock in front of my bed reads *0543*. Sunlight—pure sunlight—streams in through my already open window. I hear the scuffle of my handmaidens, already scurrying about, and sit up to rub my eyelids. The gold wedding band remains on my finger. Since Lord Acastus gave it to me two weeks ago, I have not removed it. At first, it was a reminder of the weight I will soon hold as Queen of The Realms of Infinity, but slowly it has become a comfort.

Once Lord Acastus and I returned from our unbearable trip to Omnis, he walked me to my chambers and left me with a smile and a nod. Something in me stirred at the thought of him disappearing once again, but my worries were washed away when he arrived at my chambers the next morning, two plates of breakfast in hand, and a charming smile on his face. That simple gesture sent flutters to my stomach; it warmed my core.

The Lord and I have spent every moment of these past two weeks together, adding final touches to preparations for The Eternal Dance, leading strategy meetings for The Undying Army, taking all of our meals in my chambers, and training side by side as well.

To be seen with the power and strength I know I possess—it is refreshing. Lord Acastus—*my husband*—sees me for exactly what I am, and he does not shy away. Each morning he kisses the gold band on my finger, and every night as he leaves my chambers, he does so again. I think about the future that is so close—an eternity ruling at his side—it does not scare me.

But I feel like I am running out of time.

Lord Acastus does not know what will happen when he binds The Books of Infinity as one, when he saves the realms from complete destruction. I pray to Infinity that things will remain as they are, that Lord Acastus and I can continue to rule, and that my friends will remain safe. I have not seen them in weeks. Not Tor, who I last saw on our trip to Ingenium. Not Nova or Arche who I haven't seen since I found them in their new war camps. Not Alma, whose colors showed true when I visited last.

Still, I am not afraid. When I am Queen of The Seven Realms of Infinity, they will bow. Everyone will bow. The image of Lord Eric pleading at my feet plays in my mind again and again. It is enough to diminish any remnants of fear that I possess.

"General Yamanu. We are to prepare you for The Eternal Dance." My handmaiden speaks softly, her words but a mere whisper compared to the volume of my thoughts.

It is the twenty ninth day of the tenth star cycle, in the nine hundred and ninety ninth year of the ninety ninth millennia. Tonight, is The Eternal Dance.

My shower is short and I only allow the coldest water to stream down my body as I wash. I scrub my hair so it can be straightened once more. I scrub my face so it can be painted in makeup not of my choosing, and I scrub my body so it can be adorned by a dress that may as well be a gift straight from Infinity.

When I am done, I wrap myself in towels and take a seat at the sofa in front of my fireplace. As I eat, I relish in the crackle and pop of the fire. The simplicity of an action such as this—the same thing that I have done every morning for my entire life, in the Lost wing as a child, in The Academy's bathing chamber as I grew, and now in my own personal chambers—is more complex than ever this morning. I feel it in my soul—the change—I know it will be grand and terrifying, but I also know that Lord Acastus will be there with me through it all.

A handmaiden walks over to me and feels my hair, checking if it is dry yet. When she declares that it is, I rise and take my usual seat in front of the vanity. I look into the mirror, but I do not see myself.

Not *Soleil Yamanu* that grew up in The Castle, under the care of The Women of the Lost. Not *Soldier Soleil Yamanu* that studied at The Academy, relishing in the clang of steel that seemed to echo through The Fortress' halls. And not *General Soleil Yamanu, second in command of The Undying Army,* who I have known for only two short star cycles.

I see someone completely other, someone blessed by Infinity, chosen by the Knight of Lex. I see the Queen of The Seven Realms at last.

Eventually, the handmaidens complete their initial stages of my preparation. When I am finally allowed to enter my closet, I let out a gasp of shock at my dress.

It is perfect. The perfect likeness of the drawing that Nelio Journee created for me after I gave him my adjustments. Currently on a mannequin, the dress is made of the velvety tulle fabric that I chose, bunching and flowing in layers of the red material. The color—in the form of a completed gown—is stunning. Tonight, I will be the rose adorning Lord Acastus arm.

Every rose must have its thorn however, and the gold, metal corset, is just that. It is just as I imagined, sharpened to a spike at its center. When I walk closer to examine, it is engraved with the same whorls of my armor. I touch my finger to the point that looks as sharp as Fate but find that it doesn't so much as prick me when I do. When I take a glance at the matching golden heels, I notice that a tag is attached to the corset. I know right away that it is from Tor.

General Yamanu,
I hope it is to your liking.
Forever your Bladesmith,
Tor Warin

A pang is sent through my chest. *Why?* This paper is the only correspondence that Tor and I have had in nearly a star cycle. While it is curt, his signing—*Forever your Blade-smith*—is enough to tell me that even if he doesn't forgive me, at the very least he understands. I stand there for a moment, rereading the same few words again and again as if in longing. It isn't until I hear a knock on the door that I set it down.

"Tell him that I'm not decent yet." I say to neither handmaiden in particular. One leaves and the other closes my closet door before moving to one of the racks to arrange what I am to wear. She pulls out a pair of red lounging thermals as well as black lace up boots, setting them on the chair in the center of my closet. When she is done, I gesture for her to leave and change quickly.

At the very least I am comfortable, though I long to get into the incredible dress that waits for me. Hastily, I lace my boots and strap both Fate and Fury to my body before stepping out to greet my husband. He is standing just outside the door, an enchanted look on his face. Emotion swirls in his grey eyes, though I cannot pinpoint exactly what it is.

"My Queen." He murmurs, pulling me to him in an embrace. I relish in the feel of his body, solid and comforting and... *infinite* against my own. When he releases me, he picks up my left hand and kisses the band of gold around my finger, my heart pounds as he does. "May I crown you?"

"Of course, my Lord." We walk back into the closet and he picks up the golden diadem and places it on my head. This gesture, the same thing he has done every morning for half a star cycle, is filled with intimacy. The raw and vulnerable emotion that only I get to see from the Lord. His fingers linger over my smooth and straight hair before he holds out a hand for me.

"Is everything prepared for tonight?" He asks.

"I have a few things to do, but everything is going according to plan." I reply casually.

"And the books?" He adds, raising an eyebrow.

"That is what I will be taking care of."

"Let me walk you out then."

I nod and take Lord Acastus' hand before walking out of my rooms.

We walk to the glass castle, the place that Tor showed me only star cycles ago. The glass castle is the perfect center mark between the ballroom and the portal room.

Unassuming, but large enough to store the false copies of The Books of Infinity.

"This is where I leave you. I will see you soon, my Queen." Lord Acastus kisses my ring once more before walking away. After a beat, I push the stone door in, shocked to find Tor sitting on a chair near the copies of The Books of Infinity. The glass windows are covered hastily with black cloth to keep away prying eyes, the only light comes from the faint glow of a candle.

"Tor." I say in shock.

"Soleil." He replies curtly.

"I—" I begin but he cuts me off.

"I do not expect an apology Soleil, nor do I need one. You have the weight of a realm on your shoulders. But still, a letter would have been nice." He jokes.

"You just decided to extend *that* pleasure to me this morning." I laugh back at him, pulling him into a warm embrace.

"How are you?" He murmurs into my hair. I forgot how much I missed him. Even though I shouldn't.

"I'm okay. What about you? I heard you had quite the task to complete." I reply, pulling away to see the books laid out on the small stone table.

"Making your armor—and the weapons at your thigh, was much worse." Tor muses.

"*Weapon,* at my thigh," I correct. "You did not *make* Fury, you fixed it."

"I beg to differ," he laughs.

"Excuse me?"

"I *made* that dagger, Soleil. It was the first weapon I made when I arrived here." There is nothing but truth in his voice—in his eyes.

"That is impossible—" I begin. He would have been twelve at the time, he would still have been in Ingenium.

"I entered The School at nine years old, Soleil. I studied for three years, and the moment I turned twelve I took the first portal here to Lex. My test—from the old head bladesmith—was to create the perfect dagger. No other instruction. So, I did, and now *that* dagger sits at your thigh." He reaches down and lets his fingers graze Fury's hilt, the movement causing my breath to hitch.

"All this time? And you didn't tell me?" I ask breathlessly.

"The day I met you, you came to me halfway to The Door of The Dusk trying to return your armor." He protests.

"And you still asked to see Fury." I reply.

"Because when I saw the hilt—I had my suspicions. But I apologize for not explaining its entire ancestry while you were bleeding out."

I glare up at him. "You had plenty of opportunities to do that," I pause. "And my name? Engraved into the blade."

"Where do you think the suspicions came from?" He laughs. "*Soleil,* is not the most common of names."

"I can't believe it."

"How else could I have engraved that pattern so perfectly."

"I knew there was something—*out of sorts* with that. You were *too* perfect." I joke, nudging him with my shoulder as I turn to examine the books.

There are seven of them, each bound in a different color leather, each equally as worn. They are incredibly large and heavy looking. Even sitting here alone, they seem full of magic. My eyes are pulled to the gold one in the center of the rest, the word *Bound* stamped into it with white ink. It is the only book that looks, *new*.

"Why is that one so perfect." I ask skeptically.

"Omnis' secrets." Tor jokes.

"Are you certain it's accurate?"

"Of course, Soleil." He assures me. "The silk is over there as well."

"Silk?" I query.

"Yes. Did Lord Acastus not tell you? The Books will be wrapped in silk when they arrive. That way the magic can't leech out onto whatever poor soul is tasked with bringing them to The Ballroom."

"That would be us." I sigh. "How much did Lord Acastus tell you?"

"Enough." Tor replies. "That there is a threat to The Books, so we need some fakes just in case."

I ache to tell him, to tell him all of it. But I know that I can't. For *my husband*, I can't.

"I will bring each book here, where you will have the fake ready. I'll take the fake and bring it to the ballroom and you will take the real book to the balcony. Once all of The Books have arrived, we are done." Tor nods along with each of my words. While I know that Lord Acastus must have told him a thousand times, I do so again. If only for my own sanity.

"And then we find out who was planning to harm The Books and The Realms are safe for another millennium."

I chuckle nervously, bringing my left hand up to twirl my hair mindlessly as I continue to examine the books. Only moments later, Tor grabs my wrist roughly.

"*What is this*, Soleil?" He asks, voice hoarse. I am backed into the wall as he overpowers me. Pain radiates out from my wrist as his brown eyes darken. *My ring.* I struggle for words as his gaze burns into my soul.

"Let go of me." I growl, my best attempt to shield the pain from reaching my voice. He obeys—as if he has no choice not to—and I twist my wrist around in an attempt to alleviate the pain.

"Soleil—" he begins.

"No." I counter. "It's *mine*. My knowledge to share *when* and *if* I decide to do so. You had no right—" My voice cracks in sadness. I trusted Tor, with my life. But the way he grabbed my wrist—I will *never* forget that. From the look in Tor's eyes, it is clear that he already knows what the ring means—*who* it is from. My stomach churns as I speak again. "I will see you tonight." I say coldly as I leave the glass castle.

The gold band burns hot on my finger—a constant reminder of all I am to gain and... all I stand to lose.

Chapter Twenty-Four

Sunlight beams through The Castle of Lex's windows, bringing me solace from the cold of my mind. I twist the ring around my finger anxiously as I walk down the halls, making my way to check the last few items on my list before preparations for The Eternal Dance are complete. The Castle is decorated more beautifully than I have ever seen. Overnight, the soldiers tasked with the preparations somehow transformed its cold and unwelcoming stone, into something of true beauty.

Eventually I make my way to the ballroom. I can't help but gasp. The ballroom is expansive and as I do not visit often, I am in utter shock when the doors open, revealing a grand room with beauty enough to rival Omnis itself. Giant windows that reach all the way to the tall ceilings, allow Lex's rare sun to stream in. The walls are covered in artwork—real artwork—so rare to find in Lex. It is similar the artwork in Omnis, but these paintings tell stories. The stories of Lex, of every Knight ever sworn to The Book of Law.

The ceiling is high and arching and beautiful golden trim swirls around its expanse. Chandeliers hang from the ceilings, illuminating the entire ballroom in a gentle glow to supplement the sunlight. The floors are wood, meticulously placed in a pattern that swirls out from the exact center of the ballroom. On the center of that swirl sits a table of pure gold—the table that will soon hold the false Books of Infinity. I look up to my left and find the balcony, currently curtained with a deep red fabric. Another table of solid gold lies there too, that is where the real books will go.

Only accessible by a back entrance which happens to be connected to the glass castle, and towering high above the ballroom, the balcony is the spot that Lord Acastus chose for his display. We can see everyone and everything from up there, and all will be able to see us, but no one can access us—not even Lord Eric whose powers will be stifled during The Alignment. I sigh as I think about the plan that will come to pass much too soon.

Near the windows on the far wall of the ballroom, sit numerous dining tables on a set of platforms. One table, with exactly eight chairs, is on the highest level of the platform. That is where The Seven Knights of Infinity will sit, where *I* will sit. I turn my head to the area directly across from the balcony and for a moment, examine the grand staircase.

The staircase is tall—as tall as the balcony—and incredibly wide. On it lies a pristine white carpet, contrasting beautifully with the dark wood. The railings are made from pure gold as well. The Knights of Infinity—as well as myself—will make their entrances there tonight, to the tune of the musicians' melodies.

When I can no longer stand being in the ballroom alone, I finally leave. A creeping inclination passes over me. It tells me that when I return, I will be a different person. The click of my boots echoes down the halls of The Castle as I walk and I let my mind wander to the melody. My daydream is interrupted however when I walk square into a pair of soldiers crossing the hall in front of me.

"Excuse me." I say. The larger of the two turns around to face me. *Arche?* I hadn't even recognized his silvery hair, now caked with dirt and…*Infinity.* His face is gaunt and his clothes are hanging off of him. The fabric is disgusting and splattered with what I hope isn't blood. Nova turns around too, her usually star bright eyes dull and sad.

"Soleil?" Arche gasps, pulling me to him. I forgot what he felt like. But this doesn't make the memory any clearer. This isn't Arche, just a shadow of him.

I have no idea what to say as I pull away from him, my hands reaching up to cup his face. "Arch—" I say softly. "What happened to you?"

"You would know. Wouldn't you?" Nova sneers.

I look at her in utter confusion. "I—I don't." I stammer, my voice merely a gasp.

"*You* are Second in Command of The Undying Army," Nova yells. "And you *don't know.*" I back away at her words, laced with venom. I have never seen her like this before. I look to Arche in exasperation. What has happened to my friends? To my brother and sister?

"She doesn't know." Arche says sternly, turning to Nova. "Look at her. Soleil has never been able to hide her surprise, Nov. Look." He gestures to me. I meet Nova's eyes.

"Typical for you to be up in your castle, away from the horrors of a real army." She hisses. "Oh! Your Lord Acastus must be so good at protecting your fragile ears from such horrible news!"

"Nova—" I plead.

"How is it possible?" Arche asks. "How do you not know? You should have been the one to make the decision in the first place. If you really don't have any idea—why?"

"I may be second in command, but Lord Acastus has a history of not telling me things. I didn't even know that he graduated half of The Academy. Not until I saw you two in the camps." My words are controlled despite the panic rising in me. Neither Nova nor Arche move to tell me anything.

Arche seems the most open to my presence, so I take my chances and ask him once more. "Tell me what happened." I beg. He looks to Nova who gives a slight shake of her head and he turns back to me with an apologetic look in his eyes. I set my jaw in determination, they are not my friends any longer—I know. They are my *soldiers*. I am their General.

"As General Soleil Yamanu, second in command of The Undying Army, I demand that you tell me everything you know." I use my General's voice, the strong and unfaltering tone that carries me through strategy meetings and court appearances. I see Nova's eyes turn from fury to pain. I stifle any pain that threatens to appear in my eyes. I am far from sorry. She left me no choice.

"We were in Aetas." Arche begins. "Two nights ago, Lord Acastus sent a message to nearly half of The Undying Army. We were to arm our legions and prepare to *take Aetas.*"

Nova huffs as Arche speaks, and she makes no effort to wipe the tears beginning to flow from her eyes. The image of the shimmering purple portal appears in my mind. So does another one, Lady Kala, slight and serious, at The Knight Court.

"Take Aetas?" I shake my head in disbelief.

"We left deep in the night—while The Castle was asleep." Arche adds. "It was a surprise attack. They had no idea we were coming."

"Lady Kala?" I ask.

"She surrendered. Too many casualties, too many of her people *dead.*" Nova replies coldly, laughing humorously as she does. "*We* killed so many people that a Knight of Infinity bowed to our legion. She *bowed* before we could touch The Ageless. For once, I understand exactly what it's like to be as cold as you are." Nova's words are poison, penetrating my skin until they hit bone.

"I am not sorry. You signed up for this when you chose to follow me to The Academy." I will not stand for her insults.

"You are right. None of this would have happened to me if I just listened to Alma and went to Ingenium instead!" She rasps. I take a defensive step back as she yells.

"Maybe. But that is not what you chose." I remind her, tears welling in my own eyes.

"I was a stupid girl, stupid to think that I could chase you to the ends of the realms. I have done nothing but chase you for my entire life! I am *done.*" She growls, unsheathing her silver sword and throwing it to the ground before walking away.

I turn away from her in hurt, she is my *sister*—not anymore. Despite my emotions I am still a General and I need this information, if at least from Arche who remains.

"Where is Lady Kala now? She is to be at The Eternal Dance tonight. The other Knights—they will know something is wrong if she doesn't show up." My words are cool and calculated. I completely disregard Nova, pushing her words away for future thought.

"The Book of Law," Arche begins. "It only took a few hours before Lady Kala relented and Lord Acastus was able to make his way to Aetas, The Book of Law in hand. No one knows what he signed into existence, but whatever it was—it is enough to keep her quiet. As if nothing happened." Arche's voice is grave and my heart breaks for the pain in his eyes.

"Why? Why take Aetas now?" I struggle.

"None of us know," Arche responds. "We're soldiers. It isn't our job to ask questions."

"You're right—it's mine." I reply.

"Do you know about tonight?" Arche asks me as I meet his broken eyes.

What did he see in Aetas? What was he forced to do to return so broken? I shiver at the thought of a realm destroyed by war and pain, of a people left in suffering.

"What about tonight?" I ask.

"We were told that you requested five hundred soldiers on a volunteer basis for security measures around The Castle."

"Yes."

"Along with Lord Acastus' message about Aetas, we were sent another. All members of The Undying Army, not on The Castle's security detail tonight, are to arm themselves and prepare to take Omnis." *No—no.* My thoughts tangle. What is *he* planning? The ring on my finger burns hot.

"Anything else I need to know?" I ask slowly.

"He gave a list. Nearly one hundred highly ranked soldiers—Nov and I included. We are all to attend The Eternal Dance." Arche replies.

Lord Acastus wishes to feign normalcy then.

"I have to go." I say quickly. "Take care of her." Arche gives me a sad smile and my heart breaks all over. I can't stand seeing him like this. Before I can do anything stupid, I turn around and begin making my way to my chambers.

When I arrive at my chamber door, I stick the key in and turn. My face turns hot when I find Lord Acastus lounging on a chair at my dining table, reading one of the books from my shelves. I stand there for a moment and stare. I know that my gaze burns. He meets my stare with curiosity, then knowing—*he knows.*

"What is it, my Queen." I can't help the way my heart thumps as he says those words. I can't help my desire to forget, to be a good General and forgive my Lord. To be a good *wife* and love my husband.

"You sent a legion of soldiers to Aetas?" My voice is quiet and I curse Infinity for it.

Lord Acastus rises and walks to me, picking up my hands in his when he arrives. "I did, Soleil." His voice is soft, comforting even. I can't look into the grey depths of his eyes.

"You *took* Aetas? Killed innocent people—" I begin. But Lord Acastus shushes me gently.

"You don't understand, Soleil. You still have so much to learn."

Tears stream down my face as I look into the light of the fire. "Lady Kala surrendered. Because you *killed* her people. She surrendered before you could touch The Ageless and do any more damage" My voice is a scratch.

"I will not deny it."

"Why?" I ask, finally meeting his eyes. "Will the power of all seven Books of Infinity not be enough?"

"Soleil, please." He is pleading, pleading with *me.* "When I bind the books tonight, it will not guarantee absolute obedience from the realms—from the other Knights. We will still need to lead our legions—*our* Undying Army—into each of the realms. We will need to fight to hold our positions as High Rulers of the realms, Soleil. This is just the beginning." He truly will take Omnis tonight then. My blood runs cold when I imagine that beautiful realm in chaos.

"They why make Lady Kala forget about the invasion?" It is the only question I dare ask.

"She did not forget, Soleil. The Book of Law made it so that until the books are bound tonight, she and her people cannot speak of it. Our soldiers cannot speak of it to anyone but fellow soldiers either."

I think of Nova and Arche. *Do they know that their tongues are held?* I suppose that the only reason they were able to tell me, is because I am a soldier myself, but that means that I am bound to the same law.

"Why now?" I demand.

"You will see, Soleil. You will see tonight when you are at my side, when you are High Queen of The Seven Realms." His voice is a whisper.

Despite the fire that rages within me, despite my anger at not being told. I forgive it all. I forgive him. I believe him, as I know I always will. The ring on my finger burns in answer and I know it is settled.

"What about the soldiers tonight?" It takes all of my effort to speak those words. Omnis means nothing to me. It disgusts me. *And still—*

"Soleil, you needn't worry about that. Once the books are bound, Omnis will be taken, and the rest of the realms will fall in line." Lord Acastus picks up my hand, raising it to his lips before kissing the gold band, his grey eyes frozen over.

As I look into Lord Acastus' eyes I see how far we have come. I have given up so much for the power I now hold, and *nothing* will stop me from taking the power I still crave. The future is laid out in front of me and I see it so clearly.

I *will* be High Queen, even if every soul in the realms has to perish as the cost.

MY HANDMAIDENS ARRIVE SHORTLY AFTER TO FINISH PREPAR-ing me for The Eternal Dance, frantic in their efforts to get me ready. I am told to shower again, scrubbing the makeup from earlier off of my face. After, my skin is slathered in a think lotion that makes my body almost shimmer as if I am the sun itself. My hair is straightened again—this time to absolute perfection—and my nails are repainted. Makeup is applied to my face, this time much heavier and more dramatic than before.

When they are done preparing my body, I pull on the required undergarments for my gown and strap Fury to my thigh. Then, my handmaidens help me into the gown itself, and the metal corset, which is secured with a gold clasp. The gown hugs my curves elegantly, and the velvet-like tulle is soft on my flawless skin. After I slide into the matching gold heels, I strap Fate to my waist and walk myself to the floor length mirror in my closet.

I am a rose—a true rose with thorns and all. The dress flows beautifully in gentle layers to the floor. My gold heels peek out ever so slightly as I shift. My skin is luminescent, turning gold in subtle changes of the light. The slit along my left leg showcases Fury and its matching scabbard of bright white. The metal corset, shining and flawless, is the perfect contrast of sharpness against the overwhelming *soft* of my gown. Fate is strapped tightly on my waist, it's golden hilt lustrous.

The makeup was done impeccably with shades of brown and gold on my lids, and a deep red—the color of my dress—on my lips. My lashes are long and dark and my eyebrows are without fault. I pull my eyes to my hair which flows well past my shoulders in a single, flawless, curtain of deep brown. The gold band around my finger gleams subtly and the only thing missing is my diadem. Knowing Lord Acastus will wish to crown me himself, I thank my handmaidens graciously for their work before dismissing them.

Lord Acastus knocks on my door at *0517*, exactly fifteen minutes after I dismissed my handmaidens. My heart skips when I take in the sight of my husband. His hair is perfectly styled to adorn his silver crown. He wears a well-tailored suit of slate grey with a matching shirt underneath. His shoes are black, matching perfectly the black stone embedded in his silver crown. It is his tie—a subtle detail but obvious enough for me to point out—of deep red that catches my eye. The tie is the exact same color as my dress. I realize the for the first time, that Lord Acastus is staking his claim over me.

The realms will know that I belong to *him*.

His eyes widen slightly when I open the door and he sees the full extent of my gown. Lord Acastus stands for a moment, examining me from head to toe. His eyes linger on the slit of the dress on my thigh, revealing the spot where Fury is strapped. Lord Acastus reaches out to touch Fury's hilt.

"This—was not here before," he moves to touch the point of my corset. "Nor was this." his movements, slow and calculated, fill me with warmth. How odd, when Lord Acastus himself radiates *ice.*

I look up at him. "I made some adjustments, my Lord."

"You didn't tell me—" he begins.

"It was a surprise." I say with a smile. It is only a half lie. I had no intention of telling him as I truly believed that that it was too trivial or that Neilo would have taken care of it. My words are mere damage control.

"It is a wonderful surprise, my Queen." Lord Acastus lifts my left hand to his lips where he kisses the gold ring. "Come, let me crown you."

Inside my closet, I move in front of the floor length mirror and watch through the surface as Lord Acastus lifts up my crown and lingers for a moment in waiting—for what, I don't know—before placing the cool metal diadem on my brow. The weight settles on my head and I simply stare at myself in the mirror, the slate grey figure of Lord Acastus towering behind me.

We are a picture—the two of us. *The High King and Queen of The Seven Realms of Infinity*—I think to myself. I watch as Lord Acastus places his hands on my shoulders, then down to my waist, clearly relishing in the picture himself. Relishing in the feel of my body next to his.

"Come, my Queen." He whispers in my ear.

"Yes, my *King*."

OUR STEPS ARE IN SYNC, OUR CHINS HIGH AND MY DRESS flowing as we walk to the portal room. I am the High Queen, the rose at Lord Acastus' side, the second in command of The Undying Army. *I am power itself.*

With a wave of Lord Acastus' hand, the doors to the portal room open for us. It is quickly nearing *0600*, I know, so Lord Acastus and I stand side by side in front of the portal to Spiritus, waiting for our first Knight to arrive.

Lady Psyche, Knight of Spiritus, steps through the portal. She is stunning, dressed in a frilly gown of pale pink, her dainty gold crown dancing in the light. She stands before Lord Acastus and I.

"My Lord," she nods to Lord Acastus who gives a curt nod in return. "General Yamanu," she nods to me. I bow deeply.

Despite my status, she is still a Knight of Infinity, and I am still mortal. As soon as the room settles from her entrance, I feel that something is off. It isn't long before I remember exactly what is in the wrapped bundle that she is cradling in her arms. The room seems to open up, to dance and almost *float*. Everything feels beautiful, everything feels new.

"My General can take The Book of Life to the ballroom for you." Lord Acastus says, gesturing to me.

"Of course," Lady Psyche smiles, handing the book to me. It is light, light as a feather, considering its size. Despite the silk wrapped around it, I feel its magic flow through the room, I feel its magic flow through *me*. This is the first time that I have ever been so close to a Book of Infinity and the power is all consuming.

It takes me a moment before I can say a word. "Thank you, my Lady. I will bring it down right now." I give a light bow and look into Lord Acastus' approving eyes before leaving.

The portal room doors open on my approach and I clutch The Book of Life tightly as I walk through the halls to the glass castle. It only takes me a couple of minutes to make it, though I know that after six round trips in high heels, it will become quite the pain. I knock twice on the door. Tor opens it and I scan the halls before walking in quickly.

"Life?" He asks indifferently.

"Mmhm. It is something else—be careful." I reply civilly.

Tor walks around the table and picks up the book of powder blue, wrapping it in a piece of white silk. We exchange books—the false Book of Life much heavier than the true one—and I give Tor a nod before leaving and beginning my trek to the ballroom.

I enter the ballroom through a back door, and simply by the feel of the room, I know that Tor has already dropped the true Book of Life off on the upper balcony. Lord Acastus is right it seems, for even though I am holding the false Book of Life, the magic from the true one flows as if I have been holding it all along. My heels click on the floor as I make it to the gold table, the false Book of Law already in its place. Quickly, I unwrap the Book of Life, lay out the silk, and place the book in the center of the fabric. I leave quickly after that.

When I arrive back at the portal room, the next Knight still hasn't arrived, though Lady Psyche is already gone.

"She went to the antechamber above the ballroom— escorted by a guard." Lord Acastus says when he meets my eyes. "How was it?"

"Perfect," I reply.

It *was.* The walk was quick enough that my heartrate didn't even raise the slightest and the books are incredibly convincing.

"Well, our next guest should be arriving soon." Lord Acastus says, raising his watch.

At his words, Lord Vale, Knight of Tellus steps through the portal of bright green. I smile at the lanky, boyish Knight who is dressed in a fine suite of emerald green to match his eyes. His crown of dark bronze—modeled after branches—sits atop his head.

"Lord Acastus, General Yamanu." He nods.

I bow deeply before Lord Vale hands me The Book of Element. I do not register the feel of the book until I hold it in my hands. It is so subtle, the feeling of life and purity, of crisp air and clean waters.

As I did with The Book of Life, I walk The Book of Element to Tor, who has the false book ready for me. I then place the false Book of Element to the right of the false Book of Life before returning to the portal room.

Lord Acastus is alone once more when I return, already standing before the glowing purple portal to Aetas. I shiver at the sight of the portal, the entrance to the world that my army destroyed. Lord Acastus must sense my rising anxiety for he takes my hand in his.

"She can't talk about it, acknowledge it, nor feel for it, Soleil. For now, it is as if it never happened. When I bind the books, she will bow to *us*." I nod my head and Lady Kala, dressed in a long and skintight gown of deep purple, steps through the portal.

"Lord Acastus, General Yamanu." She gives no nods as she acknowledges us. However, she looks as if everything is normal, as if we had not just destroyed her realm. It is when I am handed The Book of Age in utter silence— with not even a look in my direction—that I realize that she *does* remember and that she has already come to terms with just how tightly she is bound. The Book of Age almost whispers to me as I take it and I feel the power—and pain—of the stars in my hands.

Lady Fable arrives next, wearing a dress of sunset orange. Her grand crown shines brightly as she hands The Book of Wit to me with a civil smile. The Book of Wit is exactly as I imagined it to be, radiating warmth and knowing—a comforting feeling as I walk it to Tor.

Then, Lord Nasim Knight of Entis—dressed solely in black with his matching crown on his head—steps through his portal. The Book of Death is the heaviest that I have had to carry to the glass castle. It is as if the weight of every soul passed is contained in it. Lord Nasim is cold and calm when he hands me the book, barely acknowledging my presence.

By the time I walk back to the portal room for the fifth time, I am slightly annoyed with the trek. It is not long, nor difficult, though the repetitive motions combined with the act of being cordial to Knights who see me as nothing but a speck of dirt, is beginning to get to me.

Lord Acastus smiles apologetically at me when I return from delivering the false Book of Death to the ballroom. I take my place next to him in front of the welcoming, golden portal to Omnis.

In a show of light, Lord Eric Knight of Omnis steps through the portal. My bones chill as power—*his power,* not the power of The Book of The Bound—bounces around the room.

He is inexplicably beautiful. Dressed in the same deep blue that he wore to The Infinite Knight Court—this time in the form of a solid deep blue doublet lined with silver and matching pants—he is the picture of a perfect Knight. He also wears a long silver cape lined with blue embroidery. The silver crown on his head—with its sparking blue stones—is perfect. He is *perfect*.

And I hate him for it.

I make myself look into his eyes—dark and all-encompassing—as he stands before us, clutching The Book of The Bound. He meets my stare with the same intensity as he did at The Infinite Knight Court and I crack a sly smile at him in remembrance of what I did that day.

"Lord Acastus." He says, nonchalantly. "General sunshine."

"It seems that you've gotten some new attire, my Lord." I say innocently.

"I could say the same thing about you, sunshine," Lord Eric winks. His eyes trail down to the slit at my leg. The skin of my thigh exposed there. My face heats. The pure power that flows from Lord Eric is dizzying, something that I could never dream of growing used to in the way I did for Lord Acastus.

"You may give your book to my General, she will be happy to deliver it to its proper spot for the ceremony." Lord Acastus says icily. Lord Eric hands me The Book of The Bound without word and I almost gasp when it meets my hands.

It is the only book to feel *normal* in weight. Though the magic that radiates from it—*and through me*—is unexplainable. It feels like *everything.* It is perfection and imperfection, chaos and calm, beauty and pain. I feel tied to it the moment I touch it.

I am mortal, a haunting fact that I try every moment to forget. I am not infinite in the way that these Knights are. No matter the power I claim for myself, I can never amount to *them*. Holding these books—holding *this* book—reminds me of just how fragile my mortality is. Just how insignificant I am compared to these tombs that are a hundred millennia old.

In a daze, I arrive at the glass castle and let myself in. Tor is already waiting with the false Book of the Bound and we exchange quickly. He stops me before I can leave, though.

"I'm sorry, Soleil."

I turn to him and know that his apology is genuine for he has never been able to hide his true feelings. Especially not in his eyes. But what he did was horrible, I cannot forgive it. Not because I am truly still angry with him, but because I am trying to save myself from more hurt. "Its—"

"Don't say it's okay. I was wrong for what I did. *I had no right.*" He repeats my words from earlier. "I am so sorry. You don't have to forgive me now—you don't have to tell me what it all means." I see his gaze flicker to my ring. "But I will be here, waiting."

"You will know *everything* soon enough." I reply curtly and walk out of the glass castle.

I want nothing more than to tell Tor everything, to pull him close and tell him what my ring means, what I am going to be after tonight. But I can't. I have to save myself from the pain of having him ripped from me tonight. Infinity gave me a way out from him.

I chose my path. I chose my power. And I will stick to it.

I walk the fake book into the ballroom and place it in the center of the rest of the false Books of Infinity. They look utterly convincing. The feeling of the true Books of Infinity—and their magic together—is fascinating and beautiful. I linger in the company of the magic for a while before leaving.

Once I step away from the false books, I realize that I truly cannot tell *where* the flow of power is coming from. It becomes clear to me then, that Lord Acastus' plan—*our plan*—will work. I look up at the curtained balcony where I know that the true Books of Infinity sit, and I smile at the future that is so close.

CHAPTER
TWENTY—FIVE

My dress flows and my heels click as I walk down the halls of The Castle of Lex. I see the image of myself as I move, an absolute rose. It is a quick walk to the antechamber, though it would have been quicker still if I simply took the grand staircase. I avoid it though, not wanting to risk seeming disrespectful to the other Knights.

Let them have their fun. Let them enjoy their status, for by the end of the night, it will be no longer.

The antechamber doors are open and to my surprise, The Seven Knights of Infinity are getting along very well. Lord Acastus is speaking to Lady Psyche and Lord Na-sim. Lady Fable and Lord Vale are chatting excitedly to Lord Eric who—for the first time—does not look as if he is above it all. It is Lady Kala who stands, unblinking in a corner of the room that captures my attention the most.

When I walk in through the doors to the antechamber, Lady Fable's eyes light. I puzzle for a moment, as I believed that my actions at The Infinite Knight Court, were enough to seal the deal on our relationship. However, she waves her hand and gestures for me to go to her. I give Lady Fable a smile and I am about to make my way to her before Lord Acastus slide a hand around the gold corset at my waist.

"Do not forget that you are *mine* tonight, Soleil." He murmurs.

My head spins. *No one knows.* Not about us, or the ring, or our plan. And yet, Lord Acastus moves to take my hand. As he does so, he adds something that only I can hear. "You are *my* Queen. Starting now and until Infinity."

I do not resist when he guides me towards Lord Nasim and Lady Psyche. I do not struggle from his grip on my arm as we walk. Lady Psyche's eyes sparkle on my arrival. Lord Nasim glowers as always.

"My Lord, my Lady." I nod to them. Lord Nasim gives a slight tilt of his head and Lady Psyche, a deep nod.

"How are you, General Yamanu?" Lady Psyche asks, her voice carrying to me in a fresh sweep of air.

"I am very well, thank you my Lady." I reply.

"Have the General duties gotten to you yet? Legend says that General Aldera tried to—" Lord Nasim starts in a growl. He isn't able to finish as Lady Psyche elbows him in the stomach and gives him a glare.

"The General duties are fine, thank you Lord Nasim. Naturally, my transition period has been quite different than General Aldera's once was." I say with a smile.

This part comes easily to me—the preening and posturing of a court member—the snake like retorts and the hidden insults, they are all natural, something that Lord Acastus never had to teach me.

"*Naturally,*" Lord Nasim begins. "For General Aldera never had the pleasure of attending a meeting of The Infinite Knight Court."

I feel Lord Acastus tense next to me. I am still holding his arm, nothing more than a chivalrous position, but I feel Lord Nasim's gaze on me as if he knows it is something *more.*

"I wouldn't exactly call it a pleasure, Lord Nasim. Though it was an experience," I smile. Lord Nasim's face almost twists in shock, the most emotion I have ever seen from him. "My Lord, my Lady, please have a good evening." I say before unhooking myself from Lord Acastus and moving to find Lady Fable.

She is still in the same spot, thankfully, and as I walk to her, I can't help but let my eyes linger on Lady Kala. The horrors behind her eyes—the hurt. I question if it is worth it, if the power is worth the pain.

It is. It always is.

"General!" Lady Fable calls out. My head snaps to her and I quicken my pace as I approach. She pulls me into a tight and quick embrace. "You look lovely, General Yamanu." She says, looking me up and down.

"Thank you, my Lady. You do as well." I respond sweetly.

She does, her gown of sunset orange sleek along her slender frame. Her hair is tied up effortlessly and her crown gleams on her head. I look to her left and find Lord Vale, sipping from a goblet. "My Lord," I add with a nod.

"General Yamanu." He replies. Lord Vale's words are always authentic, never biting or ambiguous. His green eyes sparkle as he looks at me, I smile. "If Fable allows it, please save me a dance," he adds with a joking wink.

"Of course, I'll allow it. If only because I wish to see that wonderful gown in action" She laughs lightly.

"Oh, I am sure that General sunshine has a line of suitors just waiting for the opportunity to dance with her." Despite his casual and teasing tone, Lord Eric's voice is full of raw and unfiltered power.

I feel my inherent mortal instincts beg for reprieve at his words. My mind knows better though. He is standing directly behind me, I know. His towering frame all encompassing, though I refuse to let even my chin dip the slightest.

"Maybe they would have," I shrug. "But I choose to be *merciful* with those suitors and let them know that I am otherwise engaged before the occasion ever takes place. Otherwise, they can get quite *demanding*." I hiss.

I feel Lord Eric's cool breath on my neck as he chuckles. "Alright, Sunshine. Save me a dance." He replies, with venom lacing his tone as he walks to my side.

My very being aches to run from him, but I turned to him anyway, directly meeting the endless dark of his eyes. He is holding a goblet and I look at it for a moment. "Keep an eye on that tonight, my Lord. We would not want a *repeat incident*," I tease.

Though I feel the physical effects of his power—the constant ebb and flow of it from being in such close proximity to him—he is much less intimidating than usual. I remember his plan, his wish to destroy the realms. I curse Infinity for my ability to somehow grow *used* to the power of The Knights of Infinity. It is a dangerous game and yet the ring on my finger tells me that I have already lost.

Lord Eric tips his goblet towards me and I barley flinch before realizing that it is empty. "Don't worry sunshine, I have learned my lesson," he winks.

I turn away from him, desperate to get away from his dizzying power and his audacity to still crave more. Before I know it, I am standing in front of Lady Kala who looks through me with dull eyes. I struggle for words, but it is no use, they never come.

What can I say to her when my husband destroyed her realm? What can I say when the cost of my power is the lives of her people? I am just about to turn away when she finally speaks.

"I pity you, Soleil Yamanu." Her voice is a rasp and I hear the struggle and tightness in her throat through each word. "You are trapped and you don't even know it. You *embrace* it."

My bones chill. *Trapped?* My knees are close to giving out and her eyes move to meet mine. "You will learn, soon enough." I take a few defensive steps away and end up in Lord Acastus' arms.

"Is everything alright?" He asks.

Before I can answer, a servant of The Castle walks into the antechamber. "Lord Acastus, General Yamanu." He acknowledges both of us with a deep bow. "A word." I straighten and hold on to Lord Acastus' arm, his presence solid and secure as we walk to the servant.

"Yes?" Lord Acastus asks.

"The guests have all been escorted into the ballroom, the musicians have begun playing and the food has been laid out. We are ready to announce the Knights, my Lord." He replies.

"Are *we* ready?" Lord Acastus asks. We sit in silence for a moment until I realize that the question is for me.

"I—yes we are." Lady Kala's words still echo in my mind. When I look to my right, she is staring right at me. I feel her gaze when I turn away.

"Very well, you may begin announcing immediately." Lord Acastus replies. I look up at him and he shakes his head slightly. A silent ask of, *what's wrong?* I brush it off and look at the servant once more.

"I will deliver the message right now my Lord," he nods. "My General," he adds before leaving.

"Is everything alright, my Queen?" Lord Acastus asks.

"I am fine." I reply. It isn't convincing enough. Lord Acastus is about to counter when trumpets sound from the other side of the door that leads to the grand staircase.

The doll-like Lady Psyche takes her spot at the head of the line. She is followed by the pure Lord Vale, then Lady Kala, ghost like in her walk. Lady Fable who is as imperial as ever, the dark Lord Nasim, and Lord Eric, the perfect Knight follow. Finally, Lord Acastus and I take the honorable position at the end of the line as hosts of The Eternal Dance.

Lady Psyche's name is announced. The wooden doors open, and she steps out, music playing in her wake, then the doors close again. This continues on for each Knight, the pace of my heart quickening until it is just Lord Acastus and I in the antechamber.

"Do I wish to know what is bothering you, my Soleil?" Lord Acastus whispers.

"It is inconsequential, my Lord." I reply.

"If it is so inconsequential, you would not hide it from me."

"Lady Kala—" I begin. "Has no one wondered about her odd attitude this evening?"

"I wondered when you would ask about that," he begins. "The Knights of Infinity are *volatile;* they rarely care enough to notice slight changes in demeanor—like that of Lady Kala—and they rarely hold grudges." I think of Lady Fable, so kind and welcoming as if my outburst at The Infinite Knight Court never occurred. It must take generations for any true disputes in The Knight Court to ever form.

"Remember Soleil, tonight you are *my* Queen."

I look into Lord Acastus' eyes, aching to find the piercing blue that I saw all of those nights ago. It isn't there tonight, but I smile anyway, holding onto his arm a bit tighter before turning to face the wooden doors.

"Lord Acastus Knight of Lex, and his General Soleil Yamanu second in command of The Undying Army." The doors open at the announcement and Lord Acastus and I step out onto the grand staircase.

We take the steps slowly. Lord Acastus' presence is steadying as I do my best to remain upright and not trip over my flowing gown. Thank Infinity, my steps are sure and full of grace, as if I have done this a thousand times before. Confident that I will not fall, I look into the audience where hundreds of people crowd around the grand staircase to catch a glimpse of the Knights.

I spot Tor easily enough. He wears a black tunic lined with beautiful gold embroidery. At his waist, a leather belt holds an array of gold daggers—clearly his own work. He looks incredible but I pull my eyes from him immediately, desperate to find anyone else to look at.

As if by fate itself, I end up staring into the endless depths of Lord Eric's eyes. A slight smirk lines his face; however, it is the glimmer of *wonder* in his eyes that keeps me from looking away. From afar, without the force of his power caving in on me, without the knowledge of his plan taking center stage in my mind, I ache to know him. Our stares hold as Lord Acastus and I near the bottom of the staircase, eventually breaking once the crowd pulls away and forms a large circle of open space for Lord Acastus and I to have the first dance.

The music is slow and swaying as Lord Acastus leads me to the very center of the circle. We pull away from each other and he bows deeply. I curtsy low to the floor—my skirt billowing around me—in reply. Taking a deep breath and meeting Lord Acastus' cool eyes to steady myself, I walk to him to the tune of the music. When we reach each other, he puts one hand on my waist and takes my right hand in his. My left hand rests gently on his shoulder, and after a beat, he leads us in a dance.

Dancing is not my strong suit, though I am competent enough to follow Lord Acastus' lead as he spins me around the circle of viewers. The dance is not anything spectacular, but it is clean and simple—I suppose it embodies the attuited of Lex in a way. Slowly, the other Knights begin joining us. First Lady Psyche and Lord Nasim, who sweep in effortlessly. Then Lady Fable and Lord Vale who are beautifully in sync and finally Lord Eric and Lady Kala.

I don't care that I am not the most perfect dancer, or that Lord Acastus and I's *routine* is far from elaborate, all I see are his beautiful steel grey eyes, and the smile that slowly spreads across his face over the course of the dance.

"It will always be like this." Lord Acastus murmurs.

"I am looking forward to it, my Lord." I reply.

Eventually, the majority of the attendees find themselves dancing away and the circle of viewers fades into nothing. We begin moving and dancing around the golden table which holds the false Books of Infinity and not a single soul suspects that they are fake. Between the gentle music, the flow of the dance, and the magic of all seven Books of Infinity moving through the room, there is a sort of wonder to the night.

The music fades gently and everyone bows to their partners. As the musicians fade into the next song, I take Lord Acastus' arm and he guides us to the Knight's table on the top platform of the ballroom. We take our seats next to each other and the rest of The Knights of Infinity follow not long after. I watch in awe at the sight of so many pairs of people dancing to the wonderful music. Magic flows through the air and I know that it is not simply the magic of the books that is present.

The end of a millennium brings with it a feeling of infiniteness, the possibility for anything and everything to occur. I feel it in the air and see it with every passing second.

Lady Fable takes a seat next to me, switching spots with Lord Vale so that we do not have to talk over him. The Seven Knights of Infinity and I chat politely as we wait to be served our dinner.

While everyone else at The Eternal Dance serves themselves at the endless buffet of rich and decadent foods, the Knights—as well as me—will be served. As I watch people swarm to the buffet, servants deliver the first course to our table. Each of us get a creamy tomato soup, a salad, and some bread with an assortment of butters and jams. As my goblet was already filled with wine, I ask for water instead, not wishing to do anything stupid under the influence of that shimmering drink. Lord Acastus does the same, moving his goblet off to the side.

The Knights and I eat, they drink, and we laugh. It is odd to feel so at home in this group of people. Something in me wishes that it did not have to end so soon. Lord Eric remains relentless in his criticism of me. However, I know how to take it and I am able to dish out retorts with half a thought. The rest of the Knights get a kick out of my sharpness, leading to ridicule aimed at Lord Eric himself.

As the grand clock chimes marking fifteen-minute intervals passing, Lady Kala remains stoic and unmoving. But as the evening progresses and the magic of the books fills me, I begin to care less and less.

I no longer care about her *people* that were hurt in our siege. I don't care about Nova and her self-righteousness, considering that she chose this path knowing where it would lead. I do not care about Tor and the way he looked at me as if I had murdered someone in cold blood when he saw my ring. All I see is the power that will soon be mine.

All I see is my future.

The conversation with the Knights goes on endlessly and soon my limbs grow stiff from sitting for so long. I excuse myself from the table and walk down the platforms until I make it to the buffet. No longer hungry, I crave a drink. I find a punch bowl and pour myself a glass. I take deep sips of the sparkling red liquid. I turn to the dance floor and find people swaying gently to the music.

A look at the grand clock tells me that it is already *1045*. I shiver at the realization that The Alignment is quickly approaching. *How has the evening gone so quickly?* Deep in thought and entranced by the lull of music, I shake in fear when two hands rested on my shoulders. Nearly spilling my drink as I set it down on a table, I spin with my hand on Fate's hilt. I calm when I see that it is Arche standing before me, dressed in a well-tailored suit of black. No words come to mind, but thankfully I don't need them for Arche pulls me into a tight hug.

"How are you?" I finally ask.

"Getting used to it." He mumbles into my hair.

I sigh. It is so much easier to grow indifferent when you are surrounded by immortals who display nothing but indifference themselves. I began to feel immortal myself for a moment and I am terrified of what that might mean.

"Nova?" I rasp after a while, pulling away from him.

"She declined Lord Acastus invitation to the dance— passed it on to another Lieutenant. She is at the portals now, with the rest of our squadron. In position and awaiting orders." His eyes are hollow and I see the eyes of Lady

Kala reflected in them. With the feeling of true infinite-ness burning through me, I take Arche's hand and drag him to the dance floor.

Arche is a natural, carrying himself with the confidence of an immortal and the fluidness of a mortal all at once. He is an easy lead and slowly we are encompassed in the music. I look into his eyes—dull and without their usual sparkle—and my heart breaks again.

"I am sorry that I didn't know. I would have gone with." I murmur as we dance.

"No. If I could have kept Nova away, I would have. It's better that you weren't there. It's better that you didn't know."

Tears well in my eyes as he replies, his voice filled with whatever horrors he witnessed in Aetas. Arche is as pure as the moon after which he is named. Despite knowing it was necessary, necessary for Lord Acastus and I to secure our power, I wish that I could have shielded him from it. I wish that I could shield him from what is going to happen tonight.

"I—"

"Please don't. I chose this, Soleil. I knew what it en-tailed, as did you. The only one who didn't—*not really at least*—is Nova." I stop abruptly, a sinking feeling settling in my core.

He is right. Even if I don't want to admit it. Couples flow around us as the music continues on, but Arche and I stand still. I hastily pull him to me, squeezing him tightly.

"Please take care of her, Arche. Please. She loves you so much. Don't let anything happen to her." My words are hurried. I know what I am asking of him. I know that I am begging him to sacrifice himself again and again so that Nova will be okay. He knows it too.

"I will, Soleil. I promise. I love her just as much." With that, I know that she will be okay, that even if Nova has to witness the horrors of the war that is to come, she will live through it. My heart beats quickly as I pull away from Arche, doing my best to repress the tears from streaming down my face,

"Thank you, Arch." I say with a sad smile. "Please, tell Nov that I love her."

"I will. Take care of yourself, Soleil." At his words, I turn around and walk swiftly through the crowd of dancers. I know that Arche will not follow. We did not say goodbye, but it was one. Tonight, Nova will lead their squadron into Omnis. I can only hope that Arche will be there too.

I am selfish, selfish for pulling myself out of their lives simply because I can't handle the fact that *they* are the cost of my ache for power. I can't see it, not when I am High Queen and have to send legions of The Undying Army out to the realms to claim them as my own. My legs are leaden as I walk away. I feel the physical tear as I pull myself away from Arche and Nova.

In a daze, I walk right into the back of a man. As I apologize profusely, he turns around. My mind whirls once more when I realize that it is Tor. Needing a distraction, I place his right hand on my waist, grab his left and lead us onto the dance floor. I can't look into his eyes, though I feel them burning.

"Soleil," he mutters.

I force myself to look up at him, sadness welling in me when I do. "Sorry I bumped into you." I say, thanking Infinity that my voice carries.

"I'm not." His voice is low and filled with longing. I know that my conversation with him will be just as horrible as the one with Arche.

"Tor—" I begin.

"I am still not expecting you to forgive me. I will wait my entire life. I will spend it groveling at your feet if that is what it takes. You don't have to forgive me, not now, not ever." My heart sinks as he speaks, our bodies swaying to the rhythm of the music.

"I forgive you now, Tor. I forgive you forever." I cure my mortal emotion. I can't leave Tor allowing him to believe that I hate him. I ache to tell him the truth, to tell him that I am Lord Acastus' wife. I pray to Infinity for strength, to do what I must.

"I care for you, Soleil." *I know he does.* "The day I met you and you asked for gold armor to match your sword. Then when you were on deaths door but still insisted on returning it yourself. I cared for you then. When your face lit up the first time you entered the portal room, and again when you saw Ingenium. Soleil, *for years* I despised that realm, and then you made it perfect simply with your presence. I cared for you then and I care for you now."

I can't—my eyes water as I try to find the words to stop him. "I can't, Tor." I rasp. I care for him too. And I burn at the thought of living without him. He is my piece of warmth, the rare kindness in Lex's unforgiving landscape.

"You can, *we* can." He pleads.

But we can't. I *belong* to Lord Acastus, and in less than an hour it will be settled. My path is awaiting me and I can't let it pass. "No, Tor. I am not yours."

Hurt flashes across his face but it is for the best. I can't dare harm him any longer. Even if all I *want* is him. I curse myself for choosing power, but I have done it for *so* long, I don't know how to stop.

"Why?" He begs.

I have to tell him. He won't stop until he knows. "You saw the ring. I know that you understand what it means."

Realization floods his eyes. He knew it the first time he saw the gold band on my finger. "You don't have to," he rasps.

I think of the realms—my *home*—in total chaos because of Lord Eric's wish. I curse him for his greed, for being so ungrateful with his realm of perfection that he has to destroy and rebuild every other one to find satisfaction. I *have* to, if only for the realms. I know that Lord Acastus *could* do it alone, but would he?

The answer follows my question immediately. *He wouldn't.*

"I do."

Tor gears up for a reply as the song winds down and our dancing slows to a stop. But it is Lord Eric—hand on my shoulder—that steps in before Tor can speak.

"Do you mind if I cut in?" He asks Tor. "I wouldn't want anyone to monopolize the General's time."

I feel his power creep over my body. I pray to Infinity that Tor miraculously denies. I would prefer this conversation with Tor for Infinity over dancing with Lord Eric.

"Of course, my Lord." Tor responds dutifully—and to my utter dismay. He flashes a pained look before letting go of me and handing me off to Lord Eric.

I make myself stare into Lord Eric's endless eyes as he takes my hand and my waist and leads to the rhythm of the music.

"My apologies for stepping in. But it's nearing midnight and I want to get my promised dance." Lord Eric winks.

His typical arrogance—feeling entitled to a dance before he plans to destroy the realms. "I thought you would never ask, my Lord." I smile anyway.

"You know sunshine, you weren't kidding about your *demanding* line of suitors. A dance partner has seemed to find you every time you were in need of one." He laughs.

"I guess that makes you one of them." I say knowingly. "Even more *demanding* since you were the first to cut in."

"I suppose so." He replies, his voice low and smooth.

Power flows off of him freely and I am intoxicated by it. It is dizzying—the feeling of so much dominance. I wonder how he can stand it. So, I ask him.

"What is it like? Having all of that power." His face paints in shock—true shock—the way it looked when I poured the goblet of wine on him. "Am I the first to ask that?"

"You are." He replies, almost dumbfounded. "I never thought about it. It was always just an intrinsic part of myself." His words are genuine, not the usually shielded and rehearsed lines that he so often spews out. I wonder how this man aches for so much destruction.

After that, we simply dance, carried by the increasing tempo of the music. Slowly the music grows louder, quicker, more intense. Lord Eric remains unfazed by it, simply quickening his lead to match. I follow effortlessly, marveling at my ability to keep up. It goes on and on endlessly, Lord Eric's grip on my waist tightening slightly. Then a burst of golden magic wraps and swirls around us. It is similar to the barrier that he put up around the council room of The Infinite Knight Court, but this is as shimmering and bright as the sun.

It is perfect.

We dance to the still quickening beat until our movements grow dizzying and we are lost in the feeling—in the magic—of the music. I follow Lord Eric's lead, finding myself lost in the depths of his eyes as well. Not caring any longer, I smile and laugh as we spin, and slowly, a smile grows on Lord Eric's face as well. Dimples appear in his cheeks and his eyes light, growing—*lighter* as we dance.

His eyes grow lighter.

And lighter and lighter still. I feel my heart jolt when they turn the most incredible and bright shade of blue. That piercing blue. My mind spins in thought.

How? How? How?

But it is there, his eyes are the exact shade of blue. As deep as the oceans and as bright as the sky. And they don't change, they remain blue. I turn and blink, and we move, and they stay the same. My world burns down around me as I realize.

It is him.

Realization crashes into me as we continue to dance, the music growing louder and quicker still.

Him, him, him. The voice in my mind echoes. I recall the dream that had plagued me for my entire existence, desperate to fit the pieces together as I see them all laid out.

A stone table. The table in the council room for The Infinite Knight Court. It has to be.

Seven ornate goblets. Eight. Eight the day that I went because I was there. I remember the beauty of those metal goblets, their almost sickening perfection.

Seven gilded thrones. Eight again. I recall the throne I sat on, made for the highest of the realms' royals.

Seven shining Knights. That remained the same—seven shining Knights and a General.

A pair of piercing blue eyes. Lord Acastus' eyes—or so I thought for so long. They are Lord Eric's, the eyes that follow me everywhere. They are *his*.

"I will find a way" I don't know who said this—what it means, but it does not stop me from fitting the rest of the pieces.

One goblet lifted. Lord Acastus, always the outcast.

Six goblets rose in unison. That makes seven goblets. Seven goblets for the seven shining Knights.

I don't know what it means. But I know at least, that for my entire life I have been dreaming of The Infinite Knight Court. I was dreaming of Lord Eric. A part of me, one that has been uneasy for my whole existence, finally settles and I know I am right. Lord Eric… he has no plan to bind the books—no he couldn't have.

I recall the night when Lord Acastus told me of his plan, the way he pleaded with me. The way I relented only when I saw his eyes a piercing blue—*a trick of the light*. Unintentional, I know, for Lord Acastus has no knowledge of my dreams, no one does. But it was enough to convince me. Enough for me to blindly follow him into the dark. I won't make that same mistake again. I stare into Lord Eric's eyes and they don't change.

It was him. It was always him.

The music rises to a peak finally and in a swirl of color and dance I remain lost in my thoughts. Finally, the music stops all at once and I miss a step, stumbling—and nearly falling—to the ground. Lord Eric catches me though, steadying me before I can tumble.

"Soleil," he begins, concern in his voice. He helps me find my footing but he leaves his hands on my waist. "Are you alright?" I look up into his eyes, still that perfect blue. In them I see perfection. In them, I see *home.*

"I—" I struggle. "I am perfect." I finally push out the words, thanking Infinity for allowing me to find them.

"You were wonderful." He says, and my heart leaps at his words.

"So were you, my Lord." I reply.

"General sun—" he begins. "*Yamanu,*" he corrects. "Thank you for dancing with me. I don't think I have had a dance like that—"

"Ever." I cut him off, entranced by his eyes, by the complete *rightness* I feel near him.

The grand clock chimes. As I look up to check the time, my heart sinks when it reads *1145.* The alignment is approaching. I have less than fifteen minutes before my life changes. Less than fifteen minutes to decide what I am going to do—who I am going to trust. My mind spins. Lord Eric still holds my waist as the music and dancing picks back up around us.

Exasperated and confused I look back up at Lord Eric, his gaze trained on me. By the time I meet his piercing blue eyes, the decision is already made for me. He picks up my left hand and kisses it goodbye, completely avoiding the gold band around my finger.

CHAPTER TWENTY—SIX

I am running. Running for my life, for the lives of everyone in the realms. Running for the Knight with the piercing blue eyes—for Lord Eric. My heart pounds but I do all that I can to steady myself. Lord Acastus can't know that my allegiance has changed, he can't know that I am on any side but his. When I leave the ballroom, Lord Acastus is already long gone, no sign of him at the dining table for The Knights of Infinity.

Quickly, I move through the halls of The Castle of Lex until I make it to the glass castle. When I arrive and push the door in, I find that the curtains that once covered the glass windows are pulled down to reveal Lex's landscape one more.

I hesitate for a moment, taking a look at the only home I have ever known. Snow falls over the landscape and I smile for a moment.

"Goodbye." I whisper to my home. Not willing to waste another second, I step through the other door inside of the glass castle and walk through the dim passageway.

The passageway that connects the glass castle to the balcony of the ballroom is narrow and short. I have to bend slightly to prevent my head from scraping across the stone ceiling. It is lit only by ancient light fixtures spread nearly thirty feet apart. My mind whirls with each step that brings me ever closer to the stone door at the end of the passageway. Before opening the door, I focus my mind, handing myself over to the battle hungry soldier that lives within. And so, I enter.

Lord Acastus is hunched over the gold table that holds the true Books of Infinity. Before he realizes my presence, I am able to watch him—watch him as he is utterly *mortal* in his actions. He heaves and huffs, and I swear that I see his hands shake and hear his breath hitch. All at once, he turns to me and straightens, repressing his feelings and becoming the picture of a perfect Knight.

I send a silent prayer to Infinity, for the strength that I will need in these next minutes, as I slowly approach Lord Acastus. His grey eyes are utterly the same, as if nothing has changed when in reality, *everything* has. I despise him, with every piece of my soul—I hate him. But I am an actress enough and I never let it show.

"Soleil—" he begins, his tone frantic. "The Alignment is almost upon us, we must prepare. The Books are in perfect order, everything is right." He walks over to me and takes my left hand, kissing the gold band that now weighs heavy on my finger.

I cringe at his actions, at my ignorance for not seeing sooner.

"What if it doesn't work? What will you do then?" I ask innocently. There is still one piece of my puzzle missing. I have to know.

"Soleil, it will work." He assures me. It isn't enough, I need to hear him say it.

"And if it doesn't?" I ask, repressing the venom that threatens to coat my words.

"I will find a way."

My heart stops, time slows, and the world spins. I am *right*. It was never him and now I know for certain. The path that I followed for so long never existed—not really. The power that I craved was nothing more than an illusion. And Lord Acastus—he used me again and again. He made me feel as if I *belonged* to him. As if I was *his*.

I belong to no one. I am mine alone.

"Come, it's nearly time, my Queen." He takes me by my hand and walks me to the right of the table that holds The Seven Books of Infinity. Their power—it sings.

Sings the most beautiful of melodies, the most harmonious of ballads. Lord Acastus walks to the edge of the balcony and pulls the rope to allow the blood red curtains to finally fall, revealing the two of us. We tower over the crowd. We are larger than life itself. We are infinite.

The music fades. The dancing slows until those on the ballroom floor stand still, looking directly at the balcony. Directly at Lord Acastus and I.

I refuse to let myself pick out a single face in the crowd, refuse to find those piercing blue eyes staring at me. My gaze is unmoving, trained on Lord Acastus only. Though I ache to see Tor, to take a final look at Arche, I never relent.

"Citizens of The Seven Realms of Infinity." I detest Lord Acastus' booming tone, the confidence he carries, the *lies* he tells. "The Alignment of The Seven Realms is finally upon us." Chatter moves amongst the crowd. It is still seven minutes till midnight. How can The Alignment be happening now? I know they ask.

They don't know. They can't know that The Alignment is not seven minutes long. It is *fourteen*. The perfect mirror between millennium past and millennium future, perfect as the realms themselves.

I know that somewhere in the crowd, the other six Knights of Infinity are panicked. But there is nothing to do. With The Alignment comes the suppression of Lord Eric's magic. He can't stop us if he tried. Somewhere in the crowd below, he watches me. I *feel* his stare, *feel* the flawless blue of his eyes.

"The Seven Realms of Infinity were created by these very books, for the purpose of being *perfect*," Lord Acastus continues. "Though, as the last one hundred millennia have passed, they have moved closer and closer into chaos, into *imperfection*. Our Infinite Knight Court has crumbled into nothing. Though I have warned your Knights—they thrive on incompetence. Not one has taken my advice, not one has seen the need for change."

He is mad, he is hysterical, he is obsessed. And for so long I followed him. *I believed him.* My pulse quickens until the thump of my heart is as loud as the music that once played in this ballroom.

"On this, The Alignment of The Seven Realms of Infinity for the one hundredth millennium, I will restore perfection in these realms. I will *save* them."

I see a figure move in the crowd and realize quickly that it is Lord Eric, reaching for the books. Relenting, I allow myself a closer look and see pain and betrayal flash in his eyes once he holds the false Book of The Bound.

"Your High Knight of Infinity, Lord Eric Omnis, has betrayed all of you." He will do it then, play his false story into the end of time. Lord Acastus will tell the citizens of the realms that it was Lord Eric who wished to bind the books in the first place. Another ploy to secure his *undying majesty.* I remain unmoving.

"He wishes to *bind* The Books of Infinity. He wishes to destroy the realms and claim even more power for himself." The clock is ticking, I feel it. As I know that Lord Acastus feels it. His small window of perfection is closing. He won't dare let it go to waste.

"Lord Eric has unleashed a prophecy, one that will destroy The Realms as we know it." The crowd gasps. "I, Lord Acastus Knight of Lex will prevent the demise of The Realms. I will become High King of The Seven Realms of Infinity and you will all *kneel.*"

The pure madness that flitters from his words is enough to fill the ballroom thrice over. I know it, for after he speaks, every person in the ballroom kneels for him. The only ones who remain standing—now surrounding the table of false Books of Infinity—are the remaining six Knights themselves. I restrain myself from looking too closely at Lord Eric, not sure what will happen if I do.

"You will all kneel, to us…"

Time slows. I have only a second—a heartbeat—to draw Fate from the sheath at my side and point it at Lord Acastus as he turns to me—to aim my sword as he is on the verge of taking my hand. My arms are steady, my jaw is set, and Fate glimmers in the light.

Fate.

The same golden blade that I pointed at Lord Acastus on the day of the first battle simulation, and again on the last. The blade that was promised to me when I was crowned General and second in command of The Undying Army.

Shock darts across Lord Acastus' face, his grey eyes going light with fear, and then darkening with realization. But the shock is not long lasting. Instead, a smile takes its place, menacingly slicing across his face.

He laughs, a true and full laugh, as I glare at him. "*Soleil Yamanu,*" he hisses. "You figured it out then?" I realize a moment too late that confusion edges my eyes. *He doesn't know about my dreams.* I remind myself. He couldn't have realized that it was Lord Eric's blue eyes that have shifted my allegiance.

"So, you didn't. At least not the *whole truth.*" His words are venomous. I step closer to him. Close enough that the tip of Fate's blade sits at the center of his pale throat. "Oh, Soleil. Don't you wish to know?" I will not give him the satisfaction of my words. He will talk anyway. Always the dramatic, *he will talk.*

"*Soleil Yamanu.*" His tone is soft, as soft as when he slipped the gold band onto my finger. It takes all of my restraint not to drop my sword at his words. "An odd name. Not one that The Women of the Lost gave you. No, you were *found* with it."

How does he know? How does he know my story?

"*Yamanu.* A word of the old worlds. A word so lost that no one ever cared to find it." I see his throat bob under the tip of Fate as he talks, his tone nonchalant as if I am unarmed. "I did, though. I cared. I cared when *no one* did."

I recall the feeling of his breath on my skin, of him placing the diadem on my head, the ring on my finger and my sword in my hands. *I am his*—I fight the feelings that awake, fight the gold band from weighing my arm down.

"You and I, Soleil. We are *the same.*"

"I am *nothing,* like you." I yell, my voice booming with Infinity evoked power.

"But you are *Miss Yamanu.* For you and I, we are both *invisible.* General Soleil *Yamanu,* the hidden sun. Or, better yet, *The Invisible Sun.*"

No. No. No.

The word echoes in my mind. *Invisible.* The name that has haunted me for my whole existence, *he knows.* It is me. The Prophecy of the Invisible. It was always *me.* It was never about Lord Acastus, or Lord Eric, it is *my prophecy.* He knew—and yet he kept me alive.

"Why?" I rasp. "Why keep me alive if you knew? Why not kill me when you had the chance." *I* am begging now, damning my promise not to satisfy him. I am desperate for an answer.

"Oh Soleil," he coos. "I didn't know, not until just moments before you arrived." His huff, the way his hands shook. It makes sense. He must have looked into The Book of Wit. By that point it became too late to kill me.

"You were so, *ignorant.* So, power hungry that you never saw it yourself, never *felt it.* And I? Well, you weren't the only one *trapped."*

I recall Lady Kala's words from earlier. Not a threat, *a warning.*

"Was it real?" I plead. "Was this real?" My eyes flicker to the ring on my finger. I feel the time tick, each second stretching into minutes. The time still passes however and the window of perfection is closing.

"*My*, Soleil. Of course, it was. *All of it.* I love you, *my* Queen."

I am not in control of my body after that.

As if in dreaming, I swing my sword out and drive it in, cringing as a spray of blood—*his blood*—meets my face. It is hot and thick as it drains from his neck. A millennium passes before he finally hits the ground, though his icy stare never breaks from mine. Not as his blood drains, not as his skin pales. His grey eyes remain open—trained on me—and a sly, knowing smile is etched into his face for Infinity.

I see the image of Duncan Lex slicing the throat of his own son. I see myself as the villain. I see myself as the monster.

The air is changing again and I have no way of knowing how long I have before midnight. Settling back into myself, not caring enough to second guess my actions, I drop Fate to the ground, letting my eyes linger as the blade rings its metallic shrill on the stone floor.

I recall The Prophecy of the Invisible—an utter shot in the dark if it could have played out without me knowing the meaning of my name. Without knowing that *I* am *the one in invisibility.* I pray to Infinity, asking—no begging—for strength, for wisdom, and above all *for power.*

Power is an intoxicating thing, Soleil. I hear Alma's words echo in my mind.

It is power that brought me here, that brought me face to face with The Books of Infinity, so close to their all-encompassing strength. It was my craving for power that led me to Lord Acastus. My ache for dominance that told me to interrupt him on the first day of battle simulation only three-star cycles ago. It was my unrelenting longing for control that named me *General Soleil Yamanu second in command of The Undying Army.* And now? It is my insatiable urge for *more* that brings me here. It is fitting I suppose, for me to meet my end here, in the face of *so much power.*

An even sacrifice for my greed.

I search the depths of my mind for the instructions for The Binding, lingering on the moment where Lord Acastus pleaded for me to believe him, and how I so stupidly did. I see the sheet of parchment, the instructions so beautifully written. I see the way I read them in the dim light of the fireplace. I remember them and so I do it.

The books are stacked already—Life, Element, Age, Wit, Law, Death, Bound—perfectly stable and in the exact orientation as demanded by The Infinite Order. My hands shake as I lift them up, growing more unsteady when I study the drops of blood—*Lord Acastus' blood*—on my hands. I hesitate for a moment, before hastily pulling the gold band from my left ring finger. I throw it into the puddle of Lord Acastus' blood at my feet. *Let it die with him.*

I place my trembling hands on top of The Book of the Bound and speak.

Life. The bottom book glows a gentle blue hue.

Element. The next book a beautifully deep green.

Age. A purple that holds time itself.

Wit. Orange as the warmest sunset.

Law. Grey and cold as Lord Acastus himself.

Death. Not scary or dark, but a black so deep that it is inviting.

Bound. An all-encompassing gold that warms my hands where they touch it.

I rise, floating in the air, suspended by the power of The Seven Books of Infinity. Then they follow suit, surrounding me, encompassing me with their magic, *entrusting me with it.*

With my final wish, my final act—an apology for my greed—I beg The Books to last the realms. To use whatever power they have—whatever power I have—to save The Seven Realms.

I think of those piercing blue eyes—Lord Erics eyes—one final time, hoping that even in the darkness, they will follow me. But I know I have no power to make demands in death.

A burst of power—golden and true—washes over me at my command.

EPILOGUE

A voice, like my own, but with the strength and wisdom of the worlds speaks to me. I can't see, I can't feel my body, I can only listen.

Your spirit entered these realms as mortal…

You will feel every piece of the realms as they are part of you.

Time will never again be of consequence to you.

The knowledge of the worlds will be yours.

The power to bend the will of all but death is yours.

…but it will not leave that way.

You will bind the realms for all of eternity.

You are Infinity.

THE END OF BOOK ONE

ACKNOWLEDGMENTS

Finishing this book was a bittersweet moment for me. INFINITY LEGION was a labor of love (and tears) and every moment writing Soleil into existence was beautiful. This book took so much out of me but also gave me so much in return. For that, I will be forever grateful. It was in the quiet hours of the night, when the world was sleeping and dark, that this book came to life. It was at 3am where Soleil was formed in the words on my laptop. Writing this book was never scary or nerve-racking, it was comforting. It felt like home. Writing Infinity was the most rewarding experience I could have ever asked for. It may have been a solitary experience, but it was one that allowed me to look deep into my mind and find the beauty in my thoughts. I will never forget that as long as I live.

While I may have dedicated this book to myself and the little girl I once was, who found herself in the pages of her favorite books, I still have many people that I want to thank.

To my brother, Aimen (forever my little nugget) who let me read him the first lines that I ever wrote for Infinity. And for telling me that it "sounds like a movie." You will never know just how much those words stuck in my mind and pushed me to keep writing. Thank you for staying up till 3 in the morning with me while I typed away and for putting up with my rants and all of the times that I talk to myself. I love you, Bruber.

To Mama and Baba for always supporting me in everything I do, no matter how ambitious or crazy it may seem. To Mama for listening to my crazy ideas and wild dreams and choosing to never burst my bubble. To Baba, for keeping me grounded and keeping my ideas realistic and for giving me the means to accomplish all of my goals. I love you both!

To Tata, for sharing her story with me and unlocking a passion for writing that I never knew existed. Your book is coming, I promise. Thank you for being my Alpha reader, for reading the earliest version of this book, and all of the ones that took me from that first draft, to this final copy. You will forever be Soleil's first fan. Love you!

To Sedo, for putting up with Tata and I as we watch all of the movies (and talk about them) and read all of the books (and talk about them too!). Thank you for sitting through (most) of them with Tata. I love you!

To Khalo Ayman, Khalto Aida, Hamooda, Nunu, Abood, and Aseelo. Thank you for all of your love, support, and excitement for everything I do. I love you all!

To my beautiful and gigantic family in Jordan. Tata and Sedo and all of my aunts and uncles and cousins who keep me in their hearts, even from almost 7,000 miles (or 12 hours) away. I love you and miss you all.

To everyone who read INFINITY prior to its publishing. Thank you for opening yourselves up to this story, to my words, and to Soleil. I am Infinitely grateful.

To you reader, for letting my story into your mind and heart. I hope you enjoyed it. I hope that it felt like home.

And finally, to Soleil Yamanu herself, for letting me write you into existence. For lighting up my mind with your voice and letting your words and actions flow onto the pages. If the multiverse is real, I hope that I get to write your story in every universe. Here's to writing the rest of your legend, because I know you are far from done.

ABOUT THE AUTHOR

Raised in the South Suburbs of Chicago and now a Political Science Major at Saint Xavier University, Myah Bawadi is the author of INFINITY LEGION, the first novel in The Legends of Infinity Series. A future lawyer and an ambitious college student with a love for film, literature, theater, and art, INFINITY LEGION is a combination of everything Myah has grown to love. Always a strong willed and passionate person with an insatiable urge to make herself heard, Myah thoroughly enjoys implementing these traits into the characters she writes, making them each spitfires in their own regards.

Find Myah on her social media for updates on upcoming novels, sneak peeks, bonus content, and more!

https://linktr.ee/myahbawadi

www.ingramcontent.com/pod-product-compliance
Lightning Source LLC
Chambersburg PA
CBHW062107290726
48975CB00001B/138